THE
FALL
LINE

KENSINGTON BOOKS are published by

Kensington Publishing Corp.
850 Third Avenue
New York, NY 10022

Library of Congress Card Catalog Number: 94-077930
ISBN 0-8217-4710-X

First Printing: November 1994

Printed in the United States of America

For Betsy, who always believed

Acknowledgments

I am grateful to all those who helped me in the research that led to this book. Special thanks to skiers Scott Roach, Rick Wyatt, and Jim Colinson of Salt Lake City, Utah; Harry Baxter and Bill Briggs of Jackson, Wyoming; and Brian Taylor and Mike Sockness of Squaw Valley; as well as filmmaker Greg Stump and extremists John and Dan Egan.

My appreciation goes out as well to Rico Varjan, Ph.D., for his insight into the minds of risk takers and the emotional bereft and to my friend and fellow deep powder addict Jim Erickson, who was there when I first thought up the story.

In a strange way, I'm likewise indebted to California financier Richard Silberman for getting caught by the FBI trying to launder money for the mob; following his paper trail taught me much about the peripheral world of the drug trade. Reporters Rick Shaughnessy and David Hasymeyer were great partners and mentors during this period.

In the writing I am beholden to Jincy Willet Kornhauser and members of my weekly writers group for their constant support and criticism during the early drafts of the book; to my gracious agent, Linda Chester, and her wonderful associate, Billie Fitzpatrick, who helped me bring the manuscript under control; and above all, to my editor, Sarah Gallick, who fought long and hard to see this novel published.

THE FALL LINE . . .

The steepest line or route of descent down a slope. It is at once the most elegant and dangerous way to ski down a mountain. In the pressure of the fall line the skier's nature is revealed.

Chapter 1

O ut West, winter storms begin as collisions of cold and warm air in the Gulf of Alaska. The two battle for control, cold winning, then racing southeast to land, across the coastal mountain ranges to the deserts of the Great Basin. There the fronts accelerate and gather fury, boiling high over the purple sage and the brine flats until they draw one last infusion of moisture crossing Utah's Great Salt Lake and then slam into the chill, nearly-verticle wall of the Wasatch mountains. One canyon, the Little Cottonwood, seems to suck the dark storm clouds into itself, up its nine-mile rip, up 8,000 feet to the half-dozen peaks and ridges that form the series of alpine bowls called Alta. Trapped by the jagged crags and the frozen cirques, the clouds are squeezed as if by a giant hand milking udders and a snow like no other falls.

The snow drops on the snake-like two-lane road that climbs the canyon to the base of the mountain. It falls on the series of steel towers and cables that make up the lifts that hoist the skiers high into the alpine terrain. It covers the five small lodges at the base of Alta's spires and ridges—shelter for the powder addicts who come to fly through the perfect snow the locals call "Peruvian."

After years of experimentation, each die-hard skier develops his own system of grading powder. Jack Farrell was no different.

When he was a young man skiing at Alta for the patrol, his method of classification ran lead, dough, oatmeal, flour. Three months after his return to the canyon, after a nearly twelve-year absence, he had reappraised his system; he decided that the finest powder snow, which falls only in the Little Cottonwood during January, February, and March, resembles air more than frozen water. "White ether," Farrell called it, an infinitely elastic and friable snow that when deep—that is, measured in increments of feet rather than inches—will flood the lungs and leave the skier thrilled that he has flirted with the sensation of drowning.

By early March, four months after he'd fled his former life, Farrell had almost fully succumbed to the pleasures of choking. He compared it to nitrogen narcosis, the rapture of the deep, the hallucinatory dream state he'd entered once scuba diving far off the coast of California. There he'd twisted and sighed and almost drifted off into the blackness. Deep powder was different; in the snow he had no artificial lung to keep him sane. The deeper the powder, the more Farrell had to hold his breath and deny his brain oxygen, so that at times he felt flush with a sense of invincibility, and at others inexplicably hysterical with laughter. No matter how many turns he made through the white ether, it stirred in him a constant battle of terror and joy.

Within the estatic black dream of these past few days, as dark clouds dumped sixty inches of new powder on the steep slopes, he'd been visited by phantoms—one a skier, the other a snowboarder—who'd shadowed him as he skied off in the woods each day, dropping into chutes and gullies that swirled with fresh snow, shooting off ledges far from the marked trails, dancing on the line between control and abandon.

There! The skier darted through the trees off to his right. Then the snowboarder in a flashing arc of neon burst onto the open slope to his left. In a mad rush to lose them, Farrell let his skis run and he dropped off a twenty-foot ledge into a spruce glade, dodging the sharp branches of the trees as he sailed through the air. He landed and burst into an opening in the woods, understanding that he'd lost the snowboarder, but not the skier. Farrell accelerated and aimed himself at the thickest stand of firs he could see, recklessly disregarding the damage their thick limbs might do. He picked a tight opening and charged into it, splintering the dead branches in his path with his armored gloves and aluminum ski poles.

Farrell was out there now, approaching the extreme, where a mistaken reflex demands penance. Pressure built behind his eyes. His chest thudded with the thick blows of a boxer. A strange static noise rang in his ears. Behind him he heard branches snap as the skier followed. Farrell grunted as he popped onto a narrow shelf of snow. He took a turning leap, twenty-five feet off a quartzite cliff, made one turn on a ledge, whipping the ski tips like scythes through the brush, then fell again, fifteen feet and felt the deep snow burst over his head as he landed. Far above him someone cursed.

Farrell skied away, reconfirming a basic truth about himself: that though he loved the jolt of falling, the blast before the nod, it did not sate his need. No, Farrell knew that as much as he craved the swell in his throat as he glided through the air, what he needed most was the numbing, deep powder landing, snow fountains bursting about his head, a cold, wet opiate dulling the ache of lost love and the sick-saccharine stench of spent cordite.

He dropped down through the trees toward the run-out. An explosion rocked the valley. He jerked to a stop, bile rushing up the back of his throat. It was a sound he knew well; the patrolmen were out with dynamite to blow the high gullies and peaks so they wouldn't avalanche and kill the customers. But his thoughts continued to be haunted by the possibility that Gabriel Cortez's men might track him and attempt a direct attack. This he had learned the hard way: betrayal in love and business are things Latin men never forget. Farrell nodded to himself to affirm the idea. He recited a melodramatic list of how he might be taken: a blaze of gunfire, a merciless beating, razor blades.

Then again, he thought, as he poled his way back up the hill toward the lift line. How would they find me here? My truck is registered in Texas under the name of Nathaniel Collins, an infant who'd died of spinal meningitis in Ft. Smith, Arkansas, in 1958, the same year I was born 2,000 miles away in Bangor, Maine.

It was an easy process, one that Farrell had learned from Cortez's right-hand man, Jorge Cordova: look up the death of a baby about your age in a remote town, then ask for a birth certificate. Send away for a social security number, then establish bank accounts, credit cards, and driver's licenses. What is identity these days? Farrell asked himself. Random blips of information on a glowing screen?

It was 10 A.M. when he got into the empty line. The patrol had kept the Wildcat area closed all morning because of avalanche. But he knew the routine, it was only a matter of time. First in line. He stood stock still, his hood zipped closely around his face to shut out the biting wind, listening to powder junkies like himself taking their places in line behind him.

"Single, mon?" a voice asked.

Farrell turned to see a man twenty, maybe twenty-one, a kid really, who he decided was as close as you could come to the personification of a cubist painting: his frame was a triangle, thin hips and broad shoulders that were set off by his neon orange and yellow jumpsuit; his freckled, tanned face was a box dominated by a jaw that broke away from his neck like a brick; and topping this crash of angles were shards of pale blond hair that splintered off his forehead and cut at his neck. Dreadlocks. He'd seen kids like this all along the Southern California coast. A white rastaman. Only this kid carried a snowboard, not a surfboard; he was a thrasher. One of the phantoms.

"Why have you been following me?" Farrell demanded.

"Making a movie," the rastaman said, shaking the snow from the snakes of hair that hung from his head. "French lady I'm up here for, she don't ski much, only the mellow slopes. But she saw you doing your wild-assed shake in the trees. Told us to trail you. Said she wants you on film."

"Not interested," Farrell said.

"Not interested in glory, mon? Celluloid glory? Shit, I didn't think that was possible these days. Sigmund said the poor ego . . . it has to serve three harsh masters. I always thought ego was a slave."

Farrell stared back at the kid. "I'm no one's slave."

Through the pale goggles the rastaman wore, Farrell saw the boy's eyes twist uncomfortably.

"Right, mon," he said. "I can see that. You're no slave. Just the same, she wants you on film."

"Why doesn't she ask me herself, this French lady?" Farrell asked.

The boy snorted. "On the hill on a day like this? In the storms or when we're storming, Inez gets all pale and psycho. Just watches, mon. Inez just likes to watch."

The second phantom, the skier, skated up through the driving snow. He was long and lean, more than six feet, dressed in a navy blue snowsuit and a yellow hat and white, dark-lensed goggles. He cocked his head to one side and looked at Farrell. Then he asked the rastaman: "He in?"

"Says he's got no taste for the cameras, mon."

"Matthew Page," the other skier said, holding out his hand.

Farrell hesitated, nodded, but did not take the man's hand. He recognized the name from ski magazines. Page had been big on the scene for a few years in the mid 1980s, then mysteriously disappeared. He was an extreme skier, the sort who challenges slopes so steep, one false turn can mean death. He was somewhat famous for sickening drops off cliffs sixty feet or more. And in that moment, Farrell understood why Page held his head at an awkward angle: he had read that Page lost his left eye as a teenager.

"I've heard of you," Farrell said. "My name's Nate Collins."

Page let his hand drop. "Never heard of you, but you're what Inez wants. Newcomers or comeback boys, like me," Page said. He pointed to the snowboarder. "This is Jerry Milburn."

"The Wave, mon," the rastaman said, smiling out from under a twisted white knot of hair that jutted out over his nose.

"How's that?" Farrell asked.

"He likes to be called The Wave," Page said.

"Didn't know there was snow in Jamaica," Farrell said in a sarcastic tone.

"Never been there, mon," The Wave said. "But I'm always in a Kingston state of mind, you know? Mostly I like the look, sets me apart. People never remember Jerry Milburn. They know The Wave."

Farrell grinned in spite of himself.

"I know, mon," The Wave said. "Madison Avenue. Human as billboard. But I know the rules of celebrity and image is one of them."

"Glory in celluloid."

"Now you're on it, old one."

"Inez wants to talk," Page said.

"No desire, sorry," Farrell said. He looked up into the storm.

"Inez can be persistent," Page said. "Convinced me to try when I thought no one would want to take a chance again. The Wave, she snagged him just as they kicked him off the team at Mammoth."

"Hey, mon, difference of opinion," The Wave protested.

"Believe what you want, Wavo," Page said.

"No desire," Farrell said again.

"But mon . . ." The Wave began.

"Fuck him," Page said. "Probably couldn't cut it anyway."

Farrell leaned over his poles and watched the snow collect. It was like looking at a ceiling, the longer he studied, the more images he saw: a boat racing across open water, a tiny blue hand clutching a blanket, a bull with an egret riding its back.

"It's hypnotic, staring at snow," said a tall man in a red anorak and navy blue nylon pants who'd skied up next to Farrell.

The man turned slightly to reveal a pale face and thin gray lips. Farrell gulped. He knew the man, or had known him years before. His name was Paul Timmons and they had served together on the Alta ski patrol. Back then Timmons was a rangy kid with a startling shock of black hair. Like Farrell, he was fresh out of college with a degree in economics and the simple need to be a vagabond for a couple of years. Although Farrell couldn't say they were close friends, they had logged many hours together; they had been comrades. Last Farrell had heard, Timmons was working real estate in Texas. It had been more than ten years since they'd seen each other, but Farrell noticed in an instant the loss of weight, the weakness in Timmons's stance, and the pallor of his skin. Farrell knew Timmons was barely thirty. He looked fifty.

"It's like looking at fire," Farrell said softly.

Timmons smiled and shuffled into place next to Farrell. "These are the days we dream of, aren't they?"

Farrell nodded, praying that the slight quiver in his shoulders would not show through the heavy fabric of his parka. Though Farrell had recognized other people in the canyon since he'd arrived, he understood that the government's surgeons had done their job well. The scars would heal with time. He'd revealed his true identity to only one person, Frank Portsteiner, his old supervisor, who now worked down the road at the Snowbird ski area.

Timmons pointed up the mountain toward the flank of Wildcat Bowl, a heavily wooded area filled with chutes and ledges.

"I woke up this morning and watched a spruce grouse waddling around up there through my binoculars," he said. "They always come out at dawn to feed during the big storms. Ever seen them?"

"Just yesterday," Farrell said, aware now that Timmons didn't recognize him from Adam;

"Yeah, this old bird was just out there in the gale behind the place I rented for the week," Timmons said. "The wind turned steady out of the north. She sensed a big blow coming because she ruffled her feathers and got down in a wallow. She tucked her head under her wing and the wind blew snow over her until you could barely make her out."

Timmons let loose with a dry, hacking cough that made Farrell wince. "I'd call that a good sign," he said when he'd recovered.

Farrell stared straight ahead. "A very good sign."

Behind them the crowd had swelled to almost ninety skiers, all of them groaning to be up in fresh deep. Page stomped up and down in his tracks and howled. He landed on the back of Farrell's skis and Farrell twisted to display his practiced, cornered-animal expression. Page jerked back. Behind Page, someone in a voice loud enough for everyone to hear said: "Guy's cheesed. Been standing first in line everyday for two months. Fucking Swiss cheese."

Timmons hacked again. "That's what they used to say about me," he said. "Always had to be first up the mountain."

The lift started to creak forward. The attendant waved Timmons and Farrell on. Page and the Wave followed. The crowd roared at the thought of cutting almost two feet of virgin white.

On the long lift ride up the mountain, Farrell tolerated the silence as long as he could, then told Timmons the lie he'd created for Collins: that he was taking a couple of years off, a financial executive from New York City tired of the buy and sell, tired of the pace, in need of rejuvenation.

Timmons coughed. "Must be nice. I've got a wife and two kids back home. Couldn't afford the luxury. Have to come up here once a year though. Puts me back in touch with things."

Timmons shifted in the chair and pointed back over his shoulder into the storm. "Can't see it back there, but just about directly behind us, across the street, is Cardiac Ridge.

"I worked here a couple of years, ski patrolman," Timmons continued. "One night after a storm, must have been late January, oh, '78. Full moon. Six of us got drunk and climbed the ridge. We took off in pairs, carving huge figure eights in the snow."

Before he could stop himself, Farrell said: "A moon dance." He had been one of the six, all of them breaking off pieces of spruce and tucking them in the bands of their ski goggles, like antennas, before they skied down the mountain. The fir branches were insurance: if a skier got stuck in the deep powder, stalled in his descent, the others could swoop down and break the tension in the snow around the trapped skier and let him continue.

"How'd you know we called it that?" Timmons demanded.

Farrell coughed and pointed ahead: It was time to get off the lift. He pulled over to the side of the trail and tightened his boots. It gave Farrell time to think, time to lie.

He said, "About a month ago, I was standing in line and looked up there on the ridge and saw these perfect sets of tracks dropping down the side of Cardiac. An old guy standing in line with me, name's Portsteiner. When I pointed to them, that's what he said: 'Moon dance.' "

"I saw Frank last night," Timmons said. "Hasn't changed a bit in fifteen years. Like the mountain itself."

Page and The Wave whizzed by toward the avalanche rope. Timmons asked Farrell if wanted to ski some. Farrell said, no, without explaining. Before Farrell skied away, however, he looked back briefly over his shoulder at Timmons, who rubbed at the back of his neck, then pushed off, picking his way down the hill in a slow, smooth roll.

Farrell clenched his teeth, fought off the desire to follow Timmons, and skied down the side of the ridge into the thick of the storm, a thick, foggy cloud that pelted his face. The metal edges and plastic bottoms of his skis made a clean hissing sound running through the snow and he dropped, as if in a long, pearly elevator shaft. He wheeled and bounced off the rubbery sides, no friction under his feet. His hands flicked forward in anticipation of every turn. Snow boiled up his chest into his mouth and choked him. He rose to the surface, spit out the sky's frozen waste and angled his hips into the hill, letting the skis arc longer and faster, exiting and entering the snow so that as speed built, he jetted up and on top of the whiteness. He wanted the mental stillness that usually accompanied acceleration to come. Instead, in the milky white of his peripheral vision, the frozen image of Timmons's face appeared. Farrell's head ached. His breath shortened. His chest hurt.

Farrell scowled and pushed off into an uncut powder chute, down through the pallor, the crystals writhing about his neck, chin, lips, cheeks, over his goggles and hat. He was buried. Even submerged, gravity and acceleration kept him moving, slicing through the trough. Deep under his feet, something—a twig, the tip of a rock—grabbed at his ski and he adjusted, mindful of pitching too far forward and somersaulting over and over again; alert to the awful popping noises that could come: an ankle, a lower leg or cartilage. Or worse, the nose dive in four feet of loose snow, trapped upside down, mouth and nose stuffed and blocked. A slow, breathless collapse.

His speed allowed him to plow forward, and as he entered the fall line—the steepest, most elegant and most dangerous drop down any mountain run—he began to float. In deep powder turns, gravity granted him freedom. For a brief instant in the middle of each arc he hung weightless, like an arctic hunting bird which at the top of its climb spreads its feathers into a killing dive.

By 11 A.M., the storm had intensified, driving those not truly committed into the lodges. Farrell was solo on almost every ride up. A gust of wind grated at the side of his face, triggering the memory of his wife Lena walking alone to their old apartment in Chicago. She had tucked her chin inside the collar of her coat on the way from the hospital where she had been a nurse in a birthing ward. It was the first time in months that he'd allowed himself a clear vision of her and he began to shake, wishing she could be there to hold him. The ache at the back of his head grew stronger.

Something truly wild was necessary to erase these thoughts, to return him to the sterile, aimless state he'd achieved for a few hours almost every day since he'd returned to Alta. He edged his skis out across the High Traverse, a narrow path above Alta's high chutes. A steep run broke away to his left—the top a series of rocks called the Stone Crusher—and he swung into it, no braking, plummeting out into space.

Big plunges like that steal the breath. In the split second before liftoff, the competing fears of height and flight meet. With nothing but white below and white falling around, Farrell sailed through an illusory world of blank ceilings and walls and floors; here was the shifting rush of the billowing snowy pack, an opaque mirror to the pelting sky; here were the fir trees that swung their limbs in delayed time to the wind; here, at his nose, was the balsam fragrance of the trees and the sweet rot of his own sweat. Here, too, was the aluminum tinge of heartburn on the back of his tongue. Then impact and panic as he pitched down the hill, too acute, adjusting his stance just in time to burrow into three feet of fresh snow on the fall line.

Chapter 2

B y the time Farrell reached the bottom, the sun had broken through the clouds. He felt strong enough to walk away from the hill, but was forced to admit that the day's troubling events demanded alcohol; without it, he might not make it until sleep could bath him in black.

At a lodge down the road from the ski area, he snuck into a downstairs bathroom and changed into a bathing suit. Posing as a guest, he bought two beers and two nip bottles of Jack Daniel's, hot-footed across the icy path to the huge outdoor hot tub, waded through the fourteen guests already soaking, and sank into a dream torpor in the far corner.

While he drank and let the hot water knead his tired muscles, Farrell stared up at the rear of the three-story lodge and admired the bulging structure of glass and wood. It was here that Farrell had first come fifteen years before as a sophomore at the University of Massachusetts. He and a friend worked a deal on their spring break to wash dishes in the lodge kitchen in exchange for room and board. They had stayed nine days, during which thirteen feet of snow fell. He smiled as he recalled run after run through bleached silk on an all but abandoned mountain.

He had graduated a year early with a degree in economics and, despite his parents' protests, had come directly to the canyon and applied for a job with the ski patrol. Portsteiner had been skeptical of an Eastern boy on a radical Western slope until he'd seen Farrell ski. Farrell thought of the long hours of training Portsteiner had put him through, teaching him how a snow-covered mountain is like a giant hibernating bear: under layers left by fat storms, the body of the snow pack grumbles and turns. Every once in a while, when the pressure gets too great, the bear wakes from its sleep and shakes and roars its hunger.

"Collins? *C'est* your name, Nate Collins?"

Farrell opened his eyes, tense and alert. Few people knew even his assumed name. The loud, raucous voice, which sounded like someone gargling with tiny glass marbles, belonged to a woman in her late twenties with shiny shoulder-length hair the color of a raven's wing. She waded through the Jacuzzi toward him with her hand extended. Her face was striking, yet not what you'd call soft or beautiful. It was more exotic, composed of acute planes and a Roman nose that punctuated her high, angular cheekbones. Her hazel eyes were set off against a skin so white, it seemed translucent. She was small, about five-four, with a firm body that seemed ready to explode from the purple one-piece bathing suit she wore. Behind her stood a lithe man, well defined, about thirty. He had weird blue eyes, one of which did not seem to track correctly. Page.

But everyone in the Jacuzzi was focused on the woman. She plowed toward him through the water with such purpose, Farrell decided it would be better to talk than ignore her. "Inez, I gather . . ."

"Already, you hear of me . . ." she gushed in a thick accent. She grabbed his hand with the tips of her fingers and the ball of her thumb and shook it like a bell. "Inez Didier. I am the director of films."

Before Farrell could respond, Inez reached out and plucked his black mirrored sunglasses from his face. *"Je m'excuse,"* she said. "I like to know the person I talk to."

Farrell shook his head, dizzy from the energy that surrounded the woman. He reached for the glasses. She threw them in the snow behind her and laughed.

"Vraiment, I like to see how the people make reaction to the unexpected," Inez said. "Your face expression was without price!"

She turned. "Excuse me. I do not wish to be rude. Matthew Page."

"We met today," Farrell said. "I think I left him in difficult circumstances."

Inez squeezed in next to Farrell. Page submerged across from them.

"He tells me this," Inez said. She smiled. "And the one who dreams always of Jamaica, too. It is the truth, you know, we spy on you these past days now."

Farrell swallowed hard at the thought. "And what sort of dossier have you developed, Mata Hari?"

Inez giggled and squeezed Farrell's knee under the water. He jumped slightly.

"Very impressive, in a *dur,* oh, rough fashion, the ski technique I mean," she said. "Page says you ski in the trees, break the branches, and turn, as if . . ."

She turned to stare at Farrell, tugged at her plump lower lip, and said in a puzzled voice: "As if you hate them?"

She squeezed his knee again. "You have this quality: cowboy I think you call it."

"We all have our own style," Farrell said.

"We do, Collins," she said, pronouncing it "Cawleens." "And I find yours terribly . . ."

"Saddle sore?" Farrell said.

Page snorted. Inez waved her fingers in front of her face, confused, then continued on as if he hadn't replied. "If you miss the turn in the manner in which you ski, you break something."

Who was this woman? Farrell asked himself. Her pushiness played on him. "I know my boundaries," he said finally. "Learned them the hard way."

"Bad fall?" asked Page.

"Something like that," Farrell said.

Inez turned to face Farrell and he felt her thigh brush against his. "But you like to test them, these boundaries, no?"

"Isn't everyone interested in that fence in the dark?" Farrell replied. Under the water his toes prickled with interest. "It's only by climbing it enough times that we figure out where the posts and rails are."

Inez dropped her head to the right and opened her eyes wide, then clucked. "No, we see what is the climber of the fence. More than physical limits—that is what interest me, Collins."

"Nate," Farrell said, surprised that he was warming to her.

"Nate," Inez said. She grinned wildly at him. "I tell you the truth, such a subject is the obsession for me."

"Lot of danger freaks up here," he said, looking toward the mountains. "They'll show you where to go."

"Moi, I like to watch, not to do it," said Inez. "Divers of cliffs, the race car men, the *parachutiste,* these types. They leave me . . . to gasp."

She hoisted herself up and sat on the edge of the pool, her legs lightly touching Farrell's shoulders. "But is it not so that they are castouts in America? You worship, how would you say, the heroes that are *collectif?* No, this is not right. My English is terrible. Help me out, Page."

"Team players," Farrell said.

"Exactement!" she cried, and she slapped her thigh. "Team players."

"And Europeans?" asked Page, whose gaze had not once left Farrell.

"Almost all love the teams for football, er, soccer," she said. "But they adore the individual. Anyway, my spies, they watch you these past days and they see you ski like you want to slap the mountain's face. *Mais,* we never hear of you."

Farrell shrugged and drank from his beer can.

"After college I spent two or three years patrolling," he said. "I had a bad turn of events. Didn't want to leave Utah, but decided it had run its course. I'd have to make some money. Did that. Now I'm retired in a way. Relearning how to make turns right. As you said, they're still pretty rough."

"And, I am sorry to ask . . . the scars?"

Farrell unconsciously ran his fingers across the pink ridges about his eyes and nose. "An auto accident last spring. Made me rethink my priorities."

"What business are you in?" Page asked. Farrell noticed for the first time that Page had one of those rich baritone voices that reverberate and make strangers want to eavesdrop.

"Financial black magic," Farrell said. "Sleight of hand. First you saw it, then you didn't."

Inez tugged at her lower lip and crinkled her nose.

"Tax attorney?" Page asked.

"You guessed," Farrell lied, and he rose to leave. "I've been too long in this soup. Time for a sauna."

He reached for Page's hand and held his gaze too long. Page averted his one good eye and Farrell felt his hand go limp.

"We have the proposition for you," Inez said.

"So your spies have told me," Farrell said. He started to wade away. Two sharp fingernails inserted down the back of his bathing suit stopped him cold in his tracks.

"But you do not hear it from me," Inez said firmly.

The other people in the tub fell silent. Farrell turned and stared at her. "No, I haven't had that pleasure."

"Meet me for a drink, *alors,*" Inez said, returning his glare with such a blank expression that he almost shivered.

"Upstairs," he said. "An hour."

Dried, dressed in his trustfunder's duds, Farrell took the far bar stool next to the window under the stuffed head of a mule deer with only one antler. From this position he had an unobstructed view of the room. It was a habit Gabriel force-fed him. At first, he had considered the practice overkill, but since sprinting from the safe house, he now followed it passionately. He studied the glass behind him and decided that the bowed windows would create enough distortion in a rifle scope to throw any shot at least two feet off line. Then he thought, Is a gunshot Gabriel's style? Gabriel, lover of fine-cut clothes, speaker of five languages, consummate entrepreneur and liar. Probably not. Though Gabriel stayed far from the nitty-gritty of production, he had kept a close watch on cash flow. Gabriel would want a more intimate final audit of their affairs.

Farrell ordered a ginger-ale setup and a shot of George Dickel from his bottle. The bar was as a bar should be: lots of dark wood and a rich red carpet and enough memorabilia hung about the room to chart the eyes during a steady course of drunkeness. Over the great stone fireplace lorded the ponderous stuffed head of a bison. Farrell took the drink down in two gulps and was ordering another when he saw Portsteiner come through the door. Portsteiner had looked fine the last time he'd seen his old boss just a week ago. Today he looked like hell; the normally visible lines about his brown eyes were deeper and set off like fissures. Portsteiner stood six feet tall in his stocking feet, but seemed taller owing to the curly shock of salt-and-pepper hair that burst off his forehead. He had the sort of facial construction—protruding eyebrows, deeply etched skin—that's tritely referred to as craggy. Farrell liked to think of it as a mountain face. Although part of him was glad to see Portsteiner enter the bar, another hated it. Years ago Porsteiner had accorded himself the role of surrogate father, and Farrell, ever the rebellious child, had fought it with the chattering force of a dull ski on an icy slope.

Portsteiner grunted and slammed a thick hand on the bar and ordered a beer.

"You look well, Frank," Farrell said.

"Crap," Portsteiner said. "I look like slush and you know it."

It was typical Portsteiner speak and largely what set the older man apart. Portsteiner worshipped the alpine researcher E. R. LaChapelle with a Maoist fervor; he carried the second edition of LaChapelle's *The ABC of Avalanche Safety* everywhere he went, winter or summer, and quoted from the red book's dry prose to everyone who had ever worked for him. Portsteiner analyzed almost every facet of life through the snow metaphor.

"Life's just one big shit storm that dumps on you every two or three days," Portsteiner liked to say. "But if you're careful, you won't get too cold or damp or washed away in a slide."

Portsteiner also used a rather imprecise way of categorizing the people he met based on the tenets of LaChapelle's snow crystal chart. People with sharp wits, he called "needles." Those with no common sense were "capped columns." Arrogant men and women, he dubbed "sleet": icy shell, all wet on the inside.

Even after all these years, Farrell knew that Portsteiner had never quite figured him out. When he first met Portsteiner, the old man had slid him into the "stellar crystal" file, for as Portsteiner had later admitted one night halfway through a bottle of Jack Daniel's, Farrell was one of the few natural skiers he'd ever seen.

That all changed when Farrell took a week off one February three years after he arrived in the canyon. He was gone three months without a word to anyone. When Farrell got back, the hill was melted, down to mud. He packed his things and told Portsteiner he was quitting and heading for Africa. That day Portsteiner filed him away as a "spatial dendrite," a strange mix of feathery crystals; he never knew what Farrell would do next.

This past December, almost twelve years to the day after he'd left Utah for Africa, Farrell had slipped into Portsteiner's office with a new hairline, thinner cheeks, the roadwork of pink scars, and a pair of eyebrows that Portsteiner said made him look "like a candidate for the Politburo." Farrell told him that after Africa he'd landed a job with a bank in Chicago working in Latin America as part of their lending operation.

"Makes a shitload of sense to me," Portsteiner said. "Now I know why banks are so mucked up."

Try as Farrell might, he couldn't bring himself to tell Portsteiner what had happened, about Lena, about the Mexicans. When the old man fished around, Farrell told him cryptically that he'd been forced into a dark room a few years back and had bumped into all the furniture, even though he knew the entire layout of his house. At one point in his blind grope, he'd found a little hallway with a single light bulb and he'd run down it. Soon there were other people chasing him and he'd had to jump out a window and flee. And here he was.

Portsteiner had drawn his tongue along the inside of his lower lip and tugged on his earlobe, a sure sign of discomfort and disgust. Right then Farrell understood that he'd been further downgraded in the Portsteiner filing system. Farrell was an "irregular particle" if there ever was one.

Even so, Farrell could tell Portsteiner still liked him. He brought Farrell to his house and fed him from time to time, drank with him once a week, and skied with him when he could. For that Farrell was more than grateful. Over the past six weeks, when the headaches and the tightness in his chest became intolerable, he looked forward to talking to the old skier. As long as the dialogue did not become too personal, Portsteiner's voice calmed him.

Now Portsteiner's short, stubby fingers drummed on the varnished bar. "Bad?" Farrell asked.

"Depends on your interpretation," Portsteiner said. His face softened.

Farrell sat silent; he'd found over the years that putting one's head over an emotional cliff can be a sickening experience. Portsteiner was having trouble even approaching the rim.

"Remember a guy named Timmons?" Portsteiner said finally.

"Saw him this morning," Farrell said. "Don't think he knew who I was."

Portsteiner squinted at Farrell. "You didn't tell him?"

"Better he doesn't know."

"You're some kind of asshole, Jack," Portsteiner said. "There's a walnut on the back of his neck that a month ago was a cashew. He's got six months."

Invisible fingertips brushed the hairs on the back of Farrell's neck and he shivered. He struggled with a surge of guilt for not having stayed with Timmons that morning. He noted how few were the experiences he'd had with the dying: on a road north into the Sahara, he'd once come upon the crash of a truck carrying sheep and nomads toward the Algerian border. Farrell had run through the heat, trying to sort the man from the lamb, the crying from the weeping. There was the piercing smell of gunpowder in the living room the day he'd returned to his parents' house so many years before. There was the stubborn ticking of a china clock on a mantelpiece and the dreadful robin's egg blue of a baby's arm. Now Timmons.

"How long is he here for?" Farrell asked.

"He's got a late flight out tomorrow evening," Portsteiner said. "Maybe it will snow for him again."

"Maybe," Farrell said dully.

Portsteiner raised his eyebrows. He huffed, "You know, Jack, you seem just busted up about your old friend."

Farrell turned away, embarrassed that he didn't feel more. He finished his second drink and waved to the bartender for another.

"You know," said Portsteiner finally, shaking his head, "the more I think of it, the more I realize I don't know the first thing about you, boy. You've never talked about where you come from, or anything."

"Unimportant," Farrell said. "I've found you just live for today, no behind you, no in front of you. You do all right."

"You think that way too long, you'll start to slide," Portsteiner said. "You know why?"

"I suppose you'll tell me," Farrell said.

"No past, no future, you're like a climber way up on the ice with no belay lines to set you; sooner or later you'll make a false step and there'll be nothing to hold on to when you go."

"The way I see it, there are some ropes not worth holding on to," Farrell said. "Easier that way."

Portsteiner tugged at his earlobe and considered Farrell for a moment. Then he said: "I don't know why I'm asking, but you want some dinner? You look like you haven't eaten enough lately."

"Can't right now," Farrell said. "Some French woman wants to talk to me."

"That moviemaker?"

"That's what she says."

"Hear her ski movies are good," Portsteiner said. "She interested in you?"

"Point is that I'm not interested in her."

"Speak of the devil," Portsteiner said.

Inez strode across the room like it was a stage and she the actress everyone had come to see. She played to the crowd as she flounced toward Farrell and Portsteiner, rolling her eyes, exaggerating each step so her jeans pulled too taut, her silver-tipped boots jingled, and her mottled brown leather jacket shimmied. Behind her came Page and The Wave.

"Surfus, brainus, minimus," Portsteiner said, smiling for the first time that evening.

"The Rasta?" Farrell said. "I don't think so. He talks strange, but there's a lot going on under that wild hairdo."

Before Portsteiner could respond, Inez was upon them. She drew both arms back toward her shoulders, palms up, and gushed: "Monsieur Portsteiner! It is marvelous to see you again. When I ask you about skiers to film, you do not tell me about this Collins."

"Collins, yeah," Portsteiner coughed. "Um, he's been back only a few months. Used to be pretty good. Haven't seen him ski too much recently, so I wouldn't know."

"Perhaps he skis in my film if you ask him?"

Portsteiner quickly glanced at Farrell, who was scrutinizing his own lap. "This boy strikes me as the stubborn type. Has to make his own decisions. Anyway, got to be going."

"I'll be in touch, Frank," Farrell said.

Portsteiner nodded and left.

"Buy me a drink?" Inez asked.

"And what does a European drink?"

"Not European, Collins. French."

Farrell made a half bow, excused himself, and headed down to the lobby to the small store where they sold liquor. He thought about walking to the truck and driving east on the canyon road out of the slide path and calling it a night. Definitely not: this woman was a curiosity and he decided to see where she was heading. He picked a nice red wine from the rack and cradled it under his sore right arm. He thought of all the deep powder turns he'd made during the last four days and decided that the actions of the shoulders and the wrists are crucial to the float: keep the body perpendicular to the fall line and the snow will reward you with flight.

He daydreamed of Canada, where the rich can ski on glaciers fifty miles from the nearest civilization, making endless, unsullied arcs through the snow toward their private helicopters. Farrell recalled a story he'd heard on the ski lift earlier that week about a shoe salesman from Boston who'd saved his money for four years to have one such perfect week. He arrived in Canada to find he'd been grouped with a movie producer from Los Angeles who had brought along his novice daughter. The salesman was forced to wait at the bottom of every run while the poor girl fell her way down the mountains. On the last night of the trip, the salesman got drunk, punched the producer in the mouth, and made the daughter cry.

Inez, Page, and The Wave had slid into a high-backed booth, so they didn't see Farrell coming. The Wave was talking. "I don't know about this one. Going through the woods like that. He's got cold eyes, doing shit like that. Seen them in dudes back in L.A.; they go off."

Farrell said: "What's the matter, kid, a little scared?"

The Wave jumped. "Didn't see you there, mon. But yeah, you're damn right."

Farrell slid in next to Inez. "These cold eyes boys you knew, what did they do, steal a comic book in the malls out in the Valley?"

"Shit, mon," The Wave said. "I'm no Valley dude. Grew up in Venice Beach. I know the streets. These dudes had their finger on the trigger."

Farrell held his hands up. "No gun on me, Wave. I'm a pacifist."

Inez broke in and asked Farrell to pour the wine. He drank while The Wave nervously turned the conversation to the day and the future weather conditions. The talk turned to the techniques of taking big jumps off cliffs. Page went down and bought two more bottles. As the wine flowed, the conversation shifted to camera angles and production values and then to skiing again.

"As I say so, I think America finds her heroes on teams," Inez said to Farrell. "But in France, and very well, in most of Europe, the public has a desire insatiable for stories of the individual. They gave a skier named Tardival an entire night to himself on national television this past year."

"Fewer people like that able to do it these days," Farrell said. "I think I read that other skier, Pierre Vallençant, died rock climbing last year. His wife two months later."

"They know the risks," Inez said.

"That isn't always an excuse," Farrell said.

Inez cocked her head and studied him. "I do not understand your English," she said. "Could you explain?"

Farrell saw then that Inez hadn't been drinking glass for glass with him, and through the blur, he realized his position was somewhat precarious. He squeezed his hands together under the table. *"Ce n'est rien?"*

Inez's eyes widened and she grinned. "You speak the French, then?"

"Passable," Farrell said. "Some Spanish, too."

"Good, then you help me when I become difficult," Inez said. "Here's the plan, okay? We come to create the film on the extreme skiing descents of the Western United States for the audience which is European."

"From what I understand, they'd be bored," Farrell said. "The Europeans are into feats that just aren't allowed here: linking climbs and descents in a single day—*enchainments*, the triathalon of thrill sports, isn't that what they call it?"

Inez nodded.

"And that crazy parapenting sport, launching yourself off the side of a mountain hitched to half a parachute. Besides, the terrain here is not half as dangerous as the Alps," Farrell continued.

"Just so," Inez said, and she ran her finger in circles on the table. "But there are ways to make it more dangerous, you know."

Before Farrell could ask her what, Page said: "A lot of what we do depends on the permission we get and the way it's filmed."

The Wave's dreadlocks bobbed. "It's all in the voltage we find, mon. We get ourselves to the most electrical chutes, plug in, and turn on. She does the rest."

Farrell pursed his lips; he was interested, but didn't want to be.

"I chase something different," Inez insisted. "Many of the films you see are shot in—how would you say it?—*écervelé?*"

"Madcap," Farrell said.

"In a tone madcap," Inez went on. "You know—oh, 'we are off to ski another wonderful place.' Really, this is nothing more than advertisements for ski resorts. I think what occurs is something more serious. I chase the head of the men who ski the extreme. To understand them on the basic level. Not a story of the voyage but the art, you know? We have the money, the patrons, and if the weather helps us, the time."

"What qualifies you?" Farrell asked.

Inez's face hardened. "I make two documentaries in France. These attract much attention. And I propose the idea to some capitalists willing to give me their money for profit. How I make the film, *c'est mon affair.*"

In spite of his misgivings, Farrell asked, "And where do you plan on making this film?"

"Here, Tahoe, Grand Tetons," Page said.

"Ranier in Washington and the Brooks Range in Alaska," The Wave added.

"My patrons, they want the film in the theaters in Europe in November," Inez said. "I begin to shoot since the end of January. We finish by mid-July."

"Quite a ride," Farrell said.

"It is," she said. "I believe you called it your ski bumming days. Did you go . . . how do you say *hors de piste* in English?

"Out of bounds or backcountry," Farrell said. "Yes, a bit."

"Then you have experience?"

"It's been years. But well enough."

"With the avalanche predictions, too?"

"Two years here," Farrell said. "Took courses with LaChapelle. But it was all a long time ago."

Page said: "Do you really know this canyon like you act?"

"I'm strictly in-bounds now," he said, trying to discourage them.

"But you know the runs out-of-bounds," Inez said.

"I know where they are."

There was a silence at the table that was palpable.

Inez began slowly. "We shoot you with the video, you know. Page does this in the woods yesterday without you knowing," she said, and then pushed on before Farrell could protest. "I say again, I like this style. So primitive. It makes the eye beg to follow you. I want you."

"Not interested," Farrell said. "I'm here to ski powder. To calm myself. To relax. I don't chase adrenaline anymore."

Inez's hands flexed into fists. Her voice became insistent: "But we ask people. We know you do not work. Every morning first in the line. Every afternoon, the last person to leave the mountain. No commitments.

"We are here to make the film about where you thrive," she continued. "And let me tell you this: I pay you very, very well."

Farrell felt the unmistakable sensation of the heel of a hand on the nape of his neck, pressing him toward a cliff he had no desire to look over. He leaned forward in his seat, took a deep breath, and reached toward a basket of popcorn. He allowed his elbow to veer slightly off course, tipping the last third of the wine bottle onto the brilliant yellow of The Wave's suit.

"You freaking glue-sniffing idiot!" The Wave yelled. He leaped to his feet, his mouth wide open in disbelief as the red wine turned his pulsing neon crotch the color of mud.

"See now, I've had way too much to drink," Farrell said. He jumped up beside The Wave and brushed at him with his napkin. "I really should sleep this off."

Inez had covered her mouth with a napkin. Page sat with his chin in his hands, silent. Farrell said, "As I told your boys, I don't think I'm right for it."

He hurried out the door before she could protest. He stumbled down the stairs and out the door into the frigid night. A shooting star tore across the sky. He stood outside the camper breathing in the clear, cold air, willing his heart to calm and his mind to stop racing. After five minutes ice had formed on his upper lip. He shivered. He drove the camper a mile east to the end of the road, parked, and climbed into the camper. His head throbbed with the alcohol, and his stomach rolled at the knowledge that he'd somehow escaped a dangerous situation.

He wrapped himself in his sleeping bag and tried to sleep. But Portsteiner's words came back to him. *You're like a climber way up on the ice with no belay lines. . . .* He flipped on the light inside the camper and knelt on the bunk so he could reach above himself to the small compartment that contained his only links with his past. He slid the wood back and thrust his arm in past the envelope that contained his money and the phone number of a banker in Telluride, past the jewelry box, past Lena's nightgown, past her jewelry box, and drew Lena's diary and a photograph out. He flopped on the bunk and looked at them like museum artifacts.

He stared at the picture of Lena and their infant daughter, Jenny. He paused long on Lena's shoulder-length auburn hair that framed the high cheekbones of her face, her gentle nose, the freckles, the green light of her eyes. She was smiling, as usual, the warm, inviting smile that had followed one of her funny, cutting remarks in the early days of their marriage. Jenny was no more than four months old in the photograph, dressed in a pink jumper, her crystal blue eyes staring up at her mother in adoration.

He closed his eyes and considered how tenuous being connected really is: jobs, families, life itself can go in a blink. He wondered whether he'd ever reestablish himself as a thread in the web. He put the photograph down.

When he opened his eyes, the diary seemed to stare back at him. The fact that Lena kept a diary still amazed him. Few people wrote down their thoughts anymore. How did Lena put it the first time he saw her writing in it, the morning after their third night together? "I write only of the things that matter to me, emotional, physical, and psychological," she had said.

Farrell lay under the blankets in her apartment in Chicago. "Why limit yourself?" he asked.

"I'm ordinary," she said. "I like ordinary things."

"Hardly," Farrell said. And at that moment in the camper he recalled how vulnerable he'd felt thinking of what she may have recorded. "Where do I fit in?" he'd asked.

She stood from her desk, then crawled under the covers. "I can't tell yet, lover. But I fear you are all three."

Her words echoed to him off the camper walls. He smiled a ter-rible, chin-trembling smile. Since he was a child, he'd developed the ability to separate his experiences and box them away in his mind where they would not disturb him. Now he was torn between the need to know what words lay within the diary and the need to keep harsh memories stored away where they couldn't hurt him. He thought about that word "ordinary." He had used it as an ex-cuse for everything he had done, as if ordinary were something bad, something to take advantage of, something to run from.

Farrell gritted his teeth to quell the swelling that ran up the back of his throat. Then he stood and returned the diary to the compartment, understanding that sooner or later he'd have to lis-ten to her. Right then, though, he did not have the strength. Right then Farrell was a coward. He pulled her nightgown from the hole, balled it into a pillow so he could smell her, and fell into a deep, dark sleep.

Chapter 3

The first person Farrell saw in the lift line the next morning was Paul Timmons, who stamped his feet in anticipation of being in the first chair. Farrell looked at his stooped shoulders, then skated up to him.

"Beat me to it," Farrell said.

"Had to," Timmons grinned.

"You still need someone to ski with?" Farrell asked.

"If you can keep up," Timmons said, still smiling.

On the ride up the hill, they remarked on the breathy snow that had fallen during the night and how it wafted away from their pants with the flick of a hand. Throughout the day they explored all the nooks and crannies at Alta: Alf's High Rustler, the Eagle's Nest, Gunsight, Yellow Trail, and White Squaw glade. About two in the afternoon, the snow stopped and the sun broke through the clouds. They decided to ski out of bounds off the eastern edge of the area. To get there, they had to climb a short ridge. Timmons stopped twice and coughed violently. In a fit of guilt, Farrell told him who he was.

"Thought you looked familiar, but different with those scars," Timmons said. "And is that a wig? They say I might be needing one of those soon."

Farrell looked away. "It's not as painful as that."

They both fell quiet, the weight of Timmon's load hanging in the air between them. Farrell shuffled by Timmons and found a forty-yard stretch of untracked snow. The two men spilled into it beside each other, instinctively sensing each other's rhythm until they began to cross each other's path and cut figure eights down the side of the slope.

In late afternoon, while the patrolmen shut down the farthest lift, Supreme, Farrell turned to Timmons: "Last run—what's it gonna be?"

"Moon dance," Timmons said.

Farrell swallowed hard. "You up to it?"

"Not Cardiac Ridge," Timmons said. "We'll go into Devil's Castle."

Behind closed lips, Farrell ground his teeth together, then nodded. The Castle, a giant alpine bowl rimmed by cliffs that tower over the backside of Alta, hadn't been open all day. The snow would be loose, spillable, treacherous, an undeniable allure.

They skied down a deserted trail, ducked under a rope, and hid in the woods until the ski patrol swept by and disappeared. They took off their skis and climbed toward a particular notch in the Castle's stonework that the locals call the Apron: a hundred-yard waterfall of snow tapered at the top, fat and bulging like a pregnant woman's smock. They waited quietly in the spruces below the Apron until almost six o'clock when the sun set and the moon rose behind them, almost full, bathing the bowl in a gentle light.

Farrell broke trail on the final ascent. He stayed hard by the edge of the forest so they wouldn't be spotted from below by the men who ran the snow-grooming equipment. Halfway up, the snow became deep and slack like a dune of wind-swept sand; with every step little rivers of snow gave way and poured down the steep hill behind them. "Moves much more and we could be on a quick freight train down this hill," Farrell said.

Timmons gasped for air behind Farrell, steadied himself, then turned and plotted his position. "It's your time to go down now, anyway."

"No. Too tricky to go alone." Farrell said.

"This is my last run," Timmons insisted. "I want to drop in solo."

For a moment Farrell thought about arguing. But it all seemed stale. A tiny sapling jutted from the snow next to him. He reached out and snapped a fresh sprig off the crown. He pulled the elastic band of the goggles away from Timmons's head and slid the fir branch inside.

"Insurance," Farrell said.

Timmons nodded and patted Farrell on the shoulder. "Tear it up."

Farrell made a dozen tight turns in the moonlight, yet the snow that burst around his legs offered no pleasure. He cut left onto a ridge where he could see the entire length of the Apron. During the next twenty minutes the temperature dove and Farrell had to stamp his feet and swing his arms to stay warm. Timmons climbed close to the left wall of the cliff, using his skis as levers to pry himself higher and higher on the fabric of the Apron. His progress was slow. One time he slid six or seven feet and almost tumbled over backward, which caused Farrell to cry out: "Jesus!"

Timmons caught himself and stood for a long while until he'd regained his balance. Another fifteen minutes and he'd made it to the top, a smudge on the mountainside. His movements were careful as he put on his skis, calculated not to disturb the sleeping bear. Yet even Farrell could see fresh powder settling and rolling around the tall man. Farrell whipped his head from side to side, trying to clear it, trying to think of all the ways this could go.

Timmons got the second ski on after several tries. He picked up his poles. Without waiting, as if he knew the slope wouldn't hold much longer, he jumped. He managed to make four swoops through the powder, each turn throwing a burst of pale silver glitter behind him. He dropped to his left at an unnatural angle. His body stuttered as if the snow underneath him were trying to catch its breath before a sneeze.

Then it came—the *woomph!*—the burst of air from under the snow, the mountain's terrible exhalation. Farrell grabbed a branch for support, sure now that Timmons was a goner. The snow sloughed and rolled like milk boiling over the edge of a sauce pan. Timmons stayed centered in the middle of the froth, a blue raft breeching white water. The unseen fingers of the avalanche reached up and squeezed Timmons; he popped to the surface and crouched on top of the running snow for a full two seconds, his hands cast in front of his chest as if he were in prayer.

After running for fifty yards, the slide crested; as it did, Timmons let his left hand fall. He punched his right hand high over his head, the motion kicking him out of the course of the surging snow. The slide spread another forty yards and threw up a sparkling cloud. Timmons skied on as if nothing had happened, speeding like some old goat breaking for a ridge. Farrell stood below Timmons as he approached. Timmons flushed a spruce grouse when he came over the top of the knoll and the bird flew straight at Farrell, forcing him to duck down. Timmons schussed by. The moonlight illuminated his face: the doomed man's lips were drawn back across his teeth, his cheeks fluttered, and his eyes were glassy, wide and set, as if he'd seen a ghost and laughed.

Farrell caught up to Timmons at the parking lot. Timmons wouldn't look at him. He just bent over, stepped out of his bindings, and said, "It's seven-thirty. I need a ride to the airport; I've got an eight forty-five flight to catch."

Farrell nodded and in spite of himself he shivered; Timmons now seemed more of a phantom than ever.

They drove the first part of the twisting road out of the canyon in silence. Six miles down, the road runs due west, revealing the city lights in the basin. Timmons opened his window and stuck his head out for a moment. When he pulled back in, his eyes were watering.

"I love the way light plays off the mountains at night," Timmons said. "You know: the shadows in the ravines and the big pastures all white like that one up there. After seeing something as beautiful as the Little Cottonwood, it's hard to believe nature can be so tough."

"But not invincible," Farrell said.

"Pissing in the wind and keeping your pants dry is not the answer," Timmons said thoughtfully. He broke into a wide grin. "But it gets you close and makes you feel a sight more comfortable with the inevitable."

"I've never seen anything like it," Farrell agreed. "What now?"

"I'm going home," said Timmons. "I'm going to just be with my wife and my sons and see if simple acts, like holding them and kissing them and throwing a ball with them, are as soothing as the dramatic ones. The more I think about it, those two little boys are the best medicine I could have right now."

They arrived at the terminal thirty-five minutes later. Timmons handed his luggage to the skycap, then turned to Farrell. "You seem sick, too, my friend."

"I'm fine," Farrell said defensively.

Timmons shook his head: "One thing this has given me is a bulletproof shit detector. I'm not one to give advice, but I guess the only thing I can tell you after today is to go back to what's important. It won't cure you, but it will help."

He shook Farrell's hand, then hurried off.

Farrell started the truck and drove the streets of Salt Lake, confused and not sure where he should go. Light rain began to splatter off the windshield. He wanted to think of what Timmons had told him, to search for a lesson. Rather, every time he began to examine it, his mind jumped sideways to images of Inez, Page, and The Wave and their plan to ski the most radical terrain in the United States. Despite his resolve to find serenity in the deep-powder float, his heart fluttered at the idea of being poised high on a steep mountainside where his mind would become terribly acute, honed to the point where he could actually taste air. He knew from experience that at those moments time would drag in slow motion. He knew it was due to a tiny pink tissue in the middle of his head— the amygydal, a powerful neural organ that coats fear with chemicals that sharpen and focus the senses. In situations frought with danger, every hair on his body would stand on end, pulsing to the slightest change in temperature or pressure. His nose would become as powerful as a beagle's. His eyes as strong as a hawk's. Another juice would be secreted next door in the hippocampus— the section of the brain that controls the perception of time—and each second would seem to have the diversity and richness of an hour.

Stopped at a red light near the center of the city, Farrell longed for the feeling of perfect clarity. He tried to calm the flutter in his stomach by summoning up pictures of wispy snowfalls in Montana, the cold-smoke powder of ski areas like Big Sky and Bridger Bowl. The daydream broke, replaced by Timmons. What did he prove up there on the Apron? That he'd had his moment? Sure he did, but soon his gross motor skills would depart, followed by incontinence and life in bed and . . .

Farrell stomped on the accelerator. Ahead, lit by spot lights, he could see the Mormon Temple Square. He parked, not quite sure of his motives, went back into the camper, and retrieved Lena's diary.

A light wind kicked leaves across the cement when he passed through the south gate toward the temple. Pious music filtered through the trees, raising in him the sort of anxiety that he had previously reserved for the Stations of the Cross during Lent. The story of Judas and his thirty pieces of silver, a tale a nun taught him in the second grade, seemed especially pertinent.

A quartet in a small stone building nearby played Brahms. Farrell entered and listened, admiring the serene glow on the faces of the musicians. After ten minutes, their blissful smiles put him on edge. He left. Oak branches cracked over his head as he walked. Outside the Tabernacle, a massive building with a long, curved roof, a young woman told him that the choir was taking a break, but would begin its practice again soon. Farrell walked down the aisle with the diary under his arm, studying the dome and the balconies, running his hand along the pine benches. Choir members mingled on a raised stage in front of the bronze pipes of the organ, which rose a full two stories off the wooden floor.

One of the women told a joke he couldn't hear. Her friends laughed. Farrell resented their happiness. He tried to formulate an edge to the situation, imagining all the horrors that must occur behind the closed doors of Mormon homes: child abuse, wife beating, ignorance, drugs, racism. But the verbs to drive the nouns would not come. He slumped into a pew and glanced at the diary. He took the tiny key from his pocket and slid it into the mechanism. The click bounced off the acoustically perfect ceiling. He turned back the cover, saw Lena's fine script, and moaned.

The first page had been embossed by the company that manufactured the diary. The gold and black lettering said THE DIARY OF _____. And on the blank line, she'd written: "Me?"

Farrell squeezed his eyes shut, opened them, flipped forward past her years in college at Georgetown, past her early days as a nurse, to where he knew their story began:

October 15

I delivered twins today. Healthy twins. Nothing wrong. Two beautiful little girls. Their mom, Gwen, named them Jennifer and Theresa.

John, their dad, cried when he held them and stroked their

fine black hair. Me, too. Paula, the other nurse on duty, looked at me like I was nuts. I told her I'd just spent two years in oncology. She smiled and told me I'd get as used to this as I did to the cancer ward. I don't think so. The magic in Gwen's eyes is powerful and true and I don't think repetition can dim such light, such life.

I met this cocky guy, a banker down in the Loop at a party last week. His name is Jack Farrell and he has a sly way of peeking at your chest while he's talking. Nothing blatant, but it's there. The third time I caught his eyes dropping below my neckline, I just up and stared at his crotch, which seemed to shatter his composure; he excused himself and said he had to get a beer. I can be cocky, too: you don't survive a childhood in Quincy, Mass. being shy.

Later I was talking to my roommate, Christina, and she whispered that a guy was staring at me. Him again. I stared back until he looked away. Around midnight we started talking. I can tell he's from New England, he says Maine. Probably spent every summer sailing. Anyway, five minutes into the conversation, he asks me out on a date. I asked him why I should. (Christina says I was born cold: it's true!)

Jack said it was something about the way I smelled. I told him it sounded like he thought I needed to take a shower. His face blushed and he jabbered how he didn't mean it that way at all. I just laughed and said I needed to go outside, maybe take an air bath. When I walked away I could feel his eyes on my rear. I whipped around and told him he'd never get a date leering at me like that. The look he gave me was almost pitiful.

He followed me onto the balcony and told me this funny story about trying to work in Guatemala when his understanding of Spanish was limited to *Sí* and *Va Ya Con Dios!* We laughed and he told me he could really use another beer. He gave me this same puppy expression. I couldn't believe he wanted me to fetch him one. I asked him why I should. He said that if I didn't, he wouldn't be able to ogle my behind as I walked across the room. I told him to get his own drink, so I could study his.

We talked to almost three in the morning. And yes, I admit it—he's intriguing and handsome in his way. He's lived all over the world. He travels to Mexico and South America on his job. And when he's not being a jerk, he's almost nice. Let's face it, when you reach your mid-twenties, you're willing to overlook some male traits you can fix!

He became rather gentlemanly walking me out to find a cab at three a.m. Christina stayed the night at Wally's.

Anyway, when I was waiting for the cab, Jack stood out on Sheridan Avenue with me. He started telling me he lived in Africa. I called his bluff; his life is too fantastic. He assured me it was true, that he'd lived with nomads for two years. I'm a pushover for that kind of thing. He sensed a softening in my face, I guess, because he asked me for a date again. I said, My armpits are like magnets, huh?

His face turned all red and I thought I'd gone too far. So I told him to call me sometime, but I didn't give him the number. I left him with a research job. What's on my mind is that he hasn't called. And I kind of wish he would.

I'm happy though. Twins were born again today. I helped.

Farrell looked up wondering how it was that such a light voice had the power to thunder in his head. It had been so long since he'd heard her.

He'd never danced in the streets before, but he found himself almost skipping along the sidewalks the night he met Lena O'Rourke. He remembered how her hair hung on her shoulders, wild and yet controlled; the way her legs flexed and rolled when she walked; and as she noted, the way her smell intoxicated him, hatching butterflies in his head. She smelled like a lake in the spring just after the ice has melted. Later in the evening Farrell decided she was the fresh ginger root he'd whiffed in the markets of Africa. At the same time, he knew that if he nuzzled her, she'd hit him with a right hook and somehow that had pleased him more than anything.

The sound of someone scuffing their foot, like fine sandpaper across the varnished pine floor, broke his train of thought. Farrell opened his eyes to a little girl, no more than three, with blond hair and blue eyes, sitting in the pew in front of him. She giggled and waved. Farrell thought of Jenny and looked away. Just live one moment at a time.

More choir members crowded the stage. Some broke into song, warming their throats after their break. A woman did deep knee bends. Others thrust their arms left and right, up and back. More men with their wives and children brushed by his seat. Some of the kids hung over the back of their benches, idly tracing their fingers on the wood. Farrell flipped forward a few pages.

October 16

Jack Farrell called me at work last night. Only two moms in the beds, early labor, so I took it. He asked if I remembered him? I said, Sure, you're the guy who thinks I stink nicely. I heard some crunching on the line, but he didn't say anything. I thought I'd blown it, then he sputtered and asked. I said, Sure, I'll have dinner with you Saturday. He hung up straightaway.

October 22

I had a long night Friday with a mother named Sheila, a single woman who was bound and determined to have her baby naturally. She's one of these New Age moms who see it as a badge of honor—didn't want to be in the hospital.

At midnight I started talking Cesarean. If there'd been a knife in the room, it would have been in me. When she'd finished a tirade about the C-section being a plot by the male-dominated AMA, and, I might add, a particularly brutal contraction, I told her, Fine—you want to put your baby in danger because of some half-baked theory, you do it. I think you're going to have to learn that, as a parent, compromises are part of life. There's a whole other part of this hospital dedicated to making kids comfortable while they die of reasons that even I don't understand. You want to take a chance on your baby for some protest, you do it. Be prepared to accept the consequences. I'll be outside waiting your decision.

They performed the C-section at two-thirty. A pretty girl.

Anyway, that was on my mind when Jack Farrell knocked at the door last night with three roses in his hand. I told him that the rule of the evening was this: that if I caught him trying to get downwind of me more than twice I was leaving.

He was perfect. He told stories, he opened doors, he made me laugh. After dinner, we danced at a blues club on Sheridan Road. He told me he loves the fall, which I do, too. He said he skis, which I don't and never want to—too scary. When the night was over, he didn't push: he just saw me to the door and kissed me on the cheek.

He's going away for a week to Central America. But we made a date for next Sunday, here, dinner.

November 5

The Pinto's busted again. I called Jack to tell him he'd have to make dinner. He was waiting at the L station with three roses and a tan that should be against the law in Chicago this time of year.

He has a small, one-bedroom apartment filled with sculpture and paintings from all the places he's been. One painting is of two African women pounding cereal in a big mortar. The colors were so brilliant I thought the artist had used oil. I looked closer and realized the whole thing was made of butterfly wings.

Next to it was a photograph of Jack on skis flying off a cliff out West somewhere. He's silhouetted against the sky and my stomach flip-floped just looking. Jack said he loves the feeling of falling, of not knowing what will happen next. Me? When I go to movies I'm always begging people, even strangers!, to tell me how they think it will turn out. Not knowing is exciting, but I'd rather have an idea of the end. Mom's like that, too—two chapters into a book she peeks at the ending.

Jack made chicken breasts sautéed in cumin and garlic, then drenched them in warm avocado and salsa sauce. Jack's mom made him learn to cook when he was ten. He said she was a strong-willed woman who ruled their home more that his father did. His father died a long time ago. The muscles in his face tense when he talks of him.

I changed the subject and we sat on his couch listening to an Aretha Franklin record. We kissed. Our first.

The idiot asked me if I wanted to continue in the bedroom! I asked him if he got erections just looking at ice cream cones. He pushed back, glanced at his lap and asked me what I was talking about? I told him I read somewhere that men can get hard just looking at ice cream cones—it's just a physical response.

A grin spread across his face. He said, Lena, I'd call you a sundae. Which, in spite of myself, I kind of liked. He rode all the way home on the L with me, walked me to my door, and didn't even try to get in the apartment. When he kissed me goodnight, I thought: Jack Farrell has potential.

Farrell closed the diary. The fine hair on the back of his neck tingled until it stood on end. He had been in love after that night. In a small church ceremony the March after they met, with just his mother and Lena's parents in attendance, he married her. Lena was pregnant almost immediately. For the first time in his life, Farrell was pleasantly at anchor.

The little girl with the blond hair waved again. "Hi ya, mister," she said in a squeeky voice. "Why ya eyes red?"

She held her arms out to Farrell as if she wanted to be picked up. Without thinking, Farrell reached for her, but her mother twisted in her seat, saw Farrell's face, and pulled the girl back and turned her around in the seat. For a split second, Farrell saw his daughter Jenny lying facedown in her cradle and all the false calm he'd built for himself since fleeing San Diego begin to crack. It widened as the hundreds of voices on the stage under the organ—sopranos followed by altos and tenors and basses—raised in hymn.

Farrell swallowed. He gripped the front of the bench in front of him. The little girl shifted in her seat to place her hand on his. He pulled his hand away, thinking of all the things he had used in the past three months to ease the knots and keep his memories boxed away—the open road, the broad alpine vistas, and the falling snow. He stood. The choir conductor, a balding man sitting on a black stool, raised his hands. The voice of the choir soared. The little girl laid her head on her mother's lap, sucked at her thumb. She gazed at Farrell.

Farrell stepped drunkenly into the aisle. He walked a chalkline to the back of the hall through the doors and out into the rain. He bent over, hands on his knees for almost five minutes, willing himself not to vomit. The tempo of rain increased, the freezing droplets stinging his neck and cheeks. Farrell tucked the diary inside his coat and ran to the truck. He drove like a maniac through the streets of the city toward the mouth of the canyon. He thought of the little girl and of himself at four crying because he'd peed in his pants even though he was toilet trained and the way his father had told him to hush, first gently, then louder until he screamed at him to quiet. His father had handed Farrell to his mother—"He's got it," his father had said sadly. "Like my dad and grandmother and her father before her." Farrell remembered how his father had stomped into a back room and slammed the door shut.

A half mile up the road, the rain turned to snow.

Farrell stopped at several lodges before he found the name at the registration desk. He knocked at an oak door. Inez opened it.

"Collins," Inez said, her hazel eyes wide. She reached out to squeeze his forearm. *"Mais,* this is not a good time. I do the interview with Page."

Page stood behind her by the bed, which was covered with topographical maps. Beside him were movie and video cameras mounted on tripods. Images of the maps and one of the pillows glowed in an orange tint on a color monitor on the desk.

Farrell fought the pounding in his chest and at the back of his head. "I know a run called the Y Couloir," he said with the breathlessness of a spent sprinter. "I think it's what you're after."

Inez took Farrell's hands in hers. They were smooth hands. He did not get the warm touch he expected. Inez's hands were clammy. "All day I wish for you to come," she said. "Meet me tomorrow, nine o'clock. We talk."

She squeezed his fingers once more and closed the door.

Farrell trudged to the camper. He felt drained, yet somehow happy and relieved that he had talked to Inez again; the ripping sensation that had enveloped him in the Tabernacle was ebbing away. He drove to the end of the road again, backed the truck into the snow wall, and firmly attached the brake. He struggled to open the camper door, which had frozen shut. It gave way with a sharp crack. He climbed inside, trembling.

Farrell stood there, snow melting at his feet, running his fingertips over the cover of the diary. He slid the book back into its hiding place above the bunk, stripped, wiggled into the sleeping bag, and buried his face in the pillowcase that held Lena's nightgown. He inhaled deeply, catching only the faintest tinge of her odor. He fell asleep that way: one hand clutching the corner of his wife's nightgown, the other clamped between his legs. He drifted off into forgetfulness, amazed at the harsh, windmill turns one is forced to make on the steepness of emotional terrain.

Chapter 4

From the thick stand of cottonwoods below it, the Y Couloir resembles a long bent branch sawed from a gnarled old crab apple tree propped against a rickety old barn wall. Nearly vertical walls of limestone, in many places no more than fifteen feet apart, hem in the ravine, which, as the winter progresses, fills with snow. Still, the powder provides only a partial buffer; the stones on the sides of the chute and those that jut through the snow in the middle of the slash on the side of the mountain are sharp, silent daggers that would slash at a skier's legs if they made the slightest mistake coming down. Fifteen hundred feet up the chute, after it makes a crazy dog-leg turn to the right, there are ledges and stumps that mark the joining of the two upper arms of the run. Viewed from the bottom, it is a nightmare vision for the two arms leap almost straight up from the intersection of the Y; it is the sort of thing only a mountain goat climbs.

The danger inherent in trying to slide down such a narrow throat, dodging rock and trees, did not impress Inez.

"This is bullshit," she said, leaning back to look up the mouth of the couloir. "Where is the crevasse that waits like the open mouth to swallow the skier? Where is the cliff to jump? This is for the child. I film the limit."

The Wave kicked his boot through the fresh powder that still lay in the shade of a Jackpine about twenty feet away. "That's not child's play, lady. That's a freaking screamer run if I ever saw one."

Page nodded. "It's as harsh as I've seen in a long time."

Inez dismissed them both with a flick of her hand. "Yes, yes, it is steep. Forty, maybe forty-five degrees of pitch, but this is not radical. My audience breaks into laughter if we try to tell them this Y is extreme."

Farrell watched a crow off to his left that fluttered its wings in a clearing near the trail's end. Its feathers brushed pinpoint, stellar crystals into the air. Hearing Inez, the bird cocked its head left, then right, then left again. It hopped forward and opened its beak to reveal a ruby tongue. The crow thrust the tongue out, then snapped a solitary floating crystal. Puzzled at tasting something stronger than cold air, the bird craned its head and snapped again. Inez stepped on a branch, cracking it. Alerted, the crow stabbed a slice of jack pinecone from the snow and flew away. Farrell was mesmerized by the way the bird's lazy slap of wing stirred an eddy of transparent pink and purple and white in the air. The bird cawed, dropped its cone, and raced off through the trees.

Farrell said: "So tell me, Inez: what's extreme?"

Inez struggled back through a drift, tucking a light meter and a brown pocket notebook in her navy blue jacket. She swung her arms wildly at the three of them. "The trouble with you Americans is you think any situation where for a moment you lose the slope or leave the ground, this is extreme. It is the word used too much . . . like love. For me, the extreme is the act of balance where even the skier does not know the future."

"So," Farrell said carefully. "You have no regard for the skier."

Inez's fingers curled to their palms. It was, he decided, an involuntary act. She leaned against a tree and studied Farrell. *"Au contraire,"* she said, just as slow and just as careful. "I wish the skier success, to be a . . . a champion."

"And that occurs . . . ?"

"At the limit."

"Talk about an overused term."

Inez took a deep breath and her cheeks hardened. "You wish me to be cold?"

"Just candid."

Inez knelt, took the glove from her hand, and traced a series of interlocking circles in the snow. Her eyes went blank, her cheeks slack. She spoke in a husky voice. "I look for the place where the fall without control kills the skier," she said. "If they fall over the front of the skis, they hit the obstacle or fall off the cliff or the things about them—stumps, rocks, these things—they will crash."

"Well, fuck you, lady!" The Wave said. "You may be paying me. But I'm into keeping my body just the way you see it: solid, wise."

Inez talked on as if she didn't hear him: "I do not wish this to happen, the skier to fall. I fear this more than all, perhaps. *Mais,* I believe that most people want to see this kind of skiing. We are all the voyeurs, no? We have this urge so, so strong to peek through the little holes between the fingers we almost always press to the eyes."

She stood. "The patron, uh, how do you say? The customer? Yes, the customer demands that look at the mystery or the film is lost. There must be the danger mortal or the audience does not buy it. This is not the aesthetic only; it is the economic standard. Does my English make sense?"

In the silence after she spoke, Page crossed his arms and cleared his throat: "Perfectly," he said. "You want kamikazes like that guy I heard died in your last film."

"This was the accident!" Inez snapped, and she turned away. Her voice dropped. "Alan knows his risks and he wants to go there, beyond all who climb and ski before. It slaps me hard when he falls. But this is what it is. Yes, like him, I want skiers to not back away from . . . their fears."

An achy sensation rushed up Farrell's spine that reminded him of the drug the government's doctors had threaded into him before they repaired his face. The chemical name was scopolamine, a narcotic that leaves the patient halfway between nod and reality. The doctors called it by its nickname: Twilight Sleep.

Farrell had the same drugged reaction earlier that morning when he'd met Inez for breakfast in a restaurant on the fourteenth floor of her lodge. They had a panoramic view of the snow-capped mountains spread out before them. Inez told Farrell that her father had been an American, a respected photographer with the Associated Press who died in Vietnam. She had followed slightly to the left of his footsteps, attending film school in Paris. Afterward, she drifted into the climbing and skiing scene at the French Alps town of Chamonix, working first as a for-hire photographer for Americans who enjoyed the fact that she spoke some English. Gradually, she had built a reputation that brought in funding for her films.

She questioned Farrell closely about his past, queries which he fended off with glib responses. She pressed, and as before, he told her only that his most recent life had ended badly, that he'd come to the Utah mountains to begin again. Farrell could see his answers made Inez even more curious, but he guided the conversation away.

They negotiated an oral contract. Farrell would guide and ski in those ranges in which he was familiar: Utah's Wasatch and the Grand Tetons in Wyoming. At Tahoe, Page's home territory, Farrell would act under his direction.

"Now," she said, "I wish to begin interviews tomorrow night."

"No interviews," Farrell said. "My history is my own and I'd just as soon let it die."

"Discussion is the foundation of my films," Inez insisted. "My audience demands the skier's mind between the shots of action."

Farrell said: "No interviews or no cowboy."

Inez took a long drag off the unfiltered cigarette she was smoking, squinted, and smiled. "Of course. But you give me the opportunity to remake the negotiation, no?"

Something about her was fascinating. "How could I resist?"

Over the course of the meal, they cut the rest of the deal: if she was not happy with his services after the first leg of the shoot, she could fire him without pay, no questions asked. He got assurances they'd be finished by July. Farrell figured with five months lead time before the film hit the European market, his trail would have long since run cold. Even if the FBI or Cortez's men happened to recognize him, he'd be in the South Pacific or back in Africa.

Now, standing below the Y Couloir, Farrell wondered whether the deal would hold. He could see that The Wave and Page were thinking of cutting out; Inez seemed more than they'd bargained for. As for himself, hearing her talk about her theories made him only more intrigued.

She went on in a seductive, yet sarcastic manner: "But I see maybe I choose the wrong skiers: someone who does not wish to find his form again. The beginner without courage. The cowboy who does not wish to ride the horse."

The Wave skuffed the snow with his boot. "No one said we're going anywhere, lady."

"Just a little startled with the point of view here," Page said nervously. "Nothing that can't be handled."

"And you?" Inez demanded.

"I thought we just got started," Farrell said.

"*Bien,*" Inez replied, throwing her hands on her hips. "Now tell me about something, anything in this canyon, to scare me."

"Follow me," Farrell said. He led them back along the trail to the road. There the snow that had fallen during the night had melted. The pavement shone like a freshly waxed car. Farrell sat on the hood of one of the Japanese four-wheel trucks Inez had rented.

"People come here, to Little Cottonwood, for soft snow, not extreme skiing," he said. "It's steep, but you're right, by European standards it's benign. The problem's the mountains themselves. The Wasatch is a crumbling range. There's granite up here, but it's falling apart because of the weather patterns—hot, dry summers, cold winters, the constant wind. The rest of the peaks here are quartzite, a lot softer."

"Your point?" Inez asked.

"The point is that in Chamonix or Verbier in Switzerland or even north of here in the Tetons, the rock's hard. So you find sheer breaks, not decomposing walls. You find drops like chimney flues. Powder snow as light as falls here won't stick at truly vertical angles. You need a slope that's in the sun much of the winter, preferably south-facing, where the snow will constantly melt and freeze to compose a firm base. There's a bunch of south-facing gullies like that here in the canyon, but only one place—it's called the Hellgate—that you can get to with the type of terrain you're looking for."

"Yes?" Inez said.

"But it will be at least six weeks before it settles enough to ski."

Inez slapped the side of the truck. "You waste my time."

"I lay out options," Farrell said. "The only radical terrain available now is back-country powder skiing, which doesn't look dangerous, but is. Or something like the Y Couloir, which will look great on film, but may not measure up to European standards. Or you wait."

Inez said nothing. She climbed in the truck and slammed shut the door. She lay back against the neck rest, her eyes closed.

"This woman's out of it," The Wave said.

"You volunteered, remember?" Page said.

"Don't remind me," The Wave said.

"How'd she find you?" Farrell asked.

"Didn't," The Wave said. "A friend of hers, a photographer from New York, was out shooting pictures at Mount Bachelor in Oregon last fall—the day I got kicked off the team. Next thing I know, I get a call, Inez wants to see me. She flies in, I do a test, and she signs me. Then I don't hear a thing until two weeks ago, when I got tickets in the mail to come out here."

"What were you kicked off for, the team I mean?" Farrell asked.

The Wave grinned. "Let's say I got a real good bad attitude."

"You?" Farrell said to Page.

Page leaned back on the hood with his arms under his head. "She showed up in Taos one day about a month ago, hears I'm around and wants to talk. First person to be interested in me in years."

"Why's that?"

"Had a problem with a different kind of snow," Page said. "Kind of got me off track."

Farrell winced—he did not want to hear more.

"A guy really died in the last film?" The Wave asked.

Page nodded. "That's what they say. Haven't seen it myself. But a friend of mine said he caught it at one of those funky ski festivals at Vail. Called it an honest-to-god ski snuff film."

Farrell inspected the mountains, thinking about a daredevil who dies on film. He expected to find the idea frightening. Instead it seemed the definition of tranquility.

Inez flung the truck door open and jumped out. "Collins!" she demanded. "One can ski this Y Couloir more early than this Hellgate?"

Farrell glanced at the Y. "Even in powder, I think, but you'd want it to sit for a few days after a storm. Sure, later this week, early next."

Inez grabbed a pair of binoculars from the truck and peered at the great ravine. "How much time does it take to ski from the top of each arm down to the *carrefoure?*"

"Intersection," Farrell said.

"Yes, yes. Intersection where the two arms come together."

"Let me see those glasses a second," Farrell said. He focused them on the left of the two spindly channels and then the right.

"About the same, I should think," he said after a moment. "No, I take that back. The left arm is probably shorter, but it's steeper and requires a nasty right turn where the arms converge. The right channel is more direct, but longer. Any skier in that right shot will have to consider his speed at the junction where it dog-legs left and drops to the canyon floor. Too much acceleration and he's going to crash into that stone wall—break the skis or a neck."

"So it's not a true Y?" said Page.

"Well, look at it," Farrell said. "Not in the sense of a letter scribbled on a piece of paper. It's a Y where the fork is bent to the right off the stem."

Inez's eyes had taken on a glassy dull finish again, her voice had deepened. "Obstacles?" she asked.

"No cliffs or crevasses, as you pointed out earlier," Farrell said. "But at the junction, a fall of rock and stumps extends out between the two arms, it makes the going very tight, like picking your way through a mine field."

"And the ledge, it supports the camera, no?" she asked.

Farrell looked through the binoculars again. "No. They'd have to be higher, in pits dug in the snow or among the trees to either side of the fork. Even then you wouldn't get a clear angle all the way up either arm. You'll need a third camera from across the road or from a helicopter hovering over the whole thing."

Inez drummed her fingers on the hood of the truck, her attention still focused on the couloir. From her hip pack, she extracted a brown notebook and began to sketch. In a few quick strokes the shape of the couloir appeared. "Tell me the thing you love, Collins, the speed or steepness?" she asked, tapping the eraser on the paper.

"I don't follow."

"This Y, it is your idea," she said. "Which arm do you ski?"

"The left."

"*Alors,* then Page—he skis the right," Inez said.

"So what makes it extreme now?" The Wave asked.

Inez walked over to him and threw her arm around his shoulder. "Because, my little rastaman, they ski it at the same time. Two skiers race at forty miles an hour down two scars on the mountain. But then, they are in the same scar. One miss and . . . Oh! But what a peek through the hands!"

The Wave's mouth fell open. "Outfuckingragious!" he said. He dropped into a surfing crouch, his right hand drifting behind his head.

Page sat down hard on the truck bumper, his feelings plain in his stunned expression: it's one thing to ski radical terrain alone, quite another to play human bumper pool.

Farrell felt sleepy as if the scopolamine had finally overtaken him. Through the daze, he studied Inez, studied her the way he'd analyze a forty-degree slope in the back country, searching for the release zone that might break and send a slab of frozen snow down upon him. In spite of himself, Farrell smiled.

Chapter 5

Farrell awoke an hour before dawn the next morning. He was in a real bed for the first time in months. He'd told Inez that while he was willing to work for nothing until he'd earned his guide title, he needed a decent place to sleep. She rented him a room in the lodge he'd worked in when he first came to Alta. The room held a double bed, a table, and a basin. Shower down the hall. The wind howled and shrieked at the cracks around the window: it was March sixteenth; a new series of spring storms raced southeast from Alaska.

Unable to fall back asleep, Farrell's mind ticked with the image of Page's suddenly pale face and the weird thrill Inez seemed to get from seeing his fear. For his part, Farrell had not yet decided what he thought of the idea. A tiny voice far back in his brain screamed, No! In the tumult of his mind, though, the voice was drowned out by the trickle of adrenaline that began to seep every time he considered the race, becoming a gush the more he considered the risk, a torrent which ripped through his brain, tearing the tops off closed boxes of memory. Farrell got up and padded down the hall to the shower. He turned on the valve as hot as it would go and climbed inside. He gripped the nozzle with both hands, closed his eyes, and let the water beat on his neck. The humidity brought back memories of the Niger River in Africa and Chicago on August days and, finally, of Mexico City five years before.

It was March of 1983 and Farrell had three years' experience in Latin America. A friend in the Mexican Ministry of Finance told him of a businessman who specialized in hotels and import-export deals whom he might want to meet.

Farrell remembered crossing the hotel lobby and exiting onto a narrow walkway through a curved screen of exotic plants—yuccas and jades and delicate orange blossoms—to a broad terra cotta–tiled patio decorated with white wicker furniture. Beyond the patio rose a second screen of vegetation and then a pool. A trellis covered with vines shaded the terrace. The air was heavy with the scent of tropical flowers and another which he could not name, but which faintly smelled like curry.

It was Farrell's first trip south of the border since Jenny's birth two months before. Though he'd been gone only two days, he already missed how she cooed at him when he arrived home from work.

He entered an air-conditioned office off the patio. Gabriel Cortez was speaking on a telephone. Cortez studied Farrell for a moment, held a finger in the air, and smiled. Farrell circled the office to look at a picture of Cortez deep-sea fishing and another of him dove hunting in the desert with an enormously fat man who wore thick-framed glasses. A third showed Cortez with his arms around a beautiful, dark-haired woman; they were standing on a veranda above a sweeping lawn that led to the sea.

Gabriel hung up the phone. "How good of you to come." He rose, came around the right side of the desk with his left hand held tightly across his stomach, and extended Farrell his other. "I've heard so much about you."

Gabriel was tall and very lean, almost to the point of appearing angular. But what Farrell first noticed were his eyes: brown, warm, and inviting, the eyes of a seducer. His inky hair was slicked back in a crooner's cut. He wore a silk jacket of blue and gray fleck, which set off the crisp white cotton shirt and the steel-blue slacks. Gabriel's grip was firm, his smile genuine. Still, he unnerved Farrell by holding his gaze longer than seemed necessary.

During their conversation, Gabriel managed to impress Farrell as a man who was at once enormously interested in his audience and yet totally self-absorbed. He laughed at Farrell's jokes and listened closely to his description of his business; several times, however, his eyes flicked above and around Farrell to the enormous window that looked out onto the patio. Farrell thought later that Gabriel was evaluating the other people who coursed by. Farrell knew that Gabriel was at least five years his senior, but when he returned to Chicago and described the meeting to Lena, he told her that he'd never met a man so young who seemed to have such a firm grasp of what was essential.

"The flowers outside are fantastic," Farrell said. "My wife would be in heaven here."

"They are like miniature sunsets," he replied. "We had them flown in from my home near Manzanillo on the coast west of here."

"This is your hotel then?"

"Partly," he said. "I invested in it and I stay here when I am in the city. I think it's quite a remarkable restoration."

Farrell agreed. Gabriel said he was involved in several just like it in Mexico City and in Guadalajara where his wife, Maria Robles, was born.

"I believe in preserving the past," Gabriel said. "Tell me one thing you've helped restore. That's what lenders do, isn't it? Provide capital to either create or restore?"

The waiter arrived and Farrell took a sip of his coffee before answering. "Before I got into banking, I lived in Africa and I helped fix a well. Took me five months to restore it and put a cap on top so animals wouldn't fall in and poison the water. It's not on the scale of something like this, but it meant a lot to the villagers."

Gabriel reached for his coffee. Farrell noticed the fingers: the slender, clever mechanisms of a piano player.

"The restorations of which you speak are the most important," Gabriel said. "The revival of a hotel or a business is largely irrelevant to the majority, isn't it? Here, and even in your country, people live at the subsistence level. Their suffering goes beyond what you and I normally see. My father was intent on impressing these facts on me. We lived all over the world, mostly Europe. And he made me understand that even in the richest of cities—Paris, Rome, Buenos Aires—there is poverty.

"At least once a month, I remind myself of these things," he continued. "I ride my jeep out into the villages outside Manzanillo, which has become a great resort. Lots of money. But outside it's different. There are fishing towns nearby; we've tried to help them with the management of their fleets. Do you still work at that level, Mr. Farrell?"

"Jack, please. Actually, the bank is always after the larger projects."

"Consider the way I work, Jack," Gabriel said. "I lay out my options and figure what is best for everyone involved. Here at the hotel we need a labor pool to keep it running. I could have raided other hotels in the city for experienced workers, as I did for the managers. But I started a training program for the poor. Some are already managing. Your waiter, who may someday run the patio bar, barely finished fourth grade."

"Has it made a return yet?"

Gabriel's face lost some color and his eyes chilled.

"I didn't mean to be rude," Farrell said. "This must be a great risk."

"That's what life is about, isn't it?" Gabriel said, his hands now flashing in the air. "The risk and the resolution? This is what I enjoy about it: you never know how it will all turn out. I have a boat at my home. I take it out on the ocean and drive it too fast for Maria's taste. I love it when the hull breaks free of the water. I don't know sometimes whether it will come down. Do you understand?"

"Perfectly," Farrell said. "I'm a skier."

"Really? I have never tried this. Exciting?"

"Very fast, many obstacles."

"Wonderful."

Suddenly Gabriel's shoulders drooped. He stared over Farrell's shoulder, through the window, nodded, and excused himself. The same heavy Mexican he'd seen in the hunting photograph appeared in the doorway. Gabriel listened intently to the man, who spoke Spanish in a rapid, thick accent Farrell found difficult to follow. The fat man stood stone still during the entire recitation. Gabriel rocked back and forth from one foot to the other, then clapped the man on the shoulder, mumbled something, and shut the door.

"I'm terribly sorry," Gabriel said when he returned. "I have just been informed of trouble with one of my enterprises near Manzanillo. I'm afraid I must fly there this afternoon. Would you care to join me for the weekend?"

"I have a flight back to Chicago this evening," Farrell said.

"Next visit then," Gabriel said. "In the meantime I'd like you to take a look at this."

"Hotel project?"

"A factory, possibly in partnership with some Japanese who've invested in Tijuana."

They spent the next two hours hashing out the deal. Gabriel had a terse, lucid mind that could condense the disparate arms of a project into a five-minute description. Gabriel was a master of the pitch, not content to dwell on the broad strokes; he was as well versed in the details. Farrell agreed to take Gabriel's proposal to his superiors and they shook hands.

"You absorb these things rapidly," Gabriel said when they'd finished. "I have a good feeling about this."

Indeed, within six weeks after their initial meeting and a flurry of phone calls, Farrell swung the loan to Gabriel.

Farrell turned in the shower to fire his aching lower back. He thought how flimsy the banking business is. He had worked for one of the world's largest financial institutions, flying all over Central and South America to work on deals. At the heart of it, strangers formed a superficial relationship, then passed money back and forth on the basis of ideas. It all occurred in such a quick, anonymous fashion that Farrell wondered whether people who stuffed their cash in their mattresses were correct after all.

Someone knocked on the shower glass and Farrell sighed, turned the lever, and dried off. When he returned to his room, he found a note taped to his door:

No Y Today
We will Film The Wave at Snowbird
Page will Pick You up at 9 sharp—Inez

The tiny electric alarm clock on the table said 6:20, still another forty minutes until the dining room opened for breakfast. Farrell dressed, then flopped on the bed, took a deep breath, and reached for Lena's diary. The knot at the back of his head began to throb again. For the sake of his short-term sanity, he ignored it. He flipped ahead and found what he was looking for.

February 22, 1983

It's been a month since Jenny shot from me slick hot, screaming bloody murder. My first time to write about her and still I feel the air in that room, electric, as if God were there to brush our cheeks, mine crying, Jack's beet red.

Mind you, it's not all roses. Haven't slept right in four days, my boobs weigh a ton, nipples feel like raw meat, and my crotch still aches like I rode a horse for three weeks straight. Stinking episiotomy.

Jenny makes it worthwhile. When I look into her eyes, I believe in the word "destiny." It's a sapphire, that word, blue and sparkling like her eyes which try to follow me when I bend to her and give her my breast. She is our destiny, even if it is a future that poops, barfs and keeps me awake.

All this time working in the unit and I never really understood. I won't be able to go back without guilt for leaving her, new empathy for the women I help through the pain until their rough jewel comes out, shuddering with the first chill of life, not knowing what they're crying for. But I know now. It's what their mommies are waiting for, too: Touch.

Farrell paused. In the rough plaster on the ceiling, he saw his baby girl waving her arms at him, rolling her tongue and drooling on his shirt. He remembered the early mornings burping her after Lena had breastfed her, how he had sung to her while changing her diapers, how she belly-laughed when he made faces. He smiled thinking how quick she was to hold up her head and watch him move around the room, how by the time she was four months she'd screeched when he tickled her belly and called her "Little Miss J."

She loved to have him say the ABCs to her slowly, his mouth big and wide. She loved to have him growl on her stomach. Her mouth rounded when he did, her legs kicked, and she giggled. She loved to put her foot in her mouth when her diapers were off.

During Farrell's early mornings with Jenny, she'd made him seem like he was the most wonderful person in the world. Lena was something else again. During that first year of motherhood she seemed to grow five inches and gain twenty pounds, a powerful, joyous force that ruled their home. He guessed it's what being a new mother is to someone who specialized in birth. His throat swelled again. He almost put the diary down. He shook his head and said out loud, "You opened, now finish it."

September 12

Jack just finished putting up the gates. Jenny has a cold, but just yesterday she tried to pull herself up on the coffee table, so it's only a matter of time before she's racing around the house. We got a picture, of course.

I've been back at work a month now and am only beginning to breathe easy when Margie comes in at eight to take care of her. Jack says I don't have to work, these deals with Gabriel Cortez are going so well that he's sure to get a big Christmas bonus that could tide us over. I feel an obligation to be there, working and coaxing the women.

Jenny's been a real pain lately, waking up and crying at two a.m. Jesus, she was sleeping through the night just last month. Jack's good, for the most part—gets up and rocks her until she falls asleep on his chest. I found them there at six the other morning, Jack slumped to one side in the armchair, Jenny snoozing. I leaned against the door jam and just watched them. All the long nights and the frustration and the stinking breast pump—I hate that thing—faded away.

Mom's coming out next week for two weeks, so I'll need Margie less. Jack's mom, Peg, is coming right after that. It will be good to see them all together, though Peg's so nervous on the phone to come out here, I don't know how much help she'll be. Jack says she's always been like that. She doesn't like to leave home because she'll miss going "to see Brendan."

All these years after his suicide, she still goes to his grave almost every day. It's funny and sad: when we visit Peg, Jack never goes with her. I don't think he's ever seen the grave.

Farrell closed the book and locked it. He got off the bed and walked to the window to watch the snow fall. He remembered the *Chicago Tribune* crossword puzzle and the date above it: Sunday, November 12. He sat in the rocking chair quietly doing the puzzle.

She'd had that awful cold on and off for almost two months. An earache once. She seemed to be getting better.

He'd put Jenny in her day crib on the far side of the room near the heater while Lena took a nap. She'd worked a rare night shift the evening before and arrived home exhausted. The rain drummed so hard on the roof and the windows that it made the city deaf. Even the strikes of hammers out on the street from city workmen fixing a busted sewer line were muffled by the wind and the downpour.

It was a minute before three. He knew because the blue china clock his grandmother left him had made a tinging noise on the quarter hour and he had looked at it, wondering if the bells would wake the baby. He even remembered the crossword clue he was stuck on: *Welcome political catastrophe.* Nine letters down, starting with *L*, fourth letter *D*. The rocker creaked on the hardwood floor. Farrell tapped his pen on the newsprint, trying to will the word to tumble from his brain.

Nothing.

That's what he remembered—a dull, nagging nothing. His hand froze in space. His legs wouldn't rock anymore. The storm battered the panes on the window with sheets of rain. Inside, the dimensions and acoustics of the room seemed to have shifted. He squeezed his nose between his fingers and blew, trying to open his ears to understand the change. The blue clock ticked on the mantelpiece, the drapes fluttered, the aerator bubbled in the fish tank. At last, somewhere behind him, he heard the silence, not just quiet, but a true, ringing emptiness he'd thought was possible only deep in the woods ten seconds after a rifle shot.

They say that people can be frozen by fear; Farrell was melted by it. His shoulders sagged. His elbows gave way as if they'd been struck by a doctor wielding a rubber hammer. The heels of his hands slid off the arms of the rocker and hung heavy and limp. The pen slipped from his fingers, clattered on the floor, and rolled into the corner.

He got to his feet, balanced on spongy knees, turned, and lost control. He flailed for the support of the stone mantelpiece, unable to look across the room to the shape under the pink cotton blanket. The ticking of the clock seemed to slow and the thirty feet of floor he crossed twisted into an eternity of conflicting frames of reference. Recalling it now, he saw himself from different angles: from the hallway, he was a bent old man; from the kitchen, he was a ghost; from the ceiling, he was a very little boy.

Jenny was on her tummy when Farrell reached the crib, her tiny hand cupping the edge of the blanket. Not gripping it, though Farrell could tell that's what she'd been doing reflexively just before. Jenny's dreadful robin's egg blue hand cupped the pink blanket.

Farrell gathered her to him and ran as fast as he could go, the pounding of his footsteps drowning the chimes of the clock, back through the living room, across a shaft of light from the bathroom, into the dimly lit hall and the dark bedroom where Lena slept.

Farrell gazed at the snow building on the ledge outside his window. He couldn't remember one word that was said the day they took Jenny back to the church in Quincy where he and Lena had been married. He knew only that later, after they'd driven to the cemetery, he'd concentrated on keeping his feet moving on the long walk through the wet grass.

Billy O'Rourke, his father-in-law, had found Farrell in the backyard of his house later that evening, walking back and forth between the laundry poles, one finger on the line. Billy had walked him back into the house and Farrell had drunk two quick whiskeys. He headed for the kitchen, where he found Lena washing the dishes, every dish her mother had.

A month later, Lena announced she was returning to work.

"I'm just going on," she said in a way that made Farrell wonder just whom she was talking to. "We've just got to keep moving and it will get better."

"Are you sure?" he asked. At work, he spent hours tapping a pencil on a piece of paper until his secretary had taken it from his hand. "The doctors said this might take time."

"I don't want time," she said. "I want to make it stand still."

Even then, Farrell was stunned by her strength. He decided it was something she'd inherited from her mother, Carol, who had been struck by multiple sclerosis in her late twenties, yet refused to give in to the disease. Carol had kept her job in the local library and forced the town to build her ramps so she could do her job.

Together Farrell and Lena retreated into routine and, though he did not realize it until that moment in his room at Alta, into isolation. Rain or shine, he arose each morning to run for miles through the park by the lake. The sweat and the endorphins calmed him, kept the awful memories of that November day boxed and corded in a remote basement in his mind. Whenever he'd catch himself breaking into melancholy, he'd pinch himself or sprint until everything blurred except the sidewalk. One morning he slipped on a patch of ice and sprawled hard on the pavement. A huge bruise and raspberry developed on his skin that ached all day and made it hard to think. Each morning after that during the long Chicago winter, he intentionally sprinted near ice, so that at least once during his run he'd feel his balance go and he'd thud hard on the frozen ground.

He filled his days with details, trying to cram as much experience as he could into every minute. In this way, his mind could not wander. Phone calls to Mexico, meetings with loan officers and statisticians and Commerce Department representatives. Reports written, more phone calls, no lunch, deals consummated over the phone (he'd requested no travel), then more meetings, decisions made, notes prepared for the following day. Finally, out into the Chicago night, briskly striding through the streets toward home.

Some nights he got home first and he cooked dinner. They spoke very little to each other, preferring to find solace in routine. While Lena watched television, he opened the recipe book, preheated the oven to three hundred twenty-five degrees. Butter and oil in the casserole, and when they began to foam, he added veal, browned it lightly on all sides, removed the meat, and added the carrots and onions to the pot. Between bastes, he swept the floor, rearranged the bookcases, took out the trash, wrote checks for the bills. When the day was over, he fell into bed, grateful for the exhaustion that brought sleep, not thought.

In February, Lena looked up from her plate and said, "I've asked for a transfer. I can't take the unit anymore."

Farrell nodded. "What will you do?"

"Maybe the E.R. I like the speed of it. You just go."

"What made you decide?"

Lena twirled spaghetti on her plate, then said: "Their faces."

It was that night, Farrell remembered, that Lena wrote again in her diary. She didn't write every night like she used to. No, the daily pattern had been shattered. Now, sometimes once a week, sometimes once a month, he awoke to find her sitting at her table scribbling. He watched her shoulders move with the rhythm of the pen, then pull a pillow over his head and fall again into darkness.

Farrell turned from the window and opened the diary.

February 6

They say I can't go back. Can't tell my Mom and Dad why. Can't tell Jack. He seems to be handling it all so well, as if feeling squished inside came natural.

A baby today, she crowned perfectly. Rotated one of those textbook rotations that freed her shoulders from her mom. She was so strong, that woman. Pushed just once and her daughter slipped free, warm and bloody into the doctor's hands, from hers to mine. Margaret helped the mom while I took the girl to do the Apgar tests. A real little one, 5 pounds, 2 ounces.

I tested her, washed her, dried her. Swaddled her in blankets. I even stroked her cheeks so she instinctively turned to suck at my finger. As if it were my breast. I asked her what she thought of her new mommy and the world. I whispered, I love you.

That's when I noticed Margaret's hand on my arm. She asked me if I didn't think it was time Paula held her baby now?

I snapped back that I was going as fast as I could. Margaret looked at me with the strangest expression, as if I were speaking a language she didn't understand.

I looked at the clock. The testing and washing usually takes me ten minutes. Thirty-five had passed.

Dr. Powers says I can stay at the hospital, just not near babies. Not for a while, not unless I get help. Don't need help. I'd never hurt a baby. Never.

Farrell dropped the diary across his chest. "Oh, Jesus," he whispered. He squeezed his eyes shut and tried to remember, tried to see anything on her face that would have told him what she went through that night. Lena's face was blank. Farrell slammed his fist into the mattress.

March 6

I've begun to dream again and it scares me. Used to be I thought of dreams as something different. Awake, dreaming, now they are the same.

Last night I saw myself lying in bed while Jack sat spread-eagled on the floor, bent at the waist, hands reaching for toes in white socks.

I told him that he thrashed in his sleep, that it kept me awake. He shrugged his shoulders and said his neck hurt.

I said, you lost weight. He smiled and said, the running, it's a benefit. I sighed and asked him how an ache can help. Jack switched to a groin stretch, his feet together, back against the wall, hands on the inside of his thighs. He said he'd get through it.

I asked what he hoped to get through. Jack didn't look at me, just said he'd read somewhere that the Japanese believe that if you move steadily into pain, you will eventually pass through it as the muscles and joints become accustomed to activity.

I rolled the edge of the pillow in my hand. I somehow knew that I had read the same thing and that they talked about a promising Japanese baseball pitcher who had a strained elbow. He threw a thousand pitches a day to fix it. His arm's useless now.

I was suddenly sitting up in bed, looking at my hands. I said, you used to love my smell.

He didn't say anything. He dropped backward into a yoga pose, gasping at the effort.

Even now, awake, I think that Jack breathes through his mouth now.

April 2

E.R. moves. Never get near the young ones. Just treat adults. Better that way. Fast. So fast you leave yourself behind. It's like that physics experiment in college—as the train goes by at the speed of light, the clocks turn backward.

Jack goes to Mexico tomorrow to meet with Gabriel Cortez at his home on the coast. I told Jack tonight we need to leave Chicago. I'm slipping. He looked at me strange and said okay.

For now, though, I'm fine. Fine. I just fear the nights when time slows and I catch up to me.

Chapter 6

The walls of the tiny room seemed to breathe and press in around Farrell like a lung. He felt seasick reading her secret thoughts and told himself working with his hands might still the sensation.

He grabbed a cup of coffee and a few pastries in the dining room and climbed down the stairs to the basement, where he'd been given a locker. He pulled out his powder skis, separated them, inverted the left ski, and wrenched it tight in a block vise. Under the tip and tail of the ski, he placed three two-by-fours for support. He rooted in the bottom of the locker and withdrew a black bag. Inside he found a ten-inch, second-cut mill file and file card. The small iron nestled in its bag slid effortlessly into his hand. He rooted out the other equipment: a stick of clear, meltable plastic, a metal scraper, and a thermometer.

Trying to keep the hangover of Lena's voice from ringing in his head, Farrell stepped out the door into the driving snowstorm and stuck the thermometer in the snow, waited thirty seconds, and peered at the mercury line: 10 degrees Fahrenheit.

As Farrell began surgery on his skis, Page walked in wearing tight black stretch pants, an oversized red anorak, and a thick red and black wool hat. He shook melting snow from the hat, wiggled out of the anorak, and brushed back his hair. He was obviously about Farrell's age, early thirties, but his blond hair was still full and lank, the hair of a teenager.

"Too bad we had to cancel," Farrell said. "I was getting ready."

Page hoisted himself on top of another bench. "It will be the wildest thing I've ever done. She was pissed, but there's just too much snow. What could she do?"

"I have time for this?" Farrell asked.

"Sure," Page said. "This is The Wave's show today."

"What's she got him doing?"

"Don't know exactly," Page said. "But I'm sure it'll be good."

Farrell nodded and cut a ragged chunk of bottom from the inside edge of the ski with a pen knife, then dug at the core with a light stroke. He held the plastic stick cigar-style, shaved the tip with the knife, and lit it. An acrid odor filled the room. Farrell held the stick away from his face, watching until the black carbon dripped off and it burned clear. "Been a long time since I've seen your pictures in the magazines," Farrell said. "Three years?"

"Flying then, wasn't I?" Page said.

"Must have been a hell of a crash."

"Yeah, the ski company I was working for eventually gave me the boot—something about my bookkeeping. That night I melted our bank machine card on a shipment of fine Peruvian. Around two in the morning, my heart started to skip and blood ran from my nose.

"At the hospital, I heard the nurse tell a doctor I had chunks coming out of my nostrils, which scared the shit out of me and I tried to straighten out. Trouble was, by the time I got it together, Tina, my fiancé, was gone."

Farrell shifted uncomfortably; Page made him think too much about his own responsibility for stories such as these. He snipped small pieces of wire off a roll and laid them diagonally within the hole. He knew he had to say something, so he said: "Story of the eighties."

"Ain't it, though?" Page said, tugging aimlessly at a piece of royal blue yarn that had snagged on his sweater. He seemed to drift off.

Farrell dripped the melted plastic into the core first, then made a second pass and filled the gash to the surface. When the mass had bonded, he bent the ends of the scraper concave and removed the excess material.

Page said: "This Y thing. The way I figure it, I perform, get filmed, get seen, get sponsors, make money. It's been five years since I've been on top."

"So Inez is your redeemer."

"That's how I've got it. Those low budget movies she's made were just the start. Now she needs a class act for the show."

"And you're Mr. Marquee," Farrell said.

"Sarcastic bastard, aren't you?" Page said.

"Sorry, I have my moments," Farrell said. He held out his hand. Page flipped him the mill file. Farrell laid the rough steel at a forty-five-degree angle and pulled in long, even strokes down the ski. After five pulls, he cleaned the file, repeating the process until the ski bottom was flat.

"Inez's movies," Farrell asked. "Any good?"

"Only seen the first one, not the second, where the guy goes," Page said. He fell quiet for a moment. "The first one, the title has something to do with an eagle, it depends on how you look at it. When I was young, my dad, asshole that he was, taught me a lesson I've never forgotten. There we were. I was twelve, standing with him in some San Francisco gallery. He points to a painting: mostly blue with a couple of big splashes of grainy white in the upper left."

"The painting?"

"Yeah, the title under this thing is 'Depression's Climax Number 41,'" Page said, chuckling to himself. "Price tag: Twenty-five grand. My dad asks me do I like it? I said, I don't know, what's there to like? He picks up a brochure on the table and opens it. Inside there's a picture of this woman who looks like Mike Wallace on *60 Minutes*, standing in a dirty pair of overalls with a paintbrush in her hand. It said she was the rage of the West Coast, pulling in thousands for everything she's done. My dad points at the dollar sign and says that's all you've got to know to like it."

"So Inez's film wasn't that good."

"Didn't say that," Page said, squinting at Farrell and blowing between his lips as if he wanted to whistle. "Part of it was interesting. Lot of interviews and crazy stuff spliced in. I guess it was what you'd call an art film, only it was a documentary. Anyway, I only saw part of it in a ski shop last year. About this old guide in Chamonix. I tried to find it after she made her offer, but they didn't have it anymore. From what I remember: experimental. Yeah, I guess that's what you'd call them. Experimental."

Farrell's interest was increasing by the moment, but he did not let Page see it. He continued to draw the melting plastic evenly along the bottom of the ski.

"The thing is," Page continued. "The guy, that guide, you know? The word is that he's a cripple now. Wheelchair. Had a bad fall in Italy a couple of months after the film was shot."

Farrell cringed and looked up at him: "That's not in the movie?"

"No."

"And the other one, the one your friend saw?"

Page cracked his neck. "About some younger kid starting out. Good skier, into real steep, real hairy shit. My friend said the movie's crazy, even before he bites it. She's buff with him in one scene."

"Completely?"

"Must be," Page said. "He said her tits are nice."

"That's comforting," Farrell said. They both laughed, then Page's expression became somber.

"The other thing, you know when he eats it, I didn't want to hear too much about," Page said. "Can't take it. I get the same feeling when they show replays of football players breaking their legs. When it's all said and done, all I know is I've seen the line of credit backing this. Some German group. You don't get bucks like that unless someone believes you're good. That, my friend, is all you have to know about Inez Didier."

"So now you and I play pinball for art," Farrell said.

"And money, best money I've seen in years," Page said. He stretched his head low over his knee and grunted. "Besides, what'd she say the other night? I know the risks."

"Not scared?"

Page didn't respond until he'd touched his head on his knee. "Didn't say that."

They were quiet for a moment. Farrell spit on the iron, satisfied at the way it crackled like birdshot off barbed wire. He turned the iron tip down over the ski and held the wax to the flat. He laid the iron on the base, smoothing the wax in, which made a pleasurable hiss.

"You thinking about backing out?" Page asked.

"Not yet," Farrell said.

Page rubbed his jaw, then said softly: "All those years before. Did some crazy shit. But I've never heard of anything like this."

Page gathered his knees to his chest and leaned his head back against the wall. "I need it, though. Can't be some full-time salesman in some sporting goods store this early in life. You?"

"I got nothing else. . . ." Farrell began. "No, that's not true. . . . It's something about her, Inez . . ."

Page's head bobbed. "You can feel it, can't you?"

"Yeah," Farrell said. Farrell wrenched the vise open and caught the ski as it popped out, angry at himself for opening up too much. He inspected the second ski, noticed no major irregularities, and flat-filed.

Page watched him. "She'll come at you strange, though."

Farrell kept his head down, eyes on the track the file made; he'd learned long ago that if people have something on their minds, they will tell you things if you keep your mouth shut.

Page came upright out of the stretch. "She asks you about everything. She's over there with The Wave right now. She did some kind of word game with me the other night. She said Black. I said Red. She said Pine, I said Red. She said Lethal, I said definitely Red."

Farrell glanced up from his work. Page was craning his head to see Farrell with his good eye. He had an idiotic grin plastered across his face. "I believe in keeping people off-balance. You ever sold anything, Collins?"

"In a way."

"Been through a sales program?"

"Never."

"All sorts of ways to throw people off or bring them to you," Page said. "I've practiced almost all of them."

"Sense of purpose. Get that from your dad?"

Page froze. "Hey, fuck you, Collins."

"Sorry again," Farrell said. "Didn't know that was sensitive."

Page was quiet for a minute. "I've done good for myself in spite of it all, you know?"

"I'm sure you have."

"Jesus, you're a real asshole. Let me tell you, bud. My mom, last time I talked to her, still waits tables at an all-you-can-eat buffet at one of those casinos on the Nevada side. My old man? Bastard was a fireman in Sacramento when I was a kid. But he likes the mountains, so we move to Tahoe. Only he finds out he likes playing cards more than he did putting out fires. My mom, she got fired once, just for bringing home leftover chicken for me. I've done good for myself, remember that."

"I'll remember," Farrell said.

Page stared until he was sure Farrell wasn't lying. "So what's your rap?"

Farrell bent low over the ski and filed carefully. He figured he owed Page something. "Had a couple of bad years and decided to come back to the only thing that makes me calm—deep powder. Hope the big empty will wash away the particulars."

"Some kind of poet, huh?"

"Me?" Farrell snorted. "Not sensual enough."

"So tell me the particulars."

"Nope," Farrell said, popping the second ski from the vise. "I'm not the sharing sort, Page. Better if we just stick to ourselves."

They were silent, both aware the mood had changed for the worse.

"Every man for himself, huh, Collins?" Page said.

"That's what it will be up in that Y."

"You just keep your old bones together," Page said. "I'll be through that intersection before you even see it."

"I believe I'll be waiting for you at the bottom, Page," Farrell said.

"You will," Page said. "In a heap."

Twenty minutes later, Page and Farrell stood in the massive, arching lobby of a building that resembled a bomb shelter more than a hotel. Outside the snow fell so hard they couldn't see the trees eighty yards away. They waited for Inez and The Wave and the cameramen to arrive. After ten minutes, Farrell decided to go to Inez's room. When the elevator door opened on the fourth floor, The Wave was leaning against the wall in all his neon glory. Farrell expected to see the normal cocky smirk painted across the rasta's face. What he saw was the stunned, anxious confusion of a little boy lost in the supermarket. "I feel like a trout," The Wave said.

"What're you talking about?" Farrell asked.

"I feel like a lake trout, mon," The Wave repeated, his attention focused more on the elevator door than Farrell. "I have this feeling I'm in this National Geographic Special I saw once. And there's this lamprey eel that's just chewed through my lower jaw and settled in for a long suck."

With that, The Wave pushed by Farrell into the elevator and stuck a finger into the panel. Farrell jogged down the hall to find Inez, dressed in a bulky, full-length down parka, locking the door to her room.

"The Wave says he's a freshwater game fish," Farrell said.

"He is the fish?" she said.

"He seemed dazed."

Inez screwed up her face in disgust. "Ah, he admits to me during our conversation that he gets out of his bed this morning and he smokes the marijuana," she said. "I tell him he smokes, I throw him off the team. He shows me his weakness. Just now he does not yet understand that this is also his strength. I show him today."

"He looked like he was about to fall over just now."

"No, no. He has . . . how do you say, *Il a la frousse.*"

"I think it's the jitters."

"*C'est ça.* He has the jitters of the sequence I wish to shoot today. But you watch, when he thinks of me, he is going to understand."

With that, Inez hooked her arm through Farrell's and dragged him down the hall as if she were a dog and he a sled. "This will be something, I swear to you," she said. "I think I prepare him well for this extreme."

The next few hours passed as Inez worked with her camera crew to get the equipment ready. Tony Carbone was forty-two, with sleepy eyes under a shank of steel gray hair that fit him like a helmet. He stood well over six feet, had a chest like a beer keg and tree-trunk legs. He could chug through thigh-deep powder like a broad-sterned boat breaking lake ice. Ann Queechee, his partner, was only a fraction over five-feet-four, and no more than 110 pounds, yet she moved with the agility of a trained dancer and the strength of an ant; she could carry as much as Carbone: a Panaflex movie camera, gear bag, and a miniature video camera that attached to the side of the rig so Inez would have a daily assessment of the footage she'd shot. Farrell guessed Queechee to be no more than thirty even though the long plait of brown hair that hung out from underneath her hat was flecked with gray.

During the introductions in the plaza near the giant aerial tram that services the upper reaches of Snowbird, Inez said that she'd recruited Carbone and Queechee from Seattle, where they'd been running a marginal video production business specializing in mountaineering documentaries.

"You don't have your own people from France?" Farrell asked Inez.

"Same eyes, same film," she said. "I try to do each film new each time. *Alors*. Make attention, if you please! The Forest Service gives us the permission to shoot outsides the boundaries of the ski area out from the Thunder Bowl. They tell me no one has ever snowboarded there. This is a first."

A booming voice broke in: "A first piece of sheer idiocy!" It was Portsteiner striding across the plaza. "Just wanted to warn all you folks that I was against this permit. You've got a lot of fresh snow falling on one bitch of a steep slope in the woods."

"The rangers of the forest tell me your concerns," Inez said dismissively. "But your market department says I go. We sign all waivers of liability, no?"

"You did," Portsteiner said. "Wanted to make sure your crew did."

The Wave, Page, Ann, and Tony shook their heads no.

"We need this shot!" Inez cried. "You are being paid well. I expect loyalty to my decision."

There was a moment of silence while Inez and Portsteiner all examined their faces for reaction. Farrell said, "Shit, Frank. You've probably already put explosives out there, what's the big deal?"

Portsteiner tugged at his earlobe. "Didn't know you'd joined in. What's your name? Collins?"

"She made me an offer I couldn't refuse."

Portsteiner huffed, "Sound of it, there's nothing you'd refuse to do these days."

The two of them glared at each other, until Page broke in and said: "I guess it won't hurt to go up and see it. Check it out, you know?"

Slowly, the rest of the crew nodded. Except The Wave, who stood off to one side, staring into space.

Portsteiner turned from Farrell. "Pack of fools! Well, Ms. Didiot . . ."

"Didier," Inez said.

"Whatever. I'm going along to dig you all out if I have to."

"This is your job," Inez said. "Now where is my ride?"

Inez strode off toward a black snowmobile parked on the snow at the edge of the plaza. A driver in goggles helped her move her camera on to the back of the machine. She looked back at them and said: "Well, we go then, I see you there."

"She's not skiing in?" Farrell asked.

"Can't stand heights if she can avoid it," Page said. "She'll go up in a chair or a tram if it's the only way. For all she talks about shooting the extreme, she hates coming anywhere near it."

During the grueling climb west from the ski area through the loose snow toward the forest where The Wave would surf, the storm gusted and died. Visibility was down to fifteen yards at times. Portsteiner grumbled. Farrell knew the man was thoroughly pissed; experienced mountaineers such as themselves should have been smart enough to know the sound of a storm building, should have known that slopes as radical as this don't appreciate new weight, should have known that the bear would only sit still so long until the fresh load disturbed its sleep, forcing the beast to grumble and roll.

An hour after they'd crossed the boundary rope, the gale slackened. Portsteiner called halt in a thick stand of fir trees and pointed through the thicket toward the bottom of the bowl, where Inez had erected a blaze orange flag next to the snowmobile. Carbone's radio crackled to life and Inez began shouting orders about the placement of cameras.

"He's going to surf here?" Page said softly to Farrell.

They both examined the series of chutes, rocks, and stumps that littered the hillside between the trees. Farrell looked over at The Wave, who was absentmindedly running his fingers over the bark of a tree.

"God help him," Farrell said.

"Surfo up to this?" Portsteiner asked.

"He's the best I've ever seen," Page said. "But . . . this . . . is out there."

They passed the next two hours rigging the camera shots. Carbone swung down through the deep snow off to the left and dug a pit in which he could film The Wave from a lower plane. Queechee moved to the right and down the slope to a ledge where she could capture the whole arc of his dance. Page stood off to the left behind The Wave with a radio; he'd give the kid the signal to begin. Portsteiner and Farrell skied around the rim of the bowl to a spot where they could see it all. With the snow falling faster now, the crew looked like ghosts and The Wave a distant neon beacon.

Farrell looked over at Portsteiner. He knew the old man was more pissed at him than the rest; after all, Portsteiner had been his teacher. He asked, "What's it doing, Frank?"

"What's that?"

"The snow, you know. What's it doing?" Farrell said. He liked to hear Portsteiner warm to his favorite subject. There was something pure about it, like the poetry of cowboys.

"I dug a well this morning above Little Cloud," Portsteiner chanted, as if he were reciting an often-read bedtime story to a young child. "Seventeen inches new. Been storming regular for almost a month now, you know; the upper snow pack's almost immaculate in ET Metamorphosis. Some friable depth hoar about five, five and a half feet down, but it's under pressure. The mountain is as solid as you'll see it."

"This last layer going to hold when The Wave drops in?"

"That's what we're all here to see, isn't it?" Portsteiner replied. "Whether old grizzly itches in his den."

"You talked to Inez this morning?"

"Had to know what she planned, didn't I?"

"What's the LaChapelle classification?"

Portsteiner ran his tongue along the inside of his lower lip. "Seems to me that woman's outside the crystal chart. She's a slope unto herself, my odd friend. My nose tells me she's under the stress of irregular creep and glide. And you, too. She mentioned some damn loon idea of a race in that Y Couloir down the canyon."

"That's her plan."

"And you're going along for the ride? You're as adled as that surfer kid. Look at him, sure as shit he don't wake the bear, he'll skewer himself on one of those stumps. You, too, you keep this up."

"It's his life," Farrell said. "Mine, too."

Portsteiner muttered, "That's a hell of a way to think about things."

Farrell shook his head. "You know, that's always been your problem, Frank—you think everyone has to think a certain way, act a certain way. People will do what they want to, whatever you say."

"Jack, you don't start opening up, you're going to hurt yourself."

Portsteiner had leaned over so that now his big face was right in front of Farrell's. There was something gentle and comforting about the old man's expression. Before Farrell could stop himself, he said, "I ever tell you my earliest memory?"

"You've never told me much about anything but the big dumps you've skied," Portsteiner said.

"Well, here's a first. I'm almost two and I'm standing in my crib. I see my Davy Crockett doll, my favorite toy, the thing I loved more than anything else as a kid, sitting on a chair about two feet away. I get myself over the rail of the crib and I'm hanging off the side. I can see the doll on my left, so I kick free, turn in space, and reach. Only I land on the edge of the chair and get the wind knocked out of me."

"Serves you right."

"Maybe. But you know what I remember thinking? That the feeling I had floating through the air was worth the pain of landing."

"So now you want to recapture your youth, that it?" Portsteiner scoffed. "Kind of young for that midlife crisis crap, ain't you?"

"It's not that simple," Farrell said.

"Tell me what's so complicated then."

Farrell rubbed at the knot at the back of his neck. Before he could continue, the radio crackled. "We are ready?" Inez's voice called. She was perched on top of the snowmobile, her camera the wide-angled shot.

"Ready here," said Carbone.

"Okay," said Queechee.

"Page?" Inez asked. "The Wave, he is ready?"

Through the binoculars Farrell could see Page pull the radio from his ear and lean over to talk to The Wave. "He's not answering me," Page said, "but I think he's going to go."

"I speak to him if you please," Inez replied.

Portsteiner and Farrell raised their binoculars again. The Wave had kicked his way farther east on the slope and was poised on a rise in a stand of tight black spruces. Page handed him the radio.

"Wave?" Inez said.

There was no answer.

"Listen and remember," she went on. "Think of it. All of that I say this morning. Think of me and go."

Again there was no answer. The Wave handed Page the radio back and stood, peering off into the storm.

"And action!" Inez yelled into the radio.

Through the glasses, Farrell saw The Wave stiffen at the command. He twisted his body left and right to rid his lower back of tension.

"Action! *Action!*" Inez yelled.

The Wave mouthed something, but Farrell couldn't make it out. The Wave shuffled forward to get his board in motion. He cut a marginal first turn and almost hit a tree. He leaned back hard on the tail of his board and it sank and stalled. Farrell got the sense The Wave didn't know what he was doing there on the hillside in the middle of a storm.

"This kid's toast," Portsteiner said.

In an instant that totally confused Farrell, The Wave's hands shot forward and his face contorted into a sheer red fury. He fell dead down the slope, the snow hissing behind him in a low-trajectory rooster's tail. His back was to Farrell and Portsteiner now, and he rocked his hips and knees into the hill, carving the snow in a precise arc. Near a gap in the glade, he laid his right arm at his forehead, left arm at his knees and sliced back against the grain, right at Farrell, moving very, very fast. Twenty yards across the slope, he drove the board against a drift, watching as the maneuver threw a wave of snow into the trees.

The board gathered speed. The Wave forced his weight out over the front, seducing the slope's gravity, coursing over the back of the comatose bear. Now he flew almost directly down the face of the bowl. He dodged a stump at thirty-miles an hour. He gasped for air, holding it as he ripped over a hummock toward a twist of spruce and cottonwood branches. He ducked. Not enough. His head jerked back as the fork of a limb caught one of his dreadlocks and tore it away from his scalp. A curdling scream echoed in the bowl. Blood spit into the air like fine mist behind him.

The Wave kept going. He screamed again and aimed himself at a lip in the snow, shooting across the hill, hitting the lip at full throttle. The Wave shot high into the air. During the early flight, he grabbed the tail of his board, and at the apex of the arc, he rocked his whole body forward. He seemed to hover above the snow, the tip of his board pointing straight down the hill like a juggernaut. His left hand was clutched in a fist. Blood coughed off his head. He was snarling.

"Jeeeesus H. Christ," Portsteiner whispered.

The radio crackled, the voice almost imperceptible: *"Avances, avances, tu brute."* It was Inez on the radio. Then louder, in English: "You have this Tony, no?"

"If I don't, I should be shot."

"Ann?"

"You bet."

The Wave landed and rocketed toward a thin snake of a gully. He dropped the board into it, and rushed, gliding so fast that the straight trunks of the pines appeared to slow him into a jerky pattern of movement, the way a strobe light will freeze the actions of a dancer. Farrell strained forward against the tongue of his ski boots, strained against the competing emotions of fear and love, trying to anticipate the kid's next move.

In the instant when the trees formed an impenetrable wall and he should have crashed, The Wave bent limbo, his shoulder blades digging the snow like the outrigger of a catamaran and he fired to his left. He jetted the board up an embankment and hung his limp body in space. The board crowned and he twisted his hips and threw his hand out palm down, as if he could balance there on the powder, a delicate, almost feline sculpture.

He whipped the tip over, shattering that porcelain moment, and popped back on the board, smoothing it into long, snakelike turns. He seemed to goad Inez's cameras to try to ignore him. He flew through the last sequence of arcs faster than any snowboarder Farrell had ever seen.

- -

The Wave finally reached the flat about thirty-five yards in front of Inez's camera and capsized in the deep snow. His head lolled to one side. Flecks of saliva boiled at the corners of his mouth. His eyeballs rolled. Blood from his wound trickled down between his eyes and formed a spider's web of red on his face. He touched a glove to the open sore and winced at the sting.

Inez yelled into the radio: "Cut! Cut! Everyone shoots this good?"

Before she got her answer, Inez's hands fluttered at her side as if they had a life of their own. She reached up, tore off her hood, and wrenched off the headset. She waded through the deep snow to The Wave, who crouched as she approached, tense, an animal at bay.

Portsteiner and Farrell took off and skied down toward them as soon as she had moved. Out of the corner of his eye, Farrell saw Page dropping into the basin from the opposite side. The three of them pulled up just as Inez reached The Wave. She seemed not to know they were there. She held out her hands to The Wave like a mother to a hurt child. Tears streamed down her face. "This is okay," she said in the soft, soothing tones of a nurse caring for the sick. "This is okay now . . . you know. . . . Now, you know."

The Wave wall-eyed her, as if he thought she might strike.

"Do not be like this," she begged. "Please. Do you not see? You were there. Really there. You are the champion!"

Adrenaline jellied down Farrell's spine all the way to his knees. Who was this woman? What had she said to The Wave that had sent him into such a frenzy? Farrell wanted to look away from Inez and The Wave, but couldn't. He stared at her with a longing he did not understand.

The shuddering woman hugged the white rastaman whose eyes rolled in his head. Farrell leaned over his ski poles, shaking his head to dispel the dizziness that took him. Portsteiner tugged furiously at his ear.

"Always be alert to sudden weather changes in winter," he said. "Consider what the effects will be on the snow cover, and proceed with extra caution when a stable weather period of any sort comes to an end."

"E. R. LaChapelle," Farrell mumbled.

Chapter 7

he Wave's scalp wound took twenty-three stiches to close. Sitting alone nursing a double George Dickel at the bar that night, Farrell thought how fast things had happened. Portsteiner had pried the kid from Inez's arm and over her protests rushed him down the hill on the snowmobile. Farrell had followed. A doctor stitched him in the infirmary at the base of the lodge. Try as they might, they couldn't get The Wave to talk of what had happened in the woods near the Thunder Bowl. Every time they asked, The Wave would turn away and stare at the wall.

They took him back to his room after the sewing was over. When Portsteiner left, The Wave reached into one of his long duffel bags, pulled out a bag of pot, and asked Farrell to roll it for him. Farrell saw the kid was in bad need of another reality, so he turned him a joint as thick as his middle finger. Three huge puffs into it The Wave's eyes glassed and Farrell asked again: "What the hell happened?"

The glowing ember of the joint trembled in the darkened room. "Surfed, mon. That was it."

"You like to think you're a tough ass."

"Mon, you don't even know the meaning."

"Funny. Up there you looked like one of those little snot-nosed kids on the playground who just met the bully."

The Wave sucked on the joint again, his eyes focused on the blazing tip and the popping noise it made as he sucked. He held his breath, then let the smoke go in a rush. "Never boarded like that before. Not once, not even close. Only in my dreams."

"What about the trout? What'd she say to you in her room?"

The Wave gritted his teeth. "You better leave, mon. You better leave now."

Sitting there in the bar, Farrell took a sip of the whiskey and realized he's seen the expression on The Wave's face before. He'd had it himself the day Gabriel had called and said he had a proposition he thought Farrell might be interested in. It had been nearly five months since Jenny's death. He'd come to dread returning at night to his home, an apartment of enforced quiet, where the inhabitants acted as if they feared waking a terrible guest who slept in the back room. The next thing he knew he was in pure flight, streaking south to Mexico, home and Lena aching sores he tried to salve with distance.

He purchased a ticket all the way to Manzanillo, almost 700 miles west of Mexico City on the tropical coast. But because of a storm, the local airport was closed and his flight was rerouted through Colima. The plane was cramped and packed with packages and even chickens in cages. Like old times. He'd once spent five hours in an African bush taxi ducking shit from a goat that was tied to the roof above his window. Gabriel was waiting at the airport with a jeep.

"The wind was high, but my truck is heavy," Gabriel said as he helped Farrell load his gear. For almost two hours they wove west through forests and mountains still shrouded in fog and light rain. Gabriel spoke of his projects: another hotel in Puerto Angel in Oaxaca; an import-export business in Tapuchala with a Guatemalan businessman; and a minority share in a Maquiladora factory near Tijuana. This last was a growing concern. The U.S. and Mexican governments had recently signed an agreement easing trade barriers along the border, a move which enabled businesses to erect factories in Mexico to take advantage of the cheap labor and to suffer fewer tariffs bringing the goods into the United States.

"Now you're thinking," Farrell said. "Those plants are the future."

Gabriel slapped his hand on the dashboard. "I go where there's money to be made!" he said. "I tend to work near borders. There's a chaos there. If you can create order from that, you'll profit."

They topped a ridge about two in the afternoon, just as the last of the clouds broke to allow the sun to bore down hot on the terrain which broke away for thousands of feet to the Pacific.

"Colima coast," Gabriel said. "Some of the best tuna fishing in the world. Yellow fin, blue fin, and albacore. And out there in the channel—marlin. To your left, Manzanillo."

Farrell followed his finger until he saw bleached white buildings bunched far in the distance. The bay curved in a lazy arch. What appeared a Moorish castle loomed at the tip of the curve. "The Las Hadas resort."

"Your home is there?" Farrell asked.

"North," he said, then he gunned the motor and they raced down the side of the mountains along a twisted, narrow road. At times the bank lazed into hundred-foot falls. Gabriel spun the truck through a hairpin turn. "You like this, don't you?" he bellowed.

Farrell gripped the edge of the roll bar and clenched his teeth. He wasn't the type of person who liked being out of control. He didn't like roller coasters and hated being a passenger on a motorcycle. Gabriel, however, was a master behind the wheel; Farrell grinned into the wind that tore at his cheeks.

They turned onto a rutted road twelve miles north of Manzanillo and bounced for another mile before meeting a wall of flowering camelias which hung crazily, torn asunder by the strength of the gale that had passed the previous evening. A man with a gun sat in a shack next to the gate.

"Even here the troubles of the outside world penetrate," Gabriel said. "An unfortunate repercussion of success."

The guard opened the gate and they drove up a narrow track through a thin grove of cottonwood trees. A flock of peahens and two large peacocks scavenged in the dust under the trees. "Maria's pets," Gabriel said. "Beautiful birds, but I can't stand them. The cock, he roosts on the roof each evening and calls to the stars 'A-hole! A-hole!' "

Gabriel nosed the truck through the last break in the glade to a parking spot below a white hacienda with a red tiled roof which sat on a small hill. There was a veranda on all sides, bordered by shrubs flowering red and pink. Huge oak posts, embraced by lime vines, supported the latticework, which was smothered in wild roses. The veranda itself was tiled in terra-cotta squares. Beyond, Farrell could make out a roll of grass and then the deep blue of the ocean still churning with the power of the departing storm. A light wind flitted through chimes. Somewhere bees were active. It was just like the photograph in Gabriel's office.

A lovely woman, Farrell's height, with shoulder-length ebony hair, brown eyes, and a delicate olive skin opened a glass and rose-wood door. She wore a lavender cotton jumpsuit she'd cinched at the waist with a sash of indigo. She walked directly to Gabriel and kissed him.

"My wife, Maria," Gabriel said.

"Mr. Farrell, how good of you to come and be our guest," she said in flawless English. "For a few hours very early this morning we thought there would be little of the house left for you to see."

She pointed out the broken limbs on the trees and the petals of the flowers strewn like a carpet across the veranda. Farrell thought of the two-bedroom apartment he and Lena were living in at the time, very comfortable by Chicago standards, but penurious compared to the Cortez's home.

"A beautiful place," Farrell said.

"It was my mother's," she said, pleased. "And her father's before. She inherited his textile factory in Guadalajara and ran it for many years. This was her retreat, her paradise."

She paused, studying Farrell. "I can see Gabriel drove with the roof down. There is red mud splattered on your shirt. Just watch out if he gets behind the wheel of the boat. I won't let him if I'm along, you know. I drive."

Inside the house, they passed through a room with a ceiling almost seven feet high. The walls were white-washed, the furniture hand-made leather. Next came a library: bookcases of the same heavy oak found throughout the hacienda and dominating the room was a ponderous desk with legs that were carved with inlays of a rising sun.

"So many books!" Farrell said.

"We spend much time here when Gabriel is not traveling," she said. "You will go crazy living so remote without these for escape."

Farrell walked to the bookcases, seeing a series of works by

Jorges Luis Borges and Gabriel Garcia Marquez in Spanish. "I wish I could read them," Farrell said. "My Spanish is primitive. I learned to read French in Africa reading the French writers I'd already studied in translation: Camus and Rimbaud and Baudelaire."

"And these—Borges and Marquez," said Gabriel. "They intrigue you?"

"Marquez has the unnerving ability to make you want to laugh and cry reading the same page. I feel uncomfortable reading him, but I do," Farrell said. "Every one of Borges's stories left me staring into space, or what did he call it, 'the crossway of the stars'?"

A small Brittany spaniel scampered into the room, across the tile onto the maroon rug, and growled at Farrell.

"Meet Cazador," Gabriel said, kneeling to rub her behind the ears. "She hunts with me in the hills here."

"Unusual," Farrell said. "I mean a Britt in Mexico."

"A friend of mine gave her to me. Said she'd run all day, and if I trained her right, she would quarter true even in dense brush. He was right. Do you hunt?"

"I used to hunt whitetail deer with my dad in Maine."

"We shall go sometime," Gabriel said. "Good quail here. Fantastic doves in Sonora."

"Enough talk," Maria said. "Why don't you get the cook going with dinner?"

"Of course," Gabriel said. "Let me get Jack settled first."

After Farrell had laid his luggage in a small room with a terracotta floor, a single bed, and a desk, he and Gabriel hiked out through the trees with one of his servants, a portly man with stubble on his chin. "We shall have fresh capon for dinner," Gabriel said as they approached a pen where a dozen chickens milled about.

The servant entered the pen, made two surprisingly quick steps, which scattered the other birds, and grabbed the capon by the neck. Hens squawked at his feet and the capon struggled frantically, the talons on the back of its legs ripping the air.

"Hold him tight," Gabriel laughed.

With a wicked twist, the bird slashed a talon into the thumb of the servant, who cursed and relaxed his grip. The bird hit the dirt and scrambled into the far corner of the pen, triumphant, with the servant in close pursuit.

"Choose another," Farrell called in his rudimentary Spanish. "Spirit like that deserves a longer life."

The servant turned and looked at his bleeding thumb.

"Señor?" the servant said, looking at Gabriel now.

"He's our dinner," said Gabriel.

"The same, señor?"

Gabriel nodded as the capon tried to take cover among the hens. "Get him."

Gabriel clapped Farrell on the shoulder. "The recipe the cook follows with capon is masterful."

They drank a Napa Valley Petit Syrah with the capon, which was served in a sauce of jalapeños, shallots, chives, and garlic. Afterward, they watched a sunset that turned the ocean and their faces crimson. It turned out that Maria had studied archeology for a year at the University of Chicago on a fellowship. She and Farrell talked about the problems on the South Side and the battleship-gray winters. Gabriel was lost; it seemed Chicago was one of the few places on Earth to which he'd never been. After dinner, they sat in the wicker chairs on the veranda, drinking port and listening to the crash of the sea. The electric lights were off, leaving only the cotton illumination of a kerosene lamp that hung from one of the oak beams.

"Is your wife also in banking?" Maria asked.

Farrell winced and realized he hadn't thought once about Lena since arriving. Guilt flooded in. "No, a nurse," he said. "She works in a hospital. We lost our child this year. She's taken it very hard."

"I'm so sorry," Maria said. "And you?"

"I'm learning my way again," Farrell said. "Do you have any children?"

"We can't," Gabriel said, with such an air of finality and sadness that Farrell did not push the issue.

"I'm sorry, too," Farrell said.

That night he slept in a guest room. He felt a genuine pang of anguish for them, this handsome couple that could not have children. He thought about Jenny and wondered if the thread that tied him to the future had been permanently snipped. He thought again of Lena, which threw a shadow of remorse across his chest bared to welcome the warm wind that coursed through the open window.

About two in the morning, he came awake and alert not knowing why. He opened the thick door, which swung silent on well-oiled hinges, and heard Gabriel's voice, steady but insistent above the buzz of an old air conditioner behind the closed door to his study. In the moonlight to his left, across the living room, he saw a movement on the veranda. It was Maria in a full-length white nightgown, leaning against one of the oak pillars. Farrell almost crossed the room. Something about the stiffness of her shoulders and the way she leaned on the railing for support froze him. Time seemed to melt away, stirring the terrible memory of how his father had turned away from him when he was seven and had hit a double in his first baseball game. Farrell had danced into the house twisting and punching the air. He reenacted the swing for his mother, who beamed with pride until his father had put down his paper and frowned. "I told you not to ever let him get excited like this," he had said firmly.

"But I hit a double, dad," Farrell said, and he skipped into the kitchen and assumed his hitting stance again.

"Maybe it would be better if you didn't play anymore," his father said.

Farrell burst into tears.

"Brendan, that's a little—" his mother began.

"What do you know about this, Peg?" he snapped. "Have you ever, ever spent a day when you see the world through a summer cloud in the morning and a charcoal curtain in the afternoon?"

"I know that a game won't hurt him," his mother insisted.

"Really?" his father said. "Look at him."

Farrell moaned and collapsed into the corner, his arms over his head.

"Come on now," his mother said, and she picked him up by his elbows and led him down the hall to his room. She washed his face.

"You know how your father feels. Now take a nap, and when you can be calm, you can come out."

Farrell laid on his bed and cried as he listened to her lock the door behind her.

He'd continued to play baseball in secret. But at those times when Farrell was unable to contain his joy, his fear, his longings, his despair—the day in 1967 when the Red Sox won the American League pennant, the afternoon his mother had a minor heart attack, the Christmas morning he'd received his first bike, the black day his beagle was struck by a car—one of his parents would step in between him and whatever object or experience had stirred his passions.

The techniques they used to calm him could be as benign as teaching him to breathe slow and deep after stubbing his toe, or as blunt as sitting him in a darkened room with quiet music after his dog had died in his arms; or standing him in a cold shower when he came home elated over seeing a beaver swimming in a stream.

As much as he wanted to, even now, he couldn't really hate them. He knew that, in their own way, they were trying to shield him from what is passed on in the genes, to battle the relentless roller coaster that haunted his father's side of the family.

In the bar, Farrell raised his whiskey glass to the mirror and examined his new face. He knew every stitch by now, yet these remained the eyes and cheeks of a stranger. He downed the drink and headed to his room, recalling how he had left Maria Robles standing in the moonlight. As he'd gone back to sleep, the croak of the peacock had echoed through the window to him: A-hole! A-hole!

Farrell shut the door to his room and got the diary out from underneath the mattress. He lay there on the bed thinking of how he'd found his wife standing in the doorway to the nursery the night before he left for Mexico.

"It would better to get Jenny's things out of here," he had said. "I'll pack it all when I get back."

Lena shook her head. "No, I'll do it while you're gone. I'll call a moving company to take it away."

Farrell tried to say more, but couldn't. He just nodded and walked back into his bedroom to finish packing.

March 3

Therapists will tell you that writing to the dead is a good thing. I can't bear to write her: you send a message, your return address goes along. They know where to find you. Sooner or later you're not home, you're not anywhere; it's dark, the world spins and hits you like a fist.

They say the coming back takes time. But I don't think you

can come back. You just go in a different direction. Jack's got the right attitude, you go away.

I looked in the room today, picked up the little music box Christina gave her, turned it on. The music made me run.

Had the day off today and slept. In my dreams the street sounds mingle with my fantasies. Had this nightmare where an old man with a rectangular head talked to me in a strange language I understood. He said, I can bring her home.

He stepped aside to show me an ambulance with siren wailing and lights flashing. We drove north along deserted highways and stopped near an abandoned lot between red brick buildings with windows that had no glass, only tattered yellow drapes that flapped in the cold wind. I stepped out onto pieces of coal and shattered glass, but my feet didn't cut. A woman wearing a white veil emerged from one of the buildings, wheeling a baby carriage. I ran to her. Through the gauze that masked the woman's face I could see she was familiar, though I know I'd never seen her before.

In the carriage was a baby dressed in the little Jemima Puddle-Duck suit my mother gave Jenny. The baby had her hands and feet and hair. The face was not hers. It was a light, opaque and shimmering, as if someone had thrown a powerful lamp against the rear of a movie screen.

Farrell let it slip from his hands onto the bed cover. The swelling had returned and he could not make it recede. In his pain, he recalled how in Mexico he had found escape. The morning after seeing her on the veranda, he found Maria and Gabriel having breakfast at a table under a tree on the lawn. A calm breeze filtered through the branches.

"You should have been here just five minutes earlier," Maria said, shielding her eyes from the sun. "A troop of dolphin passed fifty meters from the dock. It's unusual to see them this close to shore."

"Why's that?" Farrell asked, searching for some sign of the remoteness he'd sensed in her the evening before.

"The tuna fishermen have killed most of them with gill nets," Gabriel said. "It's very sad, but the people here have to make a living."

Maria turned back to the sea. Farrell followed her gaze to a thin aluminum dock that stretched from the bottom of the grassy knoll into the tiny cove. A silver powerboat was tied at the far end.

"We'll go out later," Gabriel said. "She's got twin 455 Oldsmobile engines in her. But first I want to show you some plans for an import-export project in Guatemala."

They spent the morning in the cool of Gabriel's office hashing out the financial aspects of the deal. It was straightforward. Gabriel and a Guatemalan businessman connected to one of that country's powerful families would work together. Gabriel would bring electronics south from Japanese contacts he had and the Guatemalan would ensure the gear got through customs.

"I think my bank will go for the project," Farrell said once it had been explained and he'd seen the numbers Gabriel said would be generated. "This is pretty safe stuff."

"I had hoped so, my friend," Gabriel said. "Now let's eat something before we go out on the boat."

Maria served empanadas—garlicky ground pork fried in cassava dough—pickled eggs, black olives, cherry tomatos, black radishes, and red wine for lunch. Gabriel opened a second bottle in the sun and the stories began. A lovely blond hooker in Rome introduced Gabriel to love when he was fourteen. After the initial lesson, he spent all his money on a week-long crash course. Farrell said a speed skater had taken his virginity in the back seat of a beat-up Datsun on a chilly November night in New England. Maria was coy: she said a lady never speaks of love in the presence of other men.

Gabriel said at dawn on the windy road west of Marseille, he crashed his motorcycle trying to race back from a midnight liaison to the villa his father had rented.

"I was almost there, leaning in and out of the curves." He paused to take a gulp of the wine. "A bicyclist, a very enchanting young woman with marvelous thighs, pulled out into the road. I laid the motorcycle down rather than risk her thighs."

Maria stuck her tongue out at him. He laughed.

Farrell told them he was stuck once in a border town in West Africa between a Muslim society and a pagan nation. He sat at a table on the Islamic side of the river waiting for the frontier to open. A friend and Farrell spoke to a boy who knew some English as they ate by lantern light, listening to the drums beating in the background like great hearts. People danced with scarecrows in the shadows. The boy's eyes widened. *"Médecin traditionel!"* he said. Farrell's friend's jaw hung open. Farrell had turned to find three black scorpions running across the forehead and chin of the man sitting next to him. The man plucked the poisonous arachnid from his chin, smiled, then snapped its belly with his finger.

The boy said the man was a sorcerer. He had talisman rings that would guard Farrell against the scorpion's sting. The sorcerer said if Farrell put the ring on and let the scorpions walk and they did not strike, Farrell could keep the ring.

"Do it," Farrell's friend had said. "You'll forget the pain of the bite, but never the memory that you didn't take the chance!"

The two scorpions moved through the hair on his forearm. One tried to enter the sleeve of his shirt toward his armpit. He shook them off at last, face flushed and bilious. The animist had laughed. He asked if Farrell wished to see his cobra. At that moment, a border guard placed his hand on the man's shoulder. Before the guard's gun barrel, the man danced in spirals across the bridge. The lights suspended over the center of the bridge cast his shadows in two directions, one ebony shape toward each shore of the river.

"Jack Farrell," Gabriel said after Farrell had finished his story. "You should have been born in a different time. You were meant to explore, to be an adventurer."

He poured Farrell more wine from the bottle. "I sense you don't know what to do about it."

"My job is enough. I travel," Farrell said uncertainly.

"Hotels, planes, and hurried meals in restaurants where the decor is different from your own kitchen," Gabriel scoffed. "Enough?"

"I'm happy," Farrell replied, and he wondered if he was.

"So you don't long for any kind of change?" Gabriel said.

"I hadn't thought of it," Farrell said. "The bank is good to me."

"This is a growing area of interest to me, the southwest border of your country," Gabriel said. "I know of a bank in San Diego that needs someone like you, experienced in big-time banking, yet young enough to have your own ideas."

"Domestic banking is so pedestrian," Farrell said. "I've told you I like the travel, the different cultures."

"That's the point," Gabriel said. "The bank wants to expand its work here and in Central America."

Farrell almost told him he wasn't interested, then he thought of the cold apartment in Chicago. "I'll keep an open mind."

Gabriel leaned forward as if he wanted to press Farrell for an answer when Maria broke in: "Enough business, I thought the afternoon belonged to the boat."

Gabriel gave her a sidelong glance, then made a dash for the keys. Maria was quicker and passed through the doors first. He followed her back onto the veranda with a third bottle of red wine.

"You may not get the chance to enjoy the pleasure of me driving my boat," he said, his lips drawn back in a joyous smile, "but at least we will have the thrill of another bottle of this tremendous wine!"

"More wine in the sun?" Farrell asked.

"What would the great Marquez have you do in this scene?" Gabriel roared.

Farrell had to laugh. "He'd have me drink."

The boat's engines were strong. Farrell stood in the well of the bow, gripping a nylon rope for balance as they shot out into the ensenada. Gabriel stood behind him, holding a second rope in one hand, the bottle of wine in the other. The sky was pure and blue, the sun intense with the kind of penetrating heat the body prays for during a Chicago winter. In the light chop, the boat reeled and vibrated. Inland to the north, a peninsula of chocolate mountains jogged against milk clouds.

"Have you ever seen light like this?" Gabriel roared above the throb of the engines. "It breaks all around us like we are rocks and it is a river."

"You're drunk," Farrell said.

Gabriel gazed at him in dead seriousness. "A light like this can change a man."

Farrell decided to humor him. "I've seen this light before. On boozy afternoons."

"Do you know Joaquin Sorolla?" Gabriel asked, handing Farrell the bottle. The boat surged off the wake of a passing boat from the resort and Farrell spilled some wine on his shirt.

"No," he coughed.

"A painter, Spanish, at the turn of the century. A genius and a man who made love to light. He was seduced by the play of it, the way it bends our perceptions. There is one painting I'm thinking of: two boys hang from the bow rope of a boat, just as we are. But they are in the water. The strokes of his brush are so clear and touched with love that it dazzles. Dazzles and changes the angle and shape of their bodies."

"I can't see it," Farrell said.

"I must show you then," Gabriel said. "Give me the wine."

He drank from the bottle, then handed it back. As the boat surged on a swell, just before a trough, he braced himself to the gunnel with the rope and calmly threw himself into the sea. His body bounced once on the water, which swallowed him on the next skip.

Maria screamed. Farrell panicked. He stumbled toward the stern, tripped, and slammed into the rail when Maria down-throttled and returned the boat to the spot where Gabriel had gone overboard. On his feet again, Farrell could see Gabriel treading water, spitting water from his mouth like a fountain and waving.

"What in Jesus's name were you thinking of?" Maria demanded as she steered the boat along side him.

"Sorolla," Gabriel said, grinning maniacally. "Bring the bow about. I must show Jack his genius."

Maria shot Farrell a wicked glare.

"I had no idea!" Farrell said. "Believe me!"

She sat in the driver's chair and pouted. Seeing that she had no intention of helping him explain Sorolla's art, Gabriel worked his way to the front of the boat. Farrell leaned over the edge and handed him the nylon line. Gabriel hoisted himself out of the water until his torso was free to his pelvic bone. His legs dangled under the water.

"You see?"

The sun skidded on the sea around Gabriel, then broke and bent as if it had been shone through crushed ice or a shattered prism. Below the surface, Gabriel's buttocks and legs diluted into a series of large splashes of viscous aqua and eggshell, shimmering and mutating with every lap of the choppy water.

"He got that in a painting?" Farrell asked.

"A genius, I told you," Gabriel said. "He took such risks with the brush that the canvas itself seems to move with the weight and the volume of water. It is as if light and water gave the painting its soul."

Farrell reached down and pulled Gabriel over the gunnels. He crashed to the floor, soaked and missing one of his boat shoes.

"Macho idiot," Maria said. "You could have hurt yourself."

"I jumped clear of the boat," Gabriel said, with a dismissive wave of his hand. "You must try it, Jack."

The idea of flying like a piece of bait in the tropical sun felt right.

"No!" Maria said. "We do not even know his wife. If you are hurt here, she'd never forgive me."

Gabriel shrugged. "Too bad, next time you come then, Jack."

When Maria had the boat running again, Gabriel passed Farrell the wine and whispered: "Drink. Then leap after we pass that buoy."

At the same moment Maria righted the wheel after rounding the channel marker, Farrell stepped onto the cushions. He heard her curse in Spanish, and she thrust the throttle arm forward, almost killing the engine. Which had the unwanted effect of tossing Farrell at a harsh angle away from the boat through two disconcerting rolls across the water. The landing seared his skin like a fall on smooth cement. He surfaced and gagged from the saltwater that the impact had driven up his nose.

"Magnificent!" Gabriel cried. He dragged Farrell aboard.

"Had to do it," Farrell gasped to Maria. "What a rush! Going from zero to fifty miles an hour in an instant."

The two-mile trip back to the dock took almost an hour as each man made a dozen leaps off the speeding boat. At the dock, Cazador greeted them with barks that made the men's heads ring. They endured Maria's silence while they tied the boat to the dock. She strode ahead of them up the lawn toward the house. On the grass, Gabriel stripped and walked nude behind her until she sensed him, turned, and broke into uncontrolled giggles. Farrell flopped soaking wet onto the bed. He enjoyed the way the room spun slowly, rekindling the wonderful sensation he felt flying from the boat. He passed out to the sounds of the peahens scratching outside his window.

———

The sun was setting when Farrell woke, sore from the falls he'd taken, hungover from the wine. He put on some dry clothes and walked into the main room of the house. In an eerie déjà vu, Maria stood alone on the veranda.

Cool and sweet, the evening breeze brushed at his throbbing temples. Maria leaned over the white-washed restraining wall. Morning glories, which had curled tightly to their vines, framed her lovely face.

"I'm sorry if we upset you today," he said.

She started. "I didn't hear you come out."

Holding on to one of the oak standards, she looked out at the sea and said: "My mother would sit here every day watching the sun die. Her face would turn copper in the last light. Near the end of her life, her skin was pale, except at dusk. The light—what does my husband call it, Sorolla's light?—well, it made her full and strong again. I miss her very much."

"You have no father?" Farrell asked.

"He left when I was very young," Maria said. "He was an American who my mother married on a lark. She was from a wealthy family and it was a scandal, but her parents stood by her. After she had me, I guess my father realized he didn't want to be a stranger in a strange land all his life. So he went home. So she went home."

"You've never seen him?"

"Once," she sighed. "It was in New York City. I couldn't bring myself to go and talk to him. I suppose I was afraid he wouldn't be the person my mother remembered. I decided nostalgia was better."

Out on the ocean, the sun hovered over the water. Above, the clouds melted into hues of purple and black and orange. Maria's skin began to burnish, then melt into a rich mélange of wine and sand. Farrell watched for the mythical moment when tropical sunsets flash a crisp green. Maria broke his concentration. "Do you take lovers on your travels?"

"I, I don't understand," Farrell stammered. "I'm married."

"So it does matter to some men," Maria said. "I'm sorry if I upset you."

Sitting in his room in the ski lodge, Farrell was sure that her voice had barely carried beyond the three feet that separated them. She looked at him, then out at the dying sun. "I just want to know how men pass time away from their wives."

"I read," Farrell said, studying her neck and shoulders. "I must entertain clients at times. I walk through museums. I try to study Spanish and stay fit. I'm not one of those men who takes solace in the arms of strangers, though late at night, when sleep comes, the thought crosses my mind."

The fact that he confessed this to someone who was really a stranger bewildered Farrell. He asked himself if he could have said the same in front of his own wife.

"Who do you think of, women in the streets, women you've seen before or known?" she asked.

"I've never really thought about it," he said. "I guess all three . . . at one time or another."

Maria frowned. "I've embarrassed you again. I just find it hard to figure out the minds of men."

Farrell rubbed his palm over the fabric of his trousers. "I think that's an affliction that strikes all women. But you shouldn't feel bad. We're mysteries to ourselves."

The sun sank over the horizon, leaving only the rose tints on the clouds far out on the Pacific. Cazador padded toward them over the tiles. An exotic smell Farrell could not name peppered his nose. He briefly considered that this must be the scent of all Mexican sunsets.

"Gabriel got in a rage the day before you came and he shot one of my peacocks," she said, hugging herself. "I feel sometimes when I hold him in my arms at night that I know only half of him."

At the same time, they heard the creak of a door inside the house. Cazador jumped up, wriggled, and ran into the house. Gabriel emerged bleary-eyed. "Why didn't you wake me?" he asked Maria in a grumpy tone. "It's impolite for me not to entertain our guest."

"You looked at peace," she said. In an abrupt move, she brushed by him back through the house toward the kitchen.

Gabriel slumped in one of the chairs, lit a cigarette, and smiled at Farrell. "I guess I'll never learn, Jack."

"What, not to shoot peahens?"

He looked up at him, his eyes wide. "She told you that? Well, what could I do? I had insomnia for two days and it sat outside my window calling A-hole just as I was falling asleep. Two days. I shot it."

He waved the cigarette quickly through the night air, leaving a tracer of orange light that faded instantly. "Peacocks I can deal with; you just don't think about it when you kill them," he said. "The things I always manage to screw up are art history and wine."

Gabriel leaned back his head to croak a short, racous laugh that Farrell found impossible not to join.

Farrell laughed bitterly to himself in the room at the lodge, wondering what Lena had written about during his weekend in Mexico.

March 5

Told myself I'd live in the nursery at night while Jack is gone. Force myself to surround myself with her, to see her. As if this is the only way I can look at it.

I'm making an inventory: piles of unused diapers, ten onesies, eight pairs of socks, a barrel of disposable wipes, her crib, the bumpers decorated with lambs, the balloon mobile hanging from her dressing table. The pads, the blankets, the dresser, the sweaters, the cross my mom and dad sent, the framed picture of the lake from Peg.

I went to Christina's yesterday. She's seven months now. Haven't seen her since the third month. I put my hand on her, just to check her size. When I touched her there, my best friend, she flinched and pulled back. As if I were a thief. As if what has happened to me could be like a cold, catching.

I told her I had to go. She bit at her fingernails. She got me my coat.

There are also four bibs, three sleepers, a mirror, her brush, two pairs of stiff white shoes . . .

The diary fell off the bed and slapped on the floor, the sharp noise spurring the instant recall of a cab door slamming outside their apartment building in Chicago. He'd left Gabriel's home the night after his conversation with Maria Robles, spent a day attending to other business in Mexico City, and arrived late the following evening in Chicago. Only Lena wasn't waiting for him at the airport. He called home and got no answer. He had jumped from the cab with a growing sense of dread and raced up the slick, snowy stairs.

The front rooms were dark and cold. Farrell called out to Lena. She didn't reply. He leaned against the wall, listening to the china clock, begging the darkness that he wouldn't float above himself again.

He took a deep breath, pinched his finger, and began to search. His wet shoes made a high, slick, squeeking noise as he crossed into the living room, aware as he'd been a thousand times in the last year of the blow of wind, the flutter of drapes, the bubbling of the aquarium.

A stream of light from the nursery issued into the hallway. He opened the door. Lena was curled in the corner near the crib, wrapped in the comforter from their bed. She clutched a stuffed pink elephant. She was surrounded by dirty dishes.

"Thank God, I . . ." Farrell began.

Lena picked her chin off her chest and looked at Farrell as if he had been standing in the doorway for hours. "I couldn't throw it all away."

"Okay," he said. He slid down the wall opposite her, his wet overcoat spread out underneath him.

Lena seemed to see him and yet not to. He realized she'd been awake for a very long time. She said, "Do you ever get the feeling that the vision you have of yourself doesn't jibe with the image other people have of you?"

"Sometimes," he said.

"What do you do?"

"I try to keep thinking about that person I want to be and hope it all comes true."

"Has it?"

"I suppose so," Farrell said. "I'm married to you."

She gave a wan smile, then said: "What do you want out of life?"

"I don't know," Farrell said, and he understood he was being totally honest. "Probably uniqueness. Singularity."

"You know, Jack, that's the difference between us," she sputtered. "I see things in specifics. You look at the world as a concept."

He looked at his wife during the silence that followed and realized with a pang of guilt that, though he still loved her, he had not desired her in a long time. "That's not fair," Farrell said. "She was no concept."

Lena drew her knees to her chest and hugged the elephant. "I guess that wasn't fair."

"No, it wasn't."

"I want life to be fair."

"That's like asking to be a child again," Farrell said.

"Is it?"

"Yes."

"Do you know what I want from life now, right now?" she asked.

Farrell crawled over to her. "Tell me."

"I want to leave Chicago," she said, digging her fingers into the elephant's neck. "I need to go where it's warm all the time. Cold reminds me, it surrounds me."

"You just said you can't throw it away . . ." he began.

Lena stiffened. "I've already quit my job."

Farrell stared at her, knowing that he should feel the surge of pity someone like Lena deserved at that moment. Instead he seemed to look at her from the other end of a long tunnel. He didn't know who she was anymore. "Gabriel told me about a job in San Diego," he heard himself say.

Lena nodded. "We have to go."

Farrell nodded, unsure of what else he could say. For a moment Farrell held his hands an inch away from her as if his body and hers were charged with opposing magnetic forces. He thought of Mexico again, which made him relax; and his hands rested lightly on Lena's soiled blue sweater. They fell asleep that way in the corner next to the crib.

Chapter 8

S t. Patrick's Day dawned gray and stormy, which put Inez in a foul mood because the preparations for the Y Couloir couldn't go forward. In the late afternoon, Farrell suggested a trip to a bar he knew outside of the canyon. Tony and Ann declined, saying they had to work on their equipment. On the ride down the canyon, the rest of them heard a radio report that the weather would change. The jet stream would retreat north into Wyoming over the next twenty-four hours. Forty degrees and sunshine was the forecast for the next three days. Inez leaned over the seat and planted kisses on the cheeks of Farrell and Page, who was driving.

"The time for you, he comes in just two days," she crooned. "You make the history."

Farrell's heart beat faster when she was near. He leaned away from her voice. Page gripped the steering wheel tighter and pressed harder on the accelerator.

Three shots of Old Bushmills, two beers, and a game of eight-ball later, Farrell had a tough split shot to put the seven in the right side pocket. The fact that he could look over the tops of his knuckles and see Inez's face and jet black hair framed by his skin tweaked his concentration. He scratched.

The Wave seemed to have recovered from the day before. He

was stripes. He stuck out his jaw and brayed: "You got no center, mon."

Farrell handed him the cue: "And you, dope fiend, got nothing from the Adam's apple up."

"Sure do, mon," The Wave beamed and rapped the cue off the side of his head. "Just light up there, that's all."

The clock above the bar chimed 5:30 P.M. A new crowd of revelers, some with tiny shamrocks painted on their faces, crowded in and ordered pitchers of low-alcohol beer. On the jukebox, Dwight Yokum sang of guitars and Cadillacs and hillbilly music. The Wave bent over and hit the cue ball hard. It jumped the rim of the table and bounced across the floor. The barman, a rangy man sporting a black cowboy hat, glared. The Wave shrugged: "No eye-hand, mon."

"Get some," the barkeep growled.

Farrell picked up the cue ball. He admitted to himself that Lena's diary had become a festering wound; where he had expected comfort, he found torture. When he thought of her, his stomach burned as if her fingernail dug into his side. He leaned against the wall, pretending to analyze the table; instead the room shifted and now he saw Inez, The Wave, and Page through a thin, white gauze as if he were taking photographs of them all through a soft-filter lens. Whiskey in the afternoon will get to you.

From her purse, Inez plucked a quarter, which she used to dig at the thick varnish on the wood. She looked at Farrell and said, "Why is the man like you without work so early in life?"

Inez. She cooled the burning sensation in his gut. "Why do you make movies?" Farrell asked.

"You first."

"How will I know the truth?"

"You do not," Inez said, her tone seductive. "Perhaps that is what makes it so interesting, no? To figure out the lie?"

"This is your game," Farrell said. "You tell the truth first."

Inez dug the serrated edge of the quarter into the varnish until a short dull groove appeared on the table. Farrell stared at it, thought of his father, and felt a pang of nausea. Before he could wallow, Inez sat up straight in her chair, laid her right ankle across her left knee, and grabbed her right foot. "I was to . . . no." She hesitated. "When I was young, I want to be a photographer."

Page leaned back in his chair until it rested against the wall. "Like your dad, huh?" he said. "He was some kind of journalist, wasn't he?"

Farrell noticed The Wave's shoulders bunch as he turned to the jukebox.

"Some kind," she replied. "He wins the Overseas Press Club award for international photojournalism. But really, he never succeeds in what he is after.

"When I am . . . was seven, he gives me a little automatic camera for my birthday. I go to school then on the hill in the *vieux quartier* of Lyon, the oldest part of the city. The buildings are tall and are—I think you say 'staggered'?—staggered up the hill. The streets, they are narrow and made of stone. My school is off the steep stairs that comes from the square, which has a fountain. Three roads enter the square, and when school lets out, we pour down the stairs like water. Everyone yells, so happy."

Inez paused and took a sip from the beer glass.

"I carry the camera around my neck always," said Inez. "I take many pictures, but none of them looks like the ones my father take. He looks at them and he nods. But me, I can see in his eyes they are dull: pictures of friends, of the school or Madame Kennedy, my cat. My father gives her that name. So one day, I walk down the stairs with my classmates. The sun comes through the clouds into just one half of the square. It is a good light. I step on a wall at the stair bottom to get the picture.

"I focus on the fountain because the sun cuts the water into shadow and light. A car horn sounds. I swing the camera. A boy named Richard from the class ahead of me rides his bike. He looks back to his friends. The car, a blue one, slides on the wet stone before it hits the bike and throws Richard far into the air. I take pictures snap—snap, one after the other."

Inez stopped, pulled a cigarette from her purse, and lit it. The blue smoke curled around her face. She slumped in the chair and took another long drag before continuing. "I run home through the streets, my shoes they slap on the wet stones. My lungs hurts, but I am happy. My father develops all the film. But there is only one real photograph, you know? Richard hears the car horn and he is at the angle to the car. He knows it hits him soon and his mouth is open. My father smiles when he sees this picture. He sells it to the local newspaper for eighty francs, uh, twenty dollars, and I buy a better camera."

"What happened to the kid?" The Wave asked.

Inez shifted uncomfortably in her chair. "I do not remember. It does not matter." She took another drag off the cigarette, then cocked her head at Farrell: "Your turn."

"Been retired eighteen months."

"Before you make the retirement?" Inez asked.

"Now that wasn't your question."

"You're cheating," said Page.

"I didn't think you had an imagination, Page," Farrell said. He pointed the tip of the cue at the one-eyed skier. "But I guess we can all be fooled. You got it: I was a cheater before I retired."

With a lazy motion, Inez drew a chair toward her with the tip of her boot, then rested the sole on it and lit another cigarette. The movement was sassy and lawless. It excited Farrell. "Do you run from Wall Street?" she asked. "The trader in secret information, I think."

Farrell cracked a ball across the table, sunk it, which allowed him an easy shot of the eight ball in the corner pocket. The Wave scowled. Farrell took another shot of Old Bushmills, feeling it roll through his stomach and numb the tiny flame that refused to die in his belly.

"Traitor of secret information, I like that," he said. "But not true. Basically, I got involved in some bad business deals. It's that simple. When it all blew up, I fell hard. Got these scars." He paused and ran his fingers along the red lines on his face. "Afterward, I thought, why not go back to Alta, make some good deep powder turns."

"Sounds boring to me," interrupted Page.

"That's bottle talk," said The Wave. "I think he's holding back."

"Very good, Wave," Farrell said. "We Irish talk quite a bit on St. Patrick's Day. You just have to figure out how much of that was true and how much was off-angle bullshit."

Farrell's eyes met Inez's. They locked, and with the whiskey flowing through his veins he thought, I could die there. He winked at her. She winked back. He turned away to begin a new game. He broke and scratched. Page sniggered.

"Page, the big player," Farrell said. "Put your money where your nose is."

"Teams," Page said.

"Done," Farrell said. "The Wave plays with me. You with Inez. Rack them up, I'll be back in a second."

In the men's room, the door swung open behind Farrell. The Wave slid in next to him. The white bandage was visible on the kid's head like a bow among the dreadlocks. The Wave studied the lines between the tiles, then said, "Watch yourself, mon. She knows more than she lets on."

"What's that supposed to mean?" Farrell said, and he zipped up.

The Wave, his eyes red and rheumy from too many joints, put a hand on Farrell's shoulder. "You figure that out for yourself," he said. "Just thought you should be aware that there are other rules being used."

With that The Wave granted himself a look in the mirror, shook his dreadlocks over the bandage, and left in a flash of neon.

Farrell followed behind him, with a growing need to become very drunk. As he walked to the bar, he took a sidelong glance at Inez, then turned to the barman. On closer inspection, he was in his late forties, with massive, scarred hands, a silver band about the black hat, a day's growth of beard, and a belt buckle that advertised a hunting outfitter from Jackson Hole. Farrell asked for a pitcher and three small bar glasses.

When the cowboy brought them, he said: "Watch yourselves." Then the bartender grinned and revealed a gap in his upper front teeth—the mark of an experienced street fighter.

"Always," Farrell said.

Page watched him set the shot glasses and the beer on the table. He leaned forward: "You planning on going black or something?"

Farrell looked over at the cowboy. "I think I'd rather get dragged behind a truck. This is merely to put us in the correct frame of mind."

Page selected a cue from a rack on the wall. "You break."

"Lubrication first," Farrell said, pouring from the Old Bushmills bottle he'd stashed under his chair. In the larger glasses he poured four drafts.

"Half for me," Inez said. "The weight of you I don't have."

"That's fair."

"I'll pass on the whiskey," said Page, shaking his head. "Makes my head go round and round. When you're whiskey drunk with one eye, you feel like you're the tip of a top spinning."

"If you do not mind, how does it happen—the eye," Inez asked.

Page shook his head. "I do mind. Bad memories."

"It helps to talk of memories," Inez said.

The Wave interrupted, "Some things are better left unsaid, Inez."

Inez shot The Wave a glare that in Biblical times would have turned him to stone. "I do not think this is your affair. Page?"

Page poured himself a shot and drank it fast. "Really want to know? My dad had this thing with the cards. Didn't like to lose. He played this game with my mom. I called it 'No Win, Gin, Slap Your Wife's Face In.' "

"You don't have to do this, mon," The Wave said, the anxiety in his voice palpable.

"Shut up, Wave," Page said. He poured himself another beer. "When I was thirteen, he loses big one summer night and comes home in a rare mood. Only I step in front of her as he swings. Shatters my occipital bone. I run outside into the woods and stay there all night. If I'd come in sooner, they could have saved the eye."

"Jesus," Farrell said.

"Satisfied, Inez?" The Wave asked.

Inez reached for a shot glass. Her hand shook as she drank. "For the moment."

There was an awkward moment of silence. The Wave grabbed a cue, crouched over the table, shook two dreadlocks over his eye to give himself a rear sight reference, and fired. The balls ricocheted and split well, except a five group about a foot in front of the right corner pocket. A stripe fell. The Wave sank three more balls before missing.

"Yours," The Wave said, and he handed the stick to Inez, holding on to it one second longer than necessary. He gave her a stoned leer and she was forced to tug it away from him.

Inez stood very still once she had the cue. "You smoke again, no? *Merde.* You dull your senses with this. You lose your edge."

"I'm still there," The Wave said. "Take your shot."

Inez glared at him, then leaned over the table.

The Wave said, "So, Inez, how would you make this scene work in your movie?"

"I do not use such a scene," said Inez, studying the ball.

"Just for instance. I mean, would you get low over the shooter's back and line the lens up like he sees it? Or would that be too close?"

Inez studied The Wave as if she were seeing him for the very first time. "It is perilous to get too close, Wave," she said coldly. "You place the camera back so the audience, they have the sense of the game and of the players. Their pace. If not, there is no logic."

The Wave said, "It only moves when there's a plan, a script, right? You ever operate without one, a script I mean?"

"I make the improvisations all the time," Inez said.

"Now I know you're tripping me, lady," said The Wave. "I think it's not on paper, you're lost. You don't know how to pick it up and go with it when you're ripping. We'd never see you on the hill."

"To be on the hill is not my strength," said Inez. She shot again, missing. "I tell the world what is on the hill."

"She likes to peek through her fingers," Farrell said sarcastically.

"She's cautious," The Wave chuckled.

"I create the peak through the fingers," Inez insisted. "And the critics recognize me for the chances I take with the camera."

"Inez knew the risks, mon," The Wave announced. "Tripped over the film on the editing room floor and cut her head. Tough break, but shit, she knew the risks!"

Inez pointed a finger at The Wave. "I took you to a world you never knew before," she said. "I take you there again!"

The Wave leaned against the wall. He cleared his throat and skuffed his high-top black sneaker against the wooden floor. "I was the one who went. Not you," he said. "I did it alone."

"Now who lies?" Inez snapped. "You know I show you the way!"

"You don't understand what it's like to be there," The Wave said.

"I surprise you, I think," Inez said.

"Maybe with some bullshit description," The Wave said, "or some piece of film, but since you haven't gone, you don't know."

"Oh, but many times I am there," Inez said. "In my own way, but many times. Because I know this way well, I understand how to get you to take this route." She paused to stare at the bottle of whiskey, which reflected the crazy five-tone color of the lamp above the pool table. "Or something like that."

"Close enough," Farrell said.

"You've lost me," said Page.

"By the way you've been staring at Inez's bum the last five minutes, it's no surprise," said Farrell.

"Hey, fuck you," said Page defiantly. He pivoted back toward Inez. "I mean, I have not."

"At least five minutes," Inez said, patting him on the cheek. "But I think this is a hill you have not the capacity to climb."

Page stared at her, then looked away: "Maybe I'll have some of that whiskey."

"Everybody drink," Farrell said, uncapping the bottle.

The three men flicked down their shots. Inez left hers on the table.

"I cannot drink more," she said.

Farrell waited until Page had set his glass down, then said, "Page, tell us what you think about all this."

"Everyone has a limit they can go beyond if they're pushed."

"A secure response," Inez sniffed. "It does not reveal."

"Hey, I'm on your side," Page protested.

"I am on the side of no one," Inez said.

"All for none and none for all!" The Wave cried, holding his right index finger in the air.

Page flipped his cue from his right hand to his left. "Okay, so now I know the rules."

"Took you long enough, mon," said The Wave.

Page ignored him. He faced Inez and said: "You don't even approach overload through a camera, you know, like Miles Davis on a particularly hot night."

"There you go," Farrell said. "But this music thing: that's not what we're looking for. Miles Davis, that's genius. So's a baseball slugger on a streak. They all call it being outside, or walking beyond or give it some mystical flip, call it being unconscious. It's not the same—"

Inez interrupted: "You are beside the point. To operate out

there, this demands genius whether you blow the horn or ski or parapent—"

"Nah," said Page, cutting her off. "The difference is penance. All Miles can do is bust a lip or blow a shitty off-note. And the big slugger? He fans or at worst loses the World Series. We fall, and—how did you put it the other day?—we hit an obstacle or fall off a cliff or are beaten to death by the rocks around us. Don't tell me it's the same."

Farrell raised the bottle and poured. "Well put for a con man."

Page's right upper eyelid twitched. He drank the whiskey.

Inez said, "So you think you are somehow different from me just because you play at these sports of mortality?"

The Wave laughed. "Isn't that why you're here?"

"No, I'm here to ask questions," she said, and she seemed surprised at the answer. "I feel drunk."

"She's got all the questions," The Wave mumbled. He nodded to himself and said louder: "What are the questions?"

"What's the worst that can happen if you fuck up?" Farrell said.

"That's not *the* question," said Page.

Farrell waved his hands in a circle: "Okay, okay. So it's one of them. Answer."

"You're crippled or you get your head bashed in," said The Wave.

Page slammed his hand on the edge of the pool table. "You're in the closed box, that's the worst."

"C'mon," Farrell said. "That happens all the time. How many die in Chamonix every year, Inez—forty? fifty?"

Inez ran her hand along the edge of the pool table. She closed her eyes as if she were off by herself, listening to a favorite piece of music. Farrell took a belt straight off the bottle, then whispered, "The worst is someone else suffers for the risks you take."

He weaved slightly on his feet, immediately regretting the statement. He sat down hard on the chair and held his head in his hands.

In an instant Inez snapped out of her daydream, raced over to him, and ran her hands over his shoulders. "This is okay, let it out now," she soothed. "Just let it come all out now."

Farrell raised his head. Inez's cheeks were flushed, her lips open, her breath shallow, and her pupils huge and shiny. "Tell me what happens?" she asked. "Tell me all of it."

The hair along Farrell's spine stood erect, hot. He wanted to tell her everything. Over her shoulder, The Wave appeared to draw his finger across his throat. The Wave said, "I think we're forgetting something. What about when you cause another person to die and you survive?"

Inez's pupils constricted and her fingernails dug into Farrell's shoulder. "I tell you that isn't my fault," she hissed.

"Sleep well thinking like that, Inez?" The Wave replied.

Inez reached for her pocketbook and pulled out another Gitane cigarette, which she had trouble lighting because her hand shook. She shut one eye, gazed at The Wave with the other, and blew out a cloud of smoke that turned lavender in the lamp light. *"Petit cochon,"* she said. "Do you sleep well last night thinking of your sunshine?"

The Wave took a step toward her, his fists clenched. Page stepped between them.

"That's enough!" Page said. "We'll all fall apart if we keep this up."

"You ain't gonna keep it up," said the cowboy bartender, who'd slipped up behind them. He was angry, but it was an even, professional anger, nothing personal. "Whose quarters?" he asked, pointing to the row on the edge of the pool table.

"Mine," said Farrell, who had regained enough composure to stand.

The cowboy handed them to Farrell. "People come in here St. Patrick's to have fun, not to listen to a bunch of god-damned drunken yammer about the glory of getting crunched. It was nice having your company, but that's it for tonight. Who's driving?"

"Me," Page said.

The cowboy eyeballed him. "Against my better judgment. Now, get you and your frog woman and your freako rastaman out of here, pronto. That or I'll put more scars on someone's face."

The whiskey talked to Farrell. He swung his elbow at the bartender's nose. A meatloaf of a hand caught it two inches from the intended impact point and spun Farrell around and into the wall.

"I was watching you, bright boy," the cowboy grunted. "You got that fuck-it-all look."

He grabbed Farrell by the belt and the collar to haul him across the room. Halfway to the door, Farrell reached out for a beer bottle on a table, swinging it up and over his head until he heard it strike flesh and break. The groan came loud in Farrell's ear, followed by a relaxing of the insistent tension at his collar. The bartender thudded to the ground. "Fuck it all!" Farrell yelled.

Page latched on to Farrell's arm and dragged him toward the door. They all raced to the car, Inez cursing in French, The Wave stumbling through the gravel. Behind them Farrell heard a door swing open and the sound of other feet crossing the parking lot. Page already had the truck running by the time the bartender's friends reached them. They spun out onto the main road with their headlights off and their tires squeeling.

"You shithead!" Page roared. "We could have all been arrested."

"Nervous tick in my arm," Farrell said, his face pressed against the cold window. "It's genetic."

"If you ruin my film, I sue," Inez said.

"What's the matter, Inez," Farrell said. "Get too close to the action?"

Inez swung around in her seat, her eyes blazing. "You do not know what the action is yet."

Farrell found himself wanting to strike her and hold her in the same moment. There was something in her expression, something that repulsed him and attracted him like nothing had in a long time, something totally unpredictable. She did not turn away, neither did he. The interior of the truck around Inez seemed to slowly whirl. He turned away to fight the sensation, to press his face against the window as they rushed toward the entrance to the canyon. The storm was clearing.

Behind him Inez put her fingers on the back of his neck and stroked in a light, delicate pattern. Farrell shivered to her touch, then shrugged away and rolled down the window. He stuck his head out to see if the cold air would stop the whirling. He put his hand out, too, spread his pinkie and thumb and let the tension go; it was a game he'd played as a child, pondering what the bird senses in flight. He remembered how much skiing had reminded him of being a bird. His mother's brother gave him the skis as a present his eighth Christmas. Outside on that Maine morning it was snowing hard. He bundled himself up with goggles and a scarf across his mouth. He'd crow-stepped up the hill in their backyard, held to the wooden skis by awkward cable bindings. He pushed off to sail down through the snow, feeling it hiss at his shins. The wind sang an unfamiliar song in his ears, flooding his eyes with water, squeezing his throat, buckling his knees. He collapsed into a drift. He bit the scarf, rejoicing at the buzz through his body, knowing that behind the bulky clothes his parents couldn't see his excitement from where they stood at the back door.

Then the memory began to twist. He saw his father take the skis away for almost a year. He saw himself sneaking out the door at night in winter with the skis to race down the hill in the darkness, dodging the dim forms of the trees while his parents slept.

A wracking pain in Farrell's stomach doubled him over. "Stop the car," he gasped. The beer, garlic burger, and whiskey had taken its toll. He stumbled out the door when the truck had stopped, lurched to his knees, and retched. Behind him, just before he lost consciousness, Farrell heard the crunch of a boot.

"Poor *chéri*," Inez said. "He looks like the little lost dog."

Chapter 9

It was past noon when Farrell fully regained consciousness. His head pounded. He was slung over a plastic bucket. His side ached. Page later told him that he had fallen on a log. He closed his eyes, vaguely remembering that Page and The Wave had carried him to his room and that Inez had stood against the wall watching him before he drifted off. He lay there now, listening to the conga line in his head and wondered if this was the feeling bears have coming out of hibernation.

Gripping the wall for support, he staggered down the hall to the shower, turned on the water as hot as he could stand it, and asked himself what he was doing. He grasped at the credo of his early twenties: that life was a medieval fairground and he a reveler. But the twisted backs and limbs of his particular court grotesques—of Gabriel, Cordova, and Stein, the FBI agent—kept crowding in. The words of The Wave in the bar the night before—*She knows more than she lets on*—rambled to him again. He realized that while he'd come to Alta to find peace, he was racing again. Although Farrell adored the rush, he demanded control. As usual he knew too little about the people he was involved with. Hadn't it happened the same way with Gabriel? Everything about him and the job in San Diego seemed legitimate.

In retrospect, the interviews had been too easy. San Diego First

Fidelity was a tiny bank by the standards to which Farrell was accustomed. "Silent" Jim Rubenstein had met him at the airport, a short, sallow man with a thick shock of carefully coiffed silver hair and the unnerving habit of waving his pinkie slowly under his chin as he spoke. Rubenstein was not a banker by training; he was an architect and developer of strip malls. In the mid-1980s, when the real estate market in Southern California exploded, Rubenstein and several other investors bought the bank from an old-line San Diego family whose only successor was a gay twenty-six-year-old named Ralph Cardell, who was more interested in the Los Angeles performance art scene than finance.

"I need someone with hands-on experience," Rubenstein admitted over dinner that night. "I'm the bank president, but really it's only a title. I'm a land developer, not a financier. I know Gabriel Cortez through some people who are developing land in Tijuana and he said you might just be the man I'm looking for."

The deal was this: Rubenstein needed someone to develop business in the Latino community in San Diego and northern Mexico, what he called "the great untapped market." Although Farrell's domestic experience was minimal, the six-figure salary and bonus that Rubenstein offered, not to mention the expense account, swayed him. But Lena's demand to leave Chicago made him accept the offer.

Standing in the shower, he saw once again the image of Lena sitting alone in the nursery. That stark vision was followed by the memory of the pleasant sensation of Inez's fingers on his neck. Farrell thought of Timmons and his advice to return to what was basic and important. *I'm no Timmons.* For a few minutes Farrell chilled this disturbing idea by imagining himself churning through the fine silk powder snow that gathers in the Windows glade at Vail. He thought of flurried turns in the cinched aspen groves at Steamboat. He considered a hypnotic 3,000-foot float down the Hobacks at Jackson Hole. Pristine vistas after heavy snowfalls—if things got stranger, light, dry snow still fell on the jagged peaks of Montana. There was an avenue of escape.

He decided in the process of the shower that such a monster hangover demanded penance. He would read more. It was past two when he went out to the camper. The sun was intense and had turned much of the parking lot outside the lodge into mud. He put the key in the camper door, and as he twisted the knob, he noticed with a sinking feeling that the tape he routinely placed across the corner of the door was broken.

His hand rose from the door handle. It was not a conscious action, but one linked to the image of Gabriel behind his desk in Manzanillo. He thought, Why not now? This is where it's all been leading and there is some justice in it: one last surge of adrenaline, then a roar of orange and red . . . into an eternal arcing drift through the white.

Farrell yanked the door open. The hinges squeaked. He lifted his right foot to the bumper step, but pulled it back before he put weight on it. He dropped to his knees and looked underneath for a suspended metal plate or wires, new solder or an electric switch, any evidence of a trigger. Nothing. He ran his hand around the inside of the door, searching for fishing line. Nothing.

At first glance, the camper seemed undisturbed: the drawers under the bunk bed tightly met the plywood frame; the cabinets above the door were shut tight and latched. Maybe I didn't tape the door, Farrell thought.

Then he saw it: a tiny envelope on the floor. He picked it up and looked at the address of the bank in Telluride. It had been in a drawer the night before, he was sure of it. Farrell jumped on the bed to reach along the frame until he found the gap in the plywood that betrayed his secret compartment. He tugged. Nothing—not the envelope containing his cash, not Lena's jewelry box, not the documents that listed his bank account numbers—was missing or disturbed.

Farrell jumped backward off the bunk and looked into the crawl space underneath. His bedding seemed undisturbed. He tugged it out, then stretched back to the darkest corner and up to a two-by-four brace. The white leatherette diary was as he'd left it. "Thank you," he whispered.

A more thorough investigation revealed his reading books slightly out of order. The tool box had been rifled. A flashlight was in a different drawer. Someone had opened his maps. Farrell collapsed on the bed to consider the evidence. It seemed as if the searcher had made calculated mistakes, as if he wanted Farrell's understanding to come incrementally, with a gradual, rather than an immediate, sense of shock. Or fear.

Whoever had violated the camper achieved both. Farrell ran through the possibilities: Gabriel's men could be waiting in one of the cars in the parking lot, ready to take him as he emerged. Or this could be Inez's doing, part of her peek through the fingers. Or Page. Or The Wave. Or just some broke lodge employee hustling cash.

He stayed there for almost an hour, running it all back and forth. The sharp edge of the bunk dug at his shoulder blade, but he ignored it. Part of him wanted to flee, to follow the original plan, head north to the snow fields. He imagined camping along the moist alpine meadows north of Missoula in late May, watching young elk calves trail their mothers through the blue-eyed grass and the rose-root and water-leaf. He took a deep breath and exhaled, watching it cloud and fragment toward the open door. With the next breath he recalled Inez's touch and the expression of longing on her face the night before. He didn't want to leave.

The interior of the camper swirled with the last remaining dregs of the whiskey. Farrell got to his feet, the diary in his hand, and walked to the door. His knees trembled under him as he climbed out into the bright sunshine, but no one called to him, no one watched him from any of the cars. All he heard was the dripping of water off the roof and the grinding of a truck on the road above him.

Back in his room, Farrell drank tumblers of cool water and ate aspirin. Between naps, he read.

June 1

We say good-bye to Chicago the day after tomorrow. They say San Diego has the best climate in the country, almost always seventy degrees.

Christina gave birth two weeks ago to a baby boy, Anthony James, and when she left a message on my machine, I stood there looking at it for the longest time as if I could see her words become real and heavy and I could handle them. She called three more times.

On Friday while Jack was at work for his last day, I packed. There was a knock at the door. I listened at it and heard the baby cry. She knocked again and begged me to open. I hugged the door and told her I couldn't. We both leaned against opposite sides of the door and cried.

I told Jack we had a wonderful lunch.

June 2

I watched the men pack your room today. Still can't bear to let it go. I am here in the empty nursery while daddy goes to get Chinese food before we go to the hotel. I know you are here, but am so afraid to say your name or write it down. Honestly I hate you for what you've done. So stay here, please. Stay in this room and don't come with your things. Stay.

Farrell shut the diary, stung and ashamed that he hadn't taken the time to look around, to see what was happening to his wife. But once they'd arrived in San Diego, hadn't she seemed to recover? He recalled how the day after they arrived, Lena uprooted soil in the backyard of their home in La Jolla, three blocks off Windandsea Beach, a Spanish three-bedroom house with an iron-gated driveway. She worked in the garden day and night those first few months. More than once he awoke at dawn to find her on her knees in the dirt.

Within months after taking the job, however, he knew deep down that he'd personally made a mistake. The job at the bank in Chicago had been much more challenging than he'd realized. By coming to this tiny bank, he'd forsaken the equivalent of a mid-level job at the U.S. Embassy in Paris for the Ambassadorship of Malawi, a prestigious, boring position, far from the action. His days consisted of meetings with local Mexican-American businessmen interested in small development loans and occasional day trips to Tijuana to consult with Japanese executives who were setting up factories on the other side of the border. He joined the Chamber of Commerce and the Kiwanas, which made his mother laugh when he told her over the phone—"Your father never would have believed it." He joined the Mexican-American Foundation, too, attending their luncheons, establishing ties. Gone were the days when he jetted about the hemisphere, backed by a billion dollars in capital.

In September, Gabriel sent them Punta as a present.

Her mother had thought dogs dirty, so Lena was unprepared for the experience of a new puppy. She called Farrell at work. "He's whining," she said. "What do I do?"

"Put him out," Farrell said. "Sounds like he has to go."

"Do I wash my hands afterwards?"

"Only if you hold it for him."

"Bastard!"

The dog became her baby. Farrell would arrive home and find them wrestling on the living room floor, Punta furiously trying to lick at Lena's ears while she laughed hysterically. In late October, Farrell surprised the two of them with a little female Brittany he'd seen advertised in the newspaper. They named her Rabo, or Tail. The two dogs were referred to as Punta y Rabo. Tip to Tail. Their neighbors joked about the English hunting dogs with the Spanish names who would gambol and twist the leash in Lena's hand, sometimes spinning her in circles when she took them for walks along the beach.

Farrell could see that the move was good for his wife, so he kept his growing frustration to himself, taking refuge in the scuba gear and lessons Lena bought for him shortly after they arrived. Out under the sea, moving with the unseen currents, he felt some of the same thrills he'd had the first day he'd raced down the side hill on his wooden skis. Under water, he would recall how his parents had discovered his nighttime ski forays. They were furious. But seeing he would not quit the sport, they gave him the skis back. Away from their watching eyes, Farrell felt free. He took school trips to go skiing, thrilling at the way the steep Maine hillsides could make the wind whistle, at the way his spectacular crashes made him breathless.

Despite the kicks scuba diving gave him, Farrell was going crazy by December of the first year in San Diego. There was very little to be done to keep the bank running. One day Farrell tried to pry from Rubenstein exactly how he wanted the bank to grow. Rubenstein stayed true to his nickname, saying very little other than, "You can do what you want with it. Be creative!"

Farrell shifted in the bed in the lodge, then forced the diary under the mattress, walked down to the lobby, and took a seat in front of the floor-to-ceiling bay windows. He gazed up at the High

Rustler run that dropped off the face of one of Alta's peaks. Was it all a set up? Probably, he thought. By the time he'd left for San Diego, he and Gabriel had worked through three deals. It was long enough for Gabriel to see what turned Farrell on.

Gabriel's partner, Jorge Cordova, came to visit in January. Farrell knew Cordova was a big man, yet until the moment when Silent Jim knocked on the door to Farrell's office, he'd never seen him up close. Cordova was in his late thirties, about five feet, eight inches tall, and of tremendous girth, perhaps 300 pounds, one of those interesting physical specimens, who despite being obese, are able to move remarkable agility and poise. His fingernails were as perfectly manicured as his moustache. His suit was black, European cut. His shoes Italian. Cordova's face had an olive, almost military tint, as though he were always lit by moonlight in the forest. With his matching tie and pocket kerchief of paisley reds and blues, and his great leg-of-lamb fists, Cordova had the anonymous, threatening quality of a freshly painted tank.

He smiled as he eased into the chair across from Farrell. His eyes slid about the office, settling briefly on the artwork the interior decorator had chosen, then the birch wainscotting, which set off the green walls and the brass frames which held pictures of Lena and the dogs and another of Farrell skiing years before.

Cordova nodded approvingly. "Mr. Cortez will be happy to hear you've settled in so well."

"How is he?" Farrell asked.

"Fine," Cordova said. "He said it is almost time for you to come south again for a visit."

"I'd like to very much," Farrell said, remembering the sounds of the peahens. "But I'm just getting up to speed here."

"You are finding the position and the city to your liking?"

"My wife is in love with the place," Farrell said, trying to sound enthusiastic. "She adores the fact that it is January and she can walk on the beach every morning."

"I usually stay at one of the resorts on Coronado or Mission Bay," Cordova said. "I like to dine in the open air, watching the water."

"Beautiful."

"It is. Do you fish?"

"Deep sea? I never have."

"One of my passions," Cordova said. He raised his right hand, then let it fall on the arm of the chair with a heavy, loud thud. "The run here used to be quite good, but has slacked off in recent years. Marlin especially."

They chatted informally of Gabriel and the factory in Tijuana and the import-export business growing steadily on the border between Mexico and Guatemala. Cordova was a very still man, unlike Gabriel, who often swung his arms in wild circles while he spoke. Cordova's only gesture was that slight raising of the right hand, followed by the weighted thud as he let it drop onto whatever object was closest.

They decided to have lunch, driving in Cordova's rented maroon Lincoln to his favorite restaurant in San Diego, an Italian place called Tentazione, which specialized in fish and was renowned for its harbor view. When Cordova opened the door to the restaurant, the pungent fragrance of onions and garlic and wine surrounded them. "Divine," Cordova murmured.

"Mr. Cordova! How good to see you!" cried the maître d', a short, intense man, who fluttered about Cordova like a white cattle egret on the back of a bull.

"What is the special?" Cordova inquired, bending over to the man.

"Your favorite," the waiter whispered conspiratorially. "Yellowtail steaks grilled three minutes each side over an open pit flame, then plunged into a broiler pan of garlic and oregano."

"Heaven," Cordova said, touching the tips of his fingers together. "I hope you have a booth, Marcello. You know how difficult a chair can be."

"Of course," the little man said. He made a half bow before leading them across the room.

Seated near the bay window, Cordova said: "My size, it bothers you, does it not?"

Flustered by so direct a question, Farrell stammered: "No, of course not. Should it?"

"For many people in your physical condition, especially here in California, the state of the body, it is a bothersome characteristic, one which they cannot seem to ignore," Cordova said. "But I'm afraid I'm stuck with it, an addiction more psychological than physiological."

Cordova continued, suddenly animated, and like all great story-tellers, he sent Farrell drifting into a waking dream. He spoke of a town in Sonora, dry and beautiful, lined with grain fields and Spanish oaks, of his parents' wooden grocery store, which burned down one night—arson—leaving Cordova alone at six in an orphanage.

Imagine a place, Cordova said, where the air was clean and the hallways always swept, but where no one smiled and meals were single slices of bread, fatty pork, and beans.

"When you are eight, you lie awake at night and try to ignore the hollowness in your stomach and you begin to plot your escape," Cordova said. "You force yourself to pay attention in the school, forcing yourself to be the best reader, the best in English class and in math, searching in what is given freely for a guide who will lead you away.

"It's funny, when you find the guide, it is not in a book on history or even in Cervantes or Neruda. No, what leads you out is a dove, a plump, white-wing dove that with its brothers and sisters flocks to the fields outside of town and draws the shooters from Mexico City and Arizona every August, shooters that pay well for a guide."

Cordova became a student of fields, of guns and of shooters. He was up long before dawn every day to clean the rich men's double barrell shotguns and to prepare their baskets for the long days of hunting. He led them at first light to ditches by the fields, listening for the whistle of the birds as they raced to water, then hissing to men: *"Palomas! Palomas! Señors!"* The boy watched, satisfied, when the men in the crisp khakis begin their rhythmic, inevitable swings. He slapped his thigh with each crack of the gun, beating time to the death of the birds. When guns fell silent, he sprinted into the fields, looking for smudges of gray and white.

One August morning when Cordova was eleven, a diplomat and his son, also eleven, came to shoot. Despite the dozens of birds that coursed overhead, the son never hit a one. "You could see the pain in his eyes," Cordova recalled. "He wanted so much to impress his father."

In the late afternoon, while the father and the other rich men slept off the thick red wine they drank at lunch, Cordova took the boy out into the field and showed him what he had stolen over the years from the shooters: how to curl the front foot into the path of the bird, how to swing and cover the smudge with the barrel of the gun, how to follow the path of the bird even when it has fallen. "Never aim, just point and lead."

Cordova climbed one of the Spanish oaks with a pocket full of shards he'd gathered and sailed them across the diplomat's son's field of vision until, after twenty or thirty tries, the gun roared and the shards shattered into fine dust in the waning light of day.

When the doves flew the next morning, ten fell to the diplomat's son. This is the part Cordova never fully understood: the diplomat threw his arms first around his son, then around Cordova. From that point on, there were smiles for Cordova at the orphanage, there were new clothes and freshly bound books. And every year, a week of hunting doves with the diplomat and his son, until finally, when Cordova turned eighteen, there was an offer of escape. The diplomat, who knew Cordova was the best student in town, offered to pay for his education. Cordova obtained a bachelor's degree in economics from the University of Texas at Austin and an MBA at the University of Houston.

"Despite the comparative luxury of my life today, I find it impossible to shake the ghosts of my childhood," Cordova said. "To be frank, I don't want to. I have much money, enough to buy boats to fish. More than that, with every bite of good food, I remind myself from what hell I've escaped."

The waiter came. Cordova requested three orders of yellowtail, two for himself, and a bottle of Chardonnay.

"But Gabriel told me you and he work together to improve orphanages and clinics and help basic industries in towns like the one you grew up in," Farrell said.

"Just because I've buried the child doesn't mean I don't visit his grave," Cordova said, putting a harsh period on the sentence by dropping his hand harder than usual on his thigh.

"I'm sorry if I offended you," Farrell said.

"Not at all," Cordova said, his right hand suspended in the air. "In fact, you have raised one of the issues Mr. Cortez asked me to speak with you about."

Farrell leaned back to allow the waiter to place a salad on the table.

"Chiapas, Mexico, you've been there, have you not?" Cordova asked between bites.

"Once about two years ago to look at a hydroelectric project," Farrell said.

"There's a region—the coffee-growing mountains outside of Escuintla—where the people have no running water, no health care, a rudimentary school, and little hope of getting anything better. Unless they get a paved road over which adequate supplies can run."

"I've seen these kinds of villages," Farrell said. "But without government intervention, what are you going to do? As for me, I'm with a small bank now; we can't get involved in public works projects."

Cordova agreed, leaning forward to pour Farrell a glass of wine. He pointed out that the Mexican economy was in a shambles owing to the slump in oil prices and the stagnation of other industries under corrupt state control. "This is no news to you," Cordova said. "But as a result, the peso has been devalued several times in the past decade, prompting many Mexicans to move their money to the United States."

"Capital flight," Farrell said. "We saw it coming to Chicago."

Cordova opened his mouth to speak again, then stopped when the waiter arrived, this time laden with plates steaming with the fresh fish. When Cordova's double portions had been placed before him, he excused himself. "I've got to have just two bites, or I won't be able to concentrate."

Cordova paused twice while he chewed to let his nose roam over the plate. "Ambrosia," he said, looking up at Farrell through half-open eyes. "Sheer ambrosia."

When Cordova had sated himself enough to continue, he said: "As you may or may not know, Mr. Cortez and I and many of the people we work with believe the government is unable to address the needs of people living in the poorer regions of our country. Though our wealth is modest by U.S. standards, we are rich beyond the wildest imaginations of most Mexican citizens. So we try in our own small way to help with projects such as the orphanage, health care, the things you've mentioned."

He took another three bites, then looked Farrell straight in the eyes, the animation gone, replaced with a steady, undecipherable stare: "The problem we face today is extreme uncertainty on the part of many people who would ordinarily be in a position to help our cause."

"I don't follow you."

"We fear the government may soon devalue the peso again, which could shatter all the work we've done."

"More wealthy Mexicans will move their money to U.S. banks?" Farrell asked, trying to leap ahead in the argument.

"Already happening," Cordova grunted. "Look at the development projects over on Coronado Island. Much of the cash for the high-rise condominiums there came from Mexico. It is not surprising. Such investments are sound, safe from public meddling."

Again Cordova bent to the yellowtail, swirling the chunks of white meat in the garlic sauce and plopping them into his mouth with his left hand, each bite accentuated by the rising and thudding of his right. Farrell wondered if Cordova heard the roar of shotguns in his mind.

"So what can I do?" Farrell asked.

"What we want to do is this," Cordova said, his voice dropping. "We want to secretly move the profits out of Mexico to create a permanent source of capital that cannot be harmed by devaluations."

Cordova paused, wiping at his mouth with the tip of the napkin.

"At the same time, we want to construct a way to move the money back into Mexico when we need it, but not under our names, preferably in the form of loans to our companies and projects."

"Let me get this straight," Farrell said, somewhat bewildered by the proposal. "You want to move your own money to my bank and then have me loan it back to you?"

"Or through your bank to overseas accounts which we could easily access," Cordova said. "That's the concept."

"Why not just deposit the money in one of the larger banks in San Diego, then take it out when you want?"

"Ordinarily we would," Cordova said. "But many of the people we represent are highly placed in Mexican social, political, and business circles. If word were to get out that these people, including Mr. Cortez, who, because of his late father is well known in Mexico City, were moving all of their money out of the country, it could quite possibly devastate the willingness of financial institutions, such as your former employer in Chicago, to work with Mexico."

Farrell studied Cordova, looking for signs of an ulterior motive. The explanation was plausible, but something didn't sound right.

The big man's stoic face revealed nothing. Farrell ran his tongue along the bottom of his teeth and his right knee bounced in pleasure under the table. "How would it work?"

Cordova said, "Our requirements would include a method to ensure our anonymity. My understanding is that this can be done by wire-transferring capital from your bank through a series of overseas accounts.

"Some of the money would be held in investment pools under your control," he said. "Other accounts would form a loan pool, from which the capital for our operations would come."

Farrell rubbed at his left eyebrow, and though he tried to control his excitement, he seemed to detach for a moment, to float above the table, looking down at himself, at Cordova's thick fingers. This was the first time the sensation had happened to Farrell when he wasn't facing some kind of obviously dangerous situation like a steep ski slope. The texture of risk, richer than the flesh of the yellowtail, pressed in around him. Farrell breathed deep, smiled, and asked: "How much money are we discussing?"

"Initially, to see if the system works, several hundred thousand dollars over three months," Cordova said. "Most of the money would end up overseas. But if it does work, you could eventually see an increase of between three million and seven million dollars a year on account at your bank."

Farrell was stunned; such deposits would swell his division fourfold. He could expand his loan base by sixteen times. The bonus he could expect at the end of such a year was stupefying. No doubt, though, the risks involved were equally mind-boggling: Farrell would have to ride a thin line between deceit and the law to conceal the source and destination of the cash. Any mistake could mean expulsion, fines, or jail. And yet, this is what Farrell confessed to himself as he looked out the window at the lodge, watching a ski patrolman sweep through the trees on the mountain: He had liked the idea. At the back of his throat he tasted the sweet aluminum, and for the first time since Jenny, his body vibrated with expectation. "I'll do it," Farrell said.

"We'd hoped you would," Cordova said, and he smiled. "Now how about dessert?"

Chapter 10

For the next twenty-four hours, Farrell holed up in his room, unwilling to read the diary again, unable to follow through on his threat to split for Montana. He'd tried twice. Each time he left the room with his bags, the spinning sensation that had enveloped him since the night in the bar calmed. And each time, about halfway down the hall, he found himself longing for that feeling of imbalance and he'd rushed back, his mind a swirl of images, of Cordova and of Lena, who had no idea what he'd agreed to do that day at lunch, of speeding power boats and lonely Latin women, of pesos and secret accounts. On top of all of this was the picture of Inez hugging The Wave after he'd surfed. When he thought of that scene, the room would accelerate into a wonderful blur, a post-modern painting in icy blues and whites, and his past would fade.

By the time Inez and the rest of the crew had gathered in the woods below the Y Couloir the morning of the race, Farrell had to fight to remain upright; he was as excited and as scared as he was the day he'd started to illicitly move money for Cordova and Gabriel. Perhaps I am like Timmons, Farrell thought; perhaps this can be an ending.

Farrell barely heard Inez describe how she'd rented a helicopter and would hover over the giant ravine to film the race from above. The Wave would climb the ridge on the south face of the canyon with a camera mounted with a telephoto lens. Tony Carbone and Ann Queechee would climb the face of the couloir with Page and Farrell.

"Just what I need at my age, a crawl up a popsicle," Tony said.

"The audience adores it," Inez said. "They are going to remember this shot for years."

Ann shook her head: "I don't know why we just can't take a ride to the top of this thing."

Inez patted her on the arm as if Ann were a kindergartner. "A guide in Chamonix tells me once this is better to see close what you are to ski. See it face to face before you drop."

"I'm not skiing."

"But you need the same feel the skier has, no?" Inez said, gritting her teeth. "I believe that the camera must be the penetration of sympathy . . . in English, empathy? This is the word?"

Ann nodded.

"Empathy must be there or there is no point of view," Inez said in an insistent tone. "No point of view and no film. Just footage that hangs together. So boring."

The Wave said, "Gonna get a lot of empathy up there nice and cozy in that chopper, huh?"

Inez spun in her tracks. "My work is different, to film the race. I never see their expressions as they drop in. But Ann and Tony will. I wish them to feel the fear they film. It comes through, you know."

"Who said anything about fear?" Page asked.

Inez smiled. "You do not have to speak of fear. Fear has a smell."

"And you have a nose for it," Farrell said dreamily.

Inez's smile vanished. "I have the nose for drama. The question is, do you wish to be an actor?"

Time seemed to slow. Farrell couldn't have left if he'd wanted to. "I'm here, aren't I?"

"Yes," Inez said. "You are." She turned to make the final radio checks with Tony and Ann and The Wave.

Farrell strode back and forth across the glen. He shook his arms over his head, trying to loosen them. Page knelt in the snow to stretch the muscles of his thighs and lower back. Each of the men did their best not to look at the other. Inez was right: Fear had a smell both Page and Farrell were aware of, hanging in the air like the subtle tang of tarragon and anise.

Inez walked off into the woods away from the hub of activity, then barked into her headset, "Two, check." Her voice came in clear over the radios.

"Check two, loud and clear," said Tony into his radio. "Harnesses ready. Four web lines. Anchors. Carabineers. My battery pack's solid."

When the radio check was over, Ann whispered to Tony within earshot of Farrell, "I still don't know why I have to climb this."

"Because she's paying us," Tony said. "Without her, we're dead."

"I know," Ann said, her hands on her hips. "I just don't like her attitude, that's all. She's not safe. She's not even trying to be."

Tony stepped over and put his thick arm around Ann's waist.

"What's the matter, Annie, you that out of shape you can't make it?"

Ann twisted out from under his weight. "I've goated up worse and I seem to remember somebody behind me with a beard begging for mercy."

"I remember that guy, too," Tony said, and he grinned. "Let's just not screw this up, now. No money—we kiss six years of work bye-bye."

Ann stared down at the snow and kicked at it. Tony looked around. Farrell acted as if he were preoccupied with the pack that lay at his feet. Inez seemed to have leverage on everyone, he thought, except me. Who knew what she had on The Wave. He turned that idea over in his mind for a second, then discarded it. He had too many other things to consider. He and Page had loaded much of the same equipment: ski boots, water bottles, thin-nylon windbreakers—Farrell's bright yellow, Page's startling red—two coils of rope, four food bars, rigging lines for the cameras, collapsing shovels, and a second set of goggles.

The radios crackled: "This is two-four-two, they in that ravine yet?" asked a deep voice with a thick Texas drawl.

Inez pressed a button on the side of her radio. "They are about to begin."

"Fine enough, little lady," the pilot responded. "We'll put this old bird in the air as soon as you get down here."

Inez turned to the four climbers. "You all make the checks on the channels A and B on the radios? *Bien.* All climbers are on A channel during the ascent. The Wave and I monitor all talk on A. At the top, Page and Collins remain on A channel. But Tony and Ann Marie switch to B. I give the directions to Page and Collins to begin, then I switch over to B, so the skiers are not distracted. I want it silent on A during the descent."

She stopped and fished in her pocket for a cigarette. She took two big drags, looking around the glen as if she were searching for a forgotten set of keys. *"Alors* then, the climb starts now, no? With that you are above the line of trees when I come up the canyon in the helicopter."

"You going to hover the whole time?" Ann asked.

"No," Inez answered. "Maybe we put down on the north ridge opposite the couloir and try the shot. The other camera The Wave operates across the road covers the basics. After Page and Collins drop out of your range, pack up and climb to the ridge. We pick you up there."

Inez paused and looked them in the eye, one by one. When she got to Page, she leaned and hugged him. She did the same to Farrell, and when she'd pulled him close, she whispered: "I cheers for you!"

She pushed him away, picked up her hip pack, and hiked out the path toward the road. Farrell couldn't take his eyes off her. It was not until Ann said, "Well?" that he saw Page was transfixed, too.

Farrell coughed and shook his head to clear her away. He fished in his pocket for the drawing Inez had made of the couloir and given to each of them. He shut his eyes to visualize the diagram. The initial chute rose almost 800 feet straight off the canyon floor to a slight right-hand turn. Above that turn, there was a second thinner channel that climbed another 300 feet before it died. The main channel of the ravine bore to the right and arched swiftly for another 400 feet before it split into two arms. In that junction was a tangle of brush and rock and debris. Page's arm, the right channel of the Y, continued up at a consistent angle through trees to the ridge. Farrell's arm was shorter, but it was steeper and was bounded by stone walls and stunted pine trees.

The spinning lurched into effect again as Farrell thought of the race. One gear turning the whirli-gig in his mind was the competition with Page. The one-eyed skier has it easier in those first few minutes, Farrell told himself, but he's screwed if he carries too much speed down the channel to that dog leg left before it drops to the canyon floor. He's also going to be thinking of me flying at him from his right side. With only one eye, his concentration will be off going through the junction.

The bigger gear was Farrell's own line of descent: he had to ski his own steep chute, then get through the rocks and bushes that blocked part of his entrance into the main channel of the ravine without crashing or hitting Page. And then there was the motor driving the gears: Inez would be watching. Somehow that made the mechanics of his situation pulse and whine with the terrible insistence of a race car about to unwind down the straightaway.

Farrell strapped on a white half-helmet, walked to the runout of the couloir, and began to climb. They'd agreed the night before that he'd start, free climbing at first, no ropes until he decided it was necessary. Page, Ann, then Tony would follow at ten-minute intervals. If they found anything out of the ordinary, they'd alert The Wave, who was set up on the first ridge across the road, about 600 feet off the canyon floor.

Farrell wore crampons, metal devices with teeth to bite into the frozen ravine as he climbed. The first few strides he took felt awkward; in the spring air, the mound at the bottom of the couloir, which had been hard-packed snow topped with light powder two days before, was now mushy. Still, he slogged on, knowing he'd need the sharp teeth of the crampons when the snow became firmer at higher altitude.

In the channel, he kept his attention focused on the terrain directly in front of himself. He found a pattern: chop up with the ice axe for purchase, left hand on the wall for guidance, pull and stab in with the crampon. Chop up, brace the body, pull, stab in. Teardrops of sweat gathered at his neck and between his forehead and the helmet. After ten minutes he relaxed into the exertion and climbed at a steady pace.

The wind that cycled at Farrell's back was moderate, but about once a minute a gust roiled up the passage, the towering rock walls amplifying the sound, so it seemed that Farrell was not climbing, instead the couloir drew him upward like a giant vacuum cleaner sucking and clanking on a discarded penny.

The Wave's voice crackled in his earpiece: "Got you, Collins, old mon mountain, hobbling hisself into that Y Couloir."

Farrell smiled in spite of himself; he found The Wave's voice reassuring. "Preserving my energy, unlike someone I know."

"Hey, I don't regret the excesses of my troubled youth, mon," The Wave said. "I will only regret, in my chilled age, certain occasions and possibilities I didn't embrace."

"Didn't know you could be so eloquent, Wave."

"Not me, old one, that's Henry James," The Wave said.

"A well-read rastaman."

"Bartlett's Familiar, mon," The Wave said. "My favorite book as a kid—"

"Sorry, Wave," Farrell broke in. "Write this down and pass it on to Inez: at one hundred and seventy-five feet, the chute widens from five to seven yards. There's a dagger of rock protruding from the snow. And exactly what I didn't want to find—blue ice, watered and rippled. It cuts across the entire width of the couloir."

"Shit," The Wave said. "How long a piece?"

Farrell looked up the smooth face. "Probably fifteen, twenty feet of it. Pray the sun hits in here and it corns up. I'm climbing."

The static in Farrell's earpiece died and he kicked the toe spikes of the crampons into the blue ice at the edge of the wall and inched himself higher in slow, precise movements. The ice was a very bad sign. At that moment, he had no idea how he or Page would cross it coming down. He became light-headed and nervous for a second, then put the ice behind him and hoped his subconscious would develop a strategy as he climbed.

Above the ice patch, the wall on the right side of the ravine rose twenty feet on average, higher in places. Black-red lichen, fibrous and rough, splashed across the rock face, fungus that survives in the harshest conditions, yet grows only a quarter inch every fifty years. Twenty minutes had passed since he'd entered the couloir. He paused once to look down between his legs. From that perspective the undulating, almost coordinated bobbing of Ann and Tony's helmets and packs far below him reminded him of the twisting of the eight-segment back of the scorpion he'd seen crawling on the witch doctor's arm so many years before.

Farrell came across shoots of brush poking through the snow. He got out a small pair of pruning shears, snipped the branches below the snow line, then tucked the twigs into a gap between the snow and the rock wall. He didn't want to catch a tip on a twig this late in the race.

In the distance he heard a drone that became a buzz and then a growl and then a roar. A hurricane-force wind closed in around him, filling every crevice and break in the ravine. A fierce storm of fine, sharp ice bits burst off the surface of the couloir and dazzled the air around Farrell with the spark and flash of a dozen hypnotic crystal globes in a tiny dance hall. He panicked, fear wrenching him out of focus. He grabbed on tighter to the ice axe as bigger chunks of ice, these the size of BBs, broke away and stung at his face and neck. They pelted the anorak and pinged off the skis and the helmet. They slapped the heavy cordura pack. Several smashed into his goggles, which cracked into a crazy spider's web. The air filled with more of the crystals until Farrell began to choke on them.

His grip began to slip and he thought about letting go, letting it end there on the side of the mountain, when over his earpiece he heard Inez's voice cackle: "Go, Collins!"

Farrell dragged himself higher and kicked his feet into the face of the ravine. He reached down and hit the transmit button on his radio. "Jesus Christ, you bitch!" he bellowed. "Back off! I can't see a thing!"

The snow under his feet slipped and he realized he'd go down, taking Ann, Tony, and Page with him if he didn't get a better hold. He snapped the ice axe over his head, felt it grab, then strained until his weight came off the crampons. He spread his legs, kicked the toe pieces into the wall and ducked his head away from the helicopter's wash. There was no thought of letting go now, only a slowing of time, as if he were no longer a participant in these events, but a member of an audience.

As rapidly as it had come, the pulsing of the chopper blade faded. Farrell clung to the couloir by the toe piece of his right crampon and the twisted leather lanyard he'd bolted to the handle of his ice axe. His left leg dangled in space. In the steady wind he swung back and forth like a rusty weather vane atop an old barn.

The helicopter arched away to the north, circled, and hovered 200 yards behind him.

"The shot, it is incredible, Collins!" said Inez, her voice quivering. *"Vraiment,* you disappeared. You do not believe it when you see it!"

The Wave's voice broke in: "Collins! Collins, mon! Are you all right? Can you hear me, mon?"

"Wave, get off the radio," Inez said.

"You bitch!" The Wave yelled. "You almost blew him off!"

"Give me a second here," Farrell puffed. "I . . . I can't see . . . the goggles are shattered."

Farrell swung his free arm and leg to the wall and got them anchored. He leaned his helmet into the snow, shut his eyes. The slowing of time was replaced by fury. "Inez," he said. "Another stunt like that and I'll . . ."

There was silence and then Inez said: "Tell me, Collins, is that what you feel when we come too close?"

Farrell sputtered, "What the Christ does that matter . . ." Then, strangely, he remembered and whispered: "No, I wanted to sleep."

"Sleep?" Inez said, incredulous. "How—"

Page broke in: "Collins, can you still climb?"

His voice came to Farrell like a yellow light through a fog. "Yeah. Yeah. Just give me a minute."

"Collins," Inez insisted. "Tell me about the sleep."

"Fuck you, Inez!" Farrell thundered, and he reached down and shut off the radio. His hands shook violently now and it took him almost five minutes to change to sunglasses. During that time he considered backing down. But he realized he didn't have the equipment necessary to anchor a rappel. Without understanding why, he began to climb again. Yet before he did, he shifted his receiver to the B channel; he was uneasy being out of touch with the other climbers, but for his own good he had to monitor Inez.

The earpiece was silent for the next twenty yards, then he heard Inez say, "Wave, pull your camera back for the long shot of the chute. They are above the treeline now. We go back down the hill until we get the signal they tie together for the second part of the climb. The pilot says we burn too much fuel."

The chugging of the helicopter faded. The beating of blood at his temples ebbed. Farrell turned in the chute to look off in the direction of the disappearing helicopter. He was confused; as angry as he'd been at Inez just moments before, for some reason he now desperately wanted her to come back, to take him to that sleepy state of terror and glee.

She was gone. Farrell sighed. He would have to content himself with climbing the steep icy wall. He reached the turn in the stem of the Y at ten minutes past eight. The ridge cast a shadow into the junction and Farrell shivered. He wedged the pack into a pocket along the wall, released the collapsible plastic shovel and changed the radio back to the A channel.

"Collins?" The voice was familiar, but not one of the party. "Collins, it's Frank Portsteiner here with your buddy the rope head."

"Frank?" Farrell said, turning around toward the opposite ridge where he supposed The Wave's camera was positioned.

"This is some crazy shit you're into this time," Portsteiner said.

"What's E.R. going to say to this one?" Farrell responded. He fought to keep his voice from betraying how befuddled he was.

"I don't need to quote," Portsteiner said. "It's easy. You're out of your mind. The kid says you were almost off it once today."

"Frank, you must be six hundred feet off the canyon floor," Farrell said. "I didn't think you climbed anywhere you didn't have to."

"Avoiding the issue as usual."

"That's my specialty."

"Not on my mountain, you don't."

"It's not your mountain, Franko. It's not anyone's. We are out of bounds, solo and responsible for our actions in free terrain."

"Fool," Portsteiner said. "You've had a strong warm wind churning up that chute for three days now. Did you forget everything I taught you?"

"No, I haven't. In fact, I was about to dig a pit to see if it's safe to go higher when you so rudely interrupted."

There was pause, then Frank said: "What's gotten into you, boy?"

"Just an opportunity for a little fun."

"I don't think you'd know truth if it smacked you upside the head."

"What's truth, Frank?" Farrell asked, knowing full well it would tick Portsteiner off.

Porsteiner groaned and was silent. They'd had this argument before and the examples seemed to change all the time; in general, Farrell had found, truth can be bent for a price or a cause. Just ask Gabriel.

Farrell unstrapped a length of nylon climbing cord from the side of the pack. He slung a loop around his shoulders, clambered into the feeder channel, and tied himself to a young spruce. He dug an eighteen-inch-square pit with the shovel. Two inches of corn snow lay atop a consistent sublayer. When he'd finished, he flipped the shovel over so the blade faced the back wall. He sliced chunks of dense snow the width of the shovel and ten inches deep on each side, which left him with a column of snow ten inches by ten inches that jutted from the rear of the pit. The idea was this: If the column of snow broke away easy or crumbled, Farrell would know the snow pack was unstable. He held the shovel over the rear of the little pillar, sliced down, then cocked the handle toward himself. After two or three tugs, it broke away in an even, solid block. Farrell thumbed the radio. "You still there, Frank?"

"Against my better judgment."

"We're okay," Farrell said, ignoring the sarcasm. "I had a hard failure on the shear plane test. The snow in the pit looks in equi-temperature metamorphosis: a series of firm, bonded layers. I noticed some percolation coming up the chute, but no evidence of depth hoar that could break away. About the only problem we might have is powder above us."

"You're still in danger of a hard-slab failure," Frank said.

"That's always a danger. But I'm not going to call the climb on that account. I think we're clear. Talk to you at the bottom."

"Hey!"

"What's that?"

"Why *are* you doing this?"

"Now that's an easy question, as old as the hills," Farrell said. "Because it's there."

By nine-thirty, the rest of the crew were at the junction and Page, the last climber, had rested enough to begin the next phase of the ascent. Again Farrell took the lead, climbing without the security of ropes and anchors. The granite in the dog-leg channel rose almost thirty feet over their heads and curved inward, which created the illusion that they were hiking through a tunnel that had had the top ripped off. Red lichen coursed by deep purple veins covered the gray walls. Farrell stripped his glove from his left hand and touched it, amazed at its elasticity.

As he climbed, the sun filtered in and cast a strange warm glow in the passage. He never could explain it, whether it was altitude or lack of sleep or lack of food, but during the next phase of the climb a tingling sensation took hold where his spinal cord met the base of his skull; a distant murmur at first, with every step, higher, closer, clearer, and more demanding. It was like the tinkling of a small, yet distinct bell in the first minutes, spreading from the nape around his ears until it enveloped and hung about his frontal lobe, ringing when he reached the split in the Y.

Farrell stopped to wait for the others to catch up. He thought he might be sick to his stomach, so he sat and hung his head and swallowed at the bile which crept up the back of his throat. Farrell ate snow. He realized he was not afraid of the Y Couloir. That made him very nervous because he'd always managed to get through difficult situations by using fear to fine-tune his senses. Now his mind raced in many directions. He wished he'd never opened the diary. He wished he'd never met Gabriel or Cordova or Maria Robles. He wished Inez would return.

Ann reached the intersection and flopped down beside him, her breath strong and hard. "Damn, I'm not in shape for this," she gasped. "Next time you guys plan something like this, I want road camera duty."

Farrell nodded. "Me, too."

"She's spooky, you know? I think it's her father gets her doing this stuff," Ann said.

"How's that?" Farrell asked.

"Back in school I read about him, came across his book in a photography course," Ann said, struggling from the pack. "I forgot all about it until I saw it in her room the other night sticking out of a bag.

"It's been a long time, but I remember he had this theory that his pictures were better . . . no truer . . . when they were of life close to death. The book's called *The Dividing Line.*"

Farrell nodded. "It makes sense, I guess. I feel more alive when I'm out here like this, even though, you know . . ."

Ann nodded. "Great pictures."

"So she's after the same stuff?"

"That's my theory," Ann said. "But what do I know? I'm just a slave this trip."

"How'd she find you and Tony?"

"That's funny," Ann said. "I mean it was kind of known around Seattle we were having trouble making ends meet. Then one day in January, she shows up talking a lot of money."

"Seen her movies?"

"No," Ann said. "But I've heard about them and her. People said she's tough to work for—they weren't kidding—but the stuff she comes out with is brilliant. We figured we could learn something and make the money we need. You?"

"Right now, I honestly don't know."

Farrell stood and studied the left arm of the Y. A reddish-yellow ledge protruded from the snow across the better part of the channel. The more he looked at it, the more he became convinced that, if his pace allowed it, he would try to traverse just above the ledge and slip over the rocks on a tiny passage of frozen snow. He admitted, however, that the odds of finding that line at high speed were slim. So he puzzled and solved the angle he'd have to achieve in the air to leap the ledge and still land in the main channel of the Y with his shoulders pointing down the hill.

Page puffed up behind him. "Better you than me," he said.

"I don't know," Farrell said. "I'd rather be slicing down on the victim than looking up to see skis coming at my head at thirty miles an hour."

"I'll be long gone by the time you get here," said Page, his jaw punching each word.

"I think I already am long gone," Farrell said.

Page gave him a strange look and walked away.

Ann and Tony took light meter readings for their cameras, then climbed to their positions. Farrell put together the poles he'd constructed the day before from two ice axes. In the butt of each axe handle, he'd drilled a hole and threaded them so the ski pole tubes would screw in tight. Now, he thought as he hefted one in each hand, I've got a self-rescue system; if I fall back and hit the slope and slide, I have a chance of striking one of the axe heads into the hill to stop myself.

Page looked at the contraptions. "Who are you? Roboskier?"

"Kind of heavy, but effective."

"I'll stick with something simple," Page said, and he clacked two lightweight aluminum poles together. The two men looked at each other, aware that each wanted to win the race, but also aware of the perilous situation that now bonded them together.

The chunka-chunka of the helicopter came to them at the same time. As one, they peered down the canyon. Page stiffened. "Here she comes."

Farrell searched the sky, found the white dot roaring along the far ridge line, and felt the muscles in the back of his leg twitch. He told himself he should feel terrible that she had returned. At gut level, he did. Riding over the nausea, however, was the liquid co-caine of anticipation—he was numbed and jittered by the knowl-edge he didn't know what she'd do next. It was nine-fifty. Farrell turned, grabbed his gear, and climbed through the woods next to the channel. He did not want to talk, even after Page had called after him to wish him luck.

By the time Farrell reached Tony, the cameraman had devised a traveling line of webbing and cords off two trees on the right side of the chute. Farrell helped him into his harness, then clipped him to the webbing. Like a spider on the outer rim of its web, Tony ran along the face of the mountain in a broad arc between the two trees. The rope strained, but held. Farrell handed him the camera and he tried it again.

"Give me another seven feet on the higher tree and five feet on the lower or I won't be able to get you as you drop into that main chute," Tony said. "Oh, yeah: I don't want to tell you how to ski this thing. That's your problem. But when you come through this sec-tion, if you could stay along that far wall, I won't have to retreat so much to keep you in focus."

"I'll keep it in mind," Farrell said, and he trudged upward again.

His head rambled with the sort of conflicting whispers he'd pre-viously thought possible only in the chemically induced state he'd existed in after the doctors had performed the two operations on his face. One voice hissed that he'd probably never see his mother again; another said the intruder who'd broken into his camper was following his fresh tracks in the snow; the other told him that his wife had been like a river that had been dammed into a lake: the surface was barely rippled by wind, but unseen currents ripped along the bottom.

At 9,000 feet above sea level, facing due north, the upper cavity of the chute caught little sun in the early spring. The snow remained soft, deep, and unconsolidated four days after the storm. Farrell's legs plunged deep into the snowpack and the wading motion he was forced to adopt cast off tiny rivulets of rolling powder. The lichen on the rocks there, fed by the new snow, was moist, almost blood red. Farrell moved to it, not caring what Inez, hovering behind him, might think. He pressed his nose into the rough sponge, inhaling the cutting, acrid pungency of old mushrooms. His head throbbed now as if every artery and corpuscle had been flayed open. His wrists and ankles pulsed with energy. He felt superhuman, truly believed at that moment that he could run a marathon and win or write sensual poetry. He was mainlining on adrenaline.

The rush continued, intensified, as he clambered higher. He bubbled internally, offering unseen audiences cogent testimony and then rebuttal on Latin American lending policy, solo rock-climbing handholds, and the deep power chutes of the American West. He stopped, buried to his knees forty yards from the summit in a cloverleaf of rock and ice and trees. The configuration struck him as funny. He giggled, chortled, then guffawed until the tears ran down his cheeks; it occurred to him that he was careening wildly toward a stinking crevice in the glacier of his mind. He liked that.

The radio broke the fever. Two hundred feet below and one hundred yards out from the mountain's side, Inez's Bell Ranger swung on the west wind.

"Okay Page, stop," she said. "You and Collins are even in the chutes. We give you ten minutes to prepare."

Page acknowledged, but Farrell still laughed too hard to respond. He waved with the back of his hand and dropped facedown in the snow. The sharp cold sobered him enough to attempt the tasks at hand. But every few moments, some hint of lunacy broke through the surface and he snickered. He checked his watch: half past ten. He changed into the ski boots, then unstrapped the skis, 204-centimeter slalom boards mounted with green-spring, non-release bindings from a sponsor Inez had cornered.

Farrell unzipped and urinated. "Now there's truth," Farrell said to himself. "No other interpretation possible. Just piss in the snow."

With his skis on, Farrell reached into the pack and got the neon-yellow wind breaker Inez demanded he wear for clear identification during the race, then cinched the reserve pair of goggles to his head. He thrust his hands through the leather straps on his axe-poles and squeezed the handles. He placed his skis parallel to the steep slope. He drew in a deep breath, dropped the tension from the lower ski, and allowed himself to slip down the hill, shaping the snow like a sharp plane across soft pine. Satisfied, he sidestepped back up to his original position, slid down again, and returned.

The Wave's voice came over the radio: "Ooooh, danger boys. Page up there, looking fine. And Collinsmon in neon. Never thought we'd see it. Cacophonous!"

"Shut it off for once, Wave," Farrell said. He was in no mood for idle chat. He tried to strip his mind clean, to see the slope and only the slope. He let himself go, trying to use his anxiety to retreat to that primitive level he needed to be in right now. But the tranquil state—his mind a cold pristine mirror, reflecting exactly what was around him—would not come.

"Quiet time, huh?" The Wave said. "Well, from here in the booth, I'm going to be giving a few observations. First, we seem to have different ideas about how to start off this alpine sprint show: Page has driven his tails into the snow, his body is pointing dead down the mountain, chin tucked into his left shoulder. Looks like he's going for speed, Collins. Page, the old one is sideways to the hill, with a little smoothed-out pad all carved out to make a nice, whipping first turn."

The helicopter roared over the crest of the ridge. Inez's voice cut The Wave off. "We run late," she said. "Are you ready?"

Farrell exhaled and shrugged to try to stop the tremors which now coursed through his shoulders and arms. He hit the transmit button. "Ready."

"Let's get this over with," Page said.

"Très bien," she said. "Switch off the radios and leave them in the snow next to your packs where Ann and Tony can find them. I check with the other cameras. We go on the drop of the orange tape from the side of the helicopter. Thirty seconds."

Farrell reached for his earplug, but on an impulse he decided to keep the radio with him. He switched the transceiver to the B channel. He wanted to hear Inez call the race. He rotated his upper body down the hill and trained his eyes on the middle of the chute.

"Camera one?" Inez said.

"I've got Page," Ann said.

"Two?"

"Collins is in my lens," Tony said.

"Road?"

"Pulled back in full wide-angle. You're in the top of the frame, Inez," The Wave said.

"And Action!" A flutter of brilliant orange scrawled on the corn-flower blue sky. Farrell grunted and threw his body over and down the hill, windmilling through the first packed turn, cut dense powder, shifted his weight to absorb the change, and drove his left hand off his hip out over the tip of the ski.

The action slapped him into the center of the chute. He let the skis run—the crimson, scabrous walls streaking at the edge of his vision—until it all became a blur, and he slammed his heels sideways to slice into the snow. He arced and crested out of the powder, dodged a bush on the left side of the couloir, and wheeled about to let the boards under his feet gather speed: fifteen, twenty, twenty-five miles an hour.

"Way, way too fast," Farrell screamed to himself. He hopped into the air, jamming on the edges of his skis just as he became aware of Tony sliding out on the harness system toward him.

Farrell flew straight at the camera. He braked right, threw a wave of brilliant snow toward Tony's lens and let gravity take him. In the earpiece came Inez's voice, quick and throaty. *"Allez. Allez cours."* Farrell knew somewhere in the woods to his left, Page was also racing at the margin. Farrell shifted his weight, squared off, and plunged into the elevator shaft again, huffing with the effort.

His ski tips snagged on a submerged bush, and before he could compensate, he was off his feet, falling out over the front of the couloir like a cliff diver in Mexico. In that split second, he saw the fleeting smudge of the ledge above the intersection of the Y, some sixty yards below him, then his head dropped as gravity threw him over and he saw sky and trees and icy rock walls.

"Collins down! Collins down!" Inez screeched. "Bring me in!"

Farrell rolled with the momentum of the fall, instinctively kicking the skis forward when they crossed over his head. Which had the miraculous effect of popping him back on top of his skis again, but splayed back like a boxer drunk off the punch of a square jaw shot. He coursed very fast at the towering right wall of the ravine.

"Fuck it!" he howled. At the same time, he slammed both poles into the snow and righted himself. He whipped the tips around just in time and threw his padded forearm out to absorb the impact with the stone. The axe and the round of his helmet grated with the shrill keen of a speeding car's bumper against a guard rail. He bounced off the wall, thrown like a lead weight on a fishing line out into the center of the couloir, not sure how he got there, twenty yards above the intersection of the Y's arms.

The helicopter pulsed above him. "Retreat, retreat," Inez yelled.

Red neon flashed in the trees uphill and to the left. Page was skiing so fast and solid that Farrell knew in an instant that he'd be first into the tunnel unless . . .

Farrell aimed his skis toward the highest section of the ledge, made four swooping turns on the steep, pointed the tips at an oblique angle, and shot forward. Just before the outcropping, he yanked his feet to his buttocks and flew. Page reeled to get out of his way. Farrell smashed into the ravine five feet in front of Page, kneeing himself in the chin on impact.

"You asshole!" Page screamed. He whipped Farrell's right shoulder with his pole. Farrell drew his skis together and accelerated.

The passage in this reach of the couloir was tighter, the snow hardpack with an inch, maybe two of rough corn snow on top. Farrell ripped through it, throwing tiny ice cubes into the air which formed a sparkling mist around his boots, a swirling glittering cloud that rose and flurried about his shins, robbing him of depth perception.

"That's it, I've lost them," Tony said.

"Another twenty feet," said Ann. ". . . and gone."

"They are mine until they turn into the final drop," said Inez. "Wave, aim your camera toward the left turn into the bottom."

Farrell could not see his skis under the shimmering fog at his feet, so he skied by touch. He jerked and skidded once, then found a survival pattern, swinging the skis left and right on a count of one, two. Gone now was the lunacy he'd suffered up high. Gone, too, was the throbbing he'd felt climbing that section of the couloir. Now he solely focused on the left-hand turn he had to make at the end of the chute.

Behind him, Farrell heard Page jam hard on his edges, then fade; and Farrell realized that the loose snow he was kicking up must have obliterated Page's ability to see.

"Collins has won already," said Inez, the disappointment palpable.

The truth of why Page had backed off dawned on Farrell before Inez. It was borne by what little information his senses were able to gather in the shifting mist of snow—the race of a bush in his peripheral vision, the chatter his skis made on the hardpack below the glitter, the angle his upper body had adopted to maintain balance; Farrell's line of descent was too steep. He couldn't make the hard left turn at this speed without crashing.

Farrell saw the tiny feeder channel where he'd checked the snow pack suddenly appear on his right. He snapped his shoulders and head back and skidded up into it, which slowed him to a crawl almost immediately. He skidded to a halt, cranked his left pole into the snow, and jumped the skis back into the fall line just in time to see Page lay his skis on edge and hug the left wall in a brilliant tight slide into the final 800-foot drop of the Y.

Farrell flung himself after Page, fighting the swell that boiled through his stomach in reaction to the spectacular illusion the steep pitch created; he was that child on the ferris wheel again, rolling over the top, swinging out into thin air. The canyon floor seemed suspended directly beneath his skis and he found himself unable to control his body's instinctive need to retreat.

Page switched to a double-edged set turn—leaping, then biting the snow with the uphill edge of both skis. It was a physically punishing maneuver, but Farrell realized it was the only way to handle the radical slope; he adopted the tactic, too, bringing his weight to bear on both skis, sinking fully on each jarring contact with the snow, then rebounding high into the air where he could whip the skis around into the next turn. Within four revolutions, Farrell's back barked, his thighs flamed. The motion had a positive effect as well: the collision between Farrell's 170 pounds and the loose snow sent a shower of crud and ice down on Page's back and slowed his competitor's advance.

"Wave? Wave, do you have this?" Inez cried.

"Brutal, mon," The Wave responded. "A good hundred and fifty feet of the chute in the lens. But I'm going to lose them if you stay where you are."

"Stay with the shot," she demanded.

Page and Farrell drained down the precipice like two splashes of water across a window, one droplet gathering weight and streaking away, the other finding the lead droplet's path and racing behind.

Sweat burst, then streaked out from under the lip of Farrell's helmet. They still had another 350 vertical feet until the runout and his lungs felt like they'd been scored with razors.

Two hundred feet below Page and Farrell, the couloir widened and it was there that the twenty-five feet of blue, rippled ice hung, split by the dagger of rock. There the couloir constricted again to just five yards wide before flooding onto the wide snout of snow that ran to the canyon floor. Farrell hadn't figured out how to cross the ice and avoid the rock; he prayed Page had.

Fifteen yards above the water ice, Page carved left to avoid the sharp rock jutting in the middle of the chute. With a clear gap in front of him, Page pointed his skis straight down, letting the boards find their own way through the frozen throat. A breath away, Farrell made a similar decision with a slight twist; he accelerated in a quick, rattling shake over the ice, aiming for the bulge that surrounded the stone dagger. The moment his tips touched the lip, Farrell jerked his skis up, barely cleared the outcropping, and landed side by side with Page. They clattered shoulder to shoulder into the final yards of the ravine, neither of them willing to let the other pass, the ragged black lichen tearing at their glowing windbreakers.

Page grimaced, leaned, and tried to ride Farrell into the wall. Farrell shoved back, flinging the blunt end of his ice axe at Page's thigh, which killed their balance. Together they shot out of the Y Couloir onto the giant mound of snow that drained into the forest.

In the collision of metal and nylon and flesh, Page flipped forward into a series of cartwheels that bore him end over end into the forest. Farrell spiraled left. He ricocheted off the hard upper part of the mound, then skidded sideways, head first through the slush, and smashed into a stand of half-inch cottonwood saplings.

Chapter 11

Farrell groaned. His hip pinned his right arm to the ground. Two saplings gripped his head at a painful angle. A tangle of brush twisted his skis up behind him. He tasted blood, but knew nothing serious was broken.

"Who won? Can anybody hear me? Who won the damned thing?" Though Farrell's earpiece had dislodged, the helmet wall reflected enough of the sound that he knew it was Tony asking the questions.

"Last thing I saw was arms and legs wrapped together like in one of those cartoons," said The Wave. "They could be hurt real bad."

A crow glided through his field of vision, then Page appeared holding his right arm close to his side. He'd removed his helmet to reveal a gashed right cheek. "You bastard," he croaked. "You almost killed me."

"Yeah," Farrell grunted. "And you didn't smack me on the shoulder with your ski pole up there either. Get me out of here, my neck—"

"Fuck your neck," Page said. "We could have died up there."

Farrell wheezed and coughed. "You knew the risks."

Page grabbed the saplings and pulled back on them. The pressure around Farrell's neck eased. Farrell's head untwisted, then slipped downhill, further into the gap between the little trees. Page wrenched the two trees together until Farrell gagged.

"Listen now and listen good, you shithead," Page said. "When I go up a hill, I have every intention of coming down in one piece. You want to go out in some blaze of self-inflicted glory, you do it alone. Not on my time."

Farrell gulped. A garbled sound curled up from his throat. Page released the tension. Farrell's elbow slipped out from under his chest and he collapsed forward in the snow. Page was right and he thought: when had suicide become a factor? With his next breath he understood that it had been skulking around since the night he'd seen Timmons slide down the strings of the Apron. Maybe he was the next link in the Farrell chain.

Page flipped the gear on Farrell's bindings. Farrell fell away from the skis and flopped onto his side. His eyes stung from the sweat and blood that trickled from his nose.

"Give me a hand up," Farrell said, his voice like gravel.

"I don't think so," Page said. He slogged off through the slush toward the clearing.

Farrell wriggled himself into a sitting position. "Page!"

Page kept moving. "See a shrink."

Farrell unstrapped the helmet and pried it off. He looked about himself at the skis and the poles and the broken goggles that hung on a branch of a stunted spruce. He sat down hard, shivering.

Page had managed to shoulder his skis and take a few stiff steps up the trail when The Wave raced into the clearing. "Foaming dogs!" he cried. "That was absolutely rabid!"

Then he saw Page's cut face: "Mon, you look like you've been whipped. You okay?"

Page shook The Wave's hand off his shoulder and staggered away toward the road. The Wave pushed his dreadlocks back behind his ears and ran to Farrell. "Damn, old one, you're worse," The Wave said. "Your face looks like cottage cheese with raspberry sauce. You hurt bad?"

Farrell stared at The Wave for a full five seconds. "No, I'm fine. Just get me up."

"Who won?"

Farrell groaned as he stood; his hip was bruised and standing had sent the muscle there into spasm. "What?"

"Who got to the bottom first, old one?" The Wave insisted. "I lost you in my lens right near the bottom."

"Page won," Farrell said. "I never made it to the canyon floor."

"Too bad, mon," The Wave said. "When you made that last insane move to the canyon floor, I figured you had it."

"Insane . . ." Farrell repeated. Black spots appeared before his eyes, his knees buckled, and he dry heaved.

"Mon, we've got to get you to a doctor," The Wave said, grabbing Farrell's elbow.

"That's what Page says, too," Farrell mumbled.

Some of Farrell's strength returned on the hike out, and by the time they reached the road, he was walking on his own. Inez stood on the bank of snow above the trail head, her face aglow, her elbows pressed tightly together at her breasts, her hands splayed about her face like the leaves of an oleander protecting its flower.

"Outrance!" she exclaimed. "Extreme, this word does not come close to make the description of what you do! Only in the French will the language do this feat justice. It's *outrance!* Audacity!"

Her enthusiasm swept her away. She jumped the snowbank to run to Farrell as she had to The Wave the week before. She grasped Farrell's face in her hands, ignoring the blood, and kissed him full on the mouth. The Wave stood off to one side twisting one of his dreads.

"You are magnificent," Inez said. Her eyes were glassy, half-lidded, and her lips wet and parted. "Myself, I cannot take you further."

Inez trembled and she hugged him again. She seemed to surround him now the way the ocean did when he scuba-dived, a comforting force that he knew could turn ugly without warning. Inez leaned to Farrell's unbraided ear. She brushed her lips across it and whispered, "Well, perhaps I take you just a little bit further in Tahoe."

Farrell flushed. The sky spun. The black dots reappeared.

"You almost killed him up there," The Wave said.

Inez twisted away from Farrell. "I just test him. *Regardez les conséquences!"*

"Yeah, look at them!" The Wave insisted. "You almost swept him off the face when you pulled close with that chopper."

"This is our affair," Inez said. "You and I have our own."

Farrell shook his head to clear the bugs which danced in the air. He felt ill again. He brushed between the two of them to clamber up the snow embankment.

"We are in Tahoe by day after tomorrow," she called after Farrell. "We must keep up the pace or we have no more breakthrough."

Farrell didn't reply. He plodded toward Portsteiner, who had just emerged from the woods on the other side of the road.

Inez raced after Farrell and threw her arm about his shoulder. "You cannot stop now, Collins. I think you loved it. Perhaps you think you hate me now. But I think, too, you loved me when you are in the Y Couloir."

Farrell tried to say something, but couldn't find the words. He just kept walking while Inez called to him from behind, louder and louder: "Collins! Collins! I see you in Tahoe! I see you in Tahoe!"

Portsteiner swabbed alcohol on the red, raw patch under Farrell's left eye. Farrell gritted his teeth and focused on the tattered old ski posters and the Hawaii calendar on the far wall of Portsteiner's office, a jumbled affair with a battered wooden desk, four pairs of skis, and a filing cabinet badly in need of a clerk.

"Never seen a more brilliant move done in such a dumb place," Portsteiner said. "Odds say both of you should be dead right now."

Farrell didn't reply. He stared at the floor until Portsteiner grabbed him by the chin and tugged his head up. "Am I getting through to you at all, son?"

Farrell jerked his head away.

Portsteiner laid gauze along Farrell's ear and taped it. "You know, you don't talk, you might get yourself into a drainage you may never leave. Funny. Before you went off to Africa, you were the tautest SOB I ever knew."

Farrell held a piece of ice to the swelling above his eye.

"Just do me one favor," Portsteiner said. "Tell me what happened when you left here that time and disappeared for three months before you took off for Africa."

"No."

"I'm trying to be your friend, Jack. Friends talk."

Farrell saw that the old man was telling the truth, he was trying to be his friend. Farrell did not know how to start. Finally, he said: "Maybe there are some snow crystals you just couldn't understand."

"Try me," Portsteiner said, and he took a seat next to Farrell.

"My great-grandmother, father's side, had what they called 'the spells,'" Farrell began. "Her son, my grandfather, hung himself. My father was thirteen when he found him in the garage."

"I don't see—"

"Let me finish," Farrell said. "There were times when I was at the dinner table as a kid. For no reason at all, he'd go off. And my mother, she'd sit there and take it until he'd kind of gotten it out of himself. Sometimes he'd cry. She'd put down her napkin and give him his pills and he'd stay in this darkened room for a couple of days."

"What did the doctors say?"

"That it was some kind of imbalance, manic-depression," Farrell said. "He'd stay on the pills, he'd be fine. He hated them, though. Thought they made the world something it wasn't.

"So every once in a while, he'd stop taking them. He worked out of the house. He was an attorney, but because of the spells, he just got jobs writing contracts and things. Anyway, I'd come home from school and my mom would be out and he'd have the stereo blasting and would be dancing with the vacuum cleaner. Honest to god, it was real fun sometimes."

Farrell put the ice down and took a drink from the beer Portsteiner had opened for him. "I remember this, too. I must have been nine and my mom was at the drug store. I made some crack about having nothing to do. So he just loads me in the car, eight-thirty in the morning, and off we drive—three and a half hours—him singing at the top of his lungs, down to the Museum of Fine Arts in Boston.

"We come back nine hours later and there's my mom all pale, sick to her stomach, and she knows he hasn't been taking his pills."

"You got it, Jack—that what you're trying to tell me?"

"I honestly don't know."

"You went home that spring and saw them, what happened?"

Farrell turned away. "There's somethings better not talked about."

Portsteiner pursed his lips. "You hate them, your parents?"

"No," Farrell sighed. "I still love them, can't help it."

"This isn't the kind of thing you can handle alone."

Farrell stood up. "I'm finding that out. I've been reading about someone who went through an awful time, worse than me, it seems. Listening to stories worse than my own seems to help, sort of."

"I'll change those bandages tomorrow."

"Won't be here," Farrell said. "Going to Tahoe for this week, then Jackson Hole next. I'm in show business, you know."

Portsteiner grabbed Farrell by the elbow as he headed toward the door. "Not a good idea, son. The woman scares me."

"Really? I kind of like her," Farrell said. "She's wild, unpredictable. Takes me places."

"I think I know you, Jack," Portsteiner said. "You go with her, you may not be able to get away."

Farrell shook his arm free, annoyed. "What are you talking about? I can leave her anytime I want. This is one thing I know how to handle."

They stared at each other in silence. Portsteiner laid his big hand on Farrell's shoulder. "The heart of a cold victim is irritable and sensitive to jarring," he said. "Rough handling of a cold victim may cause the heart to stop or beat irregular. Gentle treatment is necessary."

Farrell lips rolled in on themselves in a grotesque version of a smile.

"E. R. LaChapelle," they both said.

Later that afternoon, the sun was warm enough that an old gray cat lay like a rug on the stone front steps of the lodge while Farrell loaded his things into the truck. Portsteiner's nonprescription painkillers had cut the edge off the ache in his hip and his chin, but his forehead and the bone around his eyes still pounded. He figured the drive to Tahoe would take him fourteen maybe fifteen hours over two days. Just as he'd told Portsteiner, if he wanted to, he simply wouldn't show up. There was always Montana. The thought of Inez's lips running across his ear returned; he would continue at least through the cliffs at Squaw Valley.

"Hey, old one," The Wave said.

Farrell started and almost fell off the truck.

"Jesus!" Farrell said. "You scared the crap out of me."

"Triggering heart attacks, it's my specialty. Here, Inez wanted me to give you the name of the motel we'll be at. How about a ride to the airport?"

Farrell took the slip of paper and said coolly, "I travel alone."

"Just to the airport, mon," The Wave said.

Farrell remembered the kid's crack in the pool room. *The woman knows more than she lets on.* "Get your stuff," Farrell said.

The Wave returned with a large duffel bag and threw it into the camper. On the ride down the canyon, Farrell's attention wavered. He found himself taking long sideways looks at the melting hillsides. He knew there was a chance he'd never be back in Little Cottonwood again and the thought depressed him. The Wave was drumming his fingers on the dashboard.

"You still got that I'm-a-lake-trout feeling?" Farrell asked.

"What's it to you, mon?"

"I'm interested in what Inez does behind closed doors."

"It's weird," The Wave said. "Maybe more than you can handle."

Farrell braked for a car full of rock climbers that pulled out onto the road. "Try me," he said.

The Wave's head rocked side to side for a minute as if he were listening to some inner reggae station. "She ever do one of these talks with you? With the cameras on? Asking questions in that bizarre English of hers—no tense but the present?"

"She's asked questions, but no cameras," Farrell said. "She's trying to renegotiate that point."

"Mon, you know, I came from nothing," The Wave said. "But she knows almost everything about nothing."

"What, that you're a surf bum who found out he liked the winter?"

"I'm telling you, mon, she knows about me, all of it, about Page and probably about you," he said.

The pain in Farrell's cheeks and hip returned, throbbing and burning. But he gave The Wave no indication of his intense discomfort.

"I don't think that's poss—" Farrell began.

"She keeps files, mon," The Wave said. "Inez keeps files. I saw them in a box last week."

"Tell me exactly what happened."

"She sat on the bed with the camera running," The Wave said. "Made me uncomfortable. I'd just smoked the better part of a killer spliff, getting ready to shred. I thought it would be an easy, go-for-it, kind of pep talk, you know? No, mon, she's in my face."

"About?"

"All sorts of crazy shit. She starts out asking me about what it was like, me growing up. I tell her I couldn't see the point. She says if I can't open up to her, we can't film. Says she wants me talking to her through the lens."

"Not so bad an idea," Farrell said.

"Yeah, yeah," The Wave said. "Never been to college, but I read, mon, a lot. I know about DeNiro and even that dude Stanislavski."

"So?"

"She asks me where I was born and I tell her the truth: somewhere in Nevada during a festival in the wilderness. My mother said she was dancing with a couple of naked people covered with mud when she felt me wrestling to get out."

"Earth child," Farrell said.

"Sunshine, that's what she named herself. Her real name is Frances Milburn. Smart, one credit shy of a Yale degree. Sunshine's . . . a pretty funky woman."

"And Inez wanted to know about her," Farrell said.

"Nothing she didn't seem to already know," The Wave said. "Took me a minute, but I picked up on that. When it hits me, I headed for the door. No use shoveling up the bad for the movies, even if I am going to be in lights. But she stops me, says it's necessary to her technique, says it—'technique'—like it's some church word."

"Then what?" Farrell asked as they left the canyon and headed north toward the highway.

"She starts asking me about my friend, Mike. I used to crash in the back of his autobody shop when I couldn't find another place to live. Same guy who got me into boarding: sidewalk, ocean, anything . . ."

"He older?" Farrell asked.

"Forties, like Sunshine, mon," The Wave said. "They were friends from way back. He was a cool dude, made me go to school. Said he didn't want me to end up like him—burnt-out surf bum working in a body shop. I'll tell you, though, I never saw him like that, a loser, you know? He liked to read, and got me into it. If I stayed in the shop, I had to read something. I did: newspapers and magazines mostly. Later, reference books, encyclopedias, and quote books. Then dudes like Kurt Vonnegut and Tom Robbins and Joseph Heller. Made me think about things.

"Anyway, I'm telling her this and she's standing behind the camera and . . ." The Wave wrapped his finger tightly around one of his dreadlocks, playing with it. He coughed. "She just asks me, right out: 'Is he, Mike, your father or something?' I said, 'Fuck this! I don't have to put up with this shit to make a fucking ski movie.' I was out of there."

The Wave leaned against the window. Farrell didn't say a word. When they'd turned onto the highway, heading west, The Wave cleared his throat. "There I am, off like a shot and that French bitch, she chases me across the room, telling me that 'We're almost done, we're almost done.' I don't know what it was—the spliff or the way she sold it to me—but I went back. And she's behind me, kneading my neck, asking me again, about Mike, about whether he's my father."

The Wave drummed his fingers again on the dashboard. "I said, there was a lot of people basking in old Sunshine's rays back in those days, why not? I could think of a lot worse people to be my old one."

"How's that?" Farrell asked.

"She didn't pick her friends too carefully, old Sunshine. Mike was about the only true one she ever had. He looked after her, thought about her, not what she could do for him."

Farrell looked over at the kid, who was furiously twisting one of his dreads. Farrell surprised himself; he felt sorry for The Wave. "You ever ask him?"

The Wave crossed his arms. "No."

"Why not?" Farrell asked.

The Wave shook his head.

"Why not?" Farrell repeated. He needed to know what Inez knew.

"I guess. . . . I guess I didn't want to hear him say no, all right?" The Wave snapped. He skuffed his sneaker very fast against the floorboard. "Anyway, Inez, she starts pumping me about Mike. Only now, she's got this folder and she's looking at it."

"What's it look like, the folder?"

"One of those long jobs with the metal prongs inside you see the D.A.s carrying around in court," he said. "Inez has hers open. She says, 'Why'd he stop coming around?' I got real nervous, because who knows that kind of stuff except for me and Sunshine and Mike?"

"Inez does," Farrell said. He wrapped his fingers so tight around the wheel that his knuckles began to turn white.

"Damn straight," The Wave said. "I decided then, it was better that I played her game, see where she was going and where she was coming from, you know, mon? I told her 1984, maybe '85, Mike left. She asked why and I said because he probably couldn't stand to see Sunshine that way, so he split. Five months later, I did, too. I was fourteen, living on the streets, digging half-munched burgers out of trash cans, crashing on the beach until I went and found Mike and he took me in."

"What's Sunshine's problem?" Farrell asked.

The Wave snorted: "What isn't? When she wasn't messing with vials and tubes, she'd start talking to the wall about stuff. I still get nightmares."

Farrell threw on his blinker to pass a slow-moving car, then veered right to get into the lane that would take him toward the airport.

The Wave said: "Last time I saw Sunshine, we got a call from the body shop from a friend of hers. We—me and Mike—we walk into the room she was renting. Paramedics working on her. They'd given her a shot of something that makes you come back from an overdose; and she's restrained because she's been speed-balling. She's wailing at them—these guys who just saved her life!—because they fucked up her high.

"When I said she should get help, she spit at me," The Wave said.

"And Inez knew all about this?"

"She had most of it," The Wave said, pursing his lips as if he couldn't quite believe it himself. "Told me Sunshine was in a treatment center, some ranch in Arizona, and then wouldn't tell me where it was or how she was doing. That's when I told her I was going to get a lawyer. That's illegal, isn't it? Checking into some-one's life like that?"

"Information has a free market, I'm afraid," Farrell said. "No such thing as privacy anymore unless you create it. Why don't you call Mike?"

"I did," The Wave said. "He said some people, like cops but not cops, came to see him. Probably private eyes. He didn't tell them much. He doesn't know where Sunshine is. Hasn't heard from her in months.

"The goddamned point is that Inez knew. She smiled, said she'd chosen me just because I was such a hard case, that she'd found out about my real good bad attitude and she thought she could use me. She tells me I've got nowhere to go except with her."

"That what you believe?"

The Wave drummed his fingers on the dashboard. "First thing I thought was that she was just power-tripping on me. The more I chewed on it, though, all I could see was me washing dishes at some resort or working a burger joint for the minimum. I want more out of life, mon."

The kid was silent for a moment, then added: "What's weird is that afterward, after the surf up there in the woods, I kept thinking about Inez—you know, the way she talked to me, the way I shred-ded."

"You think it's her technique?" Farrell asked, remembering the abandon with which he'd gone after Page in the Y Couloir.

The Wave curled his fingers tight against his palms as if he were trying to grip something that wasn't there. "Maybe. It was strange. You ever been out on the ocean just as the sun rises?"

"Yes."

"Then you know how it is that you can taste the sea, even if your head isn't in the water," he said. "Waiting to board in the storm up there at Snowbird, what she talked to me about was like the water, all around me, taunting me almost. I could taste it and her at the same time and it scared the shit out of me."

"So you want to sleep with her, so what?" Farrell said.

"It wasn't like that at all, Collins," The Wave said, deadly seri-ous. "It was more like being unable to get enough air. I wanted . . . I don't know . . . to fight back maybe? But there was no one place to go after it, so I went after the whole slope, hitting back at her on the way down."

"Her?"

He nodded and sighed. "That's it. I don't know, maybe both of them, maybe all of it."

"Inez hugged you at the bottom of the run," Farrell said. "You hugged her back."

"Can't explain it, mon," The Wave said. "It's like halfway down, I had these flashes of warm, white light in my head. They made me feel good and powerful—stoked, you know?—I couldn't do anything wrong. For that one run, I'd been taken out of shit-happens to where I was shredding the impossible like a goddamned super-hero and, for who knows why, she was the one who understood. I could tell her about it."

He rapped his hands on the roof of the camper and leaned his head against the door frame. "The thing that has me really freaked is that afterward, even now, thinking about it, replaying the whole run in my head, I might do anything to feel that way again."

Farrell realized that after the race in the Y Couloir, he felt the same way. He looked through the windshield at the late afternoon sun setting over the Uinta Mountains to the West, somehow scared and delighted at the same time. "How much of this streetwise act of yours is real?" Farrell asked.

The Wave shook back his dreads. "No act, mon."

"Then I think you owe it to yourself and me to do a little bur-glary on Inez's room when you get to Tahoe," Farrell said. "Get us some information. Don't tell Page."

The Wave smiled a harsh smile. "Cold, cold eyes," he said.

"You, too, rastaman," Farrell said as the kid got out of the truck. "You, too."

Chapter 12

March 16, 1986

Seeds thrive here in any season. New shoots will burst forth from dormant bushes, especially now that winter is dying. What I wait for is June when the neighbors say that the tree that grows outside my window, a jacaranda, will flood itself with purple blossoms.

Each morning we awake to ocean fog. My neighbors say the sea is warming. The misty veil hangs in the sky until early afternoon, when the sun shines strong enough to burn it off. Then the water on the flowers—the hibiscus and the bougain-villaea and the roses—evaporates in a heady perfume.

Some days the cloud cover never yields. And in the late afternoon, while the surfers bob for the day's last waves, Punta and Rabo and I trek to the beach. I sit on a rock, throwing sticks into the breakwater. They chase, elated. In Chicago, the fog depressed; here the mists pep up the dogs, the hibiscus, and Jack.

A few months back, I thought we'd made a mistake coming here. Jack moved about the house with his eyes half-closed, distant and dulled. I got him some scuba lessons, thought they might help. They didn't.

Ever since Jack started working with Gabriel Cortez, however, he seems more alive. He came home the other night with a big bottle of white wine, told me he'd consummated a big deal with Cortez, and that there would be more like it. Jack demanded that we drink the bottle naked in the hot tub. How California!

He had to travel a bit to set up his deal, which like most of his financial business, I don't understand. He's been to Mexico City twice to meet with Gabriel and once to Panama City.

Jack's fingers drummed on the edge of the tub and I could see the old fire in his eyes. He told me it was kind of like skiing. He didn't know what was going to happen next and that was the best part.

He has been working steady hours for the first time since we met. We sit on the patio as dusk comes or we go out for walks with the dogs. Sometimes he reaches out and holds my hands, but he says little. He can't imagine how just the touch of his fingers holds me in place. Without words he manages to stir in me once again the idea that I can just be. I suppose he does it by expecting so little of me.

We've begun to make love again. I smell his skin and hold him tight to me as if I can bring more of him inside me than already is. It only lasts for a while. Part of me drifts off and part stays alert for that moment when I feel him become anxious and determined and I push him off and reached for my diaphragm and the security of that rubber wall.

When I bend and push that barrier between us, I can see his cheeks slacken and his motions become mechanical, just searching for release. He rolls over and falls asleep.

There in the hot tub the other night, he rubbed himself against my leg. I couldn't get to the diaphragm, and I lost myself in panic, not lust. We moved without protection. Afterwards I cried, and when he asked me why, I lied and told him it was because I loved him so much.

Farrell closed the diary, stung by the idea that she had to lie to him. He grimaced: How often had he lied to her? He stepped through the door of the camper to stand underneath the stars. He was 140 miles out of Salt Lake City, in a truck stop near the Nevada line, numbed by the painkillers, muscle relaxants, three shots of tequila, and the beer he'd consumed since he'd pulled over. Still, the pungent sage cut through the fog in his head. He gazed at the stars and said to himself, "I guess I just walked around with blinders on."

Farrell listened to the wind and the snap of brush in the darkness. The Wave's conversation replayed itself in his head. He was fascinated and unnerved that Inez had been able to delve that deep into the kid's past. Why was he important? What was she up to? he asked himself. He needed to know more.

Farrell went back into the camper, got his wallet, and crossed the pavement to a pay telephone. He punched in a series of numbers that connected him to an overseas line, then eight more. A phone rang in an office in Basel, Switzerland. When the woman's voice answered, Farrell cleared his throat and read off a series of numbers and letters.

"Just one moment, sir," the woman said. The line went dead.

Farrell leaned his head against the glass, waiting for the voice of a thin man he'd met only briefly in the Bahamas. The phone clicked. "It has been quite a while, sir," the attorney said.

"It has," Farrell said. "I need some research done."

"As always, we await your instructions," the attorney said.

Farrell's head reeled. *We await your instructions!*

"Of course," Farrell said, trying to ward off the awful memories those words could generate. "I need information, anything you can get me on an Inez Didier. She makes movies about skiing and mountain climbing. I believe she grew up in Lyons, France, spent time in Chamonix."

"Inez Didier," the attorney repeated, then paused. "How much do you wish to know?"

"Beyond financials," Farrell said. "I want to get personal."

"An expensive proposition, sir," the attorney said.

"How much?"

"For the best? A thousand dollars a day, plus expenses."

Farrell didn't hesitate. "Take it from the 201A account with an initial cap and report at ten thousand dollars."

"Where can I reach you, sir?"

"You can't," Farrell said. "I'll call."

"Very good, sir," the attorney said. "And if there is more, as always, we await instructions."

Farrell sighed and hung up the phone. *Await instructions.*

How many times had he read those words after his first meeting with Jorge Cordova? As he walked back to the truck, he remembered the first time. It was near the end of March, about 11 A.M., when his secretary handed him the folder marked for his eyes only. He closed the door to his office on the twenty-first floor of the office building. He sat in his high-backed black chair and turned it toward the incredible view of the downtown skyscrapers and beyond them the clear blue of San Diego Bay. Farrell took a deep breath and flipped open the manila sleeve. Inside lay a simple light green telegram from a bank on the Bahnhofstrasse in Zurich: *RE: Account number 99236Bl. Handelsregister Namen: Buena Vista Anstalt. Cumulative total received this month: One hundred and twenty-five thousand U.S. Await instructions."*

Farrell touched the green sheaf to his nose and inhaled. He rubbed his hands together and danced about the office damn near singing to himself. His legs quivered. He knelt, his fingers on the edge of the desk, and whispered: "You ballsy bastard! You fooled them all!"

This risk had a different quality than the sort he associated with physical jeopardy. It was dreamlike, rather than immediate and sensory. Yes, he experienced the same flutters and shakes of postexperience, as if he'd free-climbed El Capitan at Yosemite or solo-shredded a fifty-five-degree slope in the Wyoming backcountry. This danger wasn't tangible, that was sure. Somehow that made it more enticing. Farrell no longer was bound by pitch of rock or steepness of slope; Farrell played with the limits of his imagination.

He settled back into his chair, waved the telegram back and forth, knowing he wanted more, to see what he could really do with the system. He flipped on his computer and punched in a series of numbers to see how much money he could make in six months. Halfway through the computations he hummed; it was as if the hypothetical figures on the screen were an indicator of the pleasures he would get taking these risks. He realized that, deep down, he didn't care about the money. The profits he made were like mountains he was able to point to after he'd skied them. Only now the mountains were dollar signs. With them he could measure how well he rode the line between success and discovery.

Suddenly, chills ran through his body. His teeth chattered. His legs jumped. What should he do now? Whom should he tell? Cordova? He lurched from his chair to race across the office to pull the file from his credenza. He dialed in the numbers of Cordova's satellite pager. The country code—502—and the city code—9—indicated the pager talked to the satellite from Quezaltenango, a Guatemalan city hard by the border at Chiapas. But Cordova could be anywhere when he received the message.

The computer tone beeped. Farrell hung up, slumped into his chair. He imagined himself far out on a winter ridge about to drop into three feet of powder.

The phone rang. "Jack?"

"Jorge, the line's bad. You sound a million miles away."

"The nature of the import-export business," he said.

To Farrell the possibilities were endless: Cordova was sweating in the jungles outside Lima, Peru, or drinking Pernod on the Île St. Louis in Paris, or sunning off Ipanema Beach in Rio. "Colon is such a shit hole," Cordova said. "Not a decent restaurant in the whole town."

Colon, Panama. It was a shit hole. Farrell told him he remembered that one of the local bistros served a passable barbecued red snapper.

"Overbroiled usually," Cordova sniffed. "But enough. To what do I owe the honor?"

"The packages have all been received."

"Magnificent," he said. "Mr. Cortez's trust has been well placed. When can we be ready to work again?"

"I figure another week until the circle is completed."

"And the freight. Can you handle more?"

"Four times as much," Farrell said.

"Slowly," Cordova said. "Let us work slowly."

To prolong the conversation, Farrell tried to discuss an article he'd read recently about the trophy fishing off the coast of Mauritania, but Cordova cut him short, saying he had a meeting to attend. The line went dead. In that moment Farrell was twelve again, far out in the woods during deer season, the thrill of hunting with a rifle alone for the first time fading as dusk approached; the boy wasn't sure how to get back to the cabin. He felt terribly alone.

Farrell traced a fingernail across the green paper, wondering if he could indeed quadruple the amount of cash without exposing himself. He hunched over the folder with a pen, drawing a diagram of the system. He had based it on a shell game: as long as he moved the cash at a rapid pace, through different accounts and banks and countries, within days only the most tenacious investigator could possibly trace the money's origin and only then with the help of Cordova or himself.

It worked like this: The U.S. government requires banks to fill out a form for any cash transaction of more than $10,000. Not filing and getting caught would bring the Internal Revenue Service or the Justice Department down on the bank but quick. Farrell needed accounts in the names of businesses that as a matter of course dealt with large sums of cash. Cordova arranged for four companies that traded currency in the U.S.-Mexico border community of San Ysidro to open twelve separate accounts with Farrell's bank.

About the same time, Farrell flew to Panama, to Colon, in fact, and met with an attorney there named Miguel Ochoa, whom he knew from deals he'd done in connection with his old job. In two days, Ochoa had organized PXZ Inc., a shell corporation the registered directors of which included Ochoa, Raul Romero—a security guard in Ochoa's office building who received $200 for signing his name—and Linda Ho, a Hong Kong notary who often worked with Ochoa.

For a $1,000-fee, Ho registered a Hong Kong parent company to PXZ Inc. that she named Peso Ltd. and opened an account in that name at a prominent Kowloon financial institution. Farrell contacted the attorney in Basel, who, in turn, contacted an attorney, Herr Luptfa, in the tiny principality of Liechtenstein. For a $2,000 fee and a $400 a year retainer, Luptfa created Bueno Vista Anstalt, with himself, the Basel attorney, and a Liechtenstein notary as directors.

In effect, the companies and countries acted as screens through which Farrell filtered the cash. The week before he received the green verification slips, armed security guards carried in the two locked, steel boxes which would become a regular sight at the bank. Inside, lay approximately $100,000 in cash. Into twelve separate accounts, sums of $9,000 were deposited—just below the federal reporting limit.

On a Friday, Farrell began a series of wire transfers to the bank in Kowloon. The Basel attorney had notified the Hong Kong bank by registered mail to expect the deposit and to directly wire the money to the Swiss bank account of Buena Vista Anstalt.

All that was needed to complete the circle was a wire transfer of cash to PXZ in Panama, or the creation of a new entity, which would accept the cash into an account in Farrell's bank or, for that matter, in an account at any of the other banks in San Diego. There the money would be. For all intents legal. Farrell's commission: 7 percent, which he arranged to deposit in a bank account set up in Basel. Of course, as the deposits accumulated in his own bank, he could expect bonuses and a substantial increase in his salary.

Now, as Farrell sat in the rear of his camper in western Utah, he remembered how smug he'd been sitting safely in his office. He'd calculated that the machine could handle as much as $250,000 a month without setting off serious alarms. Any amount beyond that would require a different kind of cash-intensive business to provide cover.

The phone rang again in his office.

"Jorge says you've hooked a marlin," Gabriel said.

"It's a beast of a fish, but all I can see is the ripples he makes on the water, a little piece of green paper," Farrell said.

"You shall have to come to Cabo soon to fish," Gabriel said.

"I'd like that," Farrell said.

With the tone of a teenage boy stealing whiskey from a liquor cabinet, Gabriel said: "There really is nothing quite so blazing as the unpredictable, is there, Jack?"

Farrell's stomach did a slight flip-flop. This man, this relative stranger, seemed to understand things about him that few others did. The odd feeling of nakedness made Farrell light-headed.

"No, Gabriel," Farrell had croaked. "Nothing."

A coyote howled somewhere out in the desert. Farrell locked the door to the camper and crawled into the bunk fully clothed. He remembered how talkative Lena had been the night after he'd completed the third transaction. He knew that she spoke of the dogs, of the garden and, of how much better she felt. He heard few of the particulars. He'd drunk too much, partly in celebration, partly to mask the uneasiness that had nagged him since speaking with Gabriel.

"Jack, you're not listening again," Lena said.

"I am, too. You were talking about bougainvillaea," he said.

"Ten minutes ago."

"I'm sorry . . . I must have been somewhere else . . ."

"You say that like it doesn't happen every day," Lena said. "I asked you to look at this." She pushed a newspaper at him. Circled in red was an a help-wanted ad for nurses in an experimental nursery.

Farrell looked out across the patio. "You haven't finished with your plans for the garden."

"I've been spending too much time out there," Lena said. "I'm about ready to let these plants grow on their own for a while."

"Maybe a nursery isn't the way to start again," Farrell said.

Lena hugged her shoulders. "A nursery is a full floor away from labor and delivery."

"That's not far," Farrell said.

"I haven't worked in eight months," Lena said. "It's a start."

Later, they had walked to the beach. They sat against the breakwall under a half-moon. The wind was blustery and cold, the air saturated with spring scent of the ocean. Lena tussled with Punta. Rabo laid her head in Farrell's lap. Farrell put a Bob Marley tape in their cassette deck and the hypnotic strains of "No Woman, No Cry" floated across the sand toward a group that stood around a bonfire.

Lena said, "I thought you'd be more supportive."

Farrell said, "I just want you to be sure." He asked himself whether it was true. As long as Lena had remained at home, he hadn't had to give her much thought. This changed everything.

Lena placed her hand on his: "Did I ever tell you that for a long time when I was young, I blamed myself for my mom's multiple sclerosis? I was seven and I'd left one of my strap-on roller-skates on the back porch. She tripped over it and landed hard on her hip. About a year later she was in a wheelchair."

Lena ran her fingers through her hair. "I thought for sure that I'd done it and I lived with it until I was thirteen, not telling anyone. I read later in a magazine that it was impossible, that MS is a hardening of tissue in the nervous system, not injury."

She kicked her heel into the sand and Punta squealed and dug at her foot. "Guilt can make us blind. I want to open my eyes again."

"I thought you were doing pretty well," Farrell said.

Lena gave him a look that struck him as strange. "Maybe I'm just doing as well as I can. What about you?"

Farrell shrugged. "The past month I've been frantic, setting up these deals for Gabriel. Today I figured out how to make it all work."

"You make that sound bad."

"Not new anymore," Farrell said. "Even though the kinks have to be worked out of it, I know it's only a matter of time before it loses its newness and I'll tire of it and look for more. Does that make sense?"

"I'm no explorer," Lena said softly. "I'm not like you."

"What does that mean?" Farrell asked defensively.

"Just that," Lena said. "Most of what I experience is here, inside."

She shifted away from him, bending forward to hug her knees. He wondered how she managed to be so strong and yet so vulnerable at the same time. He felt suddenly guilty at what he'd been doing in secret with Cortez and Cordova. He didn't allow himself to dwell on it more than a moment. He reached out to hug her. Lena tensed for a moment, then leaned back into his shoulder and shut her eyes.

April 3, 1986

I was brave last week for the first time in I don't know when. I answered that ad in the paper. Dr. Maddy Crukshank, a plump, bespeckled woman met with me. I told her straight off about Jenny. I didn't want her to find out my problems from some personnel jerk back in Chicago. She listened, and when she finally spoke, I could hear the hesitation in her voice. But I was honest and told her I would be better for those kids because of what has happened. I'll care more. There was a long silence, then she showed me around. Dr. Crukshank's ward is more of a research lab than a nursery. There are two rooms where she cares for babies with special problems—low birth weight, prematurity, congenital disorders. I'd forgotten how tiny and helpless they are, lashed down by tubes and monitors. There was a moment during the tour when time slowed. I was looking at a premie, four pounds, attached to a plastic umbilical tube to a feeding bag. Her skin was mottled. She tried to wave her hand, but it snagged on another cord that was taped to her chest. I fought off the urge to pick her up from the little crib and hold her.

Dr. Crukshank had stopped talking and I startled, thinking I'd blown the interview. She took off her glasses, wiped them on her smock, and told me not to worry: the baby's mom comes in twice a day to hold her.

Near the end of the interview, she sat me down in her office and told me the truth—that she was nervous about me. For a second I thought I'd cry, but I held it back and told her how my dad always said to stick your chin in the thing you fear most.

She hesitated again. I told her the truth: I'll never forget my daughter, but I've buried her. She studied me, her right knee wiggling back and forth, until I thought I couldn't take it anymore. She gave me two months probation.

April 21

Snipping the orchid bush yesterday, I noticed something flitting. A yellow monarch butterfly. I haven't seen one in years. Pesticides have all but wiped them out. When I was a little girl, my father would find cocoons among the pussy willows in the backyard and snip the whole branch and put it in a big caning jar for me. I'd watch until one day I'd notice a crack in the pupal case. Hours later, an orange monarch, wet and exhausted, would squeeze from the shell. I'd take it out into the driveway and twist off the top of the jar, watching as the sun dried the butterfly's wings. Once I put my finger in and it crawled on. I held it up to the breeze and it flew away. Don't know why I think this is important.

Anyway, now, instead of a nurse, I'm a researcher. Of a sort. Maddy—Dr. Crukshank wants everything informal—she has me weighing and taking notes on the behaviors of the babies for a paper she's writing. Basically, we're trying to find out which fabrics babies of low birth weight are most comfortable

with. Maddy says their skin is so sensitive that they seem irritated by anything but the softest of covers.

Some of the parents are addicts. Maddy says I will see more
of them. I can't understand.

Chapter 13

Warm dawn light shone on the sagebrush, throwing fili-
greed shadows westward on the melting snow patches
when Farrell started driving again the next morning.
Motion soothed him after so many months in one place. He drove
for hours without rest, enjoying the rattle of the steering wheel,
the piping of his tires on the road, and the fragrance of the first
desert flowers wafting through his open window.

When a rut or frost heave in the road broke the hypnotic state,
his mind cast back to Lena's writing and he was struck by the lone-
liness between the lines. He passed the turnoff to the road that led
north to Idaho, bit at the inside of his lip, and said out loud, "I'm so
sorry." But the sort of guilt he'd experienced as a child—the awkward twist in his lower abdomen, the dryness in his mouth, and the
pressure behind his eyes—would not come; he had not felt that in
years. There was only the knot at the back of his neck again and
the twitching of his cheek.

As much as he tried to calm these tics by thinking ahead to the
steep cliffs of Lake Tahoe, he could not; Lena hovered around him
constantly and he was forced to get out of the truck once near Elko
to dispell her presence. There he stared up at the vast brooding
range of desert rock known as the Rubies, where the only skiing is
by helicopter. He considered stopping for the night to see if he

could get a ride into those mountains and lose himself in deep powder turns. Overriding this whimsy was the thought of Inez. He tried again to figure out why she used her "technique." He allowed the possibility that it jarred the skiers from ordinary thoughts before they pushed off. Too easy.

He recalled his feelings in the Y Couloir, how she had overwhelmed him, how he had wanted to crush her, how he had wanted to let her take him down into her embrace. Those same longings built within him again until he ran back to the truck. He jammed hard on the gas, squeeling his tires westward ho.

He made Reno by dusk and crossed the California line in the dark. Coming back to the state where it all happened triggered a brief spell of vertigo, which he managed to quell by leaning out the window on the road toward Truckee, a twisting four-lane that races steep, then flat through forests of thick-waisted, wind-weary trees. The balsams filled the chill night air with a prickly, seductive scent that tickled Farrell's nose until he was unsure whether to sneeze or breathe in more.

The Shady Pine Motel squatted in the middle of a row of honkey-tonk pasta joints, ski shops, and curio nooks in the center of Truckee, just a few miles from Squaw Valley. It was a low, plank wood building painted white with muted blue shutters and a dark shingled roof. Farrell parked. The street was almost deserted this late in the season. He was about to go to the office to get his key when The Wave rapped him on the shoulder with his knuckles, which caused Farrell to jump.

"Don't you ever just say hello?" Farrell hissed. "I almost crapped my pants."

"Did rap, Collins mon, right on your clavicle," The Wave said, his grin so broad that Farrell couldn't stay angry with him.

"Everyone here?" Farrell asked.

"Except Inez," The Wave said. "She's down in San Francisco meeting some German who invested in the film. She'll be back first thing in the morning. We got a meeting at seven A.M. She and Page have signed all the permission contracts to let us film. I'll tell you, from the sound of it, mon, we'll be into some hairball stuff."

"Squaw's known for big air," Farrell said.

The Wave twirled his wayward dreadlock and broke into a troubled smirk that made Farrell think he'd been smoking pot again.

"Well, the way she's talking, we'll be jumping into the iono-sphere," The Wave said.

"How's that?"

"You know her, mon. She isn't saying."

"What's the book?" Farrell asked.

The grin cracked and fell away from The Wave's lips like broken pottery. "Got into the luggage she had delivered early, looking for the files," The Wave said, handing the ledger-sized volume to him. "She must have them with her. But I did find this."

Farrell glanced at the title: *The Dividing Line: Photographs by Laurence Didier.* He tucked it under his arm. "Ann told me about this. You read it?"

"Yeah, mon," The Wave said. "Part of it anyway. Figured the way your cold eyes work, you might have special understanding, see things I don't. Drop it by the room before you sleep. I'll get it back."

"You pick the lock or break a window to get this?" Farrell asked.

"Chill out, old one," The Wave said. "No need for violence if you can avoid it. I just slipped a joint to one of the maids."

Farrell locked the door behind him and flopped belly down on the bed. The cover was a black-and-white photograph: a U.S. infantryman climbing the banks of a ravine in a jungle during a rainstorm. His thick eyebrows and sunken cheeks framed huge white eyes that stared past the camera lens, obviously past Didier, who seemed to have shot the photograph from above the soldier's thin, gnarled fingers, mud-blackened, woof to the weave of the thick, tortured roots of a tree. The soldier had the simple dignity of a man who has suffered unprotected, yet had the skill to survive. It was a mesmerizing shot.

On the inside flap at the bottom, Farrell found the title to the cover piece: *Uprooted, Mekong Delta. 1966.* It was a clear homage to Dorothea Lange, the Depression-era photographer, whose work Didier cited in the book jacket copy along with Walker Evans as "influences on my style; let the facts sing."

Farrell read the entire preface to the book, searching for clues:

Like the jobless who walked the Depression's streets years before they were born, the Vietnam combatants were mostly silent in the first years of the war. We photographers were kept away from the patrols, forced to take pictures of events after they occurred. I noticed when platoons came in from the jungle, the soldiers' bodies would still carry with them the stigma of the world beyond the barbed wire.

In 1966, I was granted permission to begin accompanying patrols regularly on forays into the Mekong Delta and the Central Highlands. During these two dozen missions I discovered a shocking, moving, elusive reality: Torn from their roots, dropped into festering jungle, the soldiers on patrol entered the dividing line, a state most of us face only once, the limbo between life and death.

I have tried to photograph men on that line, pushed to an edge they should have encountered only in old age. It was hard to photograph boys within the realm of separateness. I had to manipulate my camera to register the deep change in these soldiers—what was different, what was important—not just how miserable and scared they were, or how dangerous their predicament may have been; I was after their passion, their spirit, their will. I believe I captured some of that, revealed on the dividing line where we see people stripped to what they truly are.

At the close of Didier's preface was an editor's postscript: *"On May 17, 1969, at age thirty-five, Laurence Didier, one of the world's premier combat photographers, was killed tragically while accompanying members of the 101st Airborne Division in an assault of a ridgeline in the wilds of the A Shau Valley in the mountains west of Hue. He left behind him a wife, Claudette, a seven-year-old daughter, Inez, and a haunting vision of war that leaves the viewer breathless when you consider what he might have accomplished in a longer artistic career.*

Farrell flipped through the photographs. He thought the most powerful one was *Divergencies, south of Kien Tuong, 1967.* Didier had shot it from inside a transport helicopter, using the blackened interior as a frame to the action outside where reeds taller than a man bent away from the helicopter blade's wash in a fading plume toward a foggy tree line. A single soldier crouched to the left of the helicopter door, watching two bands of soldiers stream away to either side of the plume and disappear into the screen of vegetation the helicopter wash did not reach.

Farrell brooded over the picture. He imagined Inez reading this book, idolizing and emulating her father in the way only a child who has lost a parent can. He flipped over on his back to scrutinize the patterns on the ceiling. As a boy, locked in his room, he studied the plaster for hours, seeing vast mountain ranges, Shoshone warriors on horseback, swirling whirlpools. Tonight all he saw was Inez. Clearly she was haunted by her father and his theories. What were hers? They certainly weren't the same. She'd taken it in another direction Farrell couldn't fathom. He trudged down the walkway to The Wave's room, knocked, and when the door opened, handed the book back.

"She trying to be her daddy, or what?" The Wave asked.

"We all do," Farrell said. "But there's more."

"Yeah, what?"

"I don't know. I think we should let her lead until we figure it out. You talk to Page about any of this?"

"Not me, mon," The Wave said. "He's plenty edged after that race, hasn't said much. Anyway, I figure him for the gray corporate suit: Don't thrash in the water, you might attract sharks."

"Let's keep it that way for a while," Farrell said. "I haven't got it straight where he fits in."

The Wave ran his fingers through the spare strings of his beard. "I'm off to see my strong-legged maid friend, mon. She says she has a friend, you want to come?"

Farrell shook his head. "I need some sleep."

Back in his room, he could not find unconsciousness. He flitted in that semi-drugged world between sleep and alertness, Inez's face reappearing, her lips parting, yelling *"Go, Collins!"* until Farrell jerked awake, shivering and sweating. He breathed very fast, disoriented in the new room, until he understood it was just a bad dream. He shut his eyes, he drifted, and she appeared again. Suddenly, Inez was Gabriel, who sat in the brilliant sun on a fishing boat off the tip of Baja California. Farrell had been invited south to review the deals he'd already consummated. There had been more than twenty transactions by this time and they had become almost routine. Still, in the back of his mind was a growing anxiety; he had talked to enough of his former colleagues at the international division of the bank in Chicago to know that there was little chance of a peso devaluation. Gabriel had involved him in something he did not understand and that, more than anything, had brought him to Baja. Lena had wanted to come, but at the last minute Dr. Crukshank asked her to work.

Cordova was there on the boat with Gabriel. He hung over the side of the red Bertram 43 sportfishing boat to test the temperature of the water with his fat hands. In his dream, Farrell could see Cordova clearly. He could hear again the throb of the muscular engines and the low-frequency modulation that had pulsed up the length of his spine. He could see the sun screeching off the waves like sheets of aluminum foil. He could feel the steady sweat roll from under his baseball cap to smear his sunglasses.

They'd had no bites in the early hours. Cordova had left the deck and taken a scout's perch on the flying bridge. Emmanuel, the scrawny captain, who seemed to be patched together from pieces of overripe banana peels, stood next to Cordova. To Farrell, the juxtaposition of the two made the obese dove boy seem like some bronze fishing Buddha, searching for enlightenment through the binoculars he'd plastered to his forehead ever since they'd hit deep water.

"What's he looking for?" Farrell asked.

Gabriel stroked his finger along the thick monofilament line that stretched away from the rear of the boat. "Birds," he said. "Circling birds just above the swells. You see them like that when big fish chase bait to the surface. The birds dive to the schools to feed."

Gabriel bent to an ice chest and lifted out a frozen flying fish. He opened the fish cleanly with a knife, inserted a hook and lead weight, then, last, sewed the whole thing up in four quick loops. He reeled in the left of three poles, attached the new bait, and cast it off the side.

"Too bad we couldn't get you down here earlier," Gabriel said. "The blacks and blues tend to run in November and December. Today if we're lucky, we'll hit into stripers, not as big. But who knows? We may get lucky and strike one of the brutes that run this ridge."

Farrell fingered the pole. "You think this little rig will hold on to something that big?"

Gabriel tilted his chin up, but Farrell couldn't tell where he was looking because of the thick black sunglasses he wore. "Little rig? You could pull in a fish over three hundred kilos with that."

"It just looks too delicate to do it," Farrell said. He took a long breath. "Like our system. There's more money coming in than I expected."

Gabriel reached for another fish. "This is a problem?"

"It will be unless we can find another way to explain the sudden increase in the cash the bank has had to deposit with the Federal Reserve. I think there's too much to use the currency exchange houses any longer."

Gabriel gripped the stiff pectoral fins that enable the flying fish to glide when they leap free of the water. He pushed the heavy needle through the flapping abdominal wound, accidentally sticking himself in the finger, flinched, then pulled the needle from the finger and held it up so Farrell could see the deep magenta drip to his palm.

"I've thought of this already," Gabriel said, wrapping the finger with his handkerchief. "It can be solved through a chain of jewelry stores a friend of ours owns in Los Angeles, Orange County, and San Diego."

"Wholesale?"

"In Los Angeles," Gabriel said. "The volume of work—especially in emeralds, which have such a floating value—would account for the substantial deposits. Everything would be covered in shipments of the jewels from South America that carry an invoice claiming a much heavier weight in the gemstones."

"I don't understand."

"The money we deposit with you and which you transfer overseas is actually for emeralds, gold, and the like which will only exist on paper," he said. He cast the fish off the rear of the boat.

"That still doesn't get rid of the money that is finding its way back to my vaults."

Gabriel watched the line play out in the boat's wake until it was taut. "What would you suggest?" he asked.

Farrell paused. While he wanted to know exactly what Gabriel was up to, he didn't want to anger him. He gave him an off-handed answer in hopes that his friend would reveal himself. "Real estate," Farrell said. "It's stable and the values are changing so rapidly, a lot of money could disappear."

Gabriel cupped his hands to his brow, turned, and yelled to Jorge: *"Pajaros?"*

"Tres, quatro graviotas," Jorge grunted from behind the binoculars.

"Pity, I'd thought there were more," Gabriel said, bending to take a third fish from the box. "Okay. Move a quarter of the money into deals where short-term appreciation is likely to be substantial: anything you see in San Diego that will work. The rest we will invest at Jorge's discretion in Dallas, Houston, and Denver. These places are bust, are they not?"

"Ever since oil plunged," Farrell said.

"Good," he said. "They will make decent returns in the long run. We are in no hurry."

Gabriel did not offer more. Finally, Farrell asked: "So how long will it take to get all of your friends' money out of Mexico?"

Gabriel leaned back and sailed the third bait fish far off to the left of the boat. He turned, hands on his hips, and raised his glasses so Farrell could see his brown eyes. "Are you unhappy with your compensation?"

"No," Farrell said honestly. "I just would like to know where I'm going. This all seemed so clear when we started, but with the increased cash, it just seems murky lately."

"Murky?"

"You know," Farrell said. "Dirt in the water."

Gabriel held his palms out to Farrell and smiled. "I'm taking you where you're going," he said. "You will be a wealthy man and help many people in the process. What more is there to know?"

"A lot, I think."

Gabriel drummed his fingers on his thighs, licked his lips, then said: "You told me once that your wife believed ignorance is bliss. Perhaps she is correct."

Farrell shook his head. "Ignorance is a sleepy happiness, like a sedative. Problem is, I like exhilarants, speeds, always have."

Gabriel inspected Farrell closely. "I thought bankers are taught early not to ask too many questions."

"We are," Farrell said, coming straight back at him with the thousand-yard stare. "But silence is directly proportional to the size of the bank, the local laws, and the risk."

"So it's a question of responsibility?"

"I am the sole person in charge of the international branch."

"That you are." Gabriel paused, then seemed to speak less to Farrell than to the wind. "My fear is that you are in this to satisfy some childish need for excitement. If I make it any more than that, you may falter and I may suffer. I do not like to suffer."

"That's a penetrating analysis coming from a grown man who spends his weekends throwing himself off the side of speeding boats."

Gabriel allowed himself to smile. "Yes, yes, it is well known that we of Latin blood have this problem with the *cojones.*"

"A need to prove your manhood, perhaps?"

He made a half bow. "Something like that, but more a desire to trust only those who make a commitment the same size as mine."

"I hope this doesn't mean we're about to measure something else," Farrell said.

Gabriel laughed. "No, no *pendejos* here. But you can see my predicament. For all that you've done for us, I do not know you the way I know Jorge."

"I think you read me fine," Farrell said. "You're the mystery man."

At that moment the flying bridge creaked under the stubborn weight of Cordova, who rose from his chair as he had hundreds of times as a child to point toward flocks of birds.

"Graviotas! Cientos!" he bellowed.

Gabriel leapt to his feet and Farrell after him. Even without the binoculars they could see the birds, gray and white, reeling and diving toward the churning surface of the blue water; and over the low throb of the engines came the piggish, angry cries of birds at feast.

Emmanuel tore the wheel to port and accelerated toward the flock. Within minutes they were among them, a teeming cloud that arced and spun and screamed in frenzy. The rank, oily odor of carnivorous gulls filled the air. Farrell was pelted by crap and scraps of the flesh that had been skewered from the boil just below: hundreds of the little fish snapping their tails and dorsal fins, leaping in terrorized flight before the unseen predators, driven into tight schools where the sharp beaks accelerating above the water could stab and gorge.

"Hookup!" Gabriel roared. Now over the squawk and the chuck of the birds came the high, insistent pule of the bail gear releasing yard after yard of thick line after an insistent escaping energy.

Gabriel and Cordova, who had miraculously appeared on the deck to hold one of the dense, compact rods, dragged Farrell to the fighting chair. Cordova stuck the rod into the butt plate affixed to the seat of the chair, clipping it to a harness so it wouldn't fly out of the boat when the gear was set. He leaned over Farrell, shielding him from the sun and adjusting the harness. The dove boy's bugged achromatic eyes were level with Farrell's own. Cordova's breath was more noxious than the smell of the birds.

"Breathe through your nose with the fish," Cordova advised. "Move with him as he moves. Don't rely on the strength of your equipment; sometimes the marlin shakes free no matter how hard you've set the hook."

Farrell ground his teeth together, huffed, then sneezed in anticipation. Gabriel shouted something in Spanish to Emmanuel that Farrell couldn't make out. The tenor of the engines changed from a growl to a gurgle. Cordova reached to the bail and threw it.

The engines quieted, the rod tip slackened. The only noise was the distant cry of the birds.

Farrell was saying: "We've lost him," when the first surge came, yanking him forward in the chair, a steady, cracking tension which raced into his knees and lower back. Farrell thought, this is how the moon must command the tides.

He fought from his center against the rolling gravity, body against body, Farrell's need to see the fish against the marlin's desire to be free. On Gabriel's direction, Farrell went with the fish, pitching forward as it sounded. He drove off the foot braces, becoming a lurching, pointed source of gravity himself. The boat turned to the west, to the sun. Bombs of light burst off the ocean skin and blinded him again. Farrell shut his eyes to drop into a pure physical discourse with the fish.

He felt it change direction. He opened his eyes to trace the shining line out to starboard, there, off the bow, where the marlin had run; and he leaned back, cranking the gear. With the next pitch, the marlin, a big striper, jumped free of the water 150 yards from the boat. It twisted and snaked its spear beak around and toward the boat. Out there on the water its body crashed away and flat like the victim of a judo flip, scoring the air with flaring, silver liquid.

"Brilliant!" Cordova cried from behind his binoculars. "He almost cut the line with his spike!"

"That fish is on to stay," said Gabriel, slapping Farrell on the back. "Work him toward us."

The marlin jumped twice more in the next five minutes, but now that Farrell had seen the fish, it seemed less a primal force than a fleeting thrill, a ride to be enjoyed. When the steel leader appeared, Cordova unclipped the rod and took it from the gambal. Farrell looked at his watch: the entire struggle had lasted thirty-five minutes, far more than the ten he'd estimated. His stomach was weak and hollow. His leg muscles twitched.

"He'll go a hundred, maybe a hundred and twenty-five kilos," Cordova said, peering over the side at the marlin, whose black and blue and silver head and ebony bill protruded from the water. "A trophy."

Emmanuel nudged Farrell: "You want to keep him, señor?" he asked. "Will look good over the wall."

"I'm not a trophy man," Farrell said. "Let's just get a picture."

The captain pulled from his pocket a pair of thick, leather gloves he used to work free the hook from the marlin's jaw. Farrell leaned over the gunnel. Gabriel snapped the camera. With a quick flick of his wrist, Emmanuel freed the fish, which lolled on its side for a moment, exhausted. The next swell of the ocean revived it. The marlin brushed its great fin through the water and vanished.

"We go back for more?" Emmanuel asked.

"Later," Cordova said. "We need to rest." He and Gabriel disappeared below deck.

Farrell collapsed onto one of the cushioned benches. He replayed the marlin's leap from the water, enjoying the pleasant image that massaged his temples. The image was blurred when he thought of the fish lolling alongside the boat. Now he felt confused—he was happy that he'd landed the marlin, yet depressed that he'd seen it up close, its bill scarred from battling the sea, its scales worn to a dusky blue by age.

"People go for years and never fight that well," Gabriel said.

Farrell cracked one eyelid. Cordova stood next to him holding a tray on which were two large thermoses of coffee, hunks of brown bread, and a slab of butter. Farrell warmed to the praise and poured the coffee. Gabriel bit into a hunk of the bread, chewed it thoughtfully, and asked: "Have you ever seen a starfish?"

"In aquariums," Farrell said, sipping the pungent Mexican coffee.

"Remarkable creatures," Gabriel said. "They survive in the harshest conditions—where the waves beat the shoreline. A delicate-looking thing, but strong because it is flexible and can adapt. It can lose an arm, even two or three, and grow them back."

"We are like one of those arms," Cordova said.

Farrell took short, tight breaths, the steamy coffee creating a mask about his face, as if he were underwater, inhaling through scuba gear. "Not exactly the kind of image a man wants to go to bed with," he said.

Cordova bit into a hunk of the bread and choked, "Depends on what that arm is used for, doesn't it?"

"Maybe," Farrell replied.

Gabriel stirred more cream into his coffee. Cordova opened his mouth to speak again, but Gabriel raised his spoon and shook his head. Cordova pinched his lips together. He nodded obediently.

"Let's say, for the sake of argument, that a starfish is many things for many people," Gabriel continued. "For some it is a road out of poverty. For others, it's strictly a financial mechanism. For others, a cause."

"And for you?" Farrell asked.

"A bit of all three," he said, drinking deeply from the cup, then placing it in a holder on one of the chairs. He cocked his jaw at an angle and closed his eyes as if looking inside for a place to begin. "Have I told you much of my father?" he asked.

Farrell told him what little he remembered from their first meetings nearly two years before: that he'd been a diplomat and they'd been close.

"His name was Estefan," Gabriel said.

The boat rolled in the noontime swells. Gabriel related how Estefan Cortez y Madrid had been born into the Mexico City aristocracy in 1911, educated at Harvard and in Madrid. He entered the diplomatic corps after returning from Spain and spent the better part of his twenties and thirties in a variety of attaché postings in Los Angeles, Rome, and Paris. In Rome, he married a woman, Fortuna, who died giving birth to Gabriel.

"We were happy together," Gabriel said. "My father had mistresses, but never married again. I was raised by governesses."

When Gabriel was ten, Estefan began to change for reasons the son never fully understood. He accepted posts that required him to act as a commercial liaison between Mexico and the underdeveloped countries.

"For the first time, I think, he had to begin to confront the true economics of our region," Gabriel said. "Once he understood, he became a bitter man in many ways. He thought the future of our countries and our peoples—of Central and South America—had been ransomed."

In parts of Mexico and the other countries in which they lived, Estefan would lead Gabriel through the slums, showing him the muddy, garbage-strewn streets, the crude houses without running water, the children in threadbare clothes, the people without hope. He demanded that Gabriel study economics to understand these desperate scenes.

"At first I thought it was neglect, simple and benign, that my father had—how would you say it—gone overboard?" Gabriel smiled at the image. "After all, look at what our friend Jorge rose from—simple neglect. Then people like you, bankers from the north, came and offered cash."

"Offered is the word," Farrell said.

Gabriel nodded. "I said offered. Much was taken and much good was done. But in some ways the money was like a bribe, a payoff, so we—people like me in the wealthy class—wouldn't talk about the teeming settlements of misery sprouting all over the region. Have you ever been to the Chalco neighborhood in Mexico City?"

"No."

Gabriel turned to Cordova and pointed his index finger in the air.

"You see? All those years in Mexico and never been to Chalco."

Cordova belched in agreement. Farrell shifted uncomfortably.

"It would be nice to call it a living hell, Jack," Gabriel said. "A million people stuffed into a square mile where there was no one a decade ago. They suffered worse than all of us when the petroleum market busted and the other commodities sagged. My country and my people were left blanketed with debt."

Estefan died when Gabriel was only twenty-three, leaving him a small fortune and enough connections within the sophisticated Mexico City audience that he could have survived well enough had he the slimmest of ambitions. In business school at the University of Virginia, Gabriel met a radical economist named Perez, who had fought his way out of poverty in the slums of Lima, Peru. Perez impressed upon Gabriel that the route out of debt with the developed world was not Communism, but a capitalism as ruthless as that employed in the early part of the century by U.S. companies in countries like Nicaragua, Guatemala, Peru, Ecuador, and Mexico.

"I came back to Mexico in 1976 and began to build," Gabriel said. "We started small with redevelopment efforts, such as those which you've aided, projects that gave us enough cash to begin to explore applications for my old professor's theories."

"We?"

Gabriel patted Cordova on the shoulder. "By this time, Jorge had also finished his studies and he decided to work for me."

It was not until then that Farrell became fully aware that Cordova's eyes had not left him once during the entire conversation; the dove boy was taking note of Farrell's every reaction.

"We made many trips to the States and to Europe, talking to businesses, analyzing the markets," Gabriel continued. "We came to believe that escape is the number one desire of peoples in the developed world. One example: your countrymen spend millions, billions of dollars on the cinema every year."

Gabriel stood, his hand at his brow, looking out to sea.

"But the entertainment business is locked tight," he said. "We were going nowhere, nowhere until one day almost a decade ago. It hit me. The Colombians and the Peruvians had the answer."

There it was, what Farrell had suspected, feared and anticipated all along. Seeing it twist there in the open, as if it were hooked at the end of a line, released some long-held tension in Farrell. He relaxed into a waking dream. "I knew the story about rich Mexicans didn't wash."

"I would have been disappointed had you not at least suspected," Gabriel said. "In the early 1980s, Jorge and I set up transportation links on the coast north and south of Manzanillo and in several coves and landing strips here on Baja. When the federal authorities cracked down on South Florida six or seven years ago, we were ready."

"So you work for them?" Farrell asked, fully aware how melodramatic the question sounded.

Cordova sniffed. "We work for no one but ourselves. We lease to whoever needs our equipment and services," he said. "Despite what you read, there is little in the way of centralized organization. Everyone who does what we do is freelance. We stay far, far away from production and distribution. We know how it works, but I've never had to move a brick of white powder and I pray I never will."

"How do I fit into this?"

"New services," Gabriel said. "Our friends are in almost constant need of ways to invest and move their profits. We do it, take our cut, and put it to our own use—the hotels in Mexico City, the trading companies in Chiapas and Houston, the factories in Tijuana."

Farrell pinched the bridge of his nose between his thumb and forefinger. "Let me get this straight: you fancy yourself some kind of Robin Hood, robbing from the rich Americans and giving jobs to the poor Mexicans."

"You needn't be sarcastic," Gabriel said. He yanked his sunglasses off and crossed his arms across his chest. "I'd never presume to be the leader of a personality cult. We do what we do for reasons beyond greed and ego, though we take our shares and live well. I am no saint, my friend. I believe *Madre* Teresa is nothing more than a jail warden in a white robe. I'm interested in getting these people out, not comforting them with words."

There, in the middle of the sea, as far out as one can get into the open on a day's warning, Farrell was seized with a severe fit of claustrophobia. He had the urge to dive into the ocean, to swim until he came to shore or relaxed easily down into the water. He gaped at Gabriel; it was the first time he'd ever seen him truly angry. And he thought about drowning and the fact that they say that once you are past the first unpleasant gagging gulps, drowning is a pleasant experience; you struggle for a moment, your lungs fill and you drift with the tides.

Against this picture, there arose in Farrell a strange, dangerous, and yet wonderful feeling of cross-purposes that he had never known before: there was the crash of jeopardy and moral muddiness; there was the stark idea that he was now in some remote manner a drug runner; and there was Gabriel's argument that this reviled activity had an admirable purpose beyond profit. All these things melded together to leave him in a daze.

"What do your clients think of your business?" Farrell asked.

"What's there to think?" Cordova said. "They know nothing of what we do with our profits, nor do they care. We know that some of them do similar things in the mountain villages down south, providing schools and clinics. Whether they tend for their people or not is not our concern."

"You've put me at great risk," Farrell said.

"You've put yourself at great risk," Gabriel said.

"I wasn't aware of all the facts," Farrell said.

"You want out?" Cordova asked in a way that made Farrell realize there was no way out.

"I didn't say that," Farrell replied. "But I tend to measure these kinds of risk with profit. More risk, more profit."

Gabriel and Cordova looked at each other for a long moment until Gabriel nodded. "This is negotiable."

The sky seemed bluer, less metallic, and Farrell found himself enchanted with his situation. He was an eager six-year-old who'd been given a bow and arrow over his mother's objections.

Farrell pointed out to sea. "I think I see birds circling." Gabriel and Cordova smiled and shifted their bodies to follow the stretch of his arm to the horizon.

A car horn sounded in the parking lot, snapping Farrell from his dream. The alarm clock said midnight. He stumbled to the bathroom, reliving the giddiness he'd felt returning to the harbor that afternoon. He had been as excited and as shamed as a boy who'd just stolen his first candy bar. Part of him still clung to the belief that he could somehow get himself out of the relationship at any time, cut his losses, return home without ever revealing his secret life.

As they had bounded over the swells to the dock, Farrell had one fleeting surge of panic when he thought of Lena. Farrell climbed back into bed remembering that deep down he had known he was putting her in danger. A heaviness came upon him when he forced himself to face the fact that he had ignored her perspective, that he had pushed on in the anticipation of personal thrills. The invisible weight grew heavier and pressed on his chest and behind his eyes. It hung about the muscles in his neck. For a moment he told himself it was exhaustion. In the darkness he finally realized that the sensation wasn't fatigue, but something he hadn't allowed himself to feel in many, many years: remorse.

Chapter 14

Farrell dreamed he was back in San Diego on Windandsea beach in the late afternoon. Moist sand filled the gaps between his toes like grainy paste. Lena knelt next to a faraway, wind-weathered rock. Her back was to him and she worked at a small bundle. He jogged to her. Punta and Rabo dashed out from behind the boulder, haunches low, hackles raised, teeth bared and salivating. Lena twisted into the sun, her hand at her brow. Farrell called to her, but she didn't seem able to hear. She grabbed a piece of driftwood and beat it against the rock, the sound melding with the pounding of the surf and the barking of the dogs into thunder.

He came awake with a start unsure of where he was, then groggily aware that someone was pounding on the door to the motel room. He jumped up, still half-asleep, aware of light and color, not really seeing, and wrenched the door open. He leaned against the transom to clear the fog. The Wave laughed and Inez said: *"Oooh. Quel image!"*

Farrell was naked with an early-morning erection. He snapped backward and dove for the blankets. Inez covered her mouth with her hand. The Wave wiped tears from his eyes. Even Page slapped his thigh.

"Do you always burst in on people like this?" Farrell yelled. He was less angry at them than himself because he realized he was embarrassed that Inez had witnessed his predicament.

"We waited almost an hour for you," Inez said. *"Mais,* from your appearance, you expect someone else, no?"

"Yeah, the abominable snow girl," Farrell snapped.

"That fits," Page said. "You on a date with the missing link."

"Shut the door, please."

The Wave stepped forward. "Wish you had the camera now, Inez?"

Inez smiled seductively at Farrell. "What a shot."

"Shut the door!" Farrell yelled.

Twenty-minutes later, the entire crew was gathered around a map spread on a restaurant table. Page's cheeks were covered with red and purple scabs from the scrapes he'd gotten at the bottom of the Y Couloir.

"You been up on Squaw before?" he asked Farrell in an icy voice.

"Once about twelve years ago," Farrell said, trying to ignore Page's obviously hard feelings. "Came to a patrol seminar. I remember some of it."

Page pointed to some cliffs at the top of the mountain. "I'll take you out on the hill in an hour or so to see what kind of shape you're in. I want to see you fly before you try the Palisades."

Farrell squeezed his fist under the table; Page knew the area better than he did, but after Gabriel, he didn't like being under anyone's control.

"The cliffs are more mental than technical," Page went on. "With the Chimney, one of the four lines we'll run on the Palisades, you drop through a five-foot opening straight down for forty feet, then it breaks out from under you and you drop another seventy to a wide run-out."

"Watermelon out the seventh-floor window," The Wave whistled.

"It's deceptive," Page said. "You're really only a few feet off the snow the whole time, so there's no real impact to speak of. But you'll touch down at sixty plus."

"We'll need downhill skis," Farrell said. "Minimum two hundred and twenty centimeters."

"All taken care of," Page said. "As I said before, when I go up the hill, I have every intention of coming down in one piece."

"Lead on," Farrell said with as much sarcasm as he could muster.

Page shrugged the comment off and ran his finger across the map to a second peak. "With any luck we'll do the Main Line pocket in the afternoon. It's steep and covered with rocks, really the most extreme thing up here."

Inez said: "You fall this much as off the Palisades, no?"

"Similar," Page said. "But you'll get better light for the cameras. The Palisades is rarely in the sun. Here on the Mainline, there will be great color and contrasts with the copper rocks for background."

Ann said: "When do we start shooting?"

"I push up the schedule," Inez said. "Tomorrow morning."

"Jesus," Page said, surprised by the announcement. "It will take a couple of days just to get our legs under us after the race."

Inez lit a cigarette. "I speak to my backers since two days ago. They want the rough cut of the film by the end of June, mid-July at the latest. They want to be out on the circuit by early October. *Alors,* we push."

"But—" Page began.

"We push," Inez insisted. "Tomorrow and Friday here, then we leave for Jackson Hole. Then Ranier and, depending on weather, McKinley."

"Too much, too soon," The Wave said.

Inez blew out a blue ring of smoke. "I decide what is too much, too soon. Ann and Tony come with me to prepare the gear. I suggest you three get out on that mountain for the practice."

Inez got up, ending whatever protests they might have. As she walked out, Farrell tried to figure out if there were other reasons she'd want to push them so hard, so fast. For a brief moment he entertained the idea that she was somehow connected to Gabriel, then discarded it as ludicrous. Gabriel dealt swiftly. He did not take slow revenge. Inez, she had her own secret designs.

The Wave opted to practice on the steeps below the KT-22 Chair. Page and Farrell caught a cable car, and a few minutes after ten, they swung past Broken Arrow Peak into the crisp, glorious sunshine. Page turned his back to Farrell. Below the cable car a web of structural steel lift-line cables hung and Farrell thought that, at age thirty-three, his tolerance for formal ski areas was ebbing. To stay financially solvent, the resorts had to erect so many lifts they'd scarred the natural beauty of the mountains. Alta was one of the few places left that retained a sense of wilderness. He moved to the right side of the car as they crossed Broken Arrow to gaze off into the terrain north of the ski valley. He thought of Lena and how he'd kept her in the dark for so long. He pinched his chest muscle. When Portsteiner had warned him about the cold heart in motion, he didn't believe in angina. Now he did.

Out on the hill, the downhill skis rode differently than the giant slalom and slalom boards he'd used every day since he'd arrived in snow country almost four months ago. He and Page set the big skis on edge and let them run, their weight and length absorbing and muffling the ripples, gullies, and mounds in the snow.

"A Rolls-Royce ride," Farrell said, thinking out loud. He picked spots far away, sped toward them, then, like a bobsledder, banked the skis and pressed the outside of the arc. The skis gathered speed. Farrell drew his lips back, exposing his teeth, delighted at the wind's ginger taste and its deafening whistle.

By the third run they were warmed up. Page was civil, but still clearly ticked off at him. He pointed out the Direct Chute on Granite Chief Peak, where they'd be skiing in two days, and the rock outcroppings where Inez was likely to place Ann and Tony with the cameras. They dropped into the basin below Emigrant Peak, rode the Mainline chair, and considered the Pocket, a series of narrow tubes walled with sheer granite, followed by the moody, north-facing Palisades themselves, stark cliffs cast in perpetual shadow.

Riding the lift for the fourth time that day, Farrell tried to study the four lines of descent they'd be likely to take down the Palisades. Instead, he thought of the fall he and Page had taken. Farrell lifted his ski pole and scrapped away snow that had accumulated near the toe piece of his binding.

He said: "Look, I want to apologize for acting crazy in the Y. It could have gone bad. I regret it."

Page cocked his chin away from Farrell. "The way I figure it, we don't have to be close on a slope anytime soon, so you don't matter."

"I said I regret it," Farrell said.

"I only trust what I can see."

"You trust what you see here, I mean you grew up here, right?" Farrell asked, trying to steer the conversation away from himself.

Page craned his head back toward the lake. "Seven years since I was here last and it's pretty much the same. California is Tahoe."

"How's that?"

"Pioneering spirit, greed, perversity, weirdness, it all took root in the Sierra Nevada," Page said. "You've got thousands of people swarming these hills in the mid-1800s, searching for gold. You've got the Donner party eating each other in the snow. Now it's hundreds of thousands pulling the one-armed bandits on the south side of the lake. They just recently busted the mayor for running coke."

"That surprises you?"

"Not me," Page said. He rolled his head back until it made a light popping noise. "The average person in California lives in what they call a 'unit' of say eight hundred square feet, while the newspapers display ads for garish pink mansions. Every day Mr. Joe drives to work in a beat-up Chevy or an old Honda. He's passed on the freeway by BMWs and Ferraris. And the streets are packed with women with impossibly hard bodies."

Farrell nodded. "Odds are against sanity."

They skied across the Siberia Bowl to a catwalk below the Palisades. Page looked at the stark cliff walls. "Even though you see them in the movies all the time, they're bigger than you think."

Farrell thought about the weightlessness such a drop would create. He smiled.

Page pointed at a scar in the middle of the cliff. "About ten years ago, I saw a guy come flying out of that chute there going sixty miles an hour. He couldn't see this ice ledge in the flat light and he got nailed: twenty-six stitches in the gash on his legs the skis made wind-milling him."

"Shit."

"You don't want to miss at all up here. You'll get Inez's peek through the hands."

They took another lift up the hill. Farrell asked, "This the side of the lake you grew up on?"

"The other side, near Heavenly," Page said. "Big difference, really. Here the skiing is steep and relentless, which requires concentration and a quiet nightlife. South side, it's pretty flat, so you need the honkey-tonk casinos and flashy clothes to cover up how boring the skiing really is."

"Your family still here?"

Page pursed his lips and crossed his arms.

"Mother is. Father, I don't know. Don't care."

Page swung his skis in the air underneath the chair. Farrell observed him out of the corner of his eye. He wanted to trust Page. But he figured it was unlikely Page would trust him. He decided to keep quiet about the book The Wave had found. Steep faces of the mountain towered all about them. Farrell idly wondered what Inez had in store for them. He smiled again.

Near the top of the lift, Page nudged Farrell and waved toward a steep rock wall on the ridge to their left. "They call it Adrenaline," he said. "Big drop. You game to see how these boards will handle it?"

"The unexamined life isn't worth living," Farrell said.

"Who said that?" asked Page.

"Damned if I know," Farrell laughed. "It's all this talking with The Wave. You start remembering bizarre quotes."

Page broke into his own laugh. "The kid's kind of looney tune, isn't he?"

A thick stand of spruce trees fringed the upper-right-hand lip of Adrenaline Rock. Farrell asked Page about stumps hidden under the snow at the bottom of the stone wall. Page said with the snow base at more than 130 inches, any stump or rock was buried at least three feet under. Still, they decided to ski below the cliff just to make sure. They found that, although the light was flat, the snow was still deep and unconsolidated; if they timed it right, the landing would be soft and easy.

On top again they crossed to the backside of the ridge to a saddle above Adrenaline. Page said because of the shadows, the best bet was to hug the trees, then break to the rock at an angle.

"There's a lip on it you can't see that will kick you into the air," Page said. "But the formation itself juts out a bit below the takeoff, so you'll want to drive out into space and drop your tips almost immediately."

"You go first," Farrell said. He skied along the fringe of trees to where he could see the stone ledge and the landing zone.

Page dropped very quickly through two arcs—his head cocked left so he could examine the takeoff zone with his good eye—veed his skis to control his speed, then set them together and raced straight at the rock. He hit the lip and rose like smoke, effortless; his body wafted forward; his loose, red anorak flapped in the breeze; his skis floated side to side.

"I'll be damned," Farrell said. He could see that Page had entered the state of "flow," where experts presented with a challenge stretch to the limits of their capabilities. Though he had entered the state only briefly on several occasions, Farrell loved the experience. In flow, time stops, unforeseen unities are revealed, the brain fires in rapid, even bursts. People in the chair lift gasped and pointed at Page. Farrell nodded; for both the participant and the audience, flow was the ultimate stunt—a conscious, yet unconscious, escape from reality. Page's flight over Adrenaline was clear, extended, and stable, an African gazelle in the full stretch of its bound.

When he was twenty feet from the ground, Page relaxed his hips and let his deer legs reach for the slope. He hit, drew his knees back to his center, and froze for a split second in a deep crouch. He sprang from it, up and out, pell-mell, to swallow the last fifty yards of the hill in five turns.

Farrell skied down to him and slapped him on the back. "That was incredible."

"I was up there forever," Page gasped. He swallowed and sucked for air again. "When I came over the front, I almost crapped for a second because I couldn't tell how the slope changed. I held on, though, and about halfway down my eye got wide and I could see it all, every crystal in the snow, every grain in the rock coming up at me. The skis absorbed perfectly; no need to lay your hip into it at all."

Twenty minutes later, Farrell stood above Adrenaline. For a moment he considered backing away. Usually these moments of anticipation yielded a calm, lucid screen. Not this time. Faced with the possibility of true escape, the odd weight of the evening before returned. His head turned jittery, like one of those old silent movies, every frame kicking the next, herky-jerky. In every one of those blips on the screen he saw his wife and he realized he hadn't really known her.

Farrell twisted his body left and right to rid himself of the feeling that would not yield. He told himself to just go, that fleeing into the unknown would offer relief. He forced his eyes open much wider than normal, snow-plowed the skis, then, just as Page had done, pulled them together and let them skim to the rock. The snow bulge at the edge of the cliff chucked him high into the air. He hadn't expected to be thrown so far and he gagged. His arms and legs curled toward his trunk. He fell in the fetal position.

It had been years since Farrell had sailed off something that tall. He knew that, as a matter of course, there's a shrieky list of things that races through your mind when you go over the invisible hump in the air and accelerate downward; you pray a gust of wind will not blow you sideways and crunch you; you pray that your ski tips stay parallel to the slope and do not invert; you pray that the landing is smooth and not strewn with stones.

All those responses were familiar. This retreat response—coiling up like a baby, desperate to be back on the rock instead of barreling into the air—was new and terrifying. Sure, there had always been before an instant of pure fear, then the flood of chemicals through the veins and the wicked, blazing smile as he glared the future down. Now, in those snap moments above Adrenaline, dread of the unknown slapped Farrell hard across the mouth. He panicked. He dropped like a bomb.

If his innate will to survive hadn't taken over in the last seconds, he'd have been a goner. He kicked his legs out and forward. He smacked the ground like a plank tossed carelessly from the roof of a house under construction. The muscle in his groin tugged. His balance was thrown. He ripped along at fifty, back on the tails of his skis, struggling for control. Gravity, old bear's friend and enemy, had him. He stabbed at the snow with his poles, thrust his hands forward, tried every trick he knew to recapture his stance.

Soft, dense snow did him in. It grabbed at the inside edge of his uphill ski and knocked him over as casually as a paper cup in a gale. He did two flips and landed on his back. He came to rest facedown in the snow, wondering how the hell he'd gotten out of that alive.

He was digging the snow out of the nape of his turtleneck when

Page skied up. "By all rights it should be dark right now," Farrell said, his voice shaking. "It's never happened before. Never."

Page clicked out of his bindings. He knelt next to Farrell.

"There was nothing wrong with that jump, Collins," Page said. "You punched the takeoff. Sure, the landing was shaky, but in the air I couldn't have done better myself."

Farrell trembled. "This was different. I'm going down before I hurt myself."

"What do I tell Inez?" Page asked. "Are you in or out for tomorrow?"

"I don't know what I am," Farrell said and he skied away in shaky, snow-plow turns.

Farrell paced in his room in a failed effort to soothe himself. He doused his face in cold water. Nothing helped. He'd always been able to shove his experiences and memories in separate little compartments. Now the walls were breaking down. The past was mixing with the present in ways that he did not understand, in ways that tortured him. He grabbed his jacket. He needed to move.

The narrow road to South Lake Tahoe leaves Tahoe City under a canopy of tall firs; it hugs the shore through small villages and around pristine inlets; after ten miles, it climbs into Placer County through a series of switchbacks and hairpin turns above a bank that gives way for a thousand feet to the water of Emerald Bay. Two hours before sunset, Farrell arrived at the locked gate to the Eagle Point Park, which sits on a cliff that juts a quarter mile out over the water. He parked the truck off the road behind some trees. In a drawer in the back he found the binoculars in case he wanted to examine the mountainsides. With the hands of an arthritic, he reached for Lena's diary. He did not want to read it, but he had no choice; the past was buffeting him like a high wind. He locked the camper and set off up the path toward the tip of Eagle Point. Farrell sat on a log, trying to reassure himself that his center would hold.

Tahoe's water was the color of Lena's irises, Farrell thought. He changed his mind and decided cynically that the water was a darker green like the Swiss papers that arrived on his desk at least once a week after his trip to Baja. He remembered how the sheaves crinkled, how they'd snapped like fresh ten-dollar bills between his fingers. He'd lock his door when the documents arrived. He'd read them for accuracy, then punch three holes in the pages and insert them in the black binder which he secreted in the back of his credenza. Some days, he'd examine the arc of his activities and find himself shifting unconsciously in his chair like a five-year-old waiting for recess. There was an aroma that seethed from the green sheets, an acrid fume of some European chemical agent the gnomes in Zurich and Basel used to seal the ink. Perhaps it was his imagination, but Farrell remembered that when the ledger lay open on his desk, he smelled swimming pools on summer days. Once he held the pages in a bunch, flipping through them quick, front to back, so that the line of zeros in the lower-right-hand corner of the stack seemed to pulse to the Latin beat of his secret life.

In a second binder, he kept copies of his terse orders to attorneys in distant countries, of wire transfers to the Grand Cayman accounts, to banks in Panama and Guatemala and Vanuatu and on. With each new piece of paper came the immediate rush of knowing he'd beaten the odds, that he had risked and won. Farrell got a kick out of examining the telegrams, the computer printouts, and the various deeds, loan documents, and warrants that detailed the assets of Bahia Vision, Inc., the company he had organized to channel the illegal profits of Gabriel's clients into legitimate investments. Between June 1986 and December of that year, Bahia Vision purchased a thirty-two-unit condominium development in Midlothian, Texas; a controlling interest in a shopping mall off Route 20 toward Tyler, Texas; 243 acres of commercial land near Englewood, Colorado; and ownership and development rights on four separate parcels totalling 225 acres of property southeast of San Diego along the U.S.-Mexico border. Total value: $16.5 million.

Of all the deals, the land buys along the San Diego border with Tijuana intrigued Farrell most. The thousands of desolate acres there had been talked about as a free-trade city between the two countries for so long that Farrell knew he could have bottled the saliva that had dripped from speculators' mouths over the years and watered his lawn with it until 1995.

Every parcel on Otay Mesa had flipflopped its way through dozens of hands in the previous decade, which made it almost impossible to know who owned what and why. By the time Farrell closed the second deal, he knew that an investigator would have as much success using a divining rod as parcel records to do a competent title search on the properties.

Into that dirt poker game, Farrell dumped first $2 million, then another $4 million, then $2.5 million. He watched the money seep into the dun border soil. Invisible. All but untraceable.

On the days when he consummated these deals, he'd surged with confidence. Six months after the fishing trip, Jim Rubenstein praised Farrell for how well he was running his division. He gave Farrell a raise and a bonus. In the meantime, Farrell stashed several hundred thousand dollars in his secret account. He would look at the new balance printed by some computer far off in Zurich and a warm feeling would surround him. He imagined that an athlete seeing a photograph of himself in action would feel the same way; it was an echo of the true experience. At home, he showered Lena with gifts: bracelets and clothes and a white BMW sedan. At the dinner table, he prattled like a hophead over the intricacies of his latest deal. He drank too much and giggled when Lena had to lead him to his bed.

Between deals, however, when he was breaking no new ground, Farrell became bored. Worse, the illegality of his activities gnawed at him. The symptoms were subtle: his knee vibrated under his desk; he bit at his fingernails until the quicks were raw; a tic developed under his right eye, knots formed between his shoulder blades. On those days, he left work early, got his scuba gear, and swam in the ocean. Down a fathom or more, he'd flip over on his back and float, staring at the orange sunbeams that reached him in the depths.

Farrell looked at the green waters of Lake Tahoe and thought about the fact that, in the early stages of their disease, alcoholics and addicts will deny the power of their habit. They will believe in the truth of a fabricated world. This will continue, warping everything around them, until a rock smashes the glass of lies.

Farrell wrapped his arms around himself as if he were wearing a straitjacket. He thought it somehow fitting that babies were the rocks that shattered his illusions.

November 28, 1987

I broke a glass tonight. It fell in the kitchen. Pop! It made me think of Elizabeth. It's been nine months since I've started here, nine months and now we see them every day like Elizabeth, these little junkie babies.

Only three weeks old. Heroin. She needs so much liquid to get through withdrawal that she's peed herself into second-degree burns.

Day one she shook and twisted like an 80-year-old with Parkinson's. Even today she tremors when she sucks at the bottle. In the past week she's bucked her knees and elbows so often against the sheet that she's worn her skin away. Her legs and arms are raw, fitful, and angry, as if it were possible to develop colic on the flesh.

We got a water bed for the babies last month and Maddy says they seem calmed by the warm water under their bellies. Maybe it reminds them of the womb. Maybe it reminds them of when they had a steady fix.

Elizabeth's twin, Antonia, died on day two. The first and only question of Lydia, their mother, was if their fingers and toes were all there? Lydia is exactly twenty-eight, my age, and she frightens me because I wonder if such an anonymous common denominator as the number of years on Earth we share makes me capable of being Lydia.

Elizabeth, her daughter, is six pounds now. Her hair is brown and her skin fair. I hold her in my arms and try to get her to rotate her head in the direction of my voice. Healthy babies can do this in seconds. Elizabeth's quaking eyes come to me in half a minute and she closes them, exhausted.

How much better it would be for Elizabeth that Lydia screw up the next time she wants to put a needle in her arm and leave a bubble in the needle. Pop!

Why can't I arrange that? Pop!

But I can't think like that, just can't.

Farrell looked up from the pages. The weight on his shoulders had returned. It was heavier now and had sharper angles. He had felt awkward and dull when he discovered who Lena's patients were. He did everything he could to suppress the thought that he was somehow responsible. He chose to dwell on the thrills he was getting.

One night Lena forced him to look in the mirror. It was early December. They sat in their living room before a roaring fire while rain pelted the windows. Punta and Rabo lay on the rug and snored.

"The government should go after them, put them away," Lena said.

"People will get it one way or the other," Farrell said, shifting uncomfortably. "And you're being a hypocrite, considering."

"I've smoked pot and, yes, we used cocaine a few times," Lena said. "What did we know then? Look what I know now: dozens of them every day in every hospital in the city."

A distance opened between them. Farrell imagined it was the day before and he was out scuba diving; Lena was on the surface leaning over the side of the boat talking to him. He could see her lips moving, but her voice was muffled.

Farrell yawned nervously. "I'm tired. Can't we talk about something else?"

"I always have to hear about your latest deal. But you never want to hear what happens to me."

"That's not true. It's just the talk of hospitals makes me jumpy."

"Some of the people you work with make me jumpy."

"Name one."

"That man, Cordova. He's the eeriest person I've ever met."

Cordova had come to the house the week before for dinner. Farrell and the dove boy had been in Houston to pass papers on a small apartment complex. Cordova decided to return with him for a night before flying back to Mexico City. At the time it had seemed a perfectly normal thing to do. Farrell thought that, in retrospect, Cordova may have had ulterior reasons. Had he been checking up on my home life?

"You just don't like him because he's fat," Farrell had told Lena.

"That has nothing to do with it," she said. "He has a strange way of looking just to the right or left of you when you are speaking."

"It's probably just the glasses. He doesn't see well without them."

"It's not his vision. I, well I . . . got the feeling he knows what I look like without makeup. I just don't want him here anymore."

"So now I can't have one of my most important clients to my house?"

"Take him to a restaurant."

"Fine. Who are we going to have to our house? One of your little shaking babies?"

Lena's mouth hung open.

"I shouldn't have said that . . ." Farrell said. "I . . ."

Lena had already walked from the room.

Farrell held his head in his hands, feeling the breeze pick up out on the lake. How could he have been so cold? He opened the diary.

December 5

Jack's been sleeping on the couch the past few nights. Nothing said, just agreed upon. Sometimes he's like a picture in a magazine ad; after a while it becomes familiar, but you don't know who the model really is.

He leaves tomorrow for Mexico. His last long trip of the year. I tried to make his leaving as smooth as possible, but after two or three glasses of wine I couldn't help bringing up Elizabeth again. I watch her and the other kids and don't know what to do. She's going home tomorrow. Child Protective Services say Lydia's agreed to go into rehab and the baby should go with her. She's her mother after all. I tried to tell Lydia today that Elizabeth is different, that the drugs make her too sensitive. Lydia just smiled. She tickled Elizabeth's little toes and fingers, torture for this kind of baby. It went on and on until Elizabeth threw her hands in front of her face as if to say, No more!

Lydia told me her baby was waving at her. I just turned away and prayed for Elizabeth.

Jack seemed to listen, but didn't. When I pressed him, he slammed his hand on the table, yelling at me that we had one last night together. Why couldn't we talk about something other than "those warped little kids."

He was that model in the magazine ad again. I screamed back that I had to talk about Elizabeth because it's what I see every day, not little bank account slips. Real people.

I don't know what has gone wrong with us. Maybe time apart is what we need. As awful as it sounds, I'm thankful he will be away.

A chipmunk chattered on the end of the log a few feet from Farrell's head. He watched it scamper under a branch and stare out at him with big brown eyes. Farrell tried to feel happiness at such a sight, but couldn't. He remembered how leaving the house that next morning had been like stepping into a spring rain. He could breath again. Sitting there on the cliff over Tahoe, Farrell experienced a ruthless pressure where his jaw met his skull. His eyes seemed ready to float. He realized he was grieving. Farrell stood before tears could form. He lifted the binoculars to his eyes, scanning the water and the mountainsides in an effort to still his head with the awe of late winter landscapes.

"Snowfields exposed daily to the sun are receding on the south-facing slopes," he mumbled. "Shale rock splintering into tiny chunks dislodge and roll into a ravine two hundred yards above the road. Perhaps they break away from the melting water or maybe an animal I can't see has triggered the slide."

It was comforting to think that somewhere above him, blacktail deer and sheep and coyotes and bear moved within the forest. Dusk settled around him now and in the waning light of day, the breeze strengthened, blew steady from the northwest, and puffed white caps. Farrell turned to it, enjoying the force, the crispness and within it the smell of the lake, fresh and yet ancient, like a woman after her bath.

Far below him on the lake road, a brown truck swung through the turns and switchbacks. At the bay, the road climbed in a gradual spiral from about 200 feet above the water to almost one thousand feet at the point where Farrell stood. Farrell trained the binoculars on the truck, tracking its course from almost a mile away.

Page was driving the truck, alone, bobbing his head to some local radio station. As the truck began the final ascent to the point, Farrell lost sight of the vehicle. He tracked it by the high whine of the gears which now cut the quiet scene. The truck bucked and groaned as Page downshifted by the entrance to the park. The tires crunched through the gravel and salts left by the winter snowplows and were gone.

Another vehicle, this one smaller, a blue Nissan sedan, moved into the spiral. Again Farrell watched through the binoculars. Inez was driving, her fingers firm on the wheel, advancing the car at a steady forty-five miles an hour, as if she did not want to gain on Page until it was necessary. In the last light of day, Farrell got a good look at her through the windshield: she was massaging her throat.

Farrell scrambling back through the brush and the rotting spring snow toward the truck. "Looks like someone's playing crack the whip," he told himself, "and I'm going to be at the tail end of it."

By the time he reached the truck, Farrell could barely hear the screech of the loose fan belt on Inez's Nissan as it coursed the road to the south of the point. A pitch, moonless night had fallen when he passed through the spruce flat on the road to South Lake Tahoe. Every few moments the red taillights of Inez's car would flicker and fade around a bend in the road, which widened, accommodating homes, motels, and restaurants.

They turned left on Route 50 toward the Nevada line and the traffic built. Farrell had a difficult time staying far back enough from Inez that she would not recognize his truck and yet still keep her in sight. He was seven cars behind her when he saw her signal blink. She made a right turn next to a bagel store. He followed, struggling to adjust to the dark street after the neon blare of the main strip. Inez was three blocks ahead of him when she stopped so suddenly Farrell had to slam on his brakes and spin the truck into an alley.

He turned off the headlights. He slipped from the truck with the binoculars. Crossing the alley into a yard, Farrell crouched behind a tree twenty-five yards from Inez. She had the window down and was watching a house a block away. Farrell trained the binoculars in the same direction, seeing Page's truck parked in front of a green cottage, the arched roof of which tilted well-off center. Paint strips hung from the clapboards. The yard was dominated by a bulky black car, vintage 1950s, which squatted on cement blocks next to a sagging picnic table and a rusted weight set.

No lights shone in the dwelling save a single glaring bulb on the front porch. Page appeared from around the side of the house near the old car. He mounted the front steps, and standing rigid, he knocked. Inez leaned out of the window to see better.

Page hunched over his knee and scribbled in a notebook. He stood, ripped out a piece of paper, and placed it between the battered screen door and the frame. He pivoted, walked out into the street, and did a slow 360-degree turn with his hands on his hips. He paused twice during the turn as if he were examining every tree limb and front porch on the street.

Without looking back, Page strode to the truck and climbed in. Inez laid down in the front seat of her car. Afraid of being caught in Page's headlights, Farrell sprinted back across the yard and into the dark alley. He waited to start up the camper until Inez had turned around and followed Page.

Farrell lost them in heavy traffic toward the state line. Inez's car was eight ahead of his when the light changed yellow, then red. She sped through after Page, leaving Farrell to watch their tail-lights recede up the slight grade toward the flash of the casinos. He rapped on the steering wheel. What was she up to? Why was she following Page? Then it hit him. *She keeps files.* But why?

Farrell knew he risked exposure if he blindly drove up the crowded strip to look for them. It had to be done. If he were caught, he could plead the plausible—he'd come to Tahoe to gamble.

Farrell kept the truck in first gear, double shifting through the parking lots in back of the casinos. After nearly a half hour of searching, he pulled into the rear lot of the High Sierra Casino, a three-acre affair that held hundreds of cars. Page pushed through the service entrance door to the casino. Farrell panicked; if he could see Page, Inez was close by. He threw the truck in reverse, punched the light switch off, and backed the truck as far into the rear of the lot as he could.

It took him almost ten minutes of searching with the binoculars in the cold dark, listening to the pounding at his temples, to spot Inez's car. The Nissan was about twenty rows forward and slightly off to his right. If she knew Farrell was there, she didn't show it.

An hour passed before Page emerged with a woman almost his height, who wore the white shirt and tan jumper of a banquet wait-ress. Her hair was strawberry blond, streaked with silver, twisted into a long braid and tied off with a red ribbon. Page touched the squared, once-lovely face of the woman, touched her high on the cheekbones. She shrugged away, hugging her own shoulders. It could have been the awkward lighting, but Farrell swore that her face was bruised.

They talked. At one point, Page raised his hands to his ears, then threw them out and to his side and took a few steps away. The woman reached out her hand to him, her entire upper body leaning toward Page. She stroked his neck and he flinched, but his legs didn't move. Farrell wanted to put the binoculars down, but he couldn't. He was watching the scene with the strange melange of titillation and embarrassment he'd endured when he and some teenage friends had leered in the window of a local bank teller who enjoyed making love with her bedroom drapes open and the lights on.

At last, Page held the woman's hands. He leaned his face to hers and kissed it. Even from so far away, Farrell could tell she cried. Page trudged down the stairs to his truck, waved once, and drove off.

Farrell expected Inez to follow, but she didn't. Farrell remained behind, too, watching the watcher, until she slid from her car and passed through the service entrance.

Twenty minutes later the same woman followed Inez out of the door. Inez smiled and laughed and shook the woman's hand. To the ordinary observer it would have seemed an easy meeting. Something about it bothered Farrell. He watched closely through the binoculars. Sure enough, when the woman turned and disappeared through the door, Inez's entire body language changed: she slouched; she swung her loose right hand in a series of circles in the air; and her smile—so animated a moment before—faded completely. But that didn't describe it. There was something else. He tried to figure it out as he waited in the parking lot after she'd left. The words would not come. It was not until he was driving back to the north side of the lake that he got it: Inez's entire face had virtually melted away; he had never seen anyone so devoid of expression. What haunted him throughout the rest of the drive was the fact that seeing her like that, so cold and plastic, turned him on.

Chapter 15

arrell slept fitfully that night, his dreams a mash and roll of fragmented memories, specters, and pangs in the gut. Inez was there, her face and hands like soft clay, capable of being shaped into whatever Farrell wanted her to be. First she was the powerhouse saleswoman he'd met in the Jacuzzi back in Utah. She mutated into the obsessed director taunting him from her helicopter. Her clothes melted away and she was nude and on film. Finally, the planes of her face softened into those of Maria Robles. Farrell groaned.

He sweated the sheets dreaming of Maria and Gabriel and the second trip he'd made to Manzanillo. Farrell was now fully into the world of money laundering, hooked on the rush, a junkie for danger. Before heading south, he devised a plan so daring, yet so potentially profitable, that he could barely contain himself on the jet.

Gabriel was leaning against a stanchion at the airport in Manzanillo when Farrell cleared customs. His cheeks were hollower than usual, his skin was pasty.

"The flu?" Farrell asked.

"That would be easier," Gabriel said. "The volume of business is off and there are several projects I need cash for if they are to go ahead."

Farrell smiled, cocked his head back, and showed him his palms. "I think you'll be happy to hear my plan."

Gabriel eased his dark sunglasses onto the bridge of his nose.

"Always the salesman, Jack," he said, and he smiled wanly. "Know what the customer wants to hear."

"Isn't that the trick of the trade?" Farrell said.

Maria greeted Farrell at the door, but she, too, appeared to have slept little in the past few days. She kissed him on the cheek and wandered off.

Even though a strong breeze blew off the early winter ocean, Gabriel insisted on running the air conditioner in his office. His heels rested on the edge of his desk. He smoked a cigarette and drank from a small glass of white wine. "Tell me how bold we will be," Gabriel said.

Farrell clicked open his briefcase and gave him the rehearsed pitch.

"There are places like Otay Mesa in every border town in America," Farrell began. He spread out a map of the Southwest on the desk. Gabriel dropped his feet and leaned forward with his head in his hands.

"Go on."

"Here outside El Paso, Laredo, Nogales, and even Douglas there are miles of scrub land," Farrell said, tracing the line between Mexico and the United States with his middle finger. "Much of it is owned by the government. But there are private parcels which may be developed as Maquiladora factories. Buy the land and build plants."

Gabriel screwed up his face. Before he could speak, Farrell broke in. He explained that in the short term the properties would serve as useful blinds for the cash they needed to hide. In the future, Gabriel and his clients would be positioned to develop legitimate factories and warehouses.

Farrell stood and bent over the map. "Here's the kicker. Think of the possibility of owning buildings on both sides of the border which are not subject to the normal scrutiny of either country's customs agents."

Gabriel rolled his eyes at the ceiling and took a deep inhale off the cigarette. He seemed preoccupied, so Farrell raised his voice and said: "Gabriel, I'm talking an almost open door for whatever you want to bring in or out of the States."

Gabriel blew the smoke out and gently said: "Don't patronize me, Mr. Farrell. I know exactly what you are talking about. I may be many things, but stupid isn't one of them."

This was all delivered in such a menacing tone that Farrell rubbed his jaw and sat down hard in the red leather chair. "Stupid is not what I'd call you," Farrell said.

"Whatever," Gabriel said. The cigarette smoke trailed off his hand in a lazy circle. "How much do you suppose your idea can absorb?"

Farrell paused, licked his upper lip, and said: "I'm figuring with this kind of deal, over the long haul—say five years—I know this sounds crazy, but . . . you'd be buying land. Lots of it."

"How much?"

"A billion."

Gabriel's cigarette froze in the air and suddenly his tightly pressed lips had reformed themselves into a frozen "O."

Farrell said: "Of course, there's no way my bank could ever operate as a funnel for that kind of money. But the potential exists for a webbed system of banks and corporations to handle the load."

"Beyond these border properties?"

"I suppose any sort of bargain basement real estate deal we could get our hands on."

"What's in it for you?" Gabriel asked.

Farrell thought of the expanding figure of his accounts. "Profit," he said. "And as you've said, there's nothing so blazing as the unpredictable."

Gabriel closed his eyes. His lips held the cigarette stiff and he sucked and blew until it was wasted. "America's slumlords. There's something poetic in that."

"Actually, I was thinking of properties in the midprice range, nothing fancy, nothing showy. Just meat-and-potato stuff."

"I was kidding about the slums," Gabriel said. His slender fingers began to stroke the desk top as if it were a piano keyboard. "I think it's an admirable plan, simple, yet elegant. But I have to talk this over with some other people. To be frank, I don't know if you are capable of something so audacious."

"I was audacious enough to come up with the idea," Farrell said coolly.

"You did, indeed," Gabriel said. He came around the desk and led Farrell to the door. "Why don't you keep Maria company while I make some calls. It will take me an hour."

Farrell nodded and tried to shut the door. The heavy piece of oak entered the jamb, stuck for a moment, and squeeked before closing. Outside a storm blustered. The branches of the hyacinth bushes scraped across the windows. In the distance came the muffled pounding of the surf.

Maria lay on the tooled leather sofa, reading Fuentes's *The Death of Artemio Cruz*. She had drawn her hair back tight against her temples and woven its length into an ebony braid that hung across her left shoulder and rested on the breast of the yellow cotton shift she wore. Cazador was curled at her feet. The Brittany growled when Farrell entered the room.

"Big meeting over at last?" She shifted her body to face him.

"I don't know about big," Farrell said. "The word doesn't seem to be part of my job description."

She sat up, curling her bare feet under her. She lifted a glass from the dark parotta wood coffee table to jiggle the melting ice cubes inside.

"A rum perhaps?" she asked.

"Why not?" Farrell crossed to the glass doors which opened onto the veranda. "Gabriel says the boat is down. No throwing ourselves into the sea today."

"Or tomorrow, I'm afraid," she said from behind the bar. "The mechanic said he blew the engine. The peacocks and peahens were terrified when he came chugging in the other day. It made a terrible rasping sound. They all took to roost in the thickest part of the eucalyptus trees."

"They screamed A-hole," Farrell said.

"Yes," she said, coming around the bar with his drink. "It's all an A-hole."

Farrell tried to cheer her by asking about her work. She was a part-time assistant in the archeology department at a university in Mexico City. She worked for an old man named Miguel, an expert in Mayan and Aztec cultures, whose greatest find was a perfectly intact clay dog, almost 1,000 years old. The dog had made Miguel's reputation: he had uncovered it in a pit in Mexico City where construction workers were about to lay down a cement foundation. Because of Miguel, archaeologists were now allowed into all new construction sites in Mexico.

"One day last week, I went to the laboratory late because I had forgotten a book I wanted to read," she said. "There was sweet old Miguel, sitting in the corner with the clay dog in his lap. He was petting it and talking to it about the awful places it had been relieving itself. He's terribly lonely, but romantic at the same time."

Farrell told her how Cazador's pup, Punta, now raced to jump the sea wall every night after work. And then in a fit of guilt—and a need to find out how much Maria understood—he told her briefly of Lena's job in the nursery.

"How sad," she said when he'd finished. "Poor babies. We are working on a clinic for a village up in the hills. There the children still suffer from polio and last year an outbreak of meningitis. I think it is awful, but in many ways it is the role of children to suffer."

All this was said with no outward reaction to indicate she understood the dark side of Gabriel's business. Perhaps it was that she knew and was beyond caring.

Maria said, "There are lines about your face that weren't there the last time I saw you, so flushed from throwing yourself off the boat."

"Are there?" Involuntarily, he touched his cheek.

"Deep, too, the kind that won't go away easily. You and my husband both seem tired these days. You work too hard and I think you neglect your women. Another drink?"

"Still working on this one." Farrell was now acutely aware that she was drinking very fast and had probably worked her way through more than one rum during his meeting with Gabriel. Behind him at the bar, ice cubes clinked.

"Clouds over the ocean like that—purple with an approaching rain—put me in the mood to drink," she said as she walked back toward the couch. She raised her left hand to the horizon and trailed her right hand across his shoulder, her fingers electric in a way Farrell had forgotten. Swirling in the wake of her yellow cotton shift was the suggestion of an exotic perfume, like the tinge of the spice markets of Africa. He watched her stand at the glass door—the setting sun highlighting her body under the thin dress, and at once horrified and transfixed, Farrell knew he was drawn by that which was forbidden, by that which was Gabriel's.

The ice cubes in his glass seemed to swirl on their own. He slowly took the base of the tumbler in his right hand and grabbed the top with the left to still the motion. He drank the rum to the bottom. "Maybe I will have another."

Maria glanced down the hallway that led to Gabriel's office and grinned. "I hoped you would," she said. "It's so boring and destructive to drink alone."

She crossed the room to take the glass and Farrell held it too long, so that she had to tug it from his fingers. Farrell stared into her eyes, then let the glass slip away. She walked back to the bar, a little less sure of herself. "You are a dangerous man, Jack."

"Am I?" Farrell asked, craning back over his shoulder.

"I think you try things just to see if you can get away with them."

"That's dangerous?"

"Passionate men have the tendency to become fanatics. You can predict where their zealotry will surface. Men like you, who dabble, your waters are unpredictable."

She set his drink on the table. "What shall we drink to?" Now she sat stiffer on the couch. Her attention darted about the room and she paused only briefly on Farrell before moving away. Cazador nosed his head under her hand and she rubbed it while she drank.

"I don't know," Farrell said. "To Mexico?"

"Why Mexico?"

"Because of the mystery."

"Is that what attracts you to my country, Jack? Something tawdry?" She folded her arms across her chest.

Farrell drank from the glass, then said: "The border towns, the tinny glitz, they've never interested me. It's the heart of the country that's attractive."

"The heart?" she snorted and took a gulp of the rum. "No adventurer such as yourself wants the heart. They want to bask in the heat and rhythm for a while, but they don't want the heart. It's too messy in the long run."

"I admit going native can be troublesome," Farrell said. "When I lived in Africa, I dressed as a nomad for months, hanging about in robes and a turban. I ate their food—a millet paste in an okra sauce—and even slept with their women. I woke up one day and realized I had dreamed in their language of a place where a great dune meets a granite cliff. I had never been there, but I knew it was a real place."

"So?"

"I had gone beyond the heart of things and that is messy. The dream upset me so much that I stopped wearing the turban and the robes and became obsessed with a Dutch woman who lived in the town where I did. She was quite obese, but I liked her because her white skin reminded me of the girls who sold hamburgers in my hometown."

Maria laughed, shook her head, and raised her glass. "You're quite an actor. To the heart of Mexico, then."

They stood to touch glasses. Maria ran her fingers across his hand. His heart began to beat wildly, a sound that was immediately accompanied by the creak of the door to Gabriel's office. They retreated to their chairs.

Gabriel clapped Farrell on the shoulder when he entered the room. "I have good news of which we will talk tomorrow."

He looked back and forth between Farrell and his wife, who did their best not to look at one another. He rubbed his hands together. "But I have had enough of work for today and I can see that you and Maria are already ahead of me."

Gabriel brought out two wonderful bottles of Merlot to complement the roast squab that the cook had prepared in a fennel sauce. Maria yawned deeply and excused herself around 10 P.M. Gabriel and Farrell drank Calvados in front of a low fire, listening to the wind buck the trees outside.

"I will break a rule of mine," Gabriel said, "and mix business with pleasure. Your idea has been met with some interest."

Farrell smiled, "Should I begin when I return to the States?"

"Interest, not approval," Gabriel emphasized. "My customers express the same reservations I have. They wish to hear you explain the concept yourself. They want to know you before committing the kind of resources you've mentioned."

Dulled as he was by liquor, a quiver of dread wormed through Farrell. Despite the charge he got working with Gabriel, he had no desire to know these people; he'd decided at the beginning that as long as he remained on the rim of Gabriel's activities, the odds were in his favor. Beyond the narrow risks he'd allowed himself, he knew there existed a wider, deeper set of connections that he did not want to understand.

"I thought you stayed away from these people," Farrell asked suspiciously.

"I do, except when it's necessary," Gabriel said.

"I don't see why this is necessary," Farrell replied.

"You and your bank are now working with a minor, yet significant percentage of the cash and disposable income of their business," Gabriel said. "You come to me and propose to increase that percentage. They feel that, before that happens, a certain trust must exist. I don't find that unreasonable."

Farrell watched the flames burst purple and then blue. He remembered himself as an eight-year-old backing away from a quarry in Maine because he saw a log floating. "Maybe you were right," Farrell said. "Maybe it won't work."

Gabriel took a drink and said, "It is as I thought. Perhaps you are as big as you can be."

Farrell squeezed at the edges of the fine crystal brandy snifter until he thought it would crack. When he'd regained his composure, he said, "Let me sleep on it. The thought of new people that I don't know. It's a little too much to take, that's all."

Gabriel patted Farrell on the shoulder as a professor would a student. "Understandable and agreed," Gabriel said. "We shall talk again in the morning before you leave. Another Calvados?"

The bells of the antique clock in the corner chimed midnight when Farrell said good night. Down the hallway past the library to his room, he heard Gabriel cross the living room behind him and flip on the stereo. The mournful sound of a clarinet blew through the house and Billie Holliday's voice sang: "Never had nothing, no one to care . . ."

Farrell lay in bed and listened as the clarinet seemed to melt and mingle with Holliday's voice and was finally overpowered and drowned by the beating of raindrops on the roof tiles. Farrell's head buzzed with improvised photographs of swarthy men with ebony hair slicked back in crooner's cuts. Some wore linen suits. One a diamond pinkie ring. This struck him as so foolish and melodramatic that he waved it off. He rolled over and fell into a troubled sleep.

Three years later, as he shifted in his bed in the motel in Lake Tahoe, he still had trouble clearly distinguishing between the real and the imagined. One thing he did not doubt: hours later he cracked an eyelid, understanding that within the white noise of the rain, the jazz had long since stopped and someone was in the room with him.

A match struck. Near the footboard, the light exploded, then mellowed into a glow that threw shadows across the room as a candle was lit. Maria put her finger to her lips. She seemed to float to him. Farrell tried to shake his head no. She untied the sash that held the rich blue robe to her hips and let the lapels of the garment slip away like the last wave of a high tide receding down a beach.

The bed creaked with her weight. The robe floated through the air, blew out the candle, and enveloped him. Now there was only the heady aroma of her and the feel of her guiding him, hissing to him, "We have no time. He might wake." And with the thought that Gabriel might burst in on them, Farrell cupped her with his palms, urging her to open, to quicken, and within seconds she whimpered and contracted.

She froze against him, gasping at his neck.

Then she started again, drawing her thighs tight around his hips, supporting herself on his chest. When she sensed that Farrell was about to arch, she whispered: "No, he'll know there." She reached around to move him backward to a place he'd never been before.

He shuddered when he understood and bucked too hard. She cried softly and dug her fingernails into his chest muscles.

"Delicadamente," she whispered.

Farrell let her have control. She lowered her hips, insistent and slow, and almost immediately he groaned into her breasts. How many minutes later the velvet robe slid then disappeared from his body, he couldn't remember. The door clicked. He was alone, listening to the rain on the roof. He ran his fingers across the welts her fingernails had raised on his chest. He widened his nostrils to trap the fading rumor of her perfume.

Farrell came awake at the sound of a car door slamming in the parking lot outside his motel room. It was first light. He lay there, trying not to think of Maria, or how he'd avoided looking Gabriel in the eye the next morning; or how well he'd lied to Lena when he'd returned to San Diego. He told her the trip had been routine and that he had to take a brief trip south again in a few weeks. But when Lena had reached for him that night, he pushed her away, told her he was exhausted. The truth was that he feared he'd allowed Gabriel to lure him onto a roller coaster, and he had no clue where the next hairpin turn would occur.

Farrell sat up and shivered. He looked at his watch. It was 6 A.M. He did not have to meet Inez and the crew until eight. It was early evening in Europe, time to talk to his attorney. He dressed, went out into the chill morning air, and walked down the street until he found a phone booth.

"An agent has been hired and is in Lyons as we speak," the attorney said. "You can expect the first report in thirty-six hours. I should alert you, however. There is a problem—inquires on your accounts here."

Farrell swallowed hard. "From Colorado?"

"No," the attorney said. "Los Angeles."

Farrell pressed his forehead against the cold glass. "Official requests?"

"Unclear," the attorney said. "They've come through a large credit bank, so it could be anyone. Of course, we gave them nothing."

The attorney mentioned the name of the bank. Farrell's throat dried; it was an institution that he'd used with Gabriel several times. The FBI knew about it, too. The attorney said: "If the request is made official through your government's liaison, it would take several weeks, but eventually we would have to release the information."

"Is there any way to find out who made the request?" Farrell asked.

"Professional courtesy, perhaps," the attorney said thoughtfully. "Money perhaps. But this is not an organization with which I've done business. I'll try."

"I'd appreciate it," Farrell said.

"We await your instructions, sir."

Farrell hung the phone in its cradle, stepped outside, and stared at the ice that had formed in yesterday's puddles. "Someone's after me."

Chapter 16

A tracker was following his footprints in the snow. The attorney's words tripped him; they snaked their way into his mind until his normally quick thought pattern crawled. He stumbled back across the parking lot to the room. He dressed in his ski clothes in a robotic manner while the possibilities trudged by: that nosy bank manager in Telluride, the FBI, Gabriel. He remembered Inez mysteriously following Page. He played with it for a moment, then dismissed it. How would she know? The odds favored the bank manager. The fat lout was trying to figure out how much money he had. If it wasn't the manager, and the FBI or Gabriel were involved, the end would come soon.

This fatalistic notion bore down on Farrell an hour later when he came upon the crew gathered on the deck outside the midstation at Squaw Valley. It was one of those spectacular Sierra Nevada days when the sky was tight blue and clean. Farrell didn't notice. He dwelt on Inez, calling it remarkable that a face so slack the evening before could now be bursting with animation. He watched her and the cloud of doom that had hung pregnant over him since the phone call lifted, replaced by hope for the heated moment, for the gut-wrenching weird, for the luminous, audacious act taken just for the sake of dancing the two-step on the sleeping fury of the mountain. Inez did not disappoint him.

"I decide that the ideas of Page for today are timid," Inez said. "So we introduce this thing artificial to make it . . . wild."

Page threw his hands up. "The Palisades and the Main Line Pocket are some of the hairiest jumps in the country. A couple of the lines we plan to ski will have us dropping for sixty, maybe seventy feet. How much wilder does it get?"

"Ahh, before this is all done, you will know," Inez said. "Last night I talk with a local cameraman who says every filmmaker has the shots of the cliffs with the jumpers."

"It's redundant," The Wave agreed.

"So what's this artificial thing?" Farrell asked.

From her pocket she pulled three black scarves. "Blindfolds," Inez said. With those words her eyelids drooped, her jaw relaxed, and her thighs parted.

The space in Farrell's stomach grew three times. He fought the urge to sit down quick. His arms became heavy and the air about him turned misty as if the cloud of the morning had turned to an opium fog. He smiled dreamily.

"No fucking way am I jumping blind," Page said. "Forget about it. Not going to happen."

"Do not be the fool," Inez snapped. "We use the blindfolds as you approach your position. Like this, you do not know which jump you take before you go over the edge."

"You could hurt them bad," Ann protested.

"Many are hurt crossing the street," Inez said. "This, the jump, is their skill, to soar like the bird through the air."

"I still don't see the point," Ann replied.

"They have no time to think," Inez said. "They must go on instinct, what is absolutely basic about them. And you and I, we capture it on film. That's what I chase! What is raw!"

Tony put his hand on Ann's shoulder. "You might capture more than you imagine."

"*Vraiment,* I hope it," Inez said.

"I don't know," Page said, shaking his head.

"Already I am approached by five more skiers here who wish to take your place," Inez said.

"I'll go," Farrell heard himself say.

They all turned to him. The Wave ran his fingers through his dreadlocks. "The eyes of the blind shall be opened, and the ears of the deaf shall be unstopped. Then shall the lame man leap . . ."

Inez ran to Farrell and hugged him. "I knew you would be the first, so brave." She broke away. "You others, do you let him go alone or do I find new skiers?"

Page rubbed the heel of his hand against his thigh for several seconds, then said. "Okay, he makes it, I'll do it, too."

"Wave?" Inez asked.

He nodded, but he wasn't happy.

A half hour later, Page, The Wave, and Farrell stood below the Palisades, examining the chutes they'd jump while Inez, Ann, and Tony set up their cameras. The three men would not look at each other.

"What's gotten into you, old one?" The Wave asked.

"I just don't see what the big deal is," Farrell said. "People say we go through life blind as it is. She just wants to test the idea."

"You bucking for a white cane with a red tip, too?" Page asked.

Farrell shrugged. "Why not?"

"Because I'm scared, mon," The Wave said. "I never done any shit like this. Bitch is out of her mind."

"She's trying to break you, see what you're made of," Farrell said.

Page nodded. "It's a fucking strange thought, but I think Collins is right. Don't think. Just go."

They all stood in silence for a minute. Farrell said, "Tell us how to make it, Page."

Page took a deep breath, then pointed up to his left. "The National Chute is that crack there on the right. It's not a bad draw. You'll know it because the entrance is real wide."

Farrell closed his eyes to imagine it, but all he saw was black.

"That other spit of snow up there that looks like a garden hose is the Main Chute," Page continued. "There's brown rock at the top, a lot of iron in it, I think. It's about ten feet wide at the entrance. But right after you drop in, you'll see a kink of stone. Get your feet up fast or you'll hit it and pitch out. There's nothing for at least fifty feet to stop you. Next to it, the Extra Chute, about the same. Probably a little easier."

"Jesus Christ," The Wave whined.

Farrell couldn't bring himself to look at the kid. "What's that last thing on the right there?" he asked Page.

"The Chimney," Page said. "Worst one. I don't think even she would put us up there blind. The top's called the smokestack: only five feet wide, high rock walls on either side."

"Claustrophobia," The Wave said.

"Three or four seconds locked in a cage," Page agreed. "By the time the walls come in around you where you can't turn, you'll be going so fast that you'll just kind of glide away from the earth. Stay cool if it happens. Aim true and suck the rest of it."

"Seventy feet?" Farrell asked.

"I said it was the worst," Page said.

There was a minor argument between Inez and the ski patrolmen assigned to the crew, which was resolved when the men understood that none of the skiers would go in absolutely blind; they'd be free of the black scarves ten feet before they entered the chutes. Inez had her camera running as the blindfolds went on, which Farrell didn't notice until the last second.

"Hey, I said no pictures!" he said and turned his back to her.

"I think perhaps we can renegotiate," Inez said. "My mystery man. My so-brave man. On this point we talk tonight, no?"

The scarf descended over his eyes, Farrell rested his hand on Tony's shoulder and shuffled forward on his skis toward the lift. Behind him he could hear Page and The Wave. It was a fifteen-minute ride to the top. Tony tried to talk to him several times, but Farrell told him he needed to think. In the darkness his mind wandered.

Gabriel had phoned a week after Farrell returned from Mexico and told him he'd be taking a flight out of Tijuana in early January to meet the customers. The meeting point: unknown. The pilot knew the way. Farrell spent hours alone in his office at work going over the data to support his ideas, but the more he worked at it, the more he became unsure of himself. A tremor took hold in his left hand, imperceptible at first, growing stronger by midmonth; and it was a noticeable palsy two days before Christmas when Lena came home red-eyed to tell him how she'd taken care of a baby that day that had screamed for hours. Farrell tried to turn the conversation, to try to assure himself that he had no part in the agony of those babies; that he was like a contractor to a bomb manufacturer: he supplied parts and services, not at fault for the carnage the product wrought. He was not the bombadier, he was not the pusher.

Christmas Eve morning he awoke to the sharp staccato whacking of the palm fronds on their window, a sound that told him the wind was surging out of the north.

He slipped out of bed quietly and got his tanks and wet suit and fins. He left a note on the kitchen table, then walked the two blocks to the beach. Wading into the gray churning water, the heady pickle barrel scent of early winter ocean surged around him. Over his head, the sky oscillated in shades of purple, charcoal, and magenta. He put the regulator in his mouth and rolled backward, rejoicing at the bite of the frigid December water.

Precious little light penetrated the surface. Farrell switched on his flashlight. The beam cut into the murkiness for five feet, ten in places, but the light was diffused, blurred by millions of bubbles and particles stirred up by the storm. The sand swirled around him. It beat against the glass of his face mask as steady as the snow in a freak blizzard; he inched his way forward, shutting his eyes every few moments to keep from becoming hypnotized by the steady current of grain that rushed at him.

The underwater sand storm suddenly changed directions and ran sideways. A current grabbed his body. He thought of Gabriel's customers and Lena's babies. He let the current draw him down. Icy threads of water seeped into the gaps between his wet suit and his skin. He shivered and twitched at the sting. He looked at his depth gauge on his wrist: thirty feet, now thirty-five, forty . . .

Enough, Farrell thought. He kicked to break himself free of the tide. He only succeeded in turning himself sideways in the current; he plunged deeper. At forty-five feet the storm disappeared, but unseen fingers grabbed at his legs and twisted them. He stopped, his upper body buffeted by the stiff flow; his lower body immobilized. Farrell twisted the flashlight down to see he was hopelessly tangled in a kelp bed. He tried to calm himself, to think straight, but the current was like a lasso that roped him and dragged him behind some phantom horse. He had a knife strapped to his ankle, somewhere below the wavering green mess that held him. He bent himself in two to reach it, but when he tried to use the flashlight to tear some of the seaweed aside, it slipped from his hands and drifted off, leaving him in the ink.

Farrell knew he had twelve minutes of air left in his tank; he'd gone into the sea with just half the cylinder filled. Every second became precious. Again he doubled himself against the current to dig at the tentacles gripping the outside of his legs. Some of the rubbery branches tore away like wet spinach. Some cracked and broke. Most of them held true. His glove slipped and slithered against the mat of hair that held him under.

He had no idea how long he fought. There was just a moment in that darkness when he understood he wouldn't free himself that way. He stopped to let the current swing him to and fro. He listened to the pop and hiss of his regulator. He gulped and allowed himself the thought that he was over. He shook himself in anger; if he believed he was gone, he was gone. Instead, he concentrated on the way his legs moved in the tide. And after a while he noticed that his legs could move together, but not apart. He bent double a third time, reaching down into the space next to his legs to tear at the tangle near his ankles. Leaves ripped free, then two branches. His fingers scrapped at the nylon strap that held the knife to his ankle. Another minute and he had the sheath turned around and the blunt end of the knife in his hand. He slashed at the kelp, not caring if he cut himself, too. Farrell got his right leg out first. The current grabbed it and split him like a ballet dancer on point. He strained forward to his left leg and took one great swipe, which set him free; he rushed out with the current.

Farrell fought against it with every bit of his strength, swimming what he thought was sideways, instead of up. As suddenly as he had entered it, the lasso broke. The phantom horse trotted on toward Hawaii. He kicked unsteadily to the surface, breaching into the rainstorm 200 yards from shore with only ninety seconds of air left.

It was a slow, awkward swim to the beach. He stroked, thinking how great it would be to take a hot shower and climb back into bed with his wife.

When he stood up in the surf, he noticed an eight-inch flap of wet suit hanging from his leg. Blood trickling out. He took off his flippers and looked up to see Lena standing on a bench above the sand. She wore a rain slicker over her nightgown. He smiled, waved, and tugged the tank and vest from his back.

Lena strode down the sand across a mound of kelp thrown up by the storm. She slapped him across the lips. "You selfish, unthinking bastard," she yelled. She turned and ran away crying.

"Get ready to get off," Tony said, breaking Farrell from his memories. The dreamy, floating state he'd been in before the ride was gone. Now he felt open, raw. It was what Inez wanted. What he wanted was to hear Inez's voice, to feel the fog come up around him again, washing away thought. He fantasized about her, about the way she thought up these crazy ideas. He realized she was like Gabriel; she had no limits and that soothed and stung him at the same time.

When Tony had tied the black scarf across his face, Farrell noticed almost immediately that the rest of his senses became heightened; he had heard each creak and whir in the chairlift; he had smelled Tony's stale cigarette odor; and now he sensed the spring snow softening under his ski boots as they climbed.

In the darkness, the image of Lena stomping away from the beach played over and over in his mind. He remembered wanting to run after her, to tell her how confused he was; he looked forward to the trip south, and yet, he dreaded it more than anything he'd ever had to do.

"Hopeless," Farrell said out loud when they had reached the top.

"What's that?" Tony asked.

"I'm hopeless," Farrell mumbled.

"Don't think like that," Tony said. "You got to be clear now."

Farrell laughed at the idea. "How can you be clear when you can't see?"

"You can back out of this, you know," Tony said.

"Doesn't matter," Farrell said.

"It all matters," Tony said. "The rastaman is over there, shaking like a leaf. You?"

"I'm trying not to think, okay?" Farrell said, rubbing at a tight spot in his thigh muscle. "Easier that way."

"Fine, fine," Tony said. "But I'm telling them to pull your blinds a good fifteen feet back. She'll never notice and I'm not going to be responsible for you going over the front in the black."

"That will help," Farrell said.

"Your skis are in front of you," a deep male voice said. It wasn't Tony. "Step down."

The heavy thud of the binding pulled him in tight against the skis. Poles were put in his hands and straps wrapped around his wrists.

"Your boots feel okay?"

"Yeah," Farrell said. He thought of Lena and the chill that had separated them on Christmas. He shivered.

"Everybody ready?" Tony's voice called from off to Farrell's right.

"Ready," the voice said.

"Old one!" The Wave yelled from far off to his left. "Be cool. Ski straight!"

Farrell nodded, his breath coming in rapid shallow bursts. His heart pounded. His entire body quaked. "Okay, okay," he chattered. "Let's do this thing!"

"And Action!" Tony bellowed.

Farrell leaned forward on his poles and pushed away, felt his head tug back and then light flooded in. "Oh shit!" he screamed as the skis dropped forward and down.

Farrell threw his hands after gravity, seeing in the first dots of coherent vision a line of brown rocks in front of him: Main Chute! He yanked his feet upward and fell, a meteor at dusk, out and over the rim, still half-blinded by the light, burning past the sharp limb of a bush that clung stubbornly to the cliff wall. A high-pitched flute note stung his ears.

He was vaguely aware of the rocks rushing by and the snow racing toward him. He wondered if the bottom would ever come and if he'd be able to handle the speed of the landing. "Son of a . . . !"

His moaning growl was cut short as his right ski struck hard spring snow. His head snapped back and he almost blacked out, but held on. Farrell gasped at the velocity—sixty-five, now seventy miles an hour—and the way his jaw rat-tatted like a jackhammer on the frozen terrain underneath him.

Suddenly Inez and her camera were there in a pit in the snow.

Inez pumped her hand as he barreled by. *"Magnifique!"* she cried.

Farrell got himself stopped thirty yards beyond her, then his legs went to rubber and he collapsed into the snow. His stomach ached hollow from the sudden loss of adrenaline. He felt ill, something that never happened after such a thrilling ride.

It took a full four minutes before he got his breath back, got himself out of his bindings, and stood. He scanned the ridge, looking for The Wave, then saw him, poised on his snowboard above the National Chute with another man in blue standing behind him. Ann had lashed herself to a rock several feet down into the chute so she could catch him as he blew by her. Across the ridge, Tony had sprawled himself flat so he could film The Wave dead on.

"Thank God," Farrell said to himself. "The kid's got the easiest way down."

Inez dropped her hand. The man behind The Wave gave him a shove. The black scarf fluttered. The Wave rolled over the lip and rocketed straight down and out into the air. He cast his left hand forward as if he were trying to feel his way to the ground through the brilliant sun. Farrell sucked in air; he could feel his jump all over again. The rastaman reached too far forward with his hand, which caused his tip to drop just before landing. The Wave flipped once, twice, and a third time; then stood up shaking and raised his hands over his snowy dreadlocks and screamed: "I'm a Stevie Wonder Snowboarder!"

The Wave kicked the board into motion again, and made faltering, erratic arcs down to where Farrell stood.

"Stoked jump, mon!" The Wave said. "I never been so close to shitting them in my life! I mean I was pissed when she thought it up, but what a goddamned feeling, like . . ."

Farrell grinned thinking about the jump, then suddenly frowned. The nausea returned. "There's Page," he said.

Page stood stiff on the very edge of the snow line above the Extra Chute, unaware of the cliff and rock below him. Tony was crouched at his feet with his camera ready. Without warning, he put the camera down and grabbed his radio.

"What's she doing?" The Wave asked.

Inez was crouched in the snow pit talking into her radio. The April sun, which grew stronger by the minute, illuminated her and cast a pleasing shadow of her body far out in front of her camera.

What got to Farrell was the fact that, while her jaw worked furiously, the rest of her features were devoid of tension; even her hands were open, loose.

"She's moving him," The Wave said.

Tony and one of the patrolmen helped Page shuffle back from the edge and up the hill.

"Sonofabitch," Farrell said. "She's putting him on the Chimney."

Tony held the radio up to Page, who listened then pushed it away and made as if he was going to strip off the black scarf.

"He's backing out," The Wave said.

"What'd she say?" Farrell said.

"Don't know, mon. Only she and the cameras got the talkies this time. Said she thought too many people would confuse the issue. But she hit him with something, sure as I'm standing here. For Christ's sake! Doesn't she understand this is for real?"

"I think that's the point," Farrell said.

Tony held the radio up to Page's ear again. Page's shoulders rose, then fell. Tony nodded and knelt in the snow right next to Page's boots. He pointed his camera into the cinched waist of snow below Page's skis.

"He's going," The Wave whispered.

Page pushed off, stripped of the blindfold, and fell almost immediately, a rifle bullet in a chimney flue. For a second Farrell feared that the human bullet would strike the wall, that Page would start to ricochet down the mountainside. Twenty-five feet into the slim passage, Page drifted left and his arm caught a bush. It jerked him as if a stranger had hooked his elbow while he ran through a crowd. He tilted in space for a moment; Farrell thought for sure Page would twist and spin away backward. At the moment inertia should have taken him, Page wrenched his arm free of the limb and dropped out of the flue into the open air.

Page landed so square and solid that Farrell expected him to flush triumphant and bellow. But no joy blazed in Page. His jaw was set hard as he raced by Inez, then Farrell and The Wave, and down the mountain.

Inez trudged through the snow toward them. "Bring the camera down. We continue after the lunch." She seemed disappointed.

"What'd you say to him there?" The Wave demanded.

"*C'est mon affaire,*" Inez said wearily.

"This is our affair," The Wave said. "He could be toast right now."

Inez spun, hands on her hips. "I do not ask you to do anything of which you are not the capable one. This is the film of skiing the extreme. This is not the travelogue."

"We're not skiing the extreme," The Wave said. "We're skiing your extreme, your inventions."

"And deep down, you love this or you would not still be here," Inez said. With that she climbed on the back of the snowmobile. The driver kicked it to life and they roared off down the mountain.

Farrell stared after her, mesmerized. He turned and saw The Wave felt the same way.

They found Page staring down at a bowl of fruit: bananas and sliced apples and two soggy pieces of tangerine.

"What sort of jabber was she laying on you?" The Wave asked.

"Forget about it," Page said. "It was nothing."

"I think we have a right to know," Farrell said, feeling immediately guilty that he hadn't told Page that Inez had been spying on him; but then again, he'd have to admit spying on the both of them.

Page cocked his head. "She asked me if the blindfold reminded me of the darkness in the woods the night I lost my eye."

"That's fucking cold," The Wave said in disgust.

Page nodded. "Kind of shocked me. But not because it was said cold. No, she said it warm, like she cared."

"She does care. About what I don't know," The Wave said. "She knows about us, things about you."

Page snorted and took a drink. "Not much to know about me she doesn't already know. I'm an open book. Take out the glass eye, you can look right into my head."

"I think you still have secrets," Farrell said.

"Secrets," Page repeated. "Come to think of it, we don't know the first damn thing about you, Collins."

Farrell avoided the challenge, "You jumped anyway."

"Yeah, well, I figured it was better than being on film as a chicken," Page said. "Tony told me I was on the Chimney. Even then, it was like jumping into the unknown. Never realized light could fuck you up like that. Anyway, probably made her happy."

Farrell ran his thumb over his fingers, reviewing the events of the morning. Just being apart from Inez gave him some perspective. When she wasn't around, he could see she might hurt all of them. Even so, he felt this overwhelming attraction to her. What he couldn't figure out was how to reconcile the competing emotions.

"Maybe making her happy isn't our job," Farrell began. "You could have hung up on that tree and had nowhere to go but the bottom."

"Well, look who's found the voice of reason," Page replied. "The guy who tried to hip-check me in the middle of the Y Couloir."

"I'm not saying it makes any sense," Farrell said.

"Tell me about it," Page said.

"Start by thinking like this," The Wave said. "We just make it."

Page shook his head. "I've never thought that way about anything, and I never will. Too limiting. Too damn depressing."

Page grabbed his gloves and hat and walked out the door.

By early afternoon, the granite outcroppings of the Main Line Pocket above Emigrant Peak had simmered in the sun for almost four hours. The entire crew except Inez and Tony stood at the top of the lift, examining the steep band of rocks and ledges. The snow and rock had a different look than the day before, Farrell thought. Less snow clung to the stone, and the scoring in the rock was changed by the steady light; it was more deeply etched, here and there highlights of silver and gold shone.

"How long we going have to wait?" The Wave asked when Tony came sliding off the lift.

"Said she'd be up soon," Tony said. He reached into his pack to pull out a white racing helmet with a tiny video camera strapped to the top with silver duct tape. He handed it to Page. "She wants you to wear this for the next run. Wave, she says you should rest this one out."

"Fine by me, mon," The Wave replied. "Nine lives of this cat are down to seven."

"No blindfolds?" Page said.

"No blindfolds," Tony replied.

"Nothing artificial, mon?"

"Just the helmet."

During the short climb, Farrell told himself it would be over soon; they'd finish the jumps tomorrow, get to Jackson Hole, and be in the backcountry again where Inez and the rest of the crew would again be under his orders. No need for anything artificial; the Tetons were brutal enough even for Inez. And the information from Europe would come soon. He'd begin to sort it all out.

At the top, they heard the buzz of the snowmobile below them and then another. Inez climbed off the first, 200 yards down the side of the cliff and across the slope. Her driver dug a pit in the snow. A man with silver hair, sporting a black jacket and pants got off the second machine and stood, watching her.

Inez set her camera in the deep snow a football field to the left of the Pocket. Ann and the Wave climbed to a position opposite and above Inez so Farrell and Page would be sure to be caught in the crossfire of lenses. Tony would anchor himself behind the jumpers again.

"You can pretty much pick your spot," Page said as Farrell and Tony struggled the final thirty feet to the top of the rise. "There's a whole bunch of stuff to handle. I guarantee it will all look spectacular on film: great light, great angles."

"I noticed," Farrell huffed. He threw down his pack. "Any suggestions?"

"The column on the right-hand side as you're looking up is always exposed, so stay back from it," Page said. "Other than that, it's as free and as wild as you want it."

Farrell had developed a blister on the heel of his right foot. He pulled at the stocking, trying to relieve the heat. Then he hung his head out over his knee and stretched.

"Who's that guy down there with Inez?" Page asked Tony.

"Don't know," Tony said. "She was talking with him before lunch. Older guy from around here. She said he was going to help her set up."

Farrell cupped his hands around his sunglasses to shut out the glare from the cloudless sky, to see the man with Inez. Though they were far away, Farrell could make out that he was taller than Inez and much older. The man stood in the sunny silence at a harsh angle, one leg higher up the hill than the other, slanted, and he held his elbows away from himself, akimbo, like a gunfighter's in an old movie. But Farrell couldn't make out the man's face. He seemed to be doing nothing more than watching. Farrell decided he was an investor or a local with ideas on how to film the shot.

"Looks like Collins is ready to go, Page," Tony said. He lay on clear plastic tarp he'd placed on the snow so he could get the low perspective on them as they took off.

Page was still staring off toward Inez and the man. Farrell clambered over to him. "You know that guy?"

Page jumped slightly. He'd lost some color in his face. "Didn't hear you come up."

"You know him?" Farrell repeated.

"Thought I did for a minute," Page said. "A guy I used to know. But it isn't him. That guy died a long time ago."

"This kind of light can play tricks on you," Farrell said.

"That's probably what it is," Page said, but he appeared preoccupied as he got ready. "Let's try to take first turns at an angle away from the sun, so we don't have to ski Helen Keller."

Page spoke into the radio, alerting Ann and Inez that they would be ready to ski in five minutes. Tony adjusted the helmet on Page's head, then flipped the switch that activated a red recording light.

Farrell's knees shook slightly when he stepped into his binding. His groin ached from the day before. And for the second time that day, the wonderful sense of being numb that usually preceeded an assault on a dangerous situation did not come. He was raw again. He pushed off before the shaking could begin. He leapt into an extremely steep initial loop that forced him down toward the tails of his skis. He managed to whip the tips around into the air, where he dropped thirty feet. Owing to the angle he'd taken, there was no illusion of drift or lift this time; it was a direct fall, gravity punching him between his legs, coming oh so close to spurring the same fetal position response he'd fought the day before. Farrell cracked hard on the snow beneath the ledges, lost his balance, and tumbled twice. He felt another hard tug in his groin muscle. Grimacing, he skied down to Ann and The Wave.

Back on top, Page had moved to the left of where Farrell had descended. From there Page would have to turn, glide directly into the air, drop twenty feet to a ledge, balance in an instant, and plunge for another thirty-five feet. To the left of the ledge was a clump of finger-width stumps, which could snag the tips of his skis should he approach them.

"That's a bad idea, mon," The Wave said.

Farrell surprised himself by nodding. Ordinarily, he would have wanted to see Page try the stunt, but for some reason he didn't want Page to take such a foolhardy risk. He further surprised himself by picking up Ann's radio and asked Tony to let him speak with Page.

"What's up, Collins?" Page said.

"Bad line," Farrell said. "Those saplings will get you."

Inez interrupted: "Where does he plan to ski?"

Farrell described it to her, then told Page, "When I came by that area, I thought I could see rotten snow and rock showing through."

"No problem," Page said. "I'll be light on them. Dance over."

"I'm telling you it looks funky—"

"Collins, you were not asked," Inez interrupted. "Page says go. So we film him. This is his spectacle."

"Fine, Inez, get your spectacle," Farrell barked into the radio. He tossed the device back to Ann, who scowled and slid it into her chest holster.

"She's wild when she sees this stuff about to go down, isn't she?" Ann said.

"Wild isn't the word," The Wave said.

Page handed his radio back to Tony, who had tied himself to two climbing cords, then edged out over the lip of the rock so he could hang down and get most of Page's drop in his lens.

Later Farrell would say that Page would have made the jump fine if he hadn't shifted to look down at Inez and her companion one more time. But what would have been an off-hand glance in a man with two eyes subtly changed Page's center of balance; he was out of sync before he even started. Page managed to get his boards turned into an initial glide before liftoff, but it was not far enough. He flew off the ledge poised on his uphill ski. Once airborne, his chin snapped back in the recognition he'd blundered. There came a jerking pause when Page missed the first ledge and landed in the little sapling stumps; and then he whiplashed crazy over the brow of the outcropping, over the gray ice, over the highlights of silver and gold. He continued to spin around and around in the perfect spring light against the remarkable angles in the rock until he hit. A flare of snow etched itself across the afternoon sky, then wisped and settled.

The thud echoed.

Farrell, The Wave, and Ann scrambled up the slope toward Page expecting to find him limp. Page, mainlining on adrenaline, was back on his feet within moments. He jumped around and waved to them.

"Jesus!" he stammered. "What a header! What a freaking header that was! But I'm okay, okay!"

Then he tottered. His knees buckled. He lay down in the snow, in the sun.

Farrell kept the lights low in Page's motel room that evening. Page sat propped against three pillows. He drank from a beer can in one hand and from a glass of Jack Daniel's in the other. He had just gotten out of his third bath of Epsom salts, looked like shit, knew it, but refused to admit it.

The trip to the emergency room showed Page had cracked one rib and bruised two others. He had dislocated his thumb on his right hand and driven a three-inch splinter from a branch through the other palm.

"You're a lucky man, Mr. Page," the doctor had said.

Inez had paced up and down in the hall outside the room; then broke into tears and hugged Farrell when he told her Page would be fine. She snuffled and said, "I am so worried of him since he crashes."

"Were you?" Farrell asked somewhat sarcastically.

"Like he was my brother," Inez snuffled. "I do not feel so well now. You come to my room later, no? We talk. Have the drink. Friends?"

"I don't know if I trust you," Farrell said.

"I know," Inez said. "Some things I do wrong. This has made me think. I want to talk."

Farrell nodded. He watched her as she left, excited at the notion of being alone with her despite the anger and resentment he had felt since Page jumped.

Now in Page's room Farrell remembered that after they put

Page on the toboggan for the ride down the hill, the second snow-mobile and the older man in black were gone.

"Feel like I ran into a house riding a motorcycle," Page said.

"You going to tell me who the guy with Inez was?" Farrell asked.

"This isn't so bad, two bruised ribs. Plenty of tape, I should be able to ski tomorrow," Page said. "There's no real airtime to speak of, just a deep breath, a hard left-hand turn, and stay on your edges until it's over."

"Don't be an idiot," Farrell said. "You've got as much chance of making another jump tomorrow as I do of having a full head of hair."

Page locked on an awful oil painting of the mountains that hung above the desk. His eyes quavered and almost shut. Farrell got to his feet in alarm; the doctors had said to watch for signs of shock.

Page sighed. "I'd bet that was my old man."

"It couldn't be," Farrell said, his thoughts racing back to Inez following Page the previous evening and knowing it could.

"I haven't seen him in ten years and that guy was a long way off," Page said. "He's lost a lot of weight. But I think so."

Farrell looked at the ground, not knowing what to say. Finally, he asked, "You hate him because of the eye?"

"I deserve to, don't I?" Page said. He drank from the whiskey glass. "You ever hit your old man?"

"No," Farrell said.

"After that night, the night he hit me, we kind of avoided each other until just before I split for college. It was always like he was scared to look at me. Anyway he'd been up five hundred dollars early in the evening. Left the card room past midnight seven hundred down. Over the years I'd seen the price of a beating drop: two hundred bucks would set his hands in lazy motion, seven bills a flurry.

"I stepped in again. He kind of laughed, drunk, asked me if I was looking to own a seeing eye dog the rest of my life. He didn't realize how quick you get being on the mountain every day."

Page winced and rearranged the pillows at his back. "You hit your old man with your fists, it changes everything. Worst of it is, my mom still went to him, picked him off the floor, and cleaned him up. Haven't been back there since."

"Sure you have," Farrell said. "I saw you the other night in front of an old green house on the south side of the lake."

Page's jaw dropped. "You followed me?"

"Inez was following you. I followed Inez. She talked to that same woman in the casino."

"What did they talk about?"

"No idea," Farrell said. "I didn't want to get that close."

"My mom," Page said. "She said he moved out two years ago and has been in therapy, but it's bull. Her cheek was bruised. She said it was a fall, a real fall, but I know how it is. Said she sees him in a neutral place once a week. Said he wants to talk to me."

"You think that's why he was up on the hill?"

Page dropped his right hand heavy onto his thigh. He lifted the hand and dropped it again, repeating the action for almost a minute.

"Could be," he said at last. "Then again, when I was a kid . . . I remember he used to like to watch me ski. Said it was like watching the dice run across the table."

Chapter 17

arrell left Page asleep holding the glass of whiskey in his hand. Back in his room he lay on the bed, unsure of what to do. If the man in black was Page's father, Inez was more than he'd imagined; she was an extreme. Who knew what she was capable of? With that thought, he tasted a Northern Spy apple in his mouth, tart and fresh and biting. The room began to whirl. The grain in the ugly wood paneling seemed to smear. The plaster on the ceiling turned into an ocean churning with whitecaps.

Suddenly, the taste of the twirling turned sickeningly cloy. He paced, torn between wanting to go to Inez's room for their little talk, to let her make his whole world spin, to make the air itself tart like a Northern Spy, and wanting to lock himself in the bathroom and sink in hot water until all movement stopped.

Farrell groaned. He dropped back on the bed. He reached for the diary, thinking he could put himself in neutral, all taste buds dead, listening to Lena's voice.

December 29, 1988

The day after Christmas, a local dentist, an experienced diver, got caught in the kelp beds off the coast here. It took two days to find him, and when they brought him to the surface, he was bloated.

I showed the newspaper article to Jack, who refused to read it. He said he doesn't like to think of what might have been.

I am tired of his attitude, of never looking back and barely looking forward. He seems distant and I can't get him to open up. I tried to tell him that living for the moment can strip you of your connections. He just sighed. I got dressed and went to work four hours early.

January 2

Came down with the flu the evening before New Year's. My black dress I bought for the dinner at Jim Rubenstein's house will sit unused, but I don't mind a bit. Jack left work early and stayed home to care for me, which was nice because we hadn't spoken much since the dentist drowned.

I was as sick as I've been in recent years, a forty-eight-hour bug that kept me in bed. Tending to me seemed to open him up for a while. On New Year's afternoon he shut off the football games and sat on the edge of the bed and read to me from his favorite book, Kawabata's *Snow Country*. It was the section where Shimamura, the Tokyo businessman, and Komako, the geisha who loves him but whom he cannot love, talk of the bird-chasing festival of February; how the children ten days before the celebration cut the hard snow and erect a palace. On the day of the festival, the children build a great bonfire before the palace. When the fire dies, the children sleep in the palace and in the morning they climb to the roof to sing the birdchasing song.

Jack put down the book and stared off into space.

I asked him if he was okay and he said he just remembered when he was four and his grandfather, his mother's father, held his hand in Copley Square in Boston. They were on their way to Fenway Park for a game—and pigeons flew all around them, rising into the sky. He said standing among the birds was like being in a moving cloud. He said it had been a long time since something so peaceful had soothed and moved him.

I was quiet, watching him, hoping he'd talk again, but he didn't. I said softly that I used to soothe him.

He turned to me as if I were not his wife, but an old friend, and said he still did love me, more than I could know. He said he couldn't explain it, but he was facing the fact that you can be confused about life for no real reason.

Moments like those I can't help but forget the bad times, because he's mine and that's enough. He crawled under the covers and I laid on his chest while he stroked my hair until I fell asleep.

January 5

Jack left last night, took a flight out of Tijuana. He'll be gone for four days to Mexico City. We are as well as we've been in many months. Something about this trip seemed to bother him, but he wouldn't talk about it except to say that he hoped it would be his last.

When he's gone, I drift into places that scare me. Don't want to write about this, but little Elizabeth and her mother, Lydia, are back in the hospital. Lydia overdosed and had a compound fracture of the femur falling down the stairs of her apartment. Elizabeth was thrown free; she only broke her arm and suffered a concussion. A miracle that she didn't land on the Fontanel.

Looking at the little girl, I wondered how the authorities could let Lydia have her back after she tested positive. They wince, but tell me again that a baby's best left with her mother.

I worked a double shift yesterday, night and graveyard. Went up to Lydia's room, nonpaying, back of the hall. She slept, hitched up to a morphine drip. Probably thrilled her. The narcotic droplets fell into the plastic line and mixed with saline. I prayed I'd see a tiny air bubble roll in the plastic. Better for Elizabeth. Better for Lydia. Better for me . . .

I have another graveyard in two days. It's three in the morning now and I'm frightened of seeing Lydia or Elizabeth again because I don't know what I might do. It's like the way you feel knowing your car's not driving right and the next exit is miles away and it will drop you off in a bad section of town.

When I was a girl, I'd sit in the back seat of our old black Buick on long trips, feeling trapped. I'd blow soap bubbles through a plastic ring. My father would yell when a bubble, purple and green and clear, floated into the front seat. I didn't care; the bubbles set me free. I keep thinking that if I put a little bubble in Lydia's morphine line, I could set Elizabeth free.

Farrell slammed the diary shut, unwilling, unable to read more. He pinched the bridge of his nose until he thought it would break. He could not bear the thought that his wife might have killed. Slicing through his head came the terrible realization that he had focused so tightly on his secret life that he hadn't seen the torture Lena endured long after Jenny's death. That set the room in motion again, not the easy, pleasing spin he was used to. No, the walls rocked and swayed, the furniture tilted, the ceiling lurched and crashed like a wave. He felt seasick. He buried his face in his pillow the way he would as a boy when his parents locked him in his room. He opened his mouth to the fabric, to let loose gagging screams.

Even that didn't help. Farrell pitched to his feet, careening out the door into the frigid night air.

Inez opened the door to her room before he could knock a second time. She wore a blue velvet bathrobe and had a drink in her hand.

"I think you do not come," she said, standing back so he could come inside. "Drink? It's the Pernod."

"Yes," Farrell said, taking a seat near the only clear table in the room. He held his breath while Inez poured two inches of clear liquid into the glasses, added ice from a bucket, then crossed into the bathroom to add water. Farrell made his rocking mind slow by making a quick inventory of the room: dual video-editing machines, seven hardened plastic trunks for the cameras, two sturdy tripods in the corner, and three pieces of bright aluminum luggage, expensive.

"Must be tough to lug around an entire editing setup with you from mountain to mountain," Farrell said. As she mixed the drinks, he noticed for the first time how slender her legs were. He became unhinged again. Maybe it wasn't a good idea to come here.

"The video is what is so large," she replied. "But to print what I shoot every day is a luxury I have not. This is the best of seconds."

"Have you looked at today?"

"Trés engageant." She leaned over to hand him the drink. The top of her robe opened and Farrell could see the rise of her breasts.

Her smell surrounded him. "You and Page especially. So strong in danger."

"And tomorrow?"

"This is a secret," Inez said. She sat on the bed. "Maybe I do not even know myself. I like to do the improvise."

He thought of Page and The Wave, then asked: "It's not in your files here somewhere?"

Inez stiffened, then relaxed. "Files?"

"Dossiers," Farrell said. "The Wave claims you keep them on us."

Inez waved her glass through the air so the ice rapped off the sides. *"Ce n'est pas grandes choses.* I keep notes on everything and everyone. You do not expect the journalist to interview without preparation, no? I think The Wave blows it outside of my perspective."

"He's concerned that your questions were a little too personal."

Inez leaned back. Her laugh gargled from her throat, filling the room. "The world is personal. My films are personal. You worry too much."

"If I do, then why did you follow Page last night?"

Inez flinched. "How did you—"

"I followed you, almost by accident. I was going gambling."

"Well, I . . . another drink?" Inez asked. She jumped off the bed. He couldn't help trailing her with his eyes. She was calm, much calmer than he was. He decided she would only reveal herself under pressure.

"That bothers you, that I followed you?" Farrell asked.

Inez smiled. "No, I just do not know you are interested. Another?"

"Why not?" Farrell said.

This time she put the drink on the table next to Farrell and lay down on her side on the bed so the robe shifted to display her leg to the knee. Farrell tried his best to ignore it. Success did not come easy around Inez.

"You followed him for research then?" he asked.

Inez drew a lazy circle on the corduroy bedspread. "Of course."

"What did you find?"

"A secret. To reveal now would be a cheat," Inez said. "The mystery is in the slow discovery."

Inez propped herself up on one elbow, facing him. "Did anyone ever tell you that you are too serious?"

"Not many," Farrell said. He took another pull off his drink, trying not to look at the robe, which had parted so he could see the beginning of her belly. "What secrets do you know about me?"

Inez brushed her hair back from her face and smiled. "Too little, I am afraid. You are my slow, slow mystery. So much to unravel."

"You love people's closets, don't you?"

"Closets?"

"*Les penderies . . .*" their hidden places."

"*Absolument,*" she said. "These places fascinate."

"I don't understand how it fits in with the film."

"*Alors,* I do not think it is your business," Inez said. She sat up. The robe fell off to the side so he could now see the rose of the nipple of her left breast. It jutted outward against the velvet fabric, erect.

If she noticed, she didn't seem to care. "But as I say, you intrigue me, Collins, so I tell you: By opening the hidden places, as you call them, we find the stairs. When one forces people to climb, their balance, she is not so steady. And they reveal themselves in front of the camera in ways I can never hope for in the situation ordinary."

"I still don't see—" Farrell began.

"Think of it like this," Inez interrupted. She spoke rapidly, caught up in the passion of her thoughts. "What is captured in the ordinary ski documentary interests in the sense visual. One craves to see how far the skier might jump, or how steep the slope is he attacks. The pictures are beautiful in their way.

"But they are surface, just pretty pictures." She sat upright, crossing her legs underneath her. Again, Farrell could see beyond breasts to the dim flat of her belly.

"Does my English make sense?"

"Yes," Farrell said.

Inez smiled, her cheeks flushed. She knew he was entranced by her body. "It is like to look at a pencil sketch when you want the oil paint to be added to the canvas, or the chalk wash to alter the pencil line to give it the new dimension. The new dimension, that excites me—to unlock the mystery why, why someone risks his life skiing the Y Couloir or to jump off the cliffs at the Palisades or well, whatever . . ."

He said, "I think you're looking for something that isn't there. Scientists will tell you that we thrill seekers lack an enzyme, that I go out on a limb because there's this juice in my head I lack and the only way I can make up for it is through adrenaline. I'm just chemically out of whack."

Inez spun around to sit on the edge of the bed, close to Farrell's leg. She put her hand on his knee. "Possible. But which explanation do you want to believe, that nature spins like the child's top, or the individual is something compelling . . . something sensual?"

Her hand had not left Farrell's thigh. They both glanced down.

"With me, it's just always been there," Farrell croaked. The air around her became misty. "I've always wanted to try things, to—"

"You lie to me," she said, running her index finger on the fabric of his jeans. "You have a reason, perhaps many more than one. I am content to comprehend just one. It takes time, but I understand later or sooner . . . because you wish me to."

Farrell felt himself floating. Before he was conscious of why, Farrell reached forward, pushed aside the robe, and brushed her skin. Inez shivered. Her eyes closed. He traced the weight of her right breast toward the nipple, which spurred a low moan from her lips.

Inez slid down the edge of the mattress to her knees. With her right hand she massaged the front of Farrell's jeans. Her throat caught air and released it when he arched his hips involuntarily under the weight of her fingers. She was like every risk he'd ever taken, a siren on the shore and he with no mast to lash himself to.

He kissed her neck, tasting the salt and tobacco flavor of her skin. She drew him from the chair and pushed him back onto the bed and dropped the robe to the floor. Farrell's breath grew sharp and shallow when she flipped off the light. She fumbled with his belt, drew down his pants, and muttered in French. She unbuttoned his shirt, rested her hands on his chest, then gathered her feet under her and crouched over Farrell. For a split second he heard a voice telling him to flee. But he was far, far beyond control.

As she lowered herself onto him, she whispered in a raspy voice, "Tell me what makes you go, Collins. Tell me what makes you go."

Farrell's mouth opened wide as she took him. "You do," Farrell groaned. "You make me go."

Farrell woke in the darkness a few hours later unsure where he was and, once he understood, even more unsure where he was going. Inez lay with her back to him, curled into a ball, her breathing rhythmic and slow. Inez hadn't cried out on her own the first or the second time; she waited until Farrell began. Afterward, in the languid moments, she draped herself across his chest like a soldier exhausted after battle. She ran her fingers through the hair on his chest and asked, "Who is Maria?"

Farrell stiffened.

"You cry her name the first time and mine only the second," Inez said. "So impolite."

"I'm sorry," Farrell said. Consumate liar that he was, he regained his composure. "Someone from my past."

"Tell me about her," Inez said.

"For your notes?"

Inez pinched the skin on his chest. "This is personal. You are in my bed."

"She was a lover in another life," Farrell said.

"Does she break your heart?" Inez asked.

Farrell pushed Inez away. He propped himself up on his elbow to study her. In the dim light from the bathroom he could see her face pasted with the same expression he'd seen the day before when Page was about to jump: placid and yet hungry.

"Her heart was already breaking," Farrell said. "Saying any more would be impolite."

"But . . ."

Farrell pressed his finger to her lips. Inez opened her mouth and bit at his finger. He wrenched his hand free. "That hurt!"

"Pain and pleasure are so close," Inez said, and she reached under the covers to stroke him. Despite the ache there and the sting of her teeth on his finger, he stirred. Only this time she did not cross with him; she bucked up and down, her mouth and eyes wide open, no sounds passing her lips. Even after he came, she continued the quick, sharp movements on him until he grew so sensitive that he almost cried out. He grabbed her hips to still her. She strained against them. He dug his fingernails sharply into her buttocks until he thought she'd bleed. She smiled, rolled off without a word, and curled up with her back to him.

Now as he listened to her sleep, he thought of Lena and Maria. He felt guilty, then defiant: what else could he have done? It wasn't what he wanted to do. It just happened. Something inside of him, those chemicals, whatever, had made him do it. It was beyond his control.

He closed his eyes. *Beyond his control.* He repeated the words to himself again and again. Almost instantly he was back in Tijuana the night he left to go south to meet Gabriel's customers. He had run across the wet asphalt of the runway while the engines of the corporate jet jabbed at his eardrum like a blunt, probing instrument shoved too far into the canal. As he ran, he told himself this was the last time, that after this trip he'd let the project unwind and move by itself. The liaison between he and Maria scared him. Lena's children made him think. Too many streams of information, sensory overload. He was in too deep. A firm hand reached out to assist him at the top of the stairs.

"It is very loud, is it not, señor?" asked the man. Farrell ducked through the door "My name is Hector. I'll be taking care of you on the ride down. Your passport?"

Hector was five foot ten inches and 165 pounds, with rich, shortly cut black hair. Farrell reached into the pocket of the speckled blue linen jacket he wore and handed him the passport. He figured Hector was a year younger than himself. Hector's pronounced feature was his nose, off-center and heavy, obviously broken several times. Perched between thin eyebrows on the bridge of the beak were a pair of horned-rimmed glasses. These last, supported by a well-cut charcoal business suit, created the odd impression of a former welter-weight fighter who'd gotten a job as a junior attorney with a Wall Street law firm.

"Very good, Señor Farrell." He handed Farrell back the passport. "I believe your ride will be comfortable. There is some reading material that has been provided which I'm sure you will wish to review at some point during the ride: six hours, one stop."

Farrell shifted in the narrow galley. "Our destination?" he asked, hearing the fretting tone in his voice and becoming annoyed.

"Did they not tell you?" Hector asked. "Cali, Señor Farrell. Cali, Colombia."

A sensation like the last two inches of bathwater draining from a tub enveloped the pit of his stomach. "Of course," Farrell said. "Cali."

He had tried to tell himself it would be some neutral ground in southern Mexico. He was in too deep; they were heading for the heart of it.

Farrell nervously tucked the passport back into his jacket and watched an airport worker help Hector with the stairway. He imagined a warm wind blowing in his face. His spine tingled. "Cali . . . Colombia." Hector closed the door and turned, surprised to find him still in the gangway.

"A problem, señor?" Hector asked.

"None at all," Farrell said. "Just daydreaming. A habit."

"I'm sure," Hector said. "Let me show you the way. Señor Cordova is already waiting."

Farrell pushed through the blue curtains to find Cordova sprawled across the tan loveseat that along with two airplane seats—first-class size—dominated the left side of the cabin. Opposite were six other lounge-style chairs. In the center stood a kidney-shaped coffee table of matching tan.

Cordova rose and cried: "Jack Farrell, good to see you! Not often we get to travel in such style, eh?"

"Or such mystery," Farrell said, taking his extended hand.

"Mr. Cortez thought it best not to disturb you with our destination," Cordova said with a grunt. He plopped in the loveseat and drew the opposite ends of the two seat belt sets and clipped them across his massive belly. "This meeting required so long to set up we thought you would be better off waiting to know."

"Gabriel?"

"He meets us there," Cordova said. "He had last-minute business in Sinaloa. He asked me to brief you on what to expect."

Hector interrupted to tell them they'd been cleared for take off. He knelt and flipped a lever that freed Farrell's chair so it swiveled toward the front of the cabin. He flipped the lever again, locking the chair, then repeated the process with Cordova's loveseat.

An hour later, Cordova was drinking tequila neat. Farrell had moved to a chair next to the loveseat where he could see the charts in a three-ring binder Cordova had produced from his briefcase. Cordova said Cali operated in a fundamentally different manner than the more famous Medellin organization. Like the Medellin traffickers, Cordova said, some of the people at the top in Cali came from the bleak slums of Colombia, often beginning their careers as street hustlers, thieves, or kidnappers. But in the mid-1920s they realized that Americans were demanding more cocaine than marijuana and they leapt to supply the demand.

"They made more money than they could have supposed in their wildest dreams," Cordova said. "In Medellin, a war developed almost immediately over turf. In Cali, the early members of the cartel sought the anonymity of middle- and upper-middle class life.

"Sure there are the big mansions and the estates like that owned by the Escobars," Cordova said. "But there is above all an effort to blend in. These men are interested in business, not bloodshed. If they have problems with a politician, they bribe him, not kill him."

He pointed to a pie chart, which indicated that only fifteen percent of the billions of dollars the cartel generated directly benefited Colombians. The rest passed into the hands of freelance salesmen, distributors, and service vendors such as themselves. "Too often they have no idea of the day-to-day details of the other eighty-five percent of the business," Cordova said.

"You're saying they think the system is inefficient?"

"To an extent," he replied. "The business has thrived in large part because it was based on entrepreneurship. If someone wanted to expand a market or devise a new transportation or cash-flow system, the attitude was go ahead: if you succeed, you will be rewarded."

"And now?" Farrell asked.

"They are concerned, as you said, that this approach, while successful, is too . . . sprawling?" Cordova said. "They want to invest some of the fifteen percent of the business they control to eventually take as much as thirty to thirty-five percent of the industry."

"Consolidation," Farrell said.

Cordova tapped his finger at a large section on the pie chart. "There will always be room for the entrepreneur in distribution and trafficking because these are the areas most likely to be disrupted by the Drug Enforcement Agency and the other U.S. organizations opposed to the business. As long as they create an environment that allows easy entry to the market, people well paid will take the risk, create new systems to replace those that have been destroyed."

"So where do you . . . I mean we . . . fit in?" Farrell asked.

"As we have in the past: financing, infrastructure, and warehousing," Cordova said. "Cali has long been concerned at the lack of loyal middle-level managers attending to these areas in the United States. At the same time, these men are not yet convinced it is time to bring all of the concerns—how would you say it—in-house?"

Cordova paused when Hector entered the cabin and asked them if they were ready to eat. "Fifteen minutes," Cordova said.

After Hector left, Cordova went on: "Effectively, they are interested in becoming venture capitalists for a series of small, emerging organizations that they will use as test cases."

Cordova sipped from the tequila. "That's where we fit in, Jack. Mr. Cortez and I have a solid reputation with these men, providing landing strips, planes, boats, the capital infrastructure of the business. But your methods and ideas have generated a new interest in our organization as a possible target of investment."

Farrell leaned back in the seat. He called Hector and asked for a drink, a double bourbon. He needed it. "So it rides on me."

"If you convince them, we expand," Cordova said. "If not, we go on as before. They are pleased with our services."

"What is the potential for exposure?" Farrell said. He shut his eyes and saw numbers on green sheaves of paper. "It seems to me that the only person assuming risk here is me."

"Mr. Cortez and I have discussed that," Cordova said. "Your percentage for any increase in the business, of course, will have to rise in proportion to risk. That is agreed."

Hector returned with dinner, and the conversation suspended while Cordova gorged on filet of sole cordon bleu and a bottle of white wine. Farrell ate, understanding that the tingle of misgiving he'd endured at the beginning of the flight was building. What had begun a year ago as a lark, a thrill—something with recognizable limits, a steep little snowy ridge he could run on a clear windless day—had mutated; a terrible fog now threatened to sock him in.

A half hour after dinner Hector served them brandy and told them to buckle their belts for a landing.

"We can't be there yet," Farrell said. They had only been flying for three hours. He figured a trip to Colombia would take at least seven.

Cordova thumped his fist against his chest and dislodged a bubble of gas, which he belched into the cabin. He splayed his hands. "Refueling perhaps," he said. "Maybe we take on another passenger. Who knows?"

"Any idea where we are?" Farrell asked.

Cordova checked his watch. "Oaxaca perhaps. If the pilot made good time, Guatemala," he said, reaching for the brandy bottle.

They descended. Farrell peered out the window. A sliver of moon shone in the sky, but no lights glowed below. He felt the rumble, followed by the grinding buzz of the landing gear. Still no lights.

"Jesus," Farrell said. "He's going to put this down in the pitch dark."

Cordova didn't respond. He was fixed on the brilliant green and red plumage and the luxurious tail of the quetzal, a bird of Guatemala that had been embroidered onto the textured wall at the front of the cabin. Beads of sweat rolled off his head.

"Hate to land, Jorge?" Farrell asked, somewhat amused. He had thought Cordova incapable of fear.

"Blew out a tire a few years back landing in a field near my home. Can't stand it now."

Farrell shut his eyes again, seeing the tire ruts in a field where Gabriel had hunted. The little dove boy ran through that field, chasing fallen birds. The jet shuddered. Farrell pressed his face to the black window. Where there was nothing, a single blue light flashed. A second, followed by a hundred others, a thread of blue lamps sewn to the horizon. They landed with the familiar jolt, the scorch of tires, and the winding rev of the turbines.

"We will be a few minutes, señors," Hector said. "You can get out and stretch your legs if you wish."

Before Farrell could answer, the sweated, pallid figure of Cordova hustled by Hector and through the curtains. The stairs groaned in protest, the jet leaned then righted itself.

"Hates to land," Farrell said.

"With me it is the takeoff," Hector said. "I never believe we will clear the trees."

Farrell stuck his head out the side of the jet and was blasted by the black peppercorn smell of jungle foliage mixed with the saffron odor of red clay. The blue lights cast a soft, unnatural glow on the rich grasses growing beyond the edge of the dirt runway. About eighty yards away, barely visible, a ragged tree line wavered in the mist.

Farrell climbed down the stairs and away from the jet to the grass. As his eyes became used to the pale blue light, he could make out cattle grazing. He walked further, hearing the beasts lowing, talking of their ignorance in the dark. With a great squawk! an egret kicked out from under Farrell's feet, flapping into the darkness toward the hardwoods.

"I figure we're near La Gomera," Cordova said in a raspy voice. He flashed a lighter and lit a cigarette. The red glow of the cigarette filtered through the blue lamp light to turn Cordova's mouth the shade of spring clover.

"I don't know it," Farrell said.

"Small town," Cordova said, pointing what Farrell guessed to be west with the tip of the cigarette. "We're farther south in Guatemala than I thought, almost to the border of El Salvador."

He chuckled, sucking so hard on the cigarette that the coal sparked and crackled.

"Mr. Cortez and I built this five, maybe six years ago," Cordova said. "One of our first projects. My idea for the blue lights: they cast almost no reflection on the plants. It's almost become an industry standard."

Cordova pointed down the runway. The glowing tip of the cigarette traced an arc in the humid air. "If I remember correctly there's a small dirt road off the other end of the runway that you can take about fifteen miles to a small restaurant that makes a passable paella. Of course, if your palette desires something more adventurous, you must travel further to—"

At first, they were dull snaps. The volume of the gunfire spread, snapping, strong and deadly: short flashes of orange at the tree line on the other side of the jet, followed by *ping! ping! ping!* on the fuselage. Pencil-thin cords of white light ripped the night. Behind them the jet's engines revved.

"Correz, Correz!" Run! Run! Cordova screamed.

Farrell sprinted through the grass, driving his knees as high as he could up and out of the morass of slender stalks. His pant legs soaked and flapped against his calves. Farrell wove side to side while bullets cracked around him. Cattle scattered, bounding herky-jerky, shitting and bawling as they ran. A mad bellow shook the darkness. Farrell thought Cordova had been hit, then understood that it was one of the feeding herd. The beast thundered behind them, roaring in gut-shot agony.

The tree line was closer now. Farrell was astounded to find Cordova right beside him, breaching through the tall grass, the latent moves of the dove boy surfacing under the gushing flow of adrenaline.

A frond of a large plant slapped at Farrell's wrist. He was aware of an insistent hum behind him that did not register until it ballooned into a close thunder: the jet was accelerating. They crashed into the jungle. Undergrowth clawed at their faces and shirts and pants. A vine hooked Farrell's ankle. He sprawled into a clump of bamboo, up again instinctively trailing Cordova, a supercharged bulldozer driving deep into the forest.

Sixty yards in, Cordova made a gurgling sound and stopped and clung to a tree, coughing and panting. Farrell grabbed the tree too, squinting at the salt that stung his eyes. He caught the stench of urine and realized with disgust that Cordova had pissed his pants. Through an opening in the canopy, the single red running light of the jet soared away. The jet thunder faded. The gunfire stopped. They were alone, stranded in the jungle.

Inez jerked in her sleep. Farrell was jolted into consciousness. He looked at her. It was all happening again. *Beyond control.* He was sick to his stomach. He looked at his watch. It was a few minutes past one in the morning. He slid out from under the blankets and was pulling on his pants when she stirred.

"It is gauche to leave a woman in the night, *chéri.*"

"Nothing to do with you," Farrell lied. "I can't sleep."

"I think of something to do," she said, pulling back the covers so he could see her body. The smell of her and of their sex swirled around him and he had to fight not to return.

"You wore me out," Farrell said weakly.

"Mmmmm," Inez said. "I think you have so much far to go."

"Not tonight," Farrell said, and he closed the door to her powerful odor behind him.

Chapter 18

Outside, Farrell's mind raced. It jumbled and mixed events. Time broke, fragmenting the sound of disparate voices, the smell of different lands, the sight of alien events. Cordova picked a leech from his chin in the jungle. Lena ran from him into a darkened hallway. Inez gave The Wave a malevolently maternal hug. Stern, the FBI agent, showed him his badge. His father jigged with the vacuum cleaner.

Farrell slammed the heels of both hands against his temples. He doubled over. He knew he was close to breaking. He clung to the threads that held the remaining boxes in his mind shut. He retched and retched again.

Farrell made it to his room, shut the door, and bolted it. The diary was sticking out from underneath the mattress. He became feverish looking at it, turned away, and immediately began to sweat. He climbed fully clothed under the blankets as the sweat turned cold. Chills wracked his body. His tongue turned dry. The fever returned and with it a new cycle of torture, his symptoms those of a man rung out by malaria on the second seven-hour cycle. Only he'd never had the disease. I'm like my father, he thought, a manic on the rise. He turned on a flashlight in the dark. To survive the augue that mamboed through him over the next hour he counted in a steady cadence, breathed to it, focusing on the beam of light that cut the dark room. He kept calm like this for a long time. Then Inez pierced his tranquility. How wild she was. How wild she'd made him. He imagined this was what an addict felt like after overdosing: sick, but satiated. He deluded himself for a few moments that this was the end of it. He'd had her—a double dose of a pure drug—and had lived. He could walk away now. But in his heart, he knew he wanted her again, to see if wilder than wild was within her range. That was the way he was, beyond control.

From deep inside came another voice, his wife's, telling him that ignorance was not bliss, that Inez's sensual, savage nature had roots. He had to know more about her. It was his only chance for control, the only chance to keep the lid on the boxes. Two days had passed since he'd spoken to Europe. Farrell got out from under the blankets and changed his soaking wet clothes. He grabbed two pieces of paper, went outside and down the road to the phone booth.

This time the Swiss attorney answered himself.

"Good afternoon, sir. I was just about to leave, thought you might not call us," the attorney said. "The report came in a few hours ago."

Farrell wiped the cold sweat that still clung to the nape of his neck: "First, tell me about the inquiries."

"Unfortunately, the secrecy laws seem to be functioning in both directions," the attorney said. "Nothing yet. If you are nervous, there are always more precautions we can take, the creation of intermediary corporations in Liechtenstein."

"Take them," Farrell said.

"It will be expensive," he said. "I do not ordinarily conduct this type of business over the phone, but I expect a fifteen percent increase in my fee."

"Take the steps," Farrell said, his voice almost a shout.

"Very good, sir," the attorney replied curtly. "The report?"

"What did he find?"

"The detective is a woman, actually," the attorney said. "Highly recommended. The gist of Ms. Didier to date is as follows: Born November 12, 1960, in Lyons to Laurence and Pauline Didier. Father, a photographer with the Associated Press. Dead—"

"I know the father," Farrell interrupted. "What about the mother?"

The line went silent for a long time, then, "Pauline, born June 17, 1941, in Chamonix, France, to Rene and Imogene LaCroix. Rene served in the French Army in World War I in an artillery unit. Subsequently, became a mountain guide in the Aguiles region near Chamonix.

"The parents owned a restaurant later in life, which served as a social center for climbers. Rene died in 1974, Imogene in 1980.

"The daughter, Inez's mother, left for Paris in 1958 to study. Met Laurence Didier, an American exchange student, soon after, married, quit school and gave birth to Inez. The detective believes from an interview she had with a neighbor of Pauline's in Lyons that during his time in Vietnam, Pauline and Inez spent much of their time in Chamonix.

"When Didier was killed, there was a falling out between Rene and Pauline. She and Inez moved to Lyons, where Pauline took a job as a secretary to a midlevel executive in a textile factory, silk I think.

"A neighbor said Inez was a quiet child—this is a direct quote—'who seemed to delight in taking pictures of awful things. She had a camera her father gave her before he was killed, and when my sister's husband, Pierre, died in a barge accident, that Inez walked up to her in the cemetery and snapped her picture as she stood over his open grave.' Close quote."

Farrell scribbled notes. "How did she get the neighbor to tell her that?"

"Cash does wonder for people's voices," he said in a cynical tone. "Okay, we move on. This from the sister whose picture Inez snapped. The sister, Claudette Noir, claims to have occupied the apartment next to Pauline and Inez until 1978. Noir says that in the late 1960s and early 1970s, the Didiers were cash poor, always borrowing money, on the edge of eviction. In 1973, the financial problems disappear."

"How does she know this?"

"Noir says Pauline suddenly was no longer in debt to a loan shark named Piret, Noir's cousin," the attorney said. "Pauline owed Piret a great deal of money at one time and then didn't. And there was new furniture and clothes for both Pauline and her daughter."

"Where did the money come from?"

"Not clear," the attorney said. "In the following years Pauline became something of a social traveler, accompanying high-level managers from the factories, men in their late fifties and early sixties, to various events in Lyons. I see a news clipping here of Pauline at the opera. She's gamine, but striking. The daughter is with her—striking also."

"I've seen her," Farrell said.

"Oh, of course," the attorney said. "Two other things from Madame Noir. In the mid-1970s there were several rows . . . fights I'd believe you'd call them, *chez Didier.*"

"What sort?"

"Men banging on the door, quite angry, late at night. Several developed into prolonged verbal affairs in which Pauline threatened to call the police. That usually ended them.

"But there was one that didn't end. A terrible broil. Noir thinks it was February 1976. A vice president at a local textile mill, angry at Pauline for some reason, arrived when Inez was home alone. The girl stayed two days in the hospital. Pauline's life quieted substantially after that."

Thinking of Inez, Farrell let the receiver drift away from his ear.

"Hello?" the attorney yelled.

"I'm here, any more?"

"Yes. Inez matriculates at Institute Des Cinemas and Photographies at the Sorbonne in Paris in the fall of the following year. Studies under Czechoslovakian ex-patriot director Milos Cranz. Produced three award-winning student films before leaving midway through her third year.

"Cranz, now seventy, said he remembers Didier as—quoting him now—'a nervous, dolorous young woman whose work was marked by strong visual effects.' Close quote."

The attorney continued: "Cranz dug up a copy of Didier's second-year project—*La Vague de Fer (The Iron Wave)*—a twenty-minute short about a young Parisien who was obsessed with surfing, but could never get to the sea; so he 'surfed' on top of freight trains. Cranz said she won an award for the film on the basis of one tremendous shot: the camera is behind the crouched boy as the train rounds a broad curve toward a mountain tunnel and a grassy valley opens up to the right."

"Sounds spectacular," Farrell said.

The attorney clucked noncommittally. "Cranz said Didier was involved for a time with a Lebanese Christian named Sami Aboudallah, who now makes television commercials for yogurt and bottled water companies.

"It took our person two days, but she finally arranged an interview with Aboudallah by claiming herself a reporter for a new cinema magazine. At first Aboudallah did not want to speak of Didier, but when she told him she'd keep his comments on a not-for-attribution basis, he talked."

"She's creative," Farrell said.

"You get what you pay for," the attorney said. "Anyway, quoting Aboudallah: 'We were in Cranz's early courses together. She found out I was from Beruit, wanted to know about the fighting—what it looked like, what the people thought of it. I told her what you tell anyone: that it was paradise before the fighting. Now my village in the highlands is rubble. I cannot go back.' "

"Go on," Farrell said. He took another note.

"Aboudallah claims they became lovers because they each saw themselves as different from the cliques within the institute. Aboudallah also says he was the cameraman on *La Vague de Fer*.

"Quoting him again, 'It was her idea. But I was on top of the train with the boy. Inez couldn't stomach that sort of thing. She saw the boy climbing on the iron supports of the metro. She followed him and talked to him, fed him. After that, he would do anything for her, even the train stunt which could have killed him. It wasn't like what the film made him out to be. He hadn't surfed on a train before.' "

"That's all he said about her?" Farrell asked.

"No, I've got the pages out of order. Here we are: Aboudallah said Christian, that's the boy, his attraction to Inez and her encouragement, inevitably led to friction in their relationship.

"Aboudallah said she would laugh at his frustration, say Christian's just a boy. Aboudallah thought it went further than that. He saw other women. In December of that year, Inez discovered his infidelities at the same time she discovered she was pregnant. Aboudallah told her that he was not in love with her and would not stay.

"Quoting Aboudallah here: 'How did I know it was not Christian's baby? I moved out with her screaming, throwing dishes, books. She left Paris soon after and, really, until I saw one of her ski films at a festival last summer—a very strange film—I hadn't heard a thing."

"What about the child?" Farrell asked.

"Aboudallah has no idea. No records detail a birth in Lyons or Paris to an Inez Didier that year. Our person will check in Chamonix on the off-chance that she had the baby there."

"Good," Farrell said. "When shall I hear again?"

"Five days," the attorney said.

"I'll call," Farrell said. "And set up the new corporations soon."

"Tomorrow morning, sir."

Farrell returned to his room to lay in the dark. Hearing about Inez's past allowed him to focus on something other than his own deeds. The terrible sprinting of images had slowed, the fever-chills cycle subsided. He thought about Inez as a granular substance, a powder. He thought he understood some of the grit and talc that made her tempting, almost irresistible. He admitted, however, that crucial bits and pieces remained to be discovered. Before he could make any judgments, fatigue overcame him. He slept without dreaming.

He awoke at 7 A.M. and went to check on Page. The one-eyed skier was gone. A note was pinned to Inez's door telling Farrell, The Wave, Ann, and Tony to be in position on Granite Chief as early as possible. She'd meet them up there at seven-thirty to begin the shots.

Farrell raced to get his gear, to drive as fast as he could to the mountain. As he buckled his boots, he tried to imagine Inez younger. How had she convinced the boy to surf the train? She probably didn't need to persuade him; he probably loved the idea, Farrell thought.

Farrell did not know whether to tell The Wave and Page of what he'd learned. He respected their need to understand; and he considered the possibility that the information was irrelevant; but most of all he was afraid to reveal he had the financial wherewithal to hire a foreign detective. He'd have to act on their behalf. Sometimes ignorance was best.

He found The Wave taping Page's ribs at the midstation restaurant. Over Farrell's protests, Page was determined to ski. "We've got at least a five-day layoff after today," Page said. "This is only one jump."

"That's all it takes, mon," The Wave said. "I looked up where you're going yesterday. The thing looks like an upside down boot, you know Italy's toe shoved up into Switzerland. All sorts of junk— boulders, logs, and other shit in the landing zone. Steeper than hell, too. Much worse than Palisades. Told her she was four nickels short of a quarter she thinks I'm boarding up there."

"She took that well, I bet," Page said.

"I don't think she cared," The Wave said. "She looked at me like I was an afterthought."

"Not me," Page said. "She was at my door at six, telling me this was my shot, the moment I've been waiting for."

"You ask her why she followed you?" Farrell asked.

Page looked at the floor. "I did, but she has this way of smothering what you really want to say. I—"

Inez swept into the room in a full-length, powder-blue down coat. *"Allez-y. Allez-y.* It is already the quarter hour! And you still drink coffee?"

Farrell saw her, thought immediately of her naked, and became angry with himself. Page was right. Apart from her, he could be somewhat objective. Close, she was a pleasant suffocating force. He glanced at Page again, took a deep breath, and crossed to her. He said softly, "He's still injured. Why don't you call him off. Just let me jump."

Inez touched Farrell's face. He swooned. She whispered, *"Chéri.* Last night was the wonderful experience. *Mais l'expérience même si sexuelle,* it does not give you the right to direct my film. The actor, he tells me he is ready. I respect him."

"Listen—"

"I have not the time, *chéri,"* Inez said. "Page has the rendezvous."

"With what?" Farrell demanded.

Inez tisked. "I think sometimes you are so smart . . . and then . . . well, you just do not comprehend, do you? With himself, of course."

With that Inez charged out, looking back just long enough to say, "I see you there in twenty minutes. *Allez-y."*

Page and The Wave gaped at Farrell. They knew. Farrell

jammed his hands in his pockets, irritated. "She was all over me. What could I do?"

A local filmmaker had told Inez that if she shot the sequence on Granite Chief—a brooding peak of sheer stone, wrinkled with snow and tree—later than 9:30 A.M., the sun would wash out the rock's brilliant copper and blue-gray hues and the rich green of the firs.

It was a steep climb to the top of Granite Chief, which Farrell made in total silence, listening to Tony and Ann decide how they'd shoot the sequence. He had sweated through his underwear by the time they reached the summit. A wind kicked up and he fought numbness. Page winced with every breath and leaned over his poles, trying to relax himself.

Tony crawled to the edge of the cliff and peered over. "I'd have to be one drunk mother to drop off this bastard."

Farrell lay on his stomach and inched his way to the edge. He was above the toe of the boot, a fifteen-foot straight plunge onto snow badly rippled by sun and wind. Any miss on the landing would trip the skier off into the jagged rocks under the tiny wedge of snow. He looked to his left, higher on the ridge, above the heel of the boot. There the granite wall rose a straight thirty feet off the snow. It was not as high as the Palisades jump, but as The Wave had said, the landing—into a narrow gully, fifty-five degrees steep, lined with ragged granite like saw teeth—made it twice as brutal.

Farrell slid himself back. Now that he was away from Inez, he could think clearer. "The heel entrance is just out of the question," he said to Page. "We'll jump in here at the toe. It will be tough—you'll have to skid hard right as you land, then whip left under the cliff and turn into the gully."

Page nodded, "I've only seen one guy jump straight into the heel."

"He make it?" Ann asked.

"Missed his landing spot by a good twenty feet, broke through some rotten snow, and went the hundred and fifty yards straight to the bottom. Snapped both ankles, both arms."

"Wonder he didn't break his skull," Ann said. "Wonder you didn't yesterday."

"Confidence builder, aren't you?"

"I call them as I see them," Ann said.

"I'm ready," Tony said. He snapped the last buckle on his harness.

Farrell drove a climbing bolt into a chunk of exposed rock, looped the thick nylon rope through the hole, and passed it to Tony, who rigged it through his harness. Page and Ann took up the slack, holding the rope taut as Tony moved to the edge. The cameraman blanched before kicking himself over. "Fucking things I do for a living," Farrell heard him mumble as he dropped from sight.

Five minutes later, Farrell peered over the face. Tony had lashed himself onto the rocks to the right of the toe with ropes and bolts. He was in the middle of this web, his camera mounted and set, a large hairy spider waiting for a fly.

"My turn," Ann said, nudging Farrell.

The three climbed to the other side of the heel cliff and set up a similar system to Tony's. Ann went over the front without hesitation, and by the time they'd lowered the camera to her, she was anchored on a narrow ledge where she could catch the skiers coming out of the toe, through the instep under the heel, and into the tube.

"You want me to wear the helmet?" Farrell asked Page.

"I want it," Page said. They recrossed the cornice to their skis.

"You sure? It's just one more heavy load."

"I'm getting used to it," Page said sharply.

Farrell glanced down to the flat below the chute where Inez and The Wave had dug a pit, stuck brightly colored poles in the snow, and erected the film and video cameras. Page's father stood next to the pit, gazing up at them. "He's here again," Farrell said.

Page nodded. "I smelled him ten minutes ago."

"You're first," Farrell said once they had their skis on. "You fall, I want to come in and help."

"No," Page said. "I'll use the helmet camera to get you going off the top from behind, then Tony picks you up on his."

"Yeah, and who gets you from behind?"

"No one. The audience goes for a ride with me."

Page turned away to fumble with the helmet straps, trying to get a snug fit under his chin. Farrell watched him for a moment, saw he wouldn't change his mind, then side-slid toward the tip of the ledge.

"Ready?" Page asked.

Farrell huffed to force more oxygen into his lungs. "All set."

Page picked up the radio. "All go up here . . . and Action!"

Farrell heaved himself up and sideways, falling parallel to the slope, clearing the rocks, his feet and skis cutting solid arcs in the air. Tony's camera tracked him like a shotgun after a bird. He landed with a vicious jolt on the cement surface of the frozen snow and skidded. One hand grabbed at the ripples in the ice, the other waved in the air. He slid toward the jagged rocks.

Ten feet before the snow gave out all together, the tail of his downhill ski struck sharp stone, which jerked him to his feet. Keen pieces of granite tore at the plastic bottom of the skis. He bucked across the top of them, trying frantically to free himself and return to the ice.

He lurched forward, caught by another rock. He kicked himself free of it, scooted sharply left, uphill between two exposed boulders—then angled into the instep below the heel right at Ann's waiting camera. His skis dragged under him and he understood that a good portion of their flat bottoms had been gouged; now hunks of plastic hung under his feet, pulling him in directions he didn't want to go.

Farrell knew in an instant that the skis would no longer carve precise turns. He was forced to windmill them, throwing himself, forehead to hips, out over the slope until he was on the verge of pitching and rolling into disaster. The weightlessness that occurred when he was on the edge of diving countered the effects of his damaged equipment; it allowed him to free his skis from the snow, haul them around, perpendicular to the slope, and then to throw his torso out again.

He twisted by Ann's camera in this fashion, plunging like a crippled duck into the gully that ran to the floor, a shot much steeper than the stem of the Y Couloir, which made him pray for strength.

On the fifth switchback, his tips snagged. The skis smacked the wall. Farrell relaxed on impact, slid backward, and got his skis downhill again, somehow saving himself from the worst nightmare a skier can have: tumbling backward, not knowing when the impact will come. He wheeled and smashed through the next fifty turns, his thighs burning and his groin begging for mercy. He limped his way to the bottom, then thrashed through the snow toward the cameras.

"Si cru!" Inez cried, turning the lens toward him as he trudged by. *"Si sauvage!* I know from last night how you perform for me today!"

Behind her, just out of earshot, Farrell could see SOUTH TAHOE FIRE—TRENT embroidered in red over Page's father's heart. No longer caring about the camera, Farrell tore off his hat and goggles. He growled into the lens. "What's he doing here?"

"Trent?" Inez asked, twisting the lens for a close-up. "He came to see his son make the ski jump."

"Page's all twisted inside up there," Farrell took another step closer. "Get the old man out of here."

"No," Inez said. "He wants to see his son. I do not act to break up such a reunion of family."

"This isn't about family," Farrell said, wrenching her away from the eyepiece. "Why's he here?"

"Ne touche pas!" she hissed. "I tell you once already, last night does not mean today!"

"I'm asking you!"

"His mother said he wants to see his son," Inez said. "Me, I arrange it. A problem?"

"Depends on why."

"I am the woman. I feel the other woman's pain!" Inez said. She pressed the radio set tight against the side of her head.

"Is this true?" she said slowly. Her eyes widened in pleasure. "When? One minute. Very good. We are ready."

Inez twisted her chin toward Farrell. "We continue this discussion later, no? Page tells Tony he is ready to run. So I make my film now."

Up on the ridge, Page's yellow helmet camera was visible far to the right of where Farrell had jumped. He stood on top of the heel of the boot, just above the ice fall which bulged off the cliff like a glass milk bottle.

Inez hopped from foot to foot. "Tony says he comes off the center of the heel and does a forty-foot drop tip into the channel!" She bent deeply at the knees so the camera apparatus tilted at the chute's angle.

Farrell tugged his glove free to pinch the flesh on his hand.

"Inez, call him off," Farrell pleaded. "He's held together with tape as it is. If you want someone to jump that, I'll do it."

"The decision, it is not mine," Inez replied without giving him a second glance. "Or for you. He knows his limits. We let him perform."

"This isn't some goddamned act," Farrell said, raising his voice. He took a quick second look at Page's father, who had moved away with his hand at his brow, staring up at the ridge top oblivious to what was transpiring. "This has consequences."

Inez stepped away from the camera. She laughed: "This is the point, no? If you do not understand this, then get off the set."

"You're out of bounds here, Inez."

Inez acted astonished. "Am I? I just watch, Collins. You and Page and The Wave are these ones who enjoy the doing. I am just the *spectateur.*"

She pressed her hand to the headset, her eye to the lens piece. "Okay. Five, four, three, two, and *Action!*"

Page soared off the top of the ice fall in a perfect T: his arms extended wide, skis pointed dead down the chute. He cleared the ice and hung in the air, eighty feet from the ground. Page swung his hands in broad circles as if he were breaststroking through water. Farrell knew the action was designed to retard forward lean, to prevent him from pitching into a swan dive. All he could think was that Page looked like he was praying.

"Jesus, Matty!" Trent Page cried.

It was not that Farrell wanted to watch, he was hypnotized, seduced by the sheer gall of the stunt. This was beyond flow. Page had broken through into a level of skill and daring he'd never witnessed before; the thrill seeker as a piece of art, ephemeral and unforgettable.

On the third rotation of his arms, Page drew his hands back to his hips, brought the tips of the skis up and parallel to the slope. He made a pinpoint landing. The early morning snow popped and flashed as he controlled his speed, instantly making the correct decision to alter the pattern of his turn to the windmills Farrell had used. Page bounced and wheeled on kangaroo legs down the face of the mountain. His upper body slammed over the fall line, dancing out there on the razor. All seemed well until he reached a spot some fifty yards above the exit to the chute. There the spirit of the artist at the height of his powers seemed to spill from him the way air will a child's inflatable toy. Page withered and slid to the bottom, where he sat very still.

Trent Page began to run, but Inez stopped him. "He is not broken, only overwhelmed," she said. Tears ran down her cheeks. "He comes to us in a minute."

Page's father made as if to protest, then fell silent. Page stood finally. His body quivered. He poled his way toward them.

Inez tapped Farrell on his forearm and whispered, "You hate me before he jumps. But when you watch, you love it, no?"

Farrell's eyelids drooped as if he were sedated. He nodded.

"This I knew," she said.

As if in a trance, Farrell turned from Inez to watch Page ski to his father. He decided later that if he wore the camera on the helmet, he was sure the first thing he would have seen was Trent's tilted, jittery posture.

"What are you doing here, Pop?" Page said. He didn't accept the hand his father offered.

"Thought I'd come to see you . . . like the old days," Trent said. His voice sounded like chunks of stone rubbing together. "Thought we might have a chance to talk."

"Nothing to talk about," Page said. He dropped his head away from his father to insert the pole tip in the release mechanism of his binding. "From what I've seen lately, things haven't changed."

"You'd have to come now, wouldn't you?" Trent begged. "When she really did fall?"

"C'mon, Pop, you can do better than that. You used to be more creative," Page said. He pulled the pole away from the binding as if he'd decided he didn't want to be off his skis, as if he wanted to glide away.

Trent reached out and grasped his son's forearm. The old man's cheeks fluttered. "It's the truth," he said. "I haven't touched her bad in two years. I don't live with her. I haven't been at the tables in fifteen months. I'm doing right by her. You can ask."

Page's back tensed, but he did not shake off his father's hand. He stirred snow with the other pole. "She'd lie for you."

"Sure she would," Trent said. "Always protecting me, your mother. No reason for her to lie anymore, Matt. There may not be anything left to protect. I've . . . I've got this thing in my gut."

In that moment walls were erected. It became their private, sad conversation. Farrell backed away, but not before he saw all of the bluster go out of Page. Suddenly, Page looked scrawny.

Inez stood off to one side. She knelt and drew lazy circles in the snow, observing the encounter. The tears had stopped. The muscles in her face were as slack as they had been the night outside the casino. Farrell might have mistaken the expression for pity had he not looked at her eyes; in the middle of those flacid ovals, her hazel irises were cradled by whites turned blood red. The orbs darting about the scene with menacing intent.

Chapter 19

arrell barely heard Inez's instructions for them all to meet in two days at the Elk Tine Motel in Jackson Hole. Watching Page leap back into his father's life struck with the force of a forward fall at thirty-five miles an hour in a race course. He thought of his own father, felt worse, and wandered back to his room. He napped. This time he dreamed. He saw Inez on one knee in the snow again, saw her bloodshot eyes and her lazy finger in the snow. Something about the longing that pervaded her actions triggered cramps in his hamstring. He woke to grab the back of his leg, to stop the seizure, unsure why the scene had bothered him so much. He wanted to be furious with Inez, but he could not deny that she had reunited Page and his father. What about it wasn't right?

Farrell took a shower. He leaned against the tiles, smiling at the steam that billowed around him. He unwrapped a bar of soap and smelled it. It had a sweet, flowery odor. He closed his eyes, sniffed again, letting the thick scent of the soap mix with the saturated air to spur the unmistakable memory of jungle, the humid air of Guatemala thickened by a spicy sauce of peppercorn, clove, and mustard. The sauce did not bubble in the heat; only the irregular pattern of Cordova's breathing stirred the night, a painful bellows noise accented by staggering sucks and blows.

In the minutes after the jet disappeared, Farrell had become accustomed to the dim light and could make out Cordova's form, sunk against the tree trunk, his legs splayed in a vee. Farrell feared the fat man had had a heart attack. He crawled over, put his hand on the man's sopping wet shoulder, and whispered: "Jorge?"

Cordova sucked again, nodding rapidly. He coughed, spit, and sucked again. "A moment! Just a moment."

In the distance toward the runway, they heard voices, three men calling as they approached the tree line. "We've got to move," Farrell said. "There's a bamboo thicket over there."

He got a hand under Cordova's arm. The dove boy struggled to his feet and into an opening in the bamboo just large enough to conceal the two of them. Farrell prayed that whoever they were, they didn't have dogs.

They lay quiet on their stomachs. Farrell's temples pounded. Cordova's breathing gradually slowed to his regular nasal rasp. The voices never came closer. Another ten minutes, they faded.

Now the din of the jungle at night, familiar to Farrell from his days in Africa, returned: birds shifted in their rookeries, rodents scurried through the brush, insects droned. An angry mosquito lit on Farrell's ear to feed. He reached to brush it away and discovered the reason for its interest: what he had thought was sweat was blood dripping from a two-inch gash on the side of his head. He fished in his pocket, found a handkerchief, and pressed it to the wound.

"What the hell was that all about?" Farrell whispered. "Thought you said this was a business."

"A dangerous commerce at times, my friend," Cordova replied. Bamboo cracked as he shifted. "I'm afraid this could have happened for any number of reasons."

"Name three," Farrell said, struck inexplicably with the desire to cry and pummel Cordova at the same time.

"It won't do any good to get angry at me," Cordova said. "You knew the risks. Perhaps someone forgot to pay the local policia. Perhaps there is some rift between the transporters who use the strip. Or the person we were supposed to pick up had enemies. Who knows?"

"What if they were going for us?" Farrell asked.

Cordova snorted. "You take yourself too seriously. Who are we,

Jack? Bit players. No, this was something that did not concern us. We were merely caught in the middle."

Cordova moved again. His cigarette lighter flashed, revealing the dove boy's upper torso: his skin had paled to gray and was smeared with the green and red pastels of the jungle. His tie hung askew from a ripped collar. His lower lip was split. "You look like shit, too!" Cordova said, and he snapped the lighter shut and smoked. The red amber glowed.

"What do we do now?" Farrell asked.

"We sit. Seven hours or so until dawn," Cordova said. "Then we make our way to La Gomera. You have your passport with you, yes?"

Farrell did, but couldn't bring himself to answer. He thought of Lena and knew he'd gone over the edge. He told himself if he lived through this, he'd get out. He hung his head between his knees and fought the sensation of having drunk far too much.

After a long time, the tremors in his hands stopped. He slept.

Chattering birds woke Farrell at first light. Cordova had wedged himself upright between two stands of bamboo. His lower jaw working like a bellows as he snored. An unsmoked cigarette lay on his shirt next to his tie. Bits of twig and leaf hung in his matted black hair. His eyeglasses were slightly fogged. A leech sucked on his third chin.

Farrell crossed to him and shook him awake. Cordova waved his hands wildly in front of his face, cursing in Spanish at the mist that caked his glasses like glue. Farrell's ankle ached. He pulled the pant leg of his suit up to find another wound and two of the grayish slugs feeding at it.

Farrell recoiled. He ground his teeth together, forcing himself to pick at the leeches with his fingers. Cordova tapped him on the shoulder and handed him the cigarette. Farrell touched the ember to the gray slimy flesh, the flinch immediate followed by withering and a fall, one by one. Farrell pointed to the leech on Cordova's neck, then held the cigarette to it, trying to avoid the odor of his breath.

"We should hike," Farrell said when he'd finished.

Cordova nodded and they made for the airstrip.

Farrell would remark later that he heard the animal before seeing it. The beast faltered and moaned through the second growth of vegetation at the edge of the tree line. Bushes and vines shook as it plowed through them. The horns appeared first, ears, snout, the massive neck, and after that the pale gray chest.

The bull shook and stopped. After a moment, it stepped forward into an opening and now Farrell could see the bull's right front hoof, which hung off the back of its shin by a shred of blood black skin, the stump of bone brilliant white against the clay.

The bull pressed the bone into the soil, moaned only to step again, revealing the broad flank of its torso. After another agonizing step that brought him into full view, the bull bent its head to a bush and chewed.

Farrell turned and retched. Cordova grasped a tree for support. It was the bull's stomach that made the beast cry. It hung out the side of the bull, swollen and pink like a balloon. Gnats and flies buzzed around the wound, which oozed a frothy brown liquid. With every step through the undergrowth, twigs and thorns caught the sac, tugged at it, tore at it; the bull bawled at the torture, but did not stop its progress.

"Do not move," Cordova whispered. "He's probably loco from the wounds."

Light rain began to fall, soothing, clean, and sweet-smelling.

An egret flapped through the trees and landed on the bull's back, pecking at the bugs in the sparse hair, oblivious to the misery it rode. Another egret alit on the bull's head between the horns. The animal shut its eyes. Gray ears twitched when the bird's beak clipped at the skull.

The bull stepped and faltered again and lowed. Then, as if compelled by a force greater than its pain, the bull bent to a pale green bush to eat.

"I don't think it has the strength to do anything," Farrell whispered, watching as the animal rolled its head left and right to rid itself of the egret.

Cordova held him back. "You'd be surprised what kind of stamina an animal has, even one suffering like that."

They stood still and silent while the bull continued on. It came to some water running into the forest from the pasture and it pressed its blown-off front hoof down into the moisture. The bull extended its tongue, curling its lips to the coolness.

Twenty minutes elapsed before the bull disappeared. The rain came steadier and soaked Farrell and Cordova. Finally, Cordova signaled that they should move. As they skirted the opening through which the bull had passed, Cordova picked leaves off the bush the animal had fed on.

"Eat these," Cordova said. "They will dull your appetite and give you energy for the long walk to La Gomera."

Farrell rolled the teardrop-shaped leaves in his hand. "Wild tea or something?"

Cordova snorted and cocked his head toward Farrell. "You amaze me, my friend," he said. "The bull may be many things, but he is not stupid. That's cocoa."

They waded slowly into the high grass, examining the far tree line for movement. Farrell raised his face to the rain. He wiped his cheeks and forehead with the forearm of his shirt, which came away further soiled with grit and blood. Cattle milled about, eyeing them nervously. Here and there were the prone forms of dead animals. As they grazed, the living steers and cows gave the corpses wide berth.

Farrell's torn black dress loafers made a squishing noise when he stepped out onto the tarmac in the pouring rain. He still studied the far hardwoods where the ambush had been launched. He shivered even though the rain was warm. "This place gives me the creeps," Farrell said. "Let's get this over with."

Cordova tore at the buttons of his shirt until it was open to the waist. He waddled down the runway quick and stealthy-like.

"Why do you always call Gabriel Mr. Cortez?" Farrell asked while they walked. "You've known him since he was a child."

"He is my oldest friend," Cordova said. "But he is still my patron. He and his father saved me from living in that village my whole life. I owe him my respect. It is nothing more than that."

Cordova put his hand across Farrell's chest. He pivoted to look up toward the clouds which hung over the forest. Farrell heard it, too—the hum of an approaching plane.

"*Su madre!*" Cordova swore, and for the second time in less than fifteen hours, the dove boy was sprinting again.

Only this time Farrell could see the patterns in the grass. He surged by Cordova, reaching the trees while the fat man was still halfway across the meadow. Cordova collapsed next to Farrell in the waist-high bushes, gagging, spewing, and coughing.

"It's gonna kill me, I have to do that one more time," he panted.

A navy blue corporate jet, slightly larger than the one in which they had ridden the night before, broke through the cloud cover at the far end of the opening in the jungle toward the road to La Gomera. It skimmed over the runway before touchdown, spraying a wake behind it.

The jet turned and taxied toward them. The rumbling of the engines scattered the egrets. Cattle loped south. The jet stopped and the door opened. Two men in white short-sleeved shirts and straw hats climbed out. Each of them held guns. Behind them a third man, dressed in gray slacks and an embroidered smock shirt, emerged. Gabriel followed him.

Cordova smiled. "I knew he would not abandon us."

Farrell and Cordova stepped from the tree line. The two men in the straw hats knelt, their guns trained on them. Gabriel said something quick in Spanish. The third man waved his hand. The weapons were lowered.

"Your accommodations were to your liking, I see," Gabriel called as they waded to him through the grass. "The food gourmet, Jorge?"

Cordova grunted. Farrell didn't reply.

"The pilot got the wrong strip," Gabriel said. "You landed in the middle of a scheduled pickup and the locals knew the jet was wrong. They decided to let you know they didn't appreciate your presence."

"Lucky you weren't killed," said the third man. "I'm sorry this had to happen."

He extended his hand to Farrell.

"Señor Farrell, my name is De La Leon, Fernando De La Leon."

Farrell took his hand. Farrell's grip was limp.

"Let's get you on the plane and on to our destination," Gabriel said, grimacing in the downpour.

There was no reluctance on Cordova's part. He grabbed the railing to the gangway and was climbing the stairs when the words were barely out of Gabriel's mouth.

Farrell turned at the bottom of the stairs and looked out toward the jungle. The bull stood away from the herd. Its head was down. Two egrets perched on its back, pecking.

"Give me your gun a moment," Farrell said to one of the guards, who hesitated until De La Leone extended his fingers. The gun was surprisingly small and light in Farrell's hands; he'd hunted as a boy, but this was a war weapon: different, somehow deadlier.

"The safety?" Farrell asked. The guard showed him a lever above the trigger guard.

Farrell crossed back into the tall grass toward the bull. When he got within fifty yards, it raised its head and bawled a weak bawl. Blood ran from its nose and Farrell saw it was near death. The bull saw Farrell and took two halting steps in his direction before Farrell raised the gun, aimed, and shot the animal between the eyes.

It buckled forward onto its knees. The jaw hit the ground first. Then the animal rolled over into the deep grass, the pink balloon of its belly deflated and plastered into the gray hair. The egret flapped away, squawking. Numb, Farrell walked back to the runway where Gabriel, Cordova, De La Leone, and the jet waited.

Farrell shut off the shower, recalling how filthy he'd felt on the ride into Colombia. Gabriel had tried to cheer him, but he'd sat by himself. He tried to see his wife in his mind, couldn't, and he realized he didn't even know himself anymore. He tried to figure out what he'd have to do to extricate himself. A plan wouldn't come on the soaring ride south to Colombia with those dangerous men. He did the next best thing—he drank.

Farrell dried himself off and dressed. He thought about drinking again, but decided it was the last thing he needed. He sat on the bed, looking at his wife's diary. He opened it, wondering if he had the guts to read how she managed to get out of her own jungle. Farrell steeled himself.

January 10

It's over between me and Lydia now. I feel as if there were a shower curtain, pink and almost transparent, between me and what is real . . .

The curtain hangs there, moldy and wet. I press my hands and body to it, but only see shadows. Of me . . . of Lydia . . . of everyone . . .

I've been sitting here four hours, bone tired, feet aching, lots of crying . . . can't figure out what to write. Wish Jack were here, but don't know what I'd say. Whether he'd listen.

Tell the truth, I say to myself. And maybe that is the way out. I came on shift before midnight, watched Elizabeth for a half hour and charted my notes. I tried to ignore the voice in me and the image of bubbles, but couldn't. This time I knew what was happening, knew there was nothing I could do to stop it.

At three in the hospital, the halls are dark. Sounds came: the moaning of the old in their beds, the beeps of the machines that keep them alive, my feet scuffing through the supply room, paper and plastic that crinkled and ripped under my fingers until I had the needle in my hand. It was so sharp and true that it kept me company when I scuffed down the hall to the elevator.

Break, I told the charge nurse. She nodded and went back to her charts. The elevator closed. A trickle of cold dripped down my back under my scrubs. The needle kept me company.

In Lydia's hall, the bell of the elevator opening was the only sound. Two nurses I know chatted at the station. I went around the back, quiet and quick, as if I were an avenging angel who belonged there in the middle of the night.

Lydia was alone in her room at the far end of the hall. The chart on the door said her moaning kept other patients awake, so they had moved her. I smelled Lydia's sweat when I pushed through the door; she was in the bed near the window. The monitor was silent, but the pulsing blue line that tracked her heart bulged and died and left traces in the darkness.

My fingers didn't feel like mine when I pulled off the blue cap over the long steel needle. Those fingers drew back the plunger an eighth of an inch, 20 ccs. I walked, thinking of Elizabeth, and then halfway to the bed, of Jenny.

Four plastic tubes ran into Lydia. Her leg hung awkward off three cables taut to the pulley and bar above the bed. The IV bag sagged with the weight of liquid. The skin on Lydia's neck—pale, moist in the moonlight—almost made me stop when I picked up the plastic tube and held the needle to it.

But then I saw my own shadow on the curtain beyond Lydia's bed and I fumbled for the v-stopper in the middle of the tube that ran to her arm. I found it and then the rubber gasket, a diaphragm through which drugs can be administered. Or air.

The gasket held off my needle, then yielded.

Lydia stirred in her sleep. She rolled toward me. Her eyelids fluttered. Her mouth opened and chopped at the air, like she wanted water. Her eyes rolled, crossed, and then she smiled. I think she thought I was bringing her more morphine. My thumb began to pressure the plunger.

She croaked, "Is just you—the one who tells me about her feet. I was scared for a moment. You see Elizabeth tonight? Tell me about my baby."

I looked into that uncovered well of a face, crying now. I began to cry, too. Tell me about my baby.

I said Elizabeth was sleeping, that I came just to tell her that.

She nodded and cried again that Elizabeth didn't deserve her, that she knew this.

Before I could say more, a monitor clicked and a drip of morphine slipped down the line. She closed her eyes, off in her dream world where all babies were not blue, but perfectly pink. I stood there, thumb—my thumb now—on the plunger, but I couldn't do it. She loved her daughter as much as I loved mine.

I pulled the needle from the gasket and put it in my pocket. I snapped the point from the barrel.

When the elevator door opened on my floor, I leaned against the wall, knowing that Jenny will always be like a clear plastic curtain around me whether I beat against it or try to cut it or just let it be.

I guess I have to learn to live with it. At least I want to. That is a start.

Farrell closed the diary. Tears collected, then ran down his face. He knew that at the time Lena wrote those words, he must have been in the jungle, begging for a way out. Only it had gotten deeper and worse, hadn't it? And in that moment, Farrell decided he didn't want his life to continue to echo on itself. He wanted to change.

The problem was he didn't know where to begin.

He lay back on the bed and considered the notion that analyzing the past will only get you so far. The trick was to solve the present. It hit him, not where to begin, but what had bothered him long after Page had floated above Granite Chief. He slammed his hand on the bedspread. "That goddamned helmet camera was on the whole time!"

Farrell could picture it: the lens panning the entire green, gray, and white valley. The field of vision shifts and staggers during Page's leap into the air where all the audience would witness was blue sky, maybe a cloud. At once the jagged rocks reel into focus. The witness splashes into the icy rush, stalls and jerks against unseen currents, yanks free, and drops again through frozen eddies.

Now the lens goes off-kilter and focuses briefly on Trent Page. He pleads for forgiveness. But the framing is off and only half the father's face is in the picture. The camera swings across the embroidery on the father's chest. It points down at the skis, now at the piñon grove in the distance, back across the black baseball jacket and up to the sky. With the mumbled words "something in my gut," the lens returns in still, dreadful focus to the gray, resigned face.

And then?

Inez opened the door, saw him, and made to shut it. "It is the late hour," Inez said. "I have much to finish before I leave in the morning."

"We have to talk," Farrell said.

"I think that is not what you want and I have much to do," Inez said.

Farrell pushed his way in. "It's not like that."

"With men, it is always like that," Inez said, turning away. She wore black jeans and a purple sweater. "Drink?"

It was his only opening. "Why not?"

Inez slid rapidly across the room to a monitor on which a video version of the day's shooting played. He saw it was Inez's camera and he was doing the windshield wiper turns in the last stretch of the chute.

"Looks good," Farrell said.

"It is enough for what do you call?—filler," Inez said. She snapped off the monitor and the video machine. "Ice?"

"Please," Farrell said.

Inez picked up the bottle of Pernod and poured two inches of the clear liquid into the glasses, added ice cubes from a bucket, then disappeared into the bathroom. She shut the door.

A San Francisco paper, that day's, sat on the table. He picked it up, the first newspaper he'd looked at since fleeing the safe house, and thumbed through it noticing how little the news changed; like a soap opera, you could slide right into the stories after months and not notice the difference in tone. There was the usual bad news from the Middle East, the blustering of politicians in Washington, the tragedy of a local fire, the hero of the latest basketball game. On page A-31, he stopped. His knee shook. He reached down and dug all the fingers of his right hand into the muscle of his thigh until he thought it would bunch and charley horse.

Gangland Slaying in Tucson Hotel

(AP)—A Mexican businessman with reputed links to drug traffickers was found slain gangland-style in a Tucson Hotel room yesterday morning.

Tucson Police said maids discovered Jorge Madrid Cordova slumped in a chair in his room at the Saguaro Inn about 9:30 A.M.

"He'd been shot twice in the head sometime last night, it looks like through the mouth, gangland style," said Lt. Peter Reeves, chief of Homicide for the Tucson Police.

Reeves said there were no witnesses and no suspects in the case. The FBI has been called in to assist in the investigation.

"The FBI said they think it could have been revenge, something having to do with the people he ran with," Reeves said. "But until someone comes forward, there's little we have to go on."

Reeves said the FBI had been probing links between Cordova and a sophisticated money laundering ring in Southern California between 1987 and 1989.

At one point, Reeves said, Cordova was under investigation by a federal grand jury interested in money laundering, but the probe was stopped when key government witnesses, Jack Allen Farrell and his wife, Lena . . .

Inez held a drink over the front of the paper, startling Farrell.

"I see that," she said, pointing to the article. "We are in the Wild West, no?"

Farrell's head bobbed. Inez swirled the milky white glass of Pernod and water and ice. "You do not want your drink then?" she said.

"No . . . it's not that, I'm just . . . tired, that's all," Farrell said.

Before he could reach for the glass, Inez had placed it on the table. He allowed his eyes to wander to the newspaper again; the story petered out after a few more inches, mostly background about himself and Cordova's business dealings in Tucson. There was no mention of Gabriel Cortez.

Inez said, "This interests?"

She inspected him now. She stood with her arms crossed, her legs more than a shoulder's width apart, the drink an inch from her mouth.

"What?" Farrell said. "No, it's just not often you hear about a—what did they call it, gangland?—gangland slaying in a sleepy town like Tucson. When I was a kid, I always used to read about the mob wars on the East Coast."

"*Vraiment?*" Inez said. "I think I read that Arizona is the place of retirement for the Mafia?"

"Never really thought of it that way," Farrell said, trying to appear nonchalant. "But I guess you're right."

He got the drink and raised the glass to his mouth fast, letting the sweet licorice and alcohol pluck and bounce off the back of his throat. In his haste, some of the liquid went down the wrong way. He choked, his eyes watered. He set the glass down quickly and coughed until the choking sensation passed. When he looked up, Inez's lower jaw had slackened and her nostrils flared. She sat down immediately on the corner of the bed opposite Farrell as she had the night before.

She said, "I ask you to forgive me for my *rudesse* at the door, *chéri*. It's just that you seemed—I think I should say—hostile for me today."

"The helmet," Farrell said, grateful for the turn in the conversation. He finished the drink.

Inez stiffened, looked away, brushed back a lock of her hair. "A wonderful technology, no?" She stood before he could answer. "Another drink perhaps?"

"Why don't you . . . well, why not?" Farrell said. He handed her the glass, happy that his nerves had steadied.

While Inez fixed the drinks, Farrell's attention darted between the noise she made and the paper: Who had killed Cordova? Cortez? Never. The Colombians? Possible. Whoever had done the deed, he wished he'd been there himself, to see the dove boy's blank eyes flash, to enjoy the terror that Cordova must have endured. Despite his decision to change, the room began to whirl.

The scent of freshly applied perfume altered the angle of the spinning sensation. Inez had changed into her blue velvet robe again. She handed him his drink, lay on the bed, and propped her head on her arm. "Now what do we do?"

"The helmet," Farrell insisted.

Her lower lip pouted, shifting her leg. "I think . . . an innovation to be explored."

"You planned that, didn't you?" Farrell said. "You planned to have Page wearing that helmet when he found his father at the bottom of the chute. And you'll use the footage somehow in the film."

Inez smiled. "But of course I use this helmet footage, it's there and adds a new angle," she said. "But this was a gift. How do I know he wears the helmet and not you? You and Page have the option to wear the head camera or no."

"You had an idea he would," Farrell said. "I think you always have an idea of where things might be going."

"The action I cannot direct," she said, waving the glass in the air. "I create documentaries. Actions occur."

"Within limits you create," Farrell said. "Your things *artificiels.*"

"Well, yes. It is necessary, you know, because I make a film about skiing the extreme; I do not discuss the architecture of Italy."

"So you think Page goes to the edge because of his father?" Farrell said. "And The Wave because of his mother?"

"Does it really matter if this is the true reason?" she said. "It just tells us more about them. Makes them complex and vulnerable, shaded in a way they cannot be if I just take pictures of them making the stares at death."

"No matter that they'd feel pain?"

"I tell you once: pain and pleasure are so close, one can say all life is a form of pain, some good, some bad," Inez shrugged. "But when life reveals herself, the audience knows it is true."

"Always for the audience," Farrell said.

"No," Inez said. "When Page walks away with his father, it is a triumph for him. Ten years they do not speak."

"And for you?"

"Yes. I said I am the woman, I feel compassion for the actor. Can you not see I feel for Page and for you, *chéri?*"

Farrell didn't answer.

Inez stood. She smiled and loosened the sash on her robe. The thick fabric slid away to hang open around her hips. She arched her chin toward him and said, "To smell you here, it makes me forget my work."

Inez took two steps toward Farrell, her fingers running up the curve of her thighs. She shivered and said in a husky voice, "When I see you today almost crash and then recover. To come so close. *Alors . . .* it made me excited. That's why I became so angry with you, *chéri.*"

She parted her thighs. She moved her legs on either side of Farrell's, then squeezed them together.

"Tell me you are not excited after you almost fall, that you do not want me afterwards, even though you hate me at the same time," she whispered as she unbuttoned his shirt.

Inez engulfed him, just as Page had said, like she was water. His decision to change faded. The old habits reasserted themselves, the idea of drowning with her so inviting. He went with the current, slid his hands behind the robe to cup her buttocks, and pulled her to him.

"Yes, *chéri.*" She fumbled at his belt and pants. "Quick now. She wants you."

Farrell ran his hand between her legs. She gasped and moved down on his fingers. She leaned forward to kiss him. He closed his eyes, imagining himself being sucked into a fierce eddy, where he tried to fight the water at first, gave up, and opened his mouth to draw it into his lungs, to drift away.

Inez's movements quickened. She shifted to move his hand away, to unzip his fly. But in the process, the edge of her robe fluttered on the erect hairs of his forearm. And his mind raced back in a terrible instant to another night long before and the fabric of another robe. He heard Page's voice describing her second movie: *"She's buff with him in one scene. Though I don't understand why."* He remembered his wife and how she had backed away from Lydia.

Inez had her fingers around him, guiding him. He was at the edge, almost incapable of fight, heated and ready when something deep inside him cooled. He went limp in her hand. He grabbed her wrists. With slow force he pushed her off.

"What is the matter, *chéri*," Inez cooed. "Whatever is, we go past. I help."

Farrell zipped up and grabbed his jacket. "You won't get your shading, or whatever you call it, like that," Farrell said, surprised at how calm he was.

"It is not like that," Inez said. But her voice had cooled so quickly Farrell knew it was like that. She drew the robe together.

"I remembered you were in bed with a guy in one of your films."

"This is different," Inez said. "You excite me."

"So you say. Funny, I can't help but get the feeling I'm a repeat performance. And the first guy who had this part had such a shitty ending."

"You pig." Inez threw the glass of Pernod and ice at him. "Get out! You are finished here, with me, with this film!"

Farrell ducked. The glass crashed on the wall above him, showering him with tiny shards and liquid. Suddenly, he felt strong.

"Oh, I don't think you really want me to go anywhere," Farrell said, drawing an invisible circle on the door with one hand while he twisted the brass knob with the other. "I'm the only mystery you've got left."

Chapter 20

arrell left before dawn and drove thirteen hours straight, backtracking through Nevada, then north to Idaho. During the long hours of driving he concluded that if he really wanted to change it wasn't enough to confront what he'd done in San Diego. He had to understand Inez, too; for she seemed to get to him in a way that no one ever had except Gabriel. She was everything he'd ever craved, everything he'd ever dreaded. There was no thought of escaping to the northern snowfields now. He'd see this through. Conquering her was his only hope for salvation.

When he crossed the Idaho state line, he stopped at a gas station next to a saloon that spit out disjointed country-western tunes. He listened for a minute while he filled the truck, the music carrying him back to Colombia. Even then he'd found it ironic that one of the men whom Gabriel had brought him to meet was a fan of the Grande Olde Oprey in Nashville. That was D. Juan Montenegras, a balding, heavy-lipped man who had the habit of shifting his hips while he talked, an unconscious physical tribute to his idol, Elvis.

Montenegras was in charge of the jungle laboratories between the Yari and Apaporis Rivers east of Cali, hard by Peru. When he wasn't working or trying to play steel guitar, Montenegras's passions were parrots and parties. The evening after Farrell and Cordova were rescued, they attended a fete in Montenegras's private aviary on the south lawn of his estate. Farrell had moved in a stupor through the crowd. He wanted to flee the party, call his wife, and tell her he was okay. But he knew he couldn't; so great was the fear that surrounded Montenegras and his partners that when the red-headed Amazons, white cockatiels, pink cockatiels, and African greys fluttered in the trees to shit on the bare shoulders of the women and the fine linen suits of the men, they smiled.

Every time Farrell tried to talk to Gabriel about wanting to get out, his friend introduced him to another of the men he'd been brought south to see. Like Montenegras, they were all well-dressed, polite men who had trim front lawns, children who attended boarding school in London, and wives who were greeted as regulars in the boutiques of Miami, New York, and Los Angeles.

Each bowed and shook hands with Farrell as if he were a respected diplomat. Each deferred to Gabriel as a prize client, someone to whom a debt was owed. After Farrell chatted with the men, after they had walked away, Gabriel would lean over and tell him of their strange pasts. There was Christian Rodriguez, a nasty-looking man with a nose as sharp as a pencil. On his right cheek he bore a thick, ugly welt he'd received as a child in the Cali slums. Rodriguez was fourteen when it happened. A contract of $200 had been placed on a marijuana smuggler who'd reneged on a deal with a grower in the hills. Rodriguez crept through the French doors that led to the balcony of the man's second-floor hotel room and got the wire around the man's neck just like his friends had shown him. But before the man died, he had managed to stick a knife through Rodriguez's cheek, knocking out two molars. Besides scarring Rodriquez, the knife had left him with a permanent, eerie trademark: when Rodriguez inhaled, you heard a slight whistle. It was said that the enemies of the cartel laid awake at night, sweating in their beds for fear that a flute note would pierce the darkness before the garrote hugged their throats. Rodriquez also knew the cargo statistics and speed of a hundred different planes and boats; besides being the company's enforcer, he was the transportation specialist.

And then Fernando De La Leone and his bitchy wife, Estelle, who broke into their conversation to demand that De La Leone fly her to Caracas or Buenos Aires for the weekend.

"Perhaps I go too far to say I knew them," Farrell said, thinking out loud as he got back in the truck and drove again. "I certainly heard the gossip and met with them, with De La Leone almost constantly."

Lithe and tall with wire-frame glasses and a pleasant smile, De La Leone was everything Rodriguez, Montenegras, and the rest of the upper-level managers of the cartel aspired to be, but could not. De La Leon was not of the slums. He was born in Bogotá and, like Gabriel, was the privileged son of the elite. Outwardly, he was a polished international economist and businessman with an advanced degree in business administration from Santiago University and banking contacts all over the world. He enjoyed gardening and grew beautiful purple orchids in a hot house attached to the side of his home. He collected rare coins that he displayed in cases in his library. He had a rare first edition of Adam Smith's *The Wealth of Nations*. And he was a news junkie; he had installed a massive satellite dish on the roof of his house so he could capture CNN updates twenty-four hours a day.

Underneath the patina, however, De La Leone was one of Cali's six financial advisors. In that capacity he served as review analyst of schemes to launder money. As Farrell would learn, his primary responsibility was to extend the organization's control of the business.

At lunch the next day, De La Leone took a sip of wine, then looked Farrell straight in the eyes. "Cocaine has made my country a flashier banana republic, Mr. Farrell. As usual, we are not getting—how would you say it?—our slice of the pie?"

Farrell nodded uneasily. De La Leone continued. "We want greater control over the flow of cash and goods inside your country. With that, more profits would return to Colombia."

"Which is where I fit in," Farrell mumbled.

"It will expand our investments in the United States and give us the physical presence to launch future efforts," said De La Leone. He laughed and turned to Gabriel and Cordova. "Imagine it: we buy the border!"

They laughed with him. Farrell scratched at a raised bump a jungle insect bite had left on the back of his hand. Through the open French doors, somewhere out in the humid night air, he thought he heard an animal cry.

Each night in Cali, Farrell had jerked awake, frightened by dreams he could not remember save the gentle patter of the rain forest and the slug that rested on Cordova's chin. He had gone over the plans with De La Leone, Montenegras, Gabriel, and Cordova because he had to. All he really wanted was to go home.

In the afternoon of his fourth and last day, he finally managed to be alone with Gabriel. They were sitting on the balcony of the twentieth floor of a downtown high-rise apartment building De La Leone and Montenegras owned. They were drinking wine, waiting for the final meeting. An explosion rocked the far quarter of the city. Dust and fire rolled high into the air, drifted, and settled.

"What the hell was that?" he asked Gabriel, who had not flinched at the roar.

"A problem solved, I should imagine," Gabriel said in a nonchalant tone. "The climate here is fabulous, like San Diego's I should think."

"Too much moisture in the air," Farrell said. "But—"

"The soil yields much to those who plant. Look at the hibiscus growing in that garden down there."

"Gabriel . . ."

"Sometimes you have to trim the weeds around these plants or they will not grow," Gabriel continued. "There are vines that can sprout, run, and throttle a plant before it is ready to flower."

Gabriel paused, looked at his hands, and rubbed them together as if he were washing. "A good gardener will cut the vine away early," he said. "Jorge said your wife is a gardener. Would she agree?"

Gabriel rarely mentioned Lena.

"I suppose," Farrell said. "I—"

"Maria sends you her best," Gabriel broke in. He was leaning against the railing now, twisting a sprig he'd plucked from a potted plant.

Farrell rubbed at the knot that was developing on the back of his neck. "Send her mine, too."

For a brief moment, across the balcony and down into the garden and even into the streets beyond, there was not a sound. Then in the distance came the wail of sirens. "I don't know if I can continue," Farrell said finally. "I'm as far as . . . well . . ."

With an easy thrust of his arm, Gabriel straightened and lowered himself into a chair. He leaned forward to the table, took the wine bottle from the bucket, and poured into the glasses. "And how far is that?"

"I've set up the system you wanted," Farrell stammered. "But the more I listen to these men, I realize the bank is too small to work the sort of deals we've discussed without suspicion."

Gabriel wet his finger in the wine. He pressed it to the rim of the glass, circling the rim until a clear, rich tone reverberated in the air.

"Perhaps it is so," Gabriel said, looking down into the wine. "The bank is no longer the place for you. I've been considering that you should resign and recruit a replacement."

Relief surged through Farrell. "It would be for the best—" he began.

Gabriel cut him off. "A private real estate development company would be better. From there you could coordinate the buys of the border properties without compromise."

Farrell splayed his fingers wide and flat on his thighs. "Actually I'd thought of leaving the business altogether. In the jungle the other night, I felt something I hadn't felt in years."

"What's that?"

"Hesitation," Farrell said. "Insecurity. I don't know exactly what to call it. Guilt maybe."

"Common enough afflictions."

"They are," Farrell said. "But not if you are preparing to test the limits of your skills."

A smirk developed on Gabriel's face. "What you are feeling is growth, my friend. I believe you are in danger of becoming stronger, not toppling over."

"It's more than that," Farrell replied. "I've always believed in understanding limits because then you act with respect. Even if you are going to the very edge of the possible, you can see the line."

"And?"

"This strikes me as having no boundaries whatsoever."

Gabriel tilted his head back, so his chin was pointed at the fading glow on the horizon. "What you are experiencing is the fear of heights," he said. "What do you call it in English?"

"Vertigo," Farrell said.

"Ahh, the same in Spanish," Gabriel said, and he ran his fingers back through his hair. "Perhaps, too, the fear of open space—agoraphobia, I believe."

Gabriel rocked forward and tapped the arm of the metal chair. "It all comes down to what you're used to, Jack," he said. "There are boundaries in all of this; you just haven't figured them out. But you will, because—and I have sensed this from the moment we met—you are a survivor."

Farrell struggled to reply, but Gabriel cut him off again. "Indeed, you must survive."

The menacing tone in Gabriel's voice shook Farrell. "Why is that?"

"Because now that you have met these men, you have no choice."

It was almost dark now. The headlights of cars flickered along the road below them. In the distance, orange flames licked sky. A gate opened and slammed shut. Farrell drank the rest of the glass and another and another as fast as he could.

Out on the dark highway beyond Twin Falls, Farrell looked for a place where he could pull over to sleep for the night. With no warning, a yellow Labrador retriever appeared in his headlights. He swerved to avoid hitting the dog. He skidded to a stop on the shoulder of the highway, his heart pounding. He looked in the rearview mirror. The dog, a puppy really, no more than seven months old, trotted down the center of the highway. Another car narrowly avoided it.

Farrell swore and got out. He jogged back on the gravel and called to the dog, which seemed disoriented. Farrell knelt and whistled. It came to him whining, head down, tail between its legs. She had no collar. When Farrell ran his fingers along the top of her back, he felt a jagged, open sore. A low growl boiled from the dog's throat.

"It's okay," Farrell said. "I'm not gonna hurt you."

He led the dog to the truck and opened the side door. She backed away at first, then jumped in, nervously sniffing the seat and the dashboard. Farrell got in the other side and turned on the light to look at the sore. It was raw and oozing. Farrell blanched when realized she'd been whipped, not cut.

He found a rest stop thirty miles beyond Twin Falls and got the dog in the back. He dug out some hydrogen peroxide and cotton to clean the wound. The lab winced once, but did not growl. When he'd finished, she curled up on a blanket near the door and looked up at him with gentle brown eyes. This pleased Farrell in a way he'd long forgotten. He rummaged around in a box until he found a can of beef stew, which he opened and gave to her. She ate it, turned, and licked his arm.

Farrell smiled then got into the bunk and turned off the light, remembering how he had found Lena digging at weeds in the garden the day he returned to San Diego.

"Hello, stranger," he had said. She raced to him and hugged him.

"I missed you so much," she said. "I felt kind of . . . well, lost without you."

Farrell stroked her cheek. He wanted to tell her, to apologize, to beg her forgiveness. Overriding his impulse was the sound of a brief, flutelike whistle in the darkness of his mind. He was ashamed and frightened.

"Me, too," he said. And that night for the first time in many months, they made love slow, tender, falling asleep in each other's arms. Holding her, Farrell told himself he had no choice. He would go forward with the plans that he had agreed to. But he knew now he was expendable. He must prepare a way to escape.

In the weeks that followed, as he bought small parcels of border land, he also set up two more Swiss and Grand Cayman accounts for himself as well as a shell corporation on the Isle of Jersey off the coast of Britain. On his way to Texas in early February, he took a side trip to Tennessee, and in a small town outside Nashville found the names of a boy, Nathaniel Collins, and a girl, Shelly Crown, both of whom had died in infancy about the same time he and Lena were born. Then came the flurry of papers and notices that became the beginning of the new identities he planned. Two weeks later he flew to Dallas, bought the camper, and arranged to have it driven to San Diego by a college kid who needed to haul his stuff home.

In the back of his mind, Farrell always knew there would come a day when he'd have to explain himself to Lena. This he feared more than anything, putting it off through the end of the month while he bought two more hundred-acre border parcels, one outside Nogales, Arizona, the other near Harlingen, Texas. On March

1, 1989, he passed papers on a third parcel near El Paso. It had been a long three days of negotiations. He flew into San Diego with eyelids that weighed two pounds each. Lena was not waiting for him at the airport. He called the house and got a recorded message saying that the phone was temporarily out of order.

In the cab on the twenty-minute ride home, Farrell dozed and dreamed of what it would be like to leave it all behind, to live in the camper, a vagabond. He tried not to think about what he'd do if she refused to go.

Farrell paid the driver at the gate. He rang the doorbell. Waited, then rang again.

Lena opened the door to the darkened front hallway. Her face was white. Her shoulders hung limp, weak, defeated. Her eyes were puffed, almost shut. "I just want to know why," she whispered.

A man appeared behind her. He was short, no more than five feet seven. Despite the boxy cut of his business suit, Farrell could tell he was thin, perhaps 140 pounds. He had curly brown hair, graying at the temples, and possessed extraordinarily large ears.

The man placed a sympathetic hand on his wife's shoulders, then slipped by Lena before Farrell could speak, his other hand thrust forward to show a black billfold. The stubby fingers flicked the billfold open. A silver badge embossed with blue enamel hung in space.

"Jacob Stern, Mr. Farrell," he said. "FBI. I think you know why we are here."

There were other men around him now, men in blue windbreakers, men who held guns, men who grabbed his elbows, men who dragged him forward. As he drifted off into sleep in the back of the camper, what Farrell remembered most was how Lena had turned to flee into the dark house like a little girl scared by a nightmare.

By the time Farrell reached Jackson the next afternoon, he'd decided we all live in tunnels of our own design, peering ahead for that little pinpoint of light that tells us we're moving in the right direction, but denying the walls that surround us.

He named the Labrador Ruby after the Nevada mountain range. Caring for her made him feel wanted in a way he hadn't in almost a year. He talked to her as he drove. On the way into the town, he pointed up at the Grand Tetons, which towered over Jackson Hole and the Snake River. He told her the ragged slash of cirques and peaks and couloirs that make up the Tetons were sculpted by glaciers 10,000 years ago. What amazed him, he said, was the fact that in geologic terms the Tetons were young and therefore still growing, not in inches, but in leaps of a foot or more. These growth spurts happened in sharp, catastrophic upheavals after years of dormancy. Not unlike the events that can upset the level planes of a life.

Farrell found the Elk Tine Motel on a side street at the edge of town. The manager said The Wave and Page had gotten in the previous evening. Inez, Tony, and Ann were due in the following day. Farrell fed Ruby. When he left, she was curled up in front of the heater.

Page and The Wave were right where he expected them to be: at a saloon in the middle of Jackson that lures tourists with blazing Las Vegas lights, a stuffed grizzly bear, a horse saddle made almost entirely of silver, and dozens of other saddles that pose as bar stools. He threaded his way through a crowd of late-season skiers and by a group of East Coast women who tittered at the local cowboys posing across the room in lank slouches for their benefit.

The Wave stood up in the stirrups of the bar stool, twisted, and raised a shot glass to Farrell. "He arrives! He who goes voyaging through strange seas of thought, alone."

"Shelly?" Farrell asked.

"Wordsworth, mon." The Wave handed Farrell a shot. "This is George Dickel."

"I'm tired. Whiskey will knock me out."

"All the more reason to do it then," Page said, raising his own glass. It was obvious he'd been through several toasts already.

Farrell shrugged and they clinked the shots together, quick dropping the liquor down their throats. Farrell slid into the saddle next to The Wave. The rastaman put his hand on Farrell's shoulder, smiled, and said: "So you prove it . . . Hell hath no fury . . ."

"What are you talking about?"

Page scoffed, "Inez. When she got to your room yesterday morning and found it empty with that note that said you'd headed for Jackson, I thought she'd bust that vein that's always bulging on the side of her neck."

"She's just pissed I won't play her game," Farrell said. "Where is she?"

"San Francisco and L.A., I think," The Wave said. "Something to do with her money men. They're getting nervous."

"So we sit here until she comes in tomorrow?"

"Not you," The Wave said. "In one of her more lucid moments she said, and I quote, 'Tell zat bastard if he has the courage enough to come, to find out where we ski off-piste. No more of zis chicken sheet leetle couloirs. Take me out of bounds!' "

Farrell smiled in spite of himself; The Wave mimicked her almost perfectly. "A bit early for zee out of bounds," he said.

"She seems set on it," Page said. "She called the stuff we have in the can so far . . . now how did she say it?"

"Caresses préliminaires," The Wave said, fumbling over the consonants.

"Foreplay," Farrell said.

"Yeah," Page mumbled. "We figured that out."

"Cold," The Wave said. He stared at his beer.

"Ours is not to reason why . . ." Page chanted. He signaled the bartender for another shot of Dickel. He drank it as soon as he poured.

Farrell jerked his head at the The Wave, who arched his eyebrow.

"Bad, huh?" Farrell said to Page.

Page set the glass down. "Hadn't seen him in ten years. Just too bad this is what it took to change him."

"You ticked off at her, mon?" The Wave asked.

"Inez?" Page said. "I don't like the way she did it, but I saw him."

Farrell ordered another round of Dickels.

"Last one for me," The Wave said. "I'm going to jump on the hill first thing in the morning."

Farrell drank as he watched tourists in neon blues and reds take to the floor to dance the two-step. "I went to her room the night before I left Tahoe."

Page rolled his eyes. "Can't stay away from the bad thing, can you?"

Farrell ignored him. "She had some equipment running. It was rude footage, but I can tell you that little helmet camera recorded in quite artistic fashion the nature and pathos of your little family reunion."

Page studied the row of bottles behind the bar while he drank the whiskey. "Figured as much the next morning. Told her she couldn't use it. She laughed and showed me a paper I'd signed that released her to use any interviews with me or my family. I never read the fine print. Bitch."

"You're still here," Farrell said.

Page's eyes were bleary. His nose ran. "You got somewhere else for me to go? Maybe I finish. Maybe a hundred thousand people or more see me jump old Granite. Who the Christ knows what she'll get me to do next!"

"In all the way," Farrell said.

"To the damned end," Page said, cracking his knuckles off the thick pinewood. "And from the way she screeched when she'd found you'd split, I see you are, too. Face it. You're just as obsessed with her as the rest of us. Maybe more, you're fucking her."

"Not anymore I'm not," Farrell said. He drained the rest of the whiskey from his glass.

"Maybe not with your cock, but you're still doing her with your head," Page said. He lurched out of the saddle. "So drink your whiskey, Collins. Get yourself good and numb, good and fucking numb before the next mental mind fuck."

The Wave hurried after him. "I'll make sure he gets home, mon."

Farrell watched them go, then stared at himself in the gilt-edged mirror behind the bar. The scars on his cheeks and below his eyes had begun to fade. He wondered if the ones inside would ever clear. He gritted his teeth at the memory of how Stern had cut at him.

"You have the right to . . . an attorney," Stern said after Lena had fled up the stairs. Farrell sat in his living room, surrounded by the men in blue windbreakers. Stern paced back and forth in front of him, talking in an unnerving speech pattern, like one of those annoying Midwestern radio announcers; the first part of Stern's sentences rushed out and then he'd stop, his eyes would dart over Farrell, his Adam's apple would bob over the knot of his tie, he'd tap his pencil twice on the yellow legal pad in front of him, and finally . . . finish.

"I waive it," Farrell replied.

Stern laid the whole thing out: they had him cold on currency transaction violations. The FBI, the Treasury Department, and the Drug Enforcement Agency had been watching the trading houses along the border for almost a year, and when the volume increased and moved to Farrell's bank, they followed. They had a search warrant for Farrell's office, which they planned to execute at six in the morning.

"You did quite well, you know," Stern said. "We still don't know where the money went . . . after the first two wire transfers. Which, of course, as far as you're concerned, is irrelevant. We've got you on at least twenty counts of failure to file the correct documents."

Farrell leaned forward, intent on Stern's tapping pencil, all too aware of the three other agents sitting on the chairs behind him. "What's the penalty for failure to file?"

"You could do twenty years . . . Mr. Farrell," Stern said.

Twenty years. The thought of no movement, trapped for two decades, raised a dread in Farrell worse than a whistle in the night. He saw himself standing atop a cliff. Dogs had him at bay.

"But . . ." Stern began.

"But?"

"You are really not who we were after," Stern said. "If you could be of aid to us, we . . . we . . . could recommend leniency."

Farrell sank back into the cushions on the couch, knowing that an escape route had been offered, a path down off the cliff. Part of him wanted to have it done with and be punished, to take the long fall, to embrace the impact. Then came the thought of Lena and what it would do to her.

"Perhaps now you would like . . . an attorney present?" Stern said.

"I'll handle this myself," Farrell said.

The tapping on the yellow legal pad stopped briefly. "As I said, leniency is . . ."

"Full immunity for what I know," Farrell said.

"Impossible," snapped Stern. The pencil cracked off the legal pad so hard the lead tip broke off and skittered onto the glass tabletop.

"Then I'm shutting up," Farrell said.

"We've got you . . . clear-cut. My office won't go for full immunity."

"Did you see my wife climb the stairs?" Farrell asked. "I'll live with that the rest of my life."

"You should have known that before you set out to break the law, Mr. Farrell," Stern said.

"I was aware of some of it," Farrell said. "But I didn't know what I was getting into."

"And you got that awful case of gonorrhea off a toilet seat," Stern scoffed. "Cut to it."

Farrell swallowed hard, then said: "You don't know a quarter of what they do and who they are."

Stern shifted uncomfortably. "Without some indication of what you have. . . . and, you must know, I don't have that kind of power. It's up to the U.S. Attorney."

"Call him," Farrell said. "I'm not going anywhere."

"It's almost midnight," Stern said.

Farrell gambled. "You're supposed to search my office at six. You'll get some of what you're after. But you'll also alert them. You'll never understand who the players are, how it all fits together."

Stern stood and crossed to the blue china clock on the mantelpiece. He ran his finger over the dome and the intricate scrollwork above the quiet face that hadn't been wound in nearly two years. He said, "Give me something to show . . . how lousy you were."

Farrell's fingers ripped into the palm of his hand. So that's how it's going to be, he thought: enforced humility.

He swallowed twice. In as sarcastic a voice as he could muster, he said, "While Christian Rodriguez tries to come off as a sophisticated horse breeder, he is actually a sadist who has killed several prostitutes. His boss, Fernando De La Leon, for a fact, is henpecked."

The pencil slipped from Stern's fingers, clattering on the pale brown tiles in front of the fireplace. Behind Farrell one of the other agents whispered, "Well tie me up and fuck me cross-eyed."

Stern bent slowly to pick up the pencil. But Farrell could see he was stunned and fighting to retain his composure. "You've met with these men . . . Mr. Farrell?"

"Call your boss," Farrell said.

Chapter 21

March 2, 1989

Strange men in my house. They've looked through every corner, behind every book. It's not like I can bop them off the head with something heavy and drive them away. They have the right to be here now. Strangers.

With them this new alien. He tries to talk to me now, but all I can see are the faces in the cribs. Can all this change in a moment? I am me, but no longer Lena Farrell. But when was I? And when was he the person I thought he was?

I did a brief rotation once in a head-trauma ward. The speech pathologist used to say to the relatives: You are going to have to learn to live with a new person; he may look the same on the outside, but inside the wiring in his brain has been altered. When fully recovered he may understand your speech, but be unable to reply. He may be able to express himself beautifully, yet not understand a word you say.

Then this woman would touch the relative on the arm and say, There's still hope for a full recovery, always hope. If not, if you love him and the person he was, you'll learn to love the person he's become.

I've heard her say those words a hundred times in the past three days: *There's still hope for a full recovery.* Recovery from what? Where is the trauma? I can't see the wound!

Farrell hung his head. It was almost 10 A.M. the following day. The Wave had knocked on his door an hour earlier to tell him that Inez had called. The crew would meet that evening. She expected Farrell to have a plan. Farrell phoned a man that Portsteiner once mentioned named Dunphy, an old guide who knew the Tetons well. Dunphy's wife told Farrell the guide would meet him for lunch.

Farrell petted Ruby's back until his fingers found the sore. It was clearing. He gripped the bedsheets with his other hand, recalling how Lena's face seemed almost festered when he'd gone up to their room. A heavy fog swirled along the coast, sending rivulets of moisture down the panes of the window. Lena sat upright in bed, hugging a pillow to her chest. Her eyes were swollen and red. She did not look at him.

"I was trying to get out, to get us out," Farrell began. "But I couldn't see how."

"There was no us in this," Lena said. "There was only you."

Farrell chewed the inside of his lip. "I've agreed to tell them everything. I've been offered immunity, so little of this will ever become public."

"How wonderful for you!" Lena screamed. "I'm so glad you're safe from the effects."

"It's not like that," Farrell said. "I'm going to destroy them."

He reached for her hand, which was worrying the pillowcase. She slapped his hand away and her other hand struck him across the mouth. Farrell did not turn from that blow, nor the dozens that followed. Lena flailed until her knuckles cracked and bled, until she collapsed and curled into the fetal position. She moved her swelling hands across the sheets, staining them with arcs of red calligraphy. "I'm going home," she whispered.

"You can't," Farrell murmured. The taste of copper seeped between his lower lip and gums. A welt burned under his right eye. "Stern says if we break pattern, we'll never get them."

For a moment Farrell thought she would strike again. He flinched. "That's it, Jack, pull away!" she yelled. "Have you ever seen a baby suffer just from being held?"

"No."

"No, nothing ever breaks through to you," she said. She threw her arms in the air. "So what am I supposed to do in the meantime, Jack? Just go to work as if nothing has happened? Hello? What's new? Oh, my husband's a drug runner, but other than that not much."

"I'm no drug runner," Farrell said.

"Now there's a pretty idea to keep in your head when you're out buying me cars with your . . . money."

"I wish it were that easy," Farrell said. "I wish I could say I did it solely for greed. That was part of it, a small part. If it was everything, you'd probably understand."

"I still don't think I would," Lena said. "But please, don't tell me you were doing it for the good of mankind."

Farrell thought of Gabriel and Cordova.

"No, I didn't," Farrell said.

"Then why?"

"Have you ever walked along the edge of a cliff just to know what it feels like?"

"I've never had the urge."

"I've never not had the urge."

Lena's attention did not waver; it was if she were observing an animal in a zoo.

"I'd leave the house when I was a kid, do everything to leave the house, you know?" He pulled up his shirt to point to a faint line below his rib cage. "You see that?"

Lena nodded.

"Out in the woods, miles out, there was a quarry filled with water. We'd jump higher and higher off the cliffs. None of my friends had ever gone off the very top, this big boulder up there, they called the Cat. It was eighty feet up."

"And you went."

"I was petrified. But I did it anyway, running as fast as I could and then diving. A branch cut me on the way down. And when I hit the water, it turned red around me and two of the younger boys cried because they thought I'd gutted myself. We stopped the bleeding with a towel. My mom and dad never knew. It was my secret. I'd lift up my shirt to see the scab and smile. That sensation of having made it . . . it was like nothing I'd ever felt before."

"You're sick, Jack."

"It got me out of that house," Farrell insisted. "It was the only way I knew how. Every time I'd move, they'd be around me, watching . . ."

"I've heard it all a dozen times, Jack," Lena said. "Fear of that bad Farrell gene, boxing you in. So when something real bad happens—your dad dying—you run to Africa. Now to Mexico. Spare me."

"What would you know?" Farrell snarled. "Did dear mom and dad O'Rourke crowd you into the center, a center where nothing seems real, just soft? So the only thing that has hardness is away from that—at the edge?"

Lena's mouth dropped open slightly, taken aback at the viciousness in his voice. "Jack, I—"

"You can't live if you're always trying to be soft," Farrell said. He fought the swelling in his throat. "I learned that the hard way. There was no suicide, though it might as well have been. Just another Farrell cover-up. It was spring after my second year in Utah. I was going home for the first time. They knew I was on my way. I'd called from the road the day before. Two years since I'd seen them.

"Mom was sitting out on the front porch staring at the lake when I got to the house. She looked like everything she had was stolen. She said, 'I didn't want to tell you. But he's been bad, real bad for a month.' "

Farrell looked at his wife. "For some reason, the idea of seeing me after all that time put him over. His dad had hung himself." But he didn't wait for me to get to the house. They wrestled and the gun went off and dug a shallow groove in his forehead. He lives in a home where they care for him. My mom visits twice a week."

There was a long silence. Shocked, Lena said to herself, "That's why she could never leave Maine."

Farrell slid down the wall and rested his head in his hands.

"God, Jack . . . why didn't you tell me?"

"I've never been to see him," Farrell said. "He was so scary and beautiful when he got going. I didn't want to see him all mushy. So when mom said he'd stabilized, I went to Africa, buried him in the spices and brilliant colors and animals."

"You couldn't tell me," Lena said.

"I wanted him buried," Farrell said. "A dead man is easier to bury."

They were quiet. Farrell looked at his fingernails. Lena closed her eyes.

Farrell said, "When I first met Gabriel, I was that little kid on the Cat again. Things looked brighter and smelled better than they had since I'd been in Africa. I chased those feelings all the way in. What I was really after, I don't know. About a month ago I realized it wasn't the same anymore: it was growing dark in my little fantasy and very scary and I didn't know how I'd gotten there."

The first pelting drops of a storm struck the window. Neither of them said anything. They just listened to the rain.

"I want to sleep, Jack," Lena said. "I want you to leave."

Farrell shut the door behind him. He shuffled around the house. He bumped into a table and overturned a lamp. He tried to sleep on the couch, but couldn't. He wandered again, finding himself in the basement. He blew away the dust that had gathered on Jenny's white dresser. When it was clean, he slumped down next to it. He thought of his father, only thirteen then, and how he'd found his father hanging. Farrell squeezed his arms in tight about his ribs to control the pain, to shove it inside a box, to wrap it securely.

In the motel room, Farrell allowed himself to feel more. Gone was his ability to tape painful memories shut. The flaps in his mind gaped open. He thought about his father and mother and how much he loved them. He thought about how much he'd let Lena down. He let these recollections sift and collide until he saw the common thread: in each case, he'd abandoned the ones he cared about. He surprised himself and cried.

Peter Dunphy knew the Tetons. He was a wiry gnome of a man, short, silver-haired, peppered beard, and close to sixty, with an infectious energy that displayed itself every time his finger stabbed at the topographical map he'd laid out on the table at LeJay's 24-Hour Sportsmen's Café.

"Talked to Frank Portsteiner after you called," Dunphy said. "Says you're a bit headstrong, but sound on a mountain. Told me to tell you he'll be up here tonight if you're around."

"He coming to ski?" Farrell asked.

"By April that Frankie boy's sick of it," Dunphy said. "He's been coming up middle of the cruel month the past few years to fish the early hatch on the Yellowstone and the lakes that lose ice early."

Over the course of an hour, Dunphy laid out the three premier extreme skiing routes in the Tetons: Buck Mountain, Mount Moran, and the Grand Teton.

"Grand's the sumbitch," Dunphy said. "When a local guy named Briggs first tried it back in 1971, no one he knew had even climbed the route he came down. He left the top at fourteen thousand feet on the East snowfield, down to a throat called the Stettner Couloir toward the Black Dike ridge and on to Tepee's Glacier. Steeper than hell. Wonder he lived through it."

"What time of year he do it?"

"Started climbing June fifteenth," Dunphy said. "Now that was a big snow year, he had to wait a long time. Not as much this year, but still, you got at least three weeks 'til it's safe. I'd say first of May minimum. But you should hike in and dig some pits before you make any decision."

"I think the director, French lady, is going to want to go before then," Farrell said. "Is it possible?"

"Go anytime you want," Dunphy said. "The Forest Service don't give a damn. All of these have been climbed in winter. But you'll be wading and postholing and who knows what else. And the ridges won't be stable, that's a fact. Watch it or you'll find yourself riding the bear's back straight down the hill."

"Instability," Farrell said. "Just what the lady ordered."

"Dandy," Dunphy said sarcastically. "This attitude the Frogs and the Krauts got of letting it fly, hoping to Jesus you come through for the history books, is like throwing cow dung out the bed of a pickup and praying you get your face back behind the cab but quick. Can't close your eyes to the danger, boy. Got to face exactly what it is you're about to do. Don't believe it? Look at me."

Dunphy unbuttoned his flannel shirt and drew it down over his shoulder.

"Daydreaming up on the Middle Teton 1973," Dunphy said. "Snow broke through. Went end over end, smashed some rocks. Tore the shoulder to shreds. Held together with pins now."

Farrell grimaced, thanked Dunphy, and left him his room number at the Elk Tine in case he had any other ideas.

The meeting with the crew wasn't for hours, so he picked Ruby up at the motel and drove out of town toward the elk refuge. He parked and watched fog burst from the muzzles of many of the beasts, which were still bedded down in tight circles, rumps to the center. Others browsed. The antlers of the bulls would fall soon, Farrell thought, and the process of regeneration would begin again and last all summer until the bugling season that heralds the rut and the snows.

"I've had enough of winters," Farrell said to Ruby. "Next year we'll go someplace warm."

Ruby wagged her tail. Outside the wind stiffened, and within minutes, the clouds broke. Behind him Farrell could see the opening to Death Canyon and beyond it to Buck Mountain. The South, Middle, and Grand Teton peaks were still socked in, but Farrell could sense them there, beyond Avalanche Canyon, towering monoliths rising 7,000 feet above the valley floor. He thought of Page, The Wave, Ann, and Tony. "You don't run away," he said to himself.

For a moment he held the diary in his hand and faltered. He added another new rule: "You take responsibility."

March 9

Tonight he came home ashen and sweating. Cordova had called him, wanting to know why their precious deals haven't moved as quickly as before. Stern hasn't installed listening devices in Jack's office, but Jack took notes.

I could see he enjoyed this game of cat and mouse and told him so. His embarrassment gave way to anger. He asked me if I wanted to whip him or burn him. I told him I've stopped wanting—he doesn't love the middle where I am.

Jack said he was there for me in his own way, that he'd left the job he loved in Chicago to come to San Diego for me. On this count he was right and I had no flip answer. He made sacrifices for me. But I don't know if I can make this sacrifice. I told him the truth: he scares me.

March 12

Twice I've awoken late at night wanting to write a letter. Only I don't know who to address it to. At work, I caught myself holding the babies up to beg forgiveness.

Stern says it is important that Jack and I go through the motions. But we pass each other without speaking. I ask myself how much more I do not know about him. We eat without talking, he at the counter, me at the table. We walk the dogs on the beach at night. I stay yards away when he throws sticks into the surf. He moves carefully around me. I stare.

Last week I had a red dream. People from our past, a jury, taunted me. Lydia was there, the only one who would defend me. I woke up shivering and went to look for him. He was curled in the basement next to her things. It has become a ritual: I come in the night to punch and kick and slap him until my nightgown clings to my wet skin. He never defends. We never talk of it.

I know I still love him, but all I feel is disgust.

The last sentence gored Farrell like the sharp horn of a wounded bull. Her feelings had been there below the surface, but he'd been able to delude himself by concentrating on getting Gabriel. Now her true emotions wrapped around him. He felt unworthy, small. Bile crept up the back of his throat, filling his mouth with the acrid taste of self-pity. He thought of a conversation they'd had about a month later. Her late-night visits to the basement had tapered off. They had retreated into civility.

"What will you do when it's over?" Lena asked. She tossed salad at the counter.

The question surprised him. Since Stern had barged into their life, he'd done nothing but try to order and explain the past. He hadn't considered the future. "How does a restaurant in Montana sound?"

"I'm being serious," she said.

"The north shore of Kauai then," Farrell said. "It's so far from anything you have to drive on one-way bridges to get there. We could—"

"We?" she asked.

Farrell took the blow. "I thought there might still be a we."

"You shouldn't think like that."

Farrell was quiet. "What will you do?"

"Go away. Maybe home. Begin again."

"Will you tell them?"

"At some point I'll have to," she said.

"Stern says some of the information is so powerful it could cripple all of them, Gabriel, Cordova, those others," he said to impress her.

"So you said." Lena crossed to the table, chewing a piece of carrot. "Do you think she knows?"

"Who?"

"His wife, Maria."

Farrell knew then that if he were ever to bring up what transpired between them, this was the time. But he knew that if he did, that "we" that lingered in his mind would surely remain a dream.

"I think of it like this," Farrell said. "Either she knows and she ignores it because it's too painful, or she justifies it by the things he does with the profits—the clinics and the programs to train the poor."

"I think it's more delicately balanced, she chooses not to know."

"Why?"

"Because she's probably something like me: she wants to believe in the man she chose to spend the rest of her life with."

A note was attached to Farrell's door when he returned to the Elk Tine: *Just a reminder: crew meeting, Inez's Room 6:30 p.m.—The Wave.*

Two hours later, Ann opened the door. Video equipment and film cameras were strewn about the floor. Inez had her back to the room, fumbling with a map that was spread across a credenza. The Wave and Tony sat in the two chairs. Page leaned against a wall, sipping a beer.

Inez pirouetted when he came through the door. She fairly danced to him across the room, a wide, friendly smile plastered across her face. She slipped her hand around his waist. "I am not so sure I find you here. But we go on, forget the past, yes?"

Farrell glanced at her sidelong. He thought to himself: this is what recovering alcoholics must go through at their first cocktail party. She batted her eyelashes and smiled again. "Why not, Inez," Farrell said.

Inez patted him on the rear, then slid back from him to the maps.

"The few days past I spend in San Francisco with one of the men who pays for the film," she announced to the room.

"Who's he?" Page asked. Farrell wasn't sure, but he thought Page had been drinking again.

"A German industrialist," Inez said. "And a fanatic for the mountains. He looks at some of the film already and other scenes on video. He calls our progress so far, the Y Couloir and the jumps—"

"We know: sticky fingers," Page mumbled.

The Wave burst out laughing.

"What do you say?" Inez demanded.

Page waved his hand at her, "Ahh nothing. Go ahead."

Inez glared at Page, who chuckled and waved at her again. "Go ahead!"

"He is angry we have no first descents," Inez allowed.

"Such is life," The Wave said.

"Not life, my *petit* Jamaica," Inez retorted. "Business. With the helicopter and the weeks in Utah and Tahoe, we're off-schedule and over budget. Perhaps he is not in anger, but he is not in happiness."

"What do *you* think," Farrell said, studying her.

Inez pulled out a cigarette and lit it. "He has reason. There are the moments of action, truly brilliant: Page in the air off Granite Chief, the last minute in the Y Couloir; but I believe that the . . . essence of the film is to come. I wish to be at the Ranier and in the Brooks Range in June."

"That's five weeks," Page said.

"Just so," Inez said. "They give me a studio for the editing in Paris July the first."

"You won't make it," Farrell said. "I checked the paper yesterday. Ranier got heavy wet snow earlier this week. Tough prospects here, too."

The tip of her cigarette seared a hunter's orange. She arched her head, let the smoke come out fast, and took another drag. "Tell me."

Farrell laid out Dunphy's scenario.

"Three weeks is bullshit," Inez said. "We go as soon as possible."

"Crazy," Farrell said.

"Les hommes laches," Inez muttered.

"Nothing to do with cowardice," Farrell said. "You go up, you want to come down."

Inez picked a bit of tobacco off the tip of her tongue and flicked it. "In France, the skiers are not thinking first how I must protect myself and then ski. Always there is a way, if there is commitment. They climb a line two, three times before to find the path. But they are not on the knees to weep 'Oh, Oh, perhaps I hurt myself.' Of course perhaps you hurt yourself. To hurt is always there. It is life."

"What's the problem?" Page slurred. "Collins said almost every peak in the Tetons been done even in winter. Let's go!"

"One gets off his knees!" Inez cried.

The Wave cracked his jaw: "It boardable. I mean these hills, mon?"

"Some of it," Farrell said. "The bowls and slopes."

"Shred city," The Wave grinned, then saw Farrell frowning at him and he stopped.

"We go in three days' time," Inez said, stubbing her cigarette out. She pointed at the map. "I think this Grand Teton, the biggest, is my destiny. I arrange another helicopter."

Farrell faced her and said, "I'm against it."

Inez's jaw froze. "I thought we declare the truce."

"Like you said, Inez: even in France, the skiers climb to see what they've got before they run."

"You already say it takes the minimum of two, maybe three days to climb this Grand and come back down. This is out of the question."

"I'll give you that," Farrell said. "But the question isn't so much the Grand as it is altitude. I'll go for a climb tomorrow to the lower slopes of Buck Mountain, dig some pits. It will give us something to go on."

Tony nodded. "It's a good idea."

"For who?" Inez demanded.

"For anyone not in the helicopter," Ann said.

Inez drew another cigarette from the pack, tapped it on the surface of the map, put it between her lips, but did not light it. "Okay, Collins. Go dig your pits. I do some research of my own. We meet back here tomorrow, same time."

Chapter 22

After the meeting, Farrell had avoided the rest of the crew and taken Ruby for a walk toward the edge of town. The full moon dimmed the stars, but lit up the valley so that the trees of early spring, leafless, stood out like calligraphy against the sky and the snow. Seeing how easy the landscape was to understand when it was just black and white triggered a fit of confusion. He knew either Stern or Gabriel or someone else was trying to track him through his Swiss accounts. He wondered how long they would hold. How long could he maintain stamina when confronted with Inez, a women composed in shades of gray? Every moment in the room with her that evening had been a struggle. The lure of skiing the Grand Teton, even this early in the year, was undeniable. For the first time in years that sort of yearning had a countervailing force; he felt an obligation now, for reasons he didn't quite understand, to protect Page, The Wave, Ann, and Tony from danger.

He thought of Stern again. Why hadn't the agent felt the same obligation? He remembered sitting in Stern's office after sneaking into the federal building downtown one morning in mid-June. He'd been startled by the size of Stern's office—barely large enough to hold a desk, its walls bare save a poster of a river with the word "Idaho" splashed across it.

Farrell cut to the point, "I can't take this much longer. My wife wants out. Me, too. Let's just bring this out into the open and get it over."

Kennerson, the U.S. Attorney assigned to his case, raised his thick eyebrows and rubbed his palm across the sleeve of his blue serge suit.

Stern rapped a pencil off the corner of his desk and said, "It's not enough . . . what you brought us."

"I've given you everything I know," Farrell protested.

Kennerson broke in, doing his best to lay out what was hearsay and what was clearly admissible in court. Farrell had done such an efficient job of burying the identities behind the different companies that owned the properties on Otay Mesa, near Nogales and El Paso, that legally Farrell and the other two attorneys in Las Vegas who'd signed on as secretary and treasurer were the only people responsible.

Farrell listened closely because he liked Kennerson as much as an informant can enjoy the company of a man who holds a sword over his head. He supposed, too, that Kennerson liked him, as much as a prosecutor can like a criminal. They were both about the same age, of similar burly build and afflicted with premature baldness. There was also the background: Farrell was from Maine, Kennerson from Rhode Island; they talked much the same language. It was not much to base a relationship on, yet it was there. Farrell could also tell that Kennerson bore him a grudging respect, for once Farrell had entered into the deal for immunity, he held nothing back; nothing except the three off-shore accounts he'd created for himself and the identity papers for him and Lena; he wanted a safety valve.

"Let me get this straight," Farrell choked. "All I've done the past four months is incriminate myself?"

Stern said, "You've got nothing with the names of Cortez or Cordova on it except for a few bank accounts and loans. All legitimate. And other than the fact that you know a lot about the furniture in the homes of Rodriguez and De La Leone, we can't place you there."

Kennerson went on, "What you've done is explain and document the pattern of activity. That was necessary and correct. We've got everything to get Cordova and Cortez, except—"

"Them," Farrell said.

Stern whacked the pencil off the desk again. "And to be honest, that is not going to be hard . . . to do."

Farrell caught something familiar in the expressions of the two men. It took him a moment, but he placed it: he'd seen a variation of it on people watching the Olympic ski race on television and the craziest Austrian was about to start on course. It was the odd mix of delight and revulsion that surfaces involuntarily in an audience when it knows someone is about to go downhill fast.

For most of Farrell's life he'd fed off that sort of energy. But now he was a lab rat in the government's experiment. Stern and Kennerson knew that if they sent enough electrical current through the wires implanted in the rodent's brain, the rat would run to sugar water or have an erection or squeal in pain.

"What do I have to do?" Farrell asked.

"You should know the risks first," Kennerson said.

Farrell's laugh was bitter.

"What's the matter?" Stern asked.

"That always comes first, doesn't it?"

Two days later, Farrell leaned against a pay phone along the trolley tracks on C Street, four blocks from his office. Rubenstein had become a regular visitor to his office of late and he didn't dare make any contact with Gabriel from there. He dialed a series of numbers, talking his way through two operators who patched him to Mexico. After five minutes, Gabriel's smooth voice came on the line.

"Jack?"

"We have to talk," Farrell replied. "Things are moving slower than I expected."

"Go on."

"I'm nervous."

"More vertigo, Jack?"

"That's not it. I'm hitting snags with the new banks we've recruited. The government auditors are cracking down on currency documents up here. We've got to devise a new system. Besides, it's been four months. I want a face-to-face."

There was a pause, then Gabriel asked: "Can you come to Manzanillo on the first?"

"Why not come north?" Farrell responded. "You haven't been to San Diego."

"Too much work here," Gabriel said. "A trip to the States will wait."

Farrell hesitated, "The first then. I'll see you sometime that afternoon. Don't bother coming over for me. I'll rent a Jeep at Colima Airport. I've never had the chance to drive that road alone."

"I look forward to it." Gabriel paused. "Maria, too."

Farrell listened to the clicks and whirs on the line fade to nothing. He hung the receiver in the cradle. "He wouldn't go for a meet here."

Stern reached into his pocket and tugged out a butterscotch candy. He popped it into his mouth, tonguing it into his cheek where it gave him the appearance of a chipmunk hoarding a nut.

"I said—"

"I heard you . . . Mr. Farrell," Stern said. "I was just telling myself how nice it would have been to put the cuffs on him right here. Now, it's extradition. Or we wait until he comes to the states. Either way, a bitch."

"This is the big coup, I imagine," Farrell said.

Stern smiled while sucking on the candy. "I'm a patient man . . . Mr. Farrell. Spend my weekends fly fishing. If we lay the right pattern on the surface, sooner or later they'll get hungry."

"Why am I always Mr. Farrell?"

Stern looked away. "Keeps it impersonal."

Farrell pursed his lips, seeing the implications behind the statement. They walked past the busy outside restaurants where dozens of office workers lunched in the warm sun. "I don't want to be there when you cuff him."

"No stomach for the confrontation?" Stern replied. "I figured you to find . . . that of interest."

"Too many bystanders could be hurt."

"Your wife will be protected," Stern said. "I promised you that, Mr. Farrell. I meant it."

"Okay." Farrell paused. "You know I wonder about it all, every night. I can't come up with an answer for why it happened."

Stern pointed a finger at him. "You'd be surprised how many of the con artists I come in contact with are like that. I always tell them . . . the same thing."

"What's that?"

"That's why the government has people like Kennerson: to tell the whole world why you did it."

Kennerson never had the chance, did he? Farrell thought on the walk back into Jackson. He bought a sandwich and a drink at a store, then went to the motel. He hadn't been back in his room five minutes when a knock came at the door. Ruby barked. It was Frank Portsteiner dressed in jeans and a khaki fishing jacket. Farrell surprised himself and the old man by hugging him.

"You been drinking again, son?" Portsteiner asked.

"No." Farrell drew his arms away from Portsteiner, embarrassed. "I guess . . . I was just happy to see a friend."

In spite of himself, Portsteiner beamed. He followed Farrell into the room, saw Ruby, and nodded. "A dog, too."

Farrell scratched Ruby behind the ears. "I guess I'm trying to change."

"A start," Portsteiner said. "How's the movie coming?"

"Getting weirder by the minute," Farrell said. He related all that had happened in Lake Tahoe as well as Inez's determination to move into the Tetons as quickly as possible.

"Was out fishing in the foothills of the Gros Ventre this afternoon," Portsteiner said. The Gros Ventre was another high mountain range near Jackson. "Heard some slabs give way. You've got to give these big hills a chance to consolidate, press down, ice up."

"Tried to tell her that, but she's got this way of twisting words so you can't think straight. I convinced her to let me climb partway up Buck Mountain tomorrow to dig some pits."

"I'll come along."

"Better I do this alone."

"LaChapelle's rule number one: Never solo in the mountains."

"That's rule number two, Frank," Farrell said. "First is always conduct a march so that only one person at a time is exposed to danger."

"Don't try to outquote me, son," Portsteiner said. "I'll just tag behind. Phelps Lake is below Buck. I've been meaning to throw a fly into it sometime on this trip."

"But . . ."

"See you at seven A.M., sharp," Portsteiner said, closing the door behind him.

Farrell listened to Portsteiner's footsteps retreat across the frozen gravel, secretly happy that the old man would accompany him the next day. Portsteiner was someone he could trust. He sighed and repeated the word. Trust. It wasn't a noun that he had used with any consistency in his life. He turned that over a few times and discovered that trust was not something to accept, only to give. He wondered at what point he had gotten the concept ass-backward. Certainly he believed he could trust Stern and Kennerson in the days leading up to his trip to see Gabriel. The two men had spent most of their time at his house, helping him review the pitch.

It was simple enough: Wired for sound, Farrell would go over the history of their accomplishments, getting Gabriel to agree and comment. There would follow in detail a discussion of the mechanics of the land purchases and how the cash moved. Farrell would move toward the hook, telling Gabriel that several banks had balked during escrow because they didn't know the identities of the directors behind his land companies.

"Good," Stern said after he'd repeated it for the tenth time. "Then you tell Cortez that a few bankers think your relationship is a conflict and they're considering going to the FDIC with it. You propose a new recruit to the system, someone outside the bank who can purchase the properties. Of course you tell him that you'll still be calling the shots. I'm the recruit, posing as an Arizona land developer with contacts in the Virgin Islands."

"He'll check on you, how I met you, what you know, how you know it."

"There will be documents on file in Arizona and Tortolla backing Art up," Kennerson said. "Beyond that you tell him that Stern knows little and wants to know less. To Cortez, he's a common-enough type."

"How's that?"

"Greedy."

On the day before he was to leave, Stern and Kennerson grilled Farrell on every possible scenario they could devise: Gabriel angered, Gabriel reluctant, Gabriel suspicious.

For more than an hour, Farrell practiced activating the recording device they'd hidden inside his briefcase. It was triggered by a latch they'd installed next to the locking mechanism. Close the latch, he completed an electronic circuit that powered the tape machine. The microphone, built into one of the brass corner braces, was hemispheric; it would gather sound forty-five degrees to each side of the direction in which the device was pointed.

"Two extra tapes, ninety minutes each," Stern said. He showed Farrell how they fit into the recorder itself. The tiny microcassette deck lay underneath a thin panel installed in the base of the case. Velcro held the false bottom in place so tightly Stern had to search for the edge with a nail file.

"Whatever you do, be calm," Kennerson said as he watched Farrell fumble with the false bottom. "Do any changes in private. Don't leave anything open or out."

It was only then, in the way the men refused to look at him, that Farrell grasped how perilous his mission was. Cotton grew on the inside of his mouth. He had the urge to curl up and sleep.

"Here's the final run for you," Stern said, and he paced to the window. Beyond the FBI agent's slender silhouette, Farrell could see Lena's BMW turning into the gate. Stern stopped to watch her spill out, her hair longer than it had been in years, glowing reddish in the late afternoon sun. Farrell could tell Stern found her attractive. He felt jealous. Turning thirty the previous month had made his wife's appearance richer, more classic; she seemed taller, more assured, strong. The dogs bounded across the yard to her, throwing their paws on her legs. She shooed them down and walked around the back.

"She will still leave you . . . Mr. Farrell?" Stern asked. His face tightened; he realized he'd made a mistake.

Farrell's stomach hollowed; they obviously had bugged the house. "We haven't spoken of it lately," he said, trying to control his anger.

Stern snapped his head around as if he was glad Farrell hadn't pursued the issue. "On the Pan Am flight to Guadalajara, a Drug Enforcement Agent will sit somewhere behind you in tourist class. He will not identify himself unless he senses trouble. In Colima one of our Mexican counterparts will take over."

"The Mexicans know?!" Farrell cried, unable to mask the panic.

"Are you out of your fucking minds? Those bastards would sell me out in a second. Forget it. Put the cuffs on now. I'll take jail."

Farrell fancied himself a very quick man. But Stern crossed the room before he'd taken a step, and the FBI agent's stubby fingers, suddenly heavy on Farrell's chest, pressed him back into the chair.

Stern leaned over Farrell. "They have no idea who you are. We've told them we suspect you are involved in a smuggling ring. That's all. If that gets to Mr. Cordova or Mr. Cortez, you have an alibi . . . you had no idea you were followed. At worst, they tell you to shut down the operation."

Kennerson stood behind Stern. "We've had two men renting a villa up the hill from Cortez's place since late April. They're posing as homosexual artists and they have a telescope trained down on the house."

"Did they see the armed guards?" Farrell demanded.

"They did," Kennerson said. "And the woman. They say she is stunning."

Farrell grunted. Stunning. He plucked the diary from his bag.

June 29

Being frightened used to be a momentary thing.

I am what Dad calls lock-joint scared. He saw it in men working the stacks of the big ships. The scaffolding would slip and they had to reach over and reattach the gear. But they wouldn't move because all they could see below them was the interior of the stack, like some old abandoned well in the woods, staring back up at them. When they'd finally take a step, they'd skip and lurch like arthritic old women leaving church.

So while Jack packs to go south, I am unable to cross to him, to tell him it will be all right. I can see that black hole between us, scared if he falls, I will be pulled in after him; scared if he doesn't fall and makes it to the other side, I'll be left behind.

We have developed an unspoken understanding. He sleeps in our bedroom, but is not welcome in my bed. He curls in the corner with a blanket. He is there now. He twitches and kicks off the blanket. I listen to the rasps from his throat. At midnight I will cover him again. It is what I can do.

July 2

Jack was gone this morning at five A.M. Before he left there was an instant between us of not knowing what to do. He left then. Before I had a chance to say everything I wanted to. Before I had a chance to hold him one more time.

The winds are out of the desert today, a scorching prelude to the fourth. If I stand near the garden wall and look south, I can see the curve of the coastline toward Mexico. I now hate the beauty of California, the perfect blue sky, the tan cliffs, the flowers.

When Stern and Kennerson left yesterday evening, the house settled into a quiet that reminded me of the electric stillness before thunderstorms. The sun was low, throwing the shadow of trees on the wall in the bedroom. I tried to imagine how my mother, who has endured for so long, would go on here. No answer except just to be.

I smelled Jack before I heard him. That's always been his primary sense. And here I am becoming him because I have to understand.

Jack stood in the doorway. His head was bowed. He scuffed his socks at the carpet. He choked that these men are capable of everything, then stopped and shook like a leaf.

At that, the sight of him defeated, alone, I could not help myself. It began by holding out my arms and drawing him into bed. I held him by his shoulders, which seem less broad than when I met him. He asked me to forgive him, but I told him I couldn't, and don't know if I ever will. But for that moment I was here. He moved closer to me. I pressed my hand to his face, feeling myself drift off to sleep, the screen behind my eyelids flickering and then fading to orange.

When I woke up, we were far apart in bed. He put his hand out on the pillow and I reached for it. It took time, but we made crippled love.

Afterward there were tears and murmurs, but little talk. In the last dark hour before he had to shower and prepare for Stern, Punta and Rabo jumped into bed and we four clung.

Farrell remembered the comfort he had taken in her touch and how lonely he'd been without it on the flight south. Before he left he had wanted to tell her how much he loved her, but he decided somehow it would ring false. He prayed he'd have the chance to prove it. He'd gone to the car meekly, which now he considered fitting for he had read that this was the way most convicted killers walked to the death chamber—with the resolve of a lamb heading to slaughter.

Chapter 23

arrell and Portsteiner signed in at the gate to the Teton National Park. They drove to the trailhead, and from there hiked the Stuart Draw through piñon pine and spruce toward the tiny lake below Buck Mountain. By nine-thirty the air had warmed into the low fifties. Around them the snow melted and revealed dark swatches of mud and moss. Before long the men were forced to strip to their T-shirts.

An hour later, they crested the ridge above the lake, a small, tidy piece of glass amid the heavy conifer. Some of the ice had melted and broken away from the shore. At the center, jigsaw pieces of ice still floated and refracted the sun, so the lake sparkled and flared like fire.

To the west, perhaps a quarter of a mile, a granite cliff rose and, above it, the peak of Buck Mountain. Farrell pointed to a gap between the northern edge of the cliff and the steep slope that ran parallel to it. "That's probably the route to the upper mountain Dunphy told me about."

"He says it's the way to go, you do it," Portsteiner said. "Peter's kind of raw, but one of the most instinctive climbers I ever saw."

"Stellar crystal?" Farrell asked.

"Nope," Portsteiner grinned. "Capped column."

"Tell you what," Farrell said. "See if you can get some of these trout to hit. I'll climb the first pitch beyond the cliff and do my tests."

"Don't ask twice," Portsteiner said, and he rushed down the trail to the edge of the lake. Ruby bobbed at his heels.

It took Farrell half an hour to circle to the far side of the lake. The idea was this: He would test the snow at the highest altitude he could reach in two hours of climbing. That would give him a clue to the stability of the snowpack at a corresponding height on the Grand Teton. The snow was thick under the strong sun. Sweat ran down the middle of his back after only one hundred yards of climbing. His boots sucked in water and weighed him down. He broke into an opening near the cliff. The sun caught him full in the eyes and he squinted, remembering how the sun had beat down on the dusty road between Colima and Manzanillo.

The peasant boys along the road had peddled their bikes with uncomfortable determination, heads down, bare feet angled off the pedals. A donkey tied to a tree next to the ditch did not shiver and quake at the flies that settled about its eyes; the animal only blinked, as if that were the limit of its capacity in the terrible heat. As he drove, Farrell had told himself that if he followed Stern's instructions, he'd come through unscathed. After all, he'd studied many of the faces on the plane and hadn't seen one remotely interested in him. Stern's people knew what they were doing.

At the gate to Gabriel's compound, the swarthy guard who had trapped the capon on his first visit greeted him with a toothless grin. "The señor and señora wait for you these past two hours," he said after a cursory glance at Farrell's luggage.

"Are they alone?" Farrell asked.

The guard slapped his stomach. "No, the one who's bigger than me, that one with the bulging eyes who treats me like shit. He's here, too."

The guard opened the gate and stepped back to let Farrell pass. Farrell drove through the gate, peering through the shade trees toward the hills, toward the villa of Stern's agents.

Gabriel stood from a white wicker love seat and came to the steps of the veranda. In the purple shadows beyond him, Farrell made out the laborious form of Cordova, who sported a white straw hat and drank from a high-ball glass.

"My friend," Gabriel said, extending his hand. "How good of you to come."

Farrell looked Gabriel right in the eye as Stern had instructed. His stomach fluttered only once, then the potential risk of the situation seized him with loving arms. He became absorbed. "I appreciate the meeting on such short notice," Farrell said.

"If it's as serious as you think, it is nothing," Gabriel said. "I had Jorge fly in from Tapuchala."

Gabriel grabbed the satchel and the briefcase from the Jeep. Farrell swallowed hard, then looked away, hoping the men would not notice the new latch near the lock. Cordova stood, grunting in the stifling air. He wiped his chin with a napkin and extended his hand.

"Jesus, señor, I don't know why this couldn't have been done in a hotel in Mexico City with an air conditioner," he said, pushing the hat back on the curve of his brow. "You made the change in Guadalajara, yes?"

"Yes, how did you know?"

Cordova shrugged. "We have much to discuss this day," he said.

Off to Farrell's left, through the ancient glass panes of the windows, he caught a flicker of green. Maria glided onto the veranda in a lime jumpsuit topped with pale red sunglasses. She reached out her hand, only the faintest hint of smile on her face. Farrell took it and leaned in to kiss her on the cheek. One of her fingers stroked his palm so lightly he jerked back.

"So good to see you again, Jack," she murmured.

Lingering in the air, competing with the blooming hibiscus and the Pacific, he caught the faint odor of liquor. And he noticed how limp her hand was in his and how she stood, stiff, yet acutely aware of her balance, like an old fence post struggling to stay upright against a winter wind.

"You, too," Farrell said, for the first time pitying Maria. "My wife asked about you."

"Did she?" Maria said. "What about?"

"Oh, this and that," Farrell fumbled. "How your dogs are doing, that sort of thing."

The enigmatic smile again. "My dogs," she said, followed by a silence, broken only by the humming of insects flitting in the vines.

Gabriel put his hand under her elbow in a manner so gentle and yet so insistent that Farrell recalled Stern's hand on his chest the previous afternoon. He prayed his own disorientation wasn't as transparent.

Cordova shook his head, coughed, and returned to the squat oak chair that someone had moved from the living room to the veranda.

"Why don't you see to some lunch for our guest?" Gabriel said to Maria as she left. He slumped into the wicker chair. "She is not herself these days, and to be honest, I don't know why. Perhaps that clinic in Palm Springs?"

Farrell almost laughed out loud at the irony. But he composed himself enough to tell Gabriel he'd read about the clinic, that it was praised as one of the best treatment centers. Gabriel looked out at the ocean. Far offshore a dinghy bobbed on the teal water. Farrell could make out two people on the boat. One crouched in the bow with a bucket and threw water into the sea.

"We all have to make difficult decisions, do we not, my friend?" Gabriel asked.

Lena's image suddenly moved into the space between them, Lena in the dark, the Lena who had rained blows on the back of Farrell's head as he dug his fingers into the carpet, a synthetic odor stinging his nostrils. Anger, deep and purple, drenched Farrell like a summer thunderstorm. You lousy stinking fuck, he thought. You don't even understand your own viciousness. He wanted to leap to his feet to strike Gabriel down. His posture must have betrayed his agitation, because Cordova shifted forward in his seat and Gabriel tensed. "Something wrong?" Gabriel asked.

"No," Farrell said, and he pinched his finger. "Nothing. These negotiations have me on edge. I just need a vacation."

Maria drifted onto the porch, carrying trays of cold tuna sandwiches and lemonade. Maria managed to get the dishes onto the table without spilling anything. She placed her hand on Gabriel's left shoulder. He covered it with his right. "I think I'll take a nap," she said. "The heat."

"That would be best," Gabriel said. He patted her hand and she floated away.

After they ate, Gabriel said: "So what is so urgent?"

"Let me get my briefcase," Farrell said, wiping at the corners of his mouth with a napkin. He rose, crossed inside the open double doors, and grabbed the case. He reached in and removed a report, a phony scenario Stern had developed. He closed the briefcase, snapped the outside latches into place, then as fast as he could, twisted the tweezer of metal over the thin metallic knob. The recorder vibrated slightly.

Farrell set the briefcase on the ground with the voice-activated sensors facing Gabriel and Cordova. He leafed through the report. He was a salesman now, speaking in a breezy, but earnest voice. They listened as he recounted the paper profits they'd posted on the land deals and the potential for future gains. Farrell didn't know what he was hoping for at that point—an affirmation, a grunt, anything audible Stern could use to establish complicity. They sat mute.

Farrell talked on, worrying that he might be babbling, worrying that he was blowing the situation.

"What's the point?" Gabriel said finally.

"I just wanted to make sure we all have the same historical perspective."

"We are well aware of the procedures and records," Cordova said.

Farrell wanted to kiss him. He leaned forward and pointed at Cordova. "That's why I'm here. We're becoming too set in our pattern."

"Go on," Gabriel said, pouring another glass of lemonade.

"The two realty trusts that I've organized to purchase the border properties are not—how shall I say this? blind enough?" Farrell said. "Given my constraints within the bank, I can't organize more than one corporate shell between the trust and myself."

"Why not?" Cordova asked. "It seems simple enough."

"Domestically, it is," Farrell said. "My fear is that if everything is organized in the States, someone with a strong nose could root out the only link. And to be frank, that's me."

Gabriel pressed his fingertips together and stared at the roof of the veranda. "What are you asking for?"

"That we move more of the documentation off-shore, in effect laundering my role out of the situation, even though I'd still be in charge."

Gabriel squinted. "How would it work?"

"Through some people I used to work with in Chicago," Farrell began. "They know a man on the island of Tortolla in the U.S. Virgin Islands, an American, who specializes in realty trusts and corporate shells. He has contacts on the Isle of Man and other safe havens. He also develops property in Arizona."

"No contact has been made yet?" Cordova asked.

"An initial phone conversation of perhaps twenty minutes," Farrell said. He thought of Stern and how he would play his role.

"What are the banks he works with?" Cordova asked.

"Mostly Grand Cayman institutions and one in London," Farrell said. "But his primary function is that of link to foreign notaries. I believe through this man we can organize a system to purchase properties along the border with so many corporate steps between us that we and our clients would be invisible."

They questioned Farrell closely on his analysis of the costs of working through a third party versus creating their own organization. Stern, Kennerson, and Farrell had discussed that scenario at length.

"I think we can go with our own people, once we understand his system," Farrell said. "Once we are educated, we cut him out."

Cordova stood and walked to the bannister of the veranda, his thick hands disappearing under the dense vines. "On the phone you mentioned problems with Customs documents," he said.

"Actually the IRS raised the issue," Farrell said. "Since the first of the year we've been contacted twice by IRS representatives to discuss the new requirements on cash deposits and cash transfers."

"And?"

"I've spoken with a number of local San Diego bankers who report similar calls," Farrell said. "My fear is that though we've managed to keep documentation to a minimum so far, they are tightening the screws. I think we're better off moving the cash in trucks across the border into Mexico, rather than continue with the wire transfers."

"Too risky," Gabriel said. "We got burned several times a few years ago when the shipments were discovered by *Federales* at the border and the money confiscated. We had to make good on the loss—almost six hundred thousand dollars."

Farrell tossed the report on the table. "And I'm telling you our old methods cannot handle the present cash volume, not to mention what we've forecast, without detection."

Gabriel traced his fingers over the blue manila surface, but did not pick up the document. He crossed his legs and said: "Why don't you go settle into your bedroom, take a shower. Jorge and I will read the report, discuss some things."

Farrell picked up the briefcase by its sides, realized the grip might appear odd, and shifted it so he held it by the handle. He wobbled when he took his first step. Gabriel half rose in alarm.

"Too damn long on the plane," Farrell said. He made a show of rubbing his right knee. "Maybe a shower would help loosen me up."

Farrell paused on the slope of Buck Mountain. His boots were sopped through. He groaned—even at this high altitude, the snow remained slushy. What sounded like distant cannon fire snapped him around. He looked frantically out into the minaret spires of granite and snow that ran out for fifty miles around him. Now came the low booming sound of the ocean against rocks. The roar built, then faded.

He examined the different peaks with the binoculars for almost five minutes before he found the evidence: a jagged line perhaps twenty-five yards long cut below the rim of a rock face; below it the bubbled and torn surface of the snow gave way to a jumble of ice and dirt and debris. It looked like a chain reaction crash of a dozen white cars on a deserted highway in a desert of soft, white sand.

Farther away came another crack, another moan, as the mountains shed their winter skin. The noise faded. Farrell climbed again, slower and more cautiously now, toward the chute that led to the snow field below the peak of Buck Mountain.

A half hour later, Farrell's thighs burned. He wedged his pack into the snow and drank from his water flask. He unstrapped his shovel and dug a three-foot trench, finding to his surprise that at least on this slope the more recent layers of the snow pack had bonded well. Deeper, however, the pack appeared fragile. The hoar, the deep frozen layer, was rotting from the water that percolated down from the surface. He crushed a handful of the brittle crystals in his hand as a small sun ball—a chunk of snow that breaks away under the direct heat of the sun—rolled past him down the chute.

Farrell looked up from where the ball had come. "This would be like climbing a pile of marbles," Farrell said, thinking out loud.

He reshouldered his pack and zigzagged slowly back down the slope, thinking of how he'd showered at Gabriel's house and returned to the porch an hour later. Dusk had crept up the sides of the hills toward the bleached white villa on the ridgeline. His blue manila report folder was in exactly the same position he'd left it. Gabriel offered him a rum. Farrell watched him pour the brown liquor over ice, add soda water and a twist of lime. Gabriel handed Farrell his glass. As Farrell raised the drink to his mouth, Cordova said, "You are still an amateur even after all this time."

Farrell lowered the glass, noticing how in the twilight the dove boy's bulging eyes seemed to glow. "How's that?"

"These IRS officials," Gabriel said. "You're telling us they didn't ask to see records?"

The ice cubes clinked against the side of Farrell's glass. He brought the tumbler down fast onto the arm of the chair and folded his hands in his lap. He cursed himself for not moving the briefcase closer; he'd left it near the door, next to a bush. With the two men in different positions now, Farrell could not tell if the microphone was pointed in the right direction.

"They didn't," Farrell said. "They called and asked about the increase in the capital reserves, which I told you about before."

"What did you say?" Cordova asked.

"That we were establishing closer relationships with the Southern California and Northern Mexico real estate development community and deposits were up. They seemed satisfied. I've had no follow-up visits. Why the amateur crack?"

Cordova said: "A professional would have figured out a way to create more distance between the corporate identities a long time ago."

"Funny, I seem to remember you being satisfied with the operation four months ago," Farrell snapped.

"No bickering!" Gabriel said sharply. "We are just upset at some of the news you brought and others that we have only just received."

"What news?" Farrell asked, watching both men carefully.

Inside, beyond the window at Gabriel's back, a light turned on; the light emanated onto the porch and, Farrell realized with discomfort, illuminated his face. Gabriel and Cordova's features, however, received only side lighting, so portions of their faces were swathed in shadows like a portrait by Rembrandt. Maria crossed the glass scrim at the back of this stage and disappeared.

"Did you know you were followed from Guadalajara and we believe from as far as San Diego?" Cordova demanded. His eyes were now those of a dead bird: opaque and dull. The golden light from inside the hacienda hit Cordova's open mouth at a peculiar angle. The effect—of purpled tongue against fluorescent teeth and flamed cheeks—was immediate; Farrell shivered and felt a short, quick stream of warm liquid in his crotch.

"My God," Farrell whispered. "My wife doesn't know anything."

"The hell with your wife," Cordova hissed. "We think they've been watching this house for months!"

Farrell's right arm twitched involuntarily and struck his glass, which crashed on the tiles. The spilled liquor spread and evaporated on the surface still hot from the day's sun. Gabriel leaned forward, staring at him. Farrell's thoughts raced to possible exits. The federal bastards had walked him through every possible scenario save this one. He seized on ignorance.

"Who's watching?" Farrell said. He began to pant and ran his fingers back through his thinning hair. "Who'd follow me? My God, the bank!"

Gabriel stood, lit a cigarette, and paced. "No auditors have been to see you?" he demanded. "No new employees?"

Farrell trembled. "No new workers. No audits other than the usual quarterly meetings with the FDIC." And this was true; neither Stern, nor Kennerson, nor any of the other federal authorities to whom he'd told his story, had ever set foot inside the bank. Farrell had smuggled out each file he thought worthy of their attention and they had copied them during the night.

"There's something missing," Cordova said. "It stinks."

"Nothing reeking on my end," Farrell snarled. "Maybe you've got the leak."

"No fighting now, I said!" Gabriel said.

"No, I want Jorge to answer that," Farrell said. "This is my butt on the line here, too."

For an instant he thought Cordova would rise out of his chair and one of his fists would swing. Gabriel flicked his fingers. Cordova relaxed back into the chair, sagging like the bag in a vacuum cleaner after the plug's been pulled. They'd been playing him, Farrell thought. Good cop, bad cop. Kennerson and Stern used the same technique.

"Almost everyone who works for us is a relative or has been known to us for a very long time," Gabriel said.

"Since when has blood or familiarity bred loyalty?" Farrell asked.

A rustling and brushing of feathers sounded in the night as the pea flock roosted. The men said nothing.

Farrell waited, studying them until their silence was intolerable. "How do you know I was followed?" he asked.

"We have our sources," Gabriel said. "An agent with the Drug Enforcement Agency rode the plane with you, approximately two seats behind yours from San Diego to Los Angeles to Guadalajara.

"From there the surveillance was continued by Alejandro Fosca, a member of the national police *narcoticos* detail, who is—how shall I say?—well known to us," Gabriel said. "Fosca was supposed to leave the trail at Colima, but he continued on at our request and noticed you were followed by one of the two *maricon* painters who rent the villa behind us."

Farrell decided bewilderment was the obvious course. "Painters? How long have they been there?"

Cordova said: "They put down a deposit on the property back in late October, early November. And then they did not take possession until mid-February. We thought nothing of it until Fosca's report. They're probably agents, too."

Gabriel dropped the cigarette stub to the ground and scuffed the sole of his shoe across it. "The DEA told Fosca they believe you are somehow involved in narcotics trafficking, but they can't figure it out exactly."

"But how?"

"They didn't offer and didn't bite when he asked," Gabriel said.

Farrell stood and crossed out of the main shaft of light, rubbing his hands together, searching for a viable lie. "It's got to be my boss, Jim Rubenstein," he said. "He's the only one with access to my records."

Cordova and Gabriel burst into laughter.

"Doubtful," Gabriel said. "Rubenstein is married to Fernando

De La Leon's second cousin, Isabel. He lives in terror that he will hear the whistling breath of Rodriguez late one night."

Farrell was speechless. The anger which had ebbed to a slow boil bubbled to the surface again; he had been played into this game as carefully as any of the marlin these two men had trolled for and fought to the deck of their boats over the years. Worse, he realized the perception of himself as a cool, dispassionate operator was pure delusion: he'd been read as a weak mark, conned. He leaned over the railing. "Rubenstein watches me. Jesus Christ."

"I'm sorry, Jack," Gabriel said. "It was just a precaution."

Farrell pressed his cheek against the cool adobe stanchion. "What are we going to do?"

"Jorge and I have discussed just that this last hour. At a minimum we shut down your operation. No action may be our safest course."

"What about the man in Tortolla?"

"I guess I wasn't making myself clear," Gabriel said in a cold, hard voice. "It stops."

Farrell considered pursuing the issue, then dropped the idea; he was thousands of miles from home and peering over the top of a very high cliff.

Cordova said: "We must operate on the assumption that our communication system has also been infiltrated. After tonight we will be severing our ties for a few months."

"Don't call us, we'll call you?" Farrell said. "Forgive me for being bitter, but this sounds like I'm being set adrift in a rot-bottom boat."

"Don't take it personally," Gabriel said soothingly. "I think upon reflection that this will be the best course for all concerned. Their interest in you may wane if your activity suddenly desists."

"And in an emergency?" Farrell asked. Thunder echoed behind him. Lightning flashed from a storm coming ashore.

Gabriel and Cordova exchanged glances. "We will arrange something," Gabriel said.

But Farrell could tell it wasn't true; in their minds, they'd already cut the rope and he was falling away from them down a very steep slope.

The memory of Mexican thunder mixed with the distant roar of snow breaking away from the mountains as Farrell slid and climbed his way back down the hill. By the time he had emerged from the trees above the lake, Portsteiner had fished his way farther along the shore. Ruby spotted him before Portsteiner did and thrashed through the snow and brush to meet him. He grinned as she sprinted toward him; she'd gained weight the past few days and the gash on her shoulder was covered with a thick scab. He slapped at her wiggling butt while she yelped and whined with pleasure.

"Saw you break out above the tree line about an hour ago and then stop," Portsteiner said. "Thought you were going higher."

"Didn't need to," Farrell said. "Friable depth hoar, no sign of a surface freeze overnight and at least one sunball."

"Shit. I thought I heard cracks up there."

"I counted five," Farrell said.

"No climb up the Teton, then?" Portsteiner asked.

"Not if I can help it," Farrell said. "How's the fishing?"

"Four macs," Portsteiner boasted.

"Enough action or you want to stay on?"

"Let's hike out," Portsteiner said. "I'm hungry."

Farrell led the way down, recalling the funeral mood at dinner at Gabriel's that night. His inclination had been to return immediately to Colima and go standby on a return flight. But Gabriel and Cordova felt such a move would raise undue suspicions on the part of the watchers on the hill.

"If you act like a courier, you'll be treated like one," Cordova said. "It could be ugly."

Maria said little during the meal. The red sunglasses were gone, and though Gabriel seemed to be rationing her wine, he had the uneasy suspicion she'd been doped. Midway through the main course, she pushed her plate back. "I have little appetite tonight," she said. "I think I'll retire."

When she rose, however, her bare toes brushed against Farrell's ankles. He ground his molars and did not look at her as Gabriel reached out to stroke her arm.

"I'll check in on you later," he said. Maria's smile was wan. She vanished into the rear of the house.

The three men spent the early evening in an awkward, forced conversation over glasses of brandy as the thunderstorm came and passed. They spoke of dove hunting, of marlin fishing, and then of the human spirit. Farrell found it bitterly amusing that Cordova thought that repeated exposure to adversity was the forge that created an indomitable character, one capable of handling any situation. Farrell demurred, noting that the strongest of men and women have their weaknesses.

"Of course," Cordova said. "But these people learn early on not to expose their soft belly, as it were."

Gabriel disagreed, arguing that the strongest of people are the ones who recognize they are weak.

"Paranoia is healthy in small doses?" Farrell asked.

"Something like that," Gabriel said. "Egos developed to the point of megalomania are often the most fragile. They consider themselves invincible and take no care to shield themselves."

Gabriel carried on in this vein for another five or ten minutes; despite the hatred Farrell now felt toward him, he enjoyed the facileness of his mind and realized he was the embodiment of the term "charming crook." Cordova added nothing more to the conversation. Farrell was aware the dove boy continued to evaluate him. *You're still an amateur at these things even after all this time.* With every ounce of effort in his body, Farrell fought to keep his composure under the scrutiny of those pallid eyes. At midnight, he pled exhaustion and excused himself. He locked the door to his room, listening at it until he was sure the two men remained in the living room. He drew the drape across the window, opened the briefcase, slid the letter opener along the base, and pulled. The tape had rolled! The second conversation may not have registered, but he was sure they had given him what he needed the first time.

He refitted the false base and locked the case tight. He slid the drape open until he could see the moonlight glistening off the rain-soaked grass. An animal, possibly Cazador, moved at the edge of the light and then vanished. Farrell turned the crank on the window and relaxed as the fresh scent of the sea flowed into the room. He lay down with his hands under his head. Thoughts and images hurtled and bumped in the darkness: Cordova's shadowed figure on the porch, Maria's vacant stare, the donkey on the road from

Colima too stifled by the heat to slap the flies, the stroke of Lena's fingers on his skin so much earlier that day.

It had been that day after all. He coveted the sensation the way one will, on the morning after the first evening with a new lover, stop amid the bustle of life and relive such tender, secret memories. "New lovers," Farrell said to himself, and the gentle reassurance of the notion gradually calmed the whirling buzz of activity. He slept.

The lock made a single clack as it moved. Farrell startled wide awake and afraid, sure in the frenzied manner of stressed logic that he would hear a man's breath come like a whistle toward him.

Maria slipped around the edge of the door and pressed it quietly shut. Farrell calmed if only for a moment; it was no pitch dark night when he could tell himself she was a dream. The moon glowed through the parted drapes. She wore no robe, only a gauzy nightgown through which were visible the dark nipples of her breast and the triangular smudge below her powerful hips. In spite of himself, he was fascinated.

She crossed the room to his bed. She raised the hem of her nightgown until the smudge became ebony hairs that seemed smooth, not crinkly in the dim light. Her smell came to him and he thought himself lost. For an instant he played with the idea of having her as revenge.

But when Maria reached forward and stroked the skin above his shorts, he sensed a bitter, callous quality in her touch. He thought of Lena's soft caress. In an instant, the situation became nonsexual and apolitical; Maria was a victim, not a perpetrator. He grasped her hand before she could pull his shorts down. With his other, he lowered the hem of her nightgown so it covered her. She sat stony on the bed.

"That's not what you need," he whispered.

"What do you know of what I need?!" she whispered angrily.

"I know enough to see you're wounded. I seem to be an expert in that field these days."

She stared at Farrell for a long time. Gradually her shoulders dropped and her hands relaxed. Tears rolled down her cheeks and splashed on his hands. He gathered her into his arms and she sobbed, her weeping muffled against his chest. By degrees her crying slowed and she started and shook into a fitful sleep. Farrell thought of his wife and how she'd managed to survive all that had happened with some dignity. He looked at Maria and found that he pitied her in a way he had not pitied anyone for years; she reminded him of every majestic animal he'd seen in zoos. Her breathing became rhythmic, hypnotic. And then he, too, drifted away into that formless state before real forgetful sleep.

So as he and Portsteiner came to the trailhead near the White Grass Ranch in midafternoon, Farrell was still unsure whether someone passed outside the open window to his room in the waning moonlight that last night in Mexico, casting a shadow across their entwined bodies and the floor and the door; and then gone.

Chapter 24

"Ridiculous," Inez snapped. "And how long do we wait? A week? Two?"

The crew was gathered again in Inez's room. Farrell had just given his report on the adverse snow conditions on Buck Mountain.

"If you want safe conditions—" Farrell said.

"What are you, a lawyer?" Page interrupted.

"What's your problem, mon?" The Wave said to Page. "Thought we decided we are all in this together."

Page blew his nose and waved his hand. "Change of heart. I'm in this for myself."

Inez smiled. She pointed at Farrell. "I sense your attitude is negative even before you come. So when you do your snow tests today, I go to a bookstore where they have the books on the Tetons. And the people at the store tell me to speak with other guides besides this Dunphy. I find them and they say that unless you have climbed above nine thousand feet, your tests will not be true. Did you go above nine thousands?"

"No," Farrell admitted. "Maybe sixty-five hundred. But I heard slides. Big ones."

Inez dismissed him. "They say we be careful on the climb, in a slow, more gentler approach to the supersteeps above nine thousand."

"And where did these guides suggest we go?" Farrell demanded.

"They say go all the way, we go the Grand," Inez replied in a smooth seductive voice. "It has never been skied so early. And we have our first descent."

The room buzzed with an intensity that had not seized the group since Page stood alone on the cliff at Granite Chief.

"That's nuts," Tony said. "All the snow on the mountain could move this time of year. One of those climax avalanches, take a whole slope right to the dirt."

Page broke in, "Inez told me about her talks at noon. I went and talked to these guys myself. Kind of young, but they claim it can be done. People climb the Grand all the way, fourteen thousand feet. But yeah, skiing it from the top this time of year would be suicidal."

Inez made as if to break in. Page cut her off. "That's what they said, Inez. They said going to the top would be laying on the sword."

Inez frowned. "Yes, but they say the Grand can be skied now."

Page nodded. "Parts of it. They said we can climb more than halfway, up toward a place called the Black Dike and into a route called the Stettner Couloir up to where it goes to a straight rock wall."

"This has been done before, so early?" Inez asked.

"As far as we know, never. You'll get your first," Page said.

"What's up at the end of the Stettner, mon?" The Wave asked.

"A nearly vertical piece of stone, a hundred and fifty feet or more. The guides said anybody who's ever skied the Grand from the top has had to do what Briggs, the first guy, did: rappel off the top of the stone until you're down in the Stettner."

"So we could get to the base of that wall?" The Wave asked.

"I think so."

"We can shoot this from the helicopter, no?" Inez asked.

Page smiled and looked at Inez. "Almost none of it. If we could climb that stone at the end of the Stettner, you'd be able to get the run off the top of the Grand. But like Collins said, it's too early to go up there. And filming the lower Stettner from above is almost impossible; on one side there's a hunk of rock that hangs over it; the route down is almost hidden."

And in that instant Farrell saw where Page was going. "You'll have to climb with us if you want to film it," Page said.

Inez's face lost all color.

"What's the matter, Inez?" Farrell asked. "Scared?"

"No peaking through the fingers this time," The Wave laughed.

"Shut up, the two of you!" Inez snarled. She paced around the room. Her hand trembled as she lit another cigarette. She paused in front of Tony and Ann. "How much weight does you carry?"

"Depends on what we're going for and how long," Ann said. Tony nodded and said, "Roughly sixty to eighty pounds."

Inez squeezed her hands into fists. "I want to know the meters vertical in total we get on film."

"I can give you that," Page said. "Four thousand, maybe forty-five hundred vertical feet. And most of it at forty to sixty degrees fall line."

The Wave whistled. Ann sat down. Tony ran his fingers through his hair. For danger junkies, the allure of the Grand was undeniable. Even in the best conditions it was arguably one of the two or three most dangerous ski descents in the United States. And no one had ever done it this early. Farrell didn't notice what was wrong at first; he saw only the gourmets of peril enjoying the anticipation of an adrenaline feast. It worked on him, however, gradually gnawing at him until he was sure something was out of sync: their motivation wasn't limited to wanting to ride the bear's back. There was something he couldn't see.

"The snow today was rotten," he said. "You all know what that means."

Neither The Wave, nor Tony, nor Ann would look at him.

Page shrugged. "Where you tested, it probably was. But we're climbing an almost totally shaded route, much higher than where you were. Sure, we'll be slogging through slush at first. But like I said, if we take the most gradual way up, stick to the shade, careful and testing as we go . . . ."

Inez's cigarette glowed. "Yes?"

"You'd be selling your movie short if you didn't at least take a look, Inez," Page said.

"How much back-country guiding have you done?" Farrell asked.

"Enough to know this is possible," Page said.

"Anything's possible," Farrell said. "The point is to play the odds."

"I thought we were making a movie about extreme skiing," Page sneered.

Farrell tried to speak again, to point out Dunphy's reservations about a climb, even from the easier eastern approach. But Inez jumped in, strung out on her plans. "How soon do we leave?"

"Day after tomorrow," Page said. "It'll take a full day to get our equipment ready. Then a day's climb to get to a hut at eleven thousand five hundred feet that will have us ready for your shots in the lower Stettner the next morning."

"What equipment do we need?"

"Bare bones," Page said. "We can hire two guys to lug stuff as far as the hut. They'll bring down our sleeping gear. We won't be coming down the same way and the skiers will want as little to carry as possible."

The Wave's voice cracked with uncertainty: "You're sure this can be boarded, right?"

"The whole thing was surfed last year by a local guy who's over in Europe now," Page said. "But he did it in early June. You'll be forced to make do with Tepee's Glacier. It's on the way down, but shred city."

Inez's cheeks had taken on a high-toned flush Farrell had never seen before. She bubbled with questions and plans, demanding to know what they'd need to pull the shot in the Stettner off. He wanted to argue again, but he saw it was beyond his control. In that moment he knew the only way he'd stop the climb was to stop Inez. He had to talk to the attorney. Farrell got to his feet and he walked to the door. The room fell silent as he twisted the knob. Inez laughed, "He is timid. He leaves us."

"Who said anything about leaving?" Farrell said, and he gave her his most maniacal leer. "I wouldn't miss seeing you take a physical risk for anything, Inez."

Inez blanched. She fumbled for a cigarette, tapped it on the side of the pack. "You relieve me," she croaked. "This is your time, you know."

Farrell watched the way she lit the cigarette, a studied, controlled series of motions designed to unnerve him. It did. His stomach flutterered, and for a second he felt a fever coming on.

"I said the Grand is your shot, your moment in the film," Inez said, more confident now. "You and I have much to discuss. Come to my room tomorrow after you have your equipment ready."

Out of the corner of his eye, Farrell saw The Wave furrow his brow. His dreadlocks shook almost imperceptibly. Farrell never let his glance waver. "Like I said, I wouldn't miss it, Inez."

He walked out into the night air, warmer now than it had been since he'd arrived. The Wave caught up to him. "Don't see her, mon," he said. "I get real bad vibes. The files."

"I'm a mystery to myself, Wavo," Farrell said, glad that The Wave cared. "What makes you think she can figure me out? Besides, you were all gung-ho to go up that hill."

The Wave hung his head. "It was pretty much a done deal even before you showed up tonight. She got to us all, said if I climbed the Grand, she'd tell me where I can find Sunshine. It's strange, but as bad as she's been, I have to see her. She may be clean now."

Farrell sighed. "The rest of them?"

"Ann and Tony get their notes written off. Page, I don't know. He's been off in his own Idaho since he saw his old man."

"You think you can board the Grand when it's this unstable?"

"How bad could it be?" The Wave said, but the usual bravado was not there.

The Wave looked up at Farrell, who did not reply. They both knew the answer without having to hear it. The Wave tugged at a dreadlock. Farrell walked away, surprised at how he felt now. He wasn't numb, he wasn't even cool; he was as furious at Inez as he had been with Gabriel. Two blocks away he found a phone booth and punched in the numbers for the Swiss attorney. In minutes, the smooth, familiar voice came on the line.

"So good to hear from you, sir," the attorney said. "The companies you requested are in place. I believe you are secure for the time being."

Farrell nodded. "The best news I've had today. The report?"

"It will be here late in the day, my time, sir," he said. "I'm afraid I have an appointment and will not be available. Do you have a number where I could fax it?"

Farrell reached down and opened the phone book. He found the name of a pharmacy with fax services. He gave the attorney the number.

"Very good, sir," the attorney said. "We await your instructions."

Farrell sat in the only chair in his room, concentrating on the throbbing in his legs and the lightness at the back of his neck. He wondered if he'd ever find stillness again, and if he really wanted to. Perhaps, life isn't supposed to be all one way, calm or chaotic. Maybe the roller coaster was the point: life is nothing but those agonizing moments climbing the first hill, waiting for the drop, your head going a million miles a minute, then over into the swirl and the blur until it slows again for another ascent. He got out the diary and turned ahead until he saw blank pages. Only a few entries left. The thought filled him with as much despair as he'd endured the morning he left Gabriel's. Maria had left his room before dawn without a word. Gabriel stood alone by his jeep two hours later as he loaded the briefcase and luggage. Gabriel patted him on the back with such an air of resignation that Farrell didn't have the strength to look at him again.

He had pulled over twice on the drive to Colima and vomited. He slept fitfully on the flights back to the United States, painfully aware that people from both sides were probably watching. It had dawned on him that while he'd breached limits and was coming back alive, people like Maria never saw the line coming; she had crossed to the other side in a waking coma. One day she opened her eyes in a foreign land where the language sounded familiar, but was not coherent. The few words she understood were laced with menace. A numbing liquid was the only thing that let her survive.

Stern was leaning against a wall in the crowded terminal when Farrell came off the plane. Stern slid through the crowd to walk next to him.

Farrell growled low: "Don't open your mouth! Don't look at me, you lousy shit! They followed your followers. And the rest they bought off. I'm lucky to be alive."

Stern allowed himself a single wide-eyed glance at Farrell. Stern was frightened.

"Do not go anywhere near my home for at least a week," Farrell said. "Then figure out a way in from the rear. Understand?"

"Yes," Stern said. He disappeared.

Farrell opened the diary and found the entry for that night.

July 4

The house was dark and the dogs whined when I opened the door. I panicked; Jack was supposed to be home hours before. My feelings about him the past two days have flip-flopped. I love him, but hate him for what he has done. I see in him a terrible link to Lydia and what I almost did to her. Could I ever want him dead the way I wanted Lydia dead?

But when I got home and found the house dark, I wanted him alive. I ran through the house flipping on the lights until I found his luggage on the floor in the kitchen. The glass door to the terrace was open. Jack was asleep on the edge of one of my flower beds, curled into the fetal position, one hand between his legs. His face and neck and hands and white shirt were smeared with soil. Yet he appeared so content, I didn't want to wake him. It's like that, isn't it, to know that waking someone can be the cruelest thing possible?

I sat down on the railroad tie and watched him sleep until Punta dashed up and licked his ears. He startled and swore at her, saw me, and looked confused as if I were a dream. I reached out and stroked his face.

He told me he had weeded my garden and planted the impatiens. I pressed my fingers in around the stems, feeling for the depth of the root systems and the density of the soil. I told him it was a good start, led him into the house, and stuck him under the shower where he told me about Mexico.

I turned green when he said they knew he'd been followed. But I took some hope: during the entire story Jack never once dropped into the quick, chopped delivery of a conspirator that would have told me he enjoyed it. Jack was terrified in Mexico.

I fixed us some dinner. He told me about Maria and how she's gone to the bottle. I asked if it was because of Gabriel. He said he thought it was part of it. I stopped stir-frying the vegetables. He was staring into his drink. And I knew now there was more than idle chat between them and I felt sick and betrayed.

I screamed at him that starting over at anything starts with confession. He got real stiff then heaved his glass across the room where it struck the blue china clock on the mantelpiece and shattered it. He ran to the mess, knelt, and picked up one of the shards. It cut him. He sat there looking at the blood in his hand, telling me in a low voice that his grandmother had left it to him because he liked to wind it when he was a kid.

I didn't say a word, just put the pieces in a paper bag. He told me about Maria. I wanted to strike him again, but didn't. I took him to the bathroom and sewed the cut up myself. With each push of the needle through his flesh, nothing to ice his pain, I thought of the bitch and how I wished his hand were hers, too.

Stern and Kennerson arrived at Farrell's home exactly seven days later in a van marked with the name of a local janitorial service. They came to the door in white overalls with mops and buckets in their hands, a sight Farrell took slight pleasure in at the time. Lena had taken the day off and, over their objections, sat with him. Since he'd confessed, she had taken over. Farrell felt impotent and lost when he looked at her. She was strong, he was weak; any decision about their future together was hers. She needed to hear everything.

Stern played back the tape, and even though it was somewhat marred by static, Cortez's voice could plainly be heard: *"We are all well aware of the procedures and records."* As Farrell had feared, the second conversation hadn't recorded clearly.

"I think you've got it in that first talk," Farrell said.

"I don't know," Kennerson said doubtfully.

"But Jack described the whole organization," Lena said.

"Sure he does," Stern said. *"He* does. God, we needed Cortez to buy the Tortolla plan."

"I got nothing then?" Farrell said, dejected.

"No. There's something," Kennerson said. "It's open to interpretation, so you'll have to testify. Grand Jury."

"What are the odds they buy it?"

"Fifty-fifty," Stern said.

"What about Rubenstein's marriage to that man from Colombia's cousin?" Lena asked.

"Shows the web," Kennerson said. "But being remotely tied to a kingpin—even by blood—is no crime."

"If I testify, they'll know," Farrell said.

"Grand Jury's secret."

"They'll know," Farrell said. "They're watching. I don't know how, but they are."

"We can compel you to testify," Stern said.

"I was offered immunity," Farrell said.

"Only if you gave us Cortez."

"You lousy bastard, Stern," Farrell said. "I'll plead the fifth."

"You'll do time," Kennerson said.

"I expect it," Farrell said. "But you won't get what you want."

Stern glanced at Kennerson, who nodded.

"Protection throughout the trial could be provided," Stern said.

Lena stood up. "Not good enough. What about this federal witness program you read about?"

"That's for people in imminent danger," Kennerson said. "And we've got no indication that these people are physical threats."

"You came to the house in janitor's overalls!" Lena said. "What do you need, a black glove in the mailbox? A kiss on his cheek?"

Kennerson sat silent for almost a minute. "Okay," he said finally. "I'll try to set it up for the both of you."

Lena cleared her throat and glanced at her husband. "Set it up for one. I'm not sure where I'm going yet."

The muscles in the backs of Farrell's legs cramped. Stern and Kennerson looked at the floor. Farrell chewed at the inside of his lip. "Set up different plans, then," he said.

Over the course of an hour, they struck a deal: in two weeks Farrell would testify. That same day, he, and possibly Lena, would fly to eastern Washington for relocation. Farrell would return under guard for trials. If Lena decided to leave, she'd be moved to another location and eventually back to Rhode Island.

When the two men left, Lena held up her hand before Farrell could speak. "I can't tell you if I'm going. I was scared when you were gone, scared worse then I've ever been. Worse than, well . . . you know."

"They said we'd be safe."

"I said I haven't decided yet, end of conversation," she said.

"What haven't you decided?"

Lena looked at him like he was a very little boy. "If you have to ask, Jack, maybe that's the problem."

Farrell turned off the light in the motel room. He listened to Ruby pant near the heater. Sorrow and lament, new emotions, pulsed up the back of his spine, soaking every thought. Face it, you snipped every strand in the web of your relationship. Worse, you didn't even do it consciously, you did it with indifference. He could see that blaming genes and his parents for his actions wouldn't wash anymore; their fear of the future could not be used to erase the responsibility of his past. Or present, for that matter.

He moaned, feeling again the hot needle as Lena sewed his cut palm. Even then, with his wife scoring his flesh, he'd told himself that the effect he'd had on Maria was somehow noble; for a brief time he'd given this lonely, self-tortured woman the gift of forgetfulness. Now he saw Gabriel and Cordova and Maria for what they really were: the vulgar reflections of his own weaknesses, of course; but more, they were the brutal weapons he'd used to hurt his wife.

Why? He turned that question over several times, and found to his horror and his shame that it was simple: Lena had had the opportunity to know him. And that he had feared more than life itself.

Chapter 25

arrell was standing outside the pharmacy at 8 A.M. The attorney's faxed report was several pages long, double-spaced. The printing was smudged, but readable. He stuffed the papers into his jacket next to the diary and drove the camper to the edge of town. He felt he needed to be outside before reading again, as if the sky and the wind could help him plot a course through the last sad yards of thicket and bramble.

He parked the truck next to a butte that hems in Jackson. He and Ruby climbed up through the sand-colored brush, skirting what snow remained under the bright warm spring sun. Two bands of mule deer lazing on the ridgeline leaped from their beds. The deer bounded across the top of the butte toward a stand of cotton-wood trees.

Farrell found a boulder on top and sat on it. The town was spread out below him, and in the distance he could make out the elk at the reserve. The herd had dwindled in the last few days as more of the animals realized the days were longer and the snow pack in the foothills thinning. One by one, the beasts crossed into the trees and left the winter meadows behind.

Despite the inherent tranquility of the scene, Farrell's breath became labored. There were only three more entries in Lena's diary. And he had the final report on Inez. He shut his eyes to concentrate on a spot above the bridge of his nose, trying to remember the meditation techniques his mother had taught him. But the musty odor of decay that rose from the thawing soil around him hampered his efforts. Ruby destroyed them, howling when a rabbit broke from a nearby bush and tore across the butte. Farrell watched her give chase, her quick, darting moves reminding him of how Punta and Rabo had torn after each other through the house while he and Lena had packed the week before he was scheduled to testify. She had been feeling sick to her stomach.

Farrell asked, "Have you decided?"

Lena refused to meet his gaze. "Not yet."

He said, "I still love you."

Lena nodded. "It's not a question of love. That would stay no matter what happened. It's whether you feel what you've done."

"I know what I've done," Farrell said.

"I think you do *know*," Lena said as she left the room. "I want you to *feel* it in the same awful hollow way I did when Stern pounded at the door with a search warrant."

Farrell hesitated. He tried to will the sensations to surge within him, but all he got was words. "I regret what I've done," he said helplessly.

She walked off without replying. Farrell listened to the echoes of her footsteps. He wanted to chase her, but his feet wouldn't move. He remembered hiking into the desert in Africa late one winter afternoon. After an hour of walking, he had come to dunes and he rolled down one, then another and another. Suddenly it was dark and the rolling had stripped him of his sense of direction. He had shivered in the sand all night, waiting for dawn, waiting for the sun to lead him back.

Sitting on the butte, Farrell shivered, enduring again the same loss of direction. He opened the diary.

August 2

I threw up twice this morning. Last night I sat upright in bed while Jack slept, fighting heartburn, trying to figure out whether to go with this cripple or leave him to hobble alone. He has left me with scars worse than Jenny, and I can't help loving him. He has abused me, but he is not a striking abuser or

even one who does it with intent. Jack's sin is that he focuses
so much on moving, he doesn't have to look at himself in
repose. He can't see anything or anybody else still and iso-
lated, for what they are. He is happiest when racing through
life, everything smeared at the edge of his vision. I tell myself I
could slow him down. I tried that once, I guess, asking him to
move to San Diego. I don't know if he can change.

The problem is I'm a nurse. And I don't know if I am callous
enough, even after all of it, to leave someone wounded by the
side of the road.

August 4

Jack talks sometimes about the nomads he saw in Africa.
He watched their ancient way collapse around them as political borders and drought and economics forced them into cities. Sedentary.

Stern says we will leave in the middle of the night. Nomads
breaking camp in the desert, stealing away to the next oasis.
Jack has spent his adulthood roaming from one place to another. I allow myself some degree of amateur analysis if I ask
whether this rootlessness contributed.

Lydia told me once that she couldn't help reaching for her
needle. She said she can see how much pain the needle might
bring her, but there's nothing she can do because she knows
it's also going to make her feel good, real good.

That's how it is with me tonight. On Friday, Maddy did
some tests on my constant nausea. She drew blood. I see blood
every day, yet the sight of my own has always chilled me. Yet
when I saw the red flow into the needle, I was like Lydia, full of
dread, full of desire.

Farrell didn't turn the page. He knew after the next entry the
pages were white. He felt damp even though he sat in the warm
sun. He closed the diary and locked it. He tried to recall the last
days before he was scheduled to testify, tried to match them up
with this entry. He figured she must have written it the day they
had made a brief appearance at a lawn party at Maddy Crukshank's
home in Del Mar. Lena made the perfunctory rounds, introducing
him to other members of her team. They were an earnest lot and all

of them smiled at him, except Crukshank, whom Lena had told; she refused to shake Farrell's hand. He went and sat in a chair away from the crowd. He drank five stiff piña coladas until the agave and desert star plants in Crukshank's garden seemed to move. Lena put her hand on his shoulder and led him to the car.

The next day, forty-eight hours before he was to testify, they left the BMW in the driveway and took the Jeep and the dogs to the mountains east of San Diego. They hiked through the pines to a point where they could look out over the whole of the Anza Borrego desert, a dusty chalkboard that melted into rock and dune on the horizon. Lena spread out a blanket. Farrell watched the dogs, who nosed pinecones over the side of ridge, only to chase them as they rolled.

"Are you ready?" Lena asked.

"I told you once I've never not had the urge to walk along a cliff," Farrell said. "I'm scared to walk along this one."

"You'll get through it."

"I don't know if I will," Farrell said. He held her hand. "I just want you to know, it wasn't ever anything to do with you."

"Yes, it was," Lena said. "Nothing takes place in isolation."

Ordinarily he would have protested. Instead, he looked at the outline of her breasts and the roundness of her hips and knew she was right somehow. In the late afternoon, Farrell tried to seduce her, but she pulled away. Lena cried on the ride back into town.

Farrell barely slept that night. He slipped down to the kitchen in the early morning and reviewed the documents Kennerson would question him about in the secret jury room the next day. There would be three days of testimony and then he'd fly. A small town outside Spokane where evergreens would shield him from curious neighbors.

Lena came into the kitchen dressed for work. She put her hand on his shoulder. "We'll talk tonight, okay?"

"We can talk now," Farrell said. "I'm done."

"Tonight," she smiled.

Relief surged through Farrell as she moved to the door that led to the garage. "So you'll go with me?"

"We'll talk tonight about it," she said again. The dogs bolted through the door after her. They thought it was play to chase her and climb into her car.

"Just a second," Farrell had called after her. "I'll get them."

Sunshine flooded into the garage as the automatic door opened. Lena moved into the light, the dogs beside her.

"You're not going to the hospital with me, sillies," she said, and she shooed the dogs away with her hands.

Now, the dampness of springtime on the butte turned to a kind of cold he could not name. And the almost imperceptible tremble that had developed in Farrell's hands during the last five minutes of reading turned to a full palsied shudder. He hugged himself, rocking back and forth to prevent the stupefying chill from reaching his heart. Ruby whined and stuck her nose under his arm.

Farrell swayed and squeezed until he felt a glimmer of warmth in his fingers. He told himself that to truly recover he had to open this last closed box in his mind; to set himself free he had to relive this final horror. But he didn't have the courage. The old escape patterns kicked in. He thought instead of Inez, crouched over him, a naked, savage force beckoning him toward recklessness. He reached into his coat to pull out the report. He pressed the flimsy pages against his knee and read.

Didier, Inez/Chamonix.

Didier arrived in Chamonix in the fall of 1981, and found work photographing tourists for three guides on the popular seven-mile glacier run. Guides names: Eric LeCompte, Paul Treynor, and Henri Rassond. This last was an accomplished mountaineer with vast expedition experience.

Rassond's most ambitious climb was in 1973. He was twenty-five, and second man on the French team to Kanchenjunga, Nepal, Himalaya range. According to members of the climbing community here, Rassond, who is nicknamed *L'Aigle* (the Eagle, for his prominent nose or swooping skiing style, depending on whom you speak to), was considered likely to lead future French assaults on Annapurna and Dhaulagiri if the Kanchenjunga assent was successful. Rassond and two other men reached the third camp at 26,000 feet on May 10, 1973, and planned to assault the summit the next day. A brutal storm rolled in and they were stuck at the high camp for four days. One of the climbers, Christophe Marginot, died. Rassond suffered pulmonary edema and was carried off.

With the death of Marginot, Rassond lost his lust for the sport, faded from the pack of top climbers. He supported himself by guiding inexperienced alpinists.

Didier seemed to have discovered what many local mountaineers had known for years: at thirty-three, Rassond was an underused, undervalued commodity. She took pictures of Rassond on his many trips across the glaciers, selling them to climbing and ski magazines. By the spring of 1982, the two were inseparable. The following winter Didier used the money she'd made on the photographs to produce a film of Rassond.

Le Retour à L'Aire (The Return to the Aerie) documents Rassond's comeback climbs and his pioneering ski routes in the Italian Dolomite mountain range. The film caused a minor sensation when it debuted at the Chamonix film festival in October 1983. The local newspaper called it "markedly different from modern mountaineering cinema. The juxtaposition of Rassond's first descents and the moody nighttime footage of the guide as he walks the streets of Chamonix talking about his triumphs and failures as a mountaineer and as a man, in effect, transcends the term *documentary* and borders on art."

In February 1984, Rassond suffered a terrible fall in the Langkofel spire group in the central Italian Dolomites, which left him paralyzed from the waist down. Didier saw Rassond through the initial phase of his recovery, but within months was seen in the cafés with Alain Valoir, a young Chamoniard who was making a name for himself as a practitioner of *enchainment* (the linking of extreme climbs, skiing routes, and parapents in a single day).

Rassond, confined to a wheelchair now, owns a café in Chamonix. He refused to talk, even to confirm a rumor that he'd asked Didier to marry him after he'd left the hospital and she'd refused.

"Inez Didier is part of my past," was all he'd say.

Valoir was nineteen when he met Didier. Between 1985 and 1988, Valoir pioneered twenty-three skiing routes in the French and Swiss Alps. He performed a series of difficult *enchainments* that garnered him commercial support, including two TV advertisements for French beer.

In secret, however, Didier was making films of Valoir in remote areas such as the Mer de Glace glacier and on couloirs in the Grandes Jorasses. The most spectacular footage of Valoir was shot in the Augilles (literally the "Needles"). Valoir was obsessed with the needles, tall sharp granite towers that dominate the Chamonix Valley. Very little snow clings to the spires, considered among the world's most perilous runs.

On March 17, 1988, Didier contracted with the aerial tramway to stop one of the cars over the 12,473-foot Auguille de Midi (the Needle of Noon) to let her film Valoir's attempt at a first descent. Valoir had climbed the route twice in the previous three days, and had commented on the lack of snow and ice as late as the evening before. Many thought he would not ski it.

He died the next day when a huge chunk of snow and rock dislodged above him while he skied. It swept him into a deep crevice. His body has never been recovered.

Didier left Chamonix soon after the accident, but returned in December to debut a film she spliced together from interviews and footage of Valoir's activities during their three years together. *Elle Le Fera Mourir (She Will Be the Death of Him)* was hailed by critics and condemned by the mountaineering community. Here's a brief review from the French publication *Cinéma:*

> Continuing with a technique that she pioneered in *Le Retour à L'Aire,* Didier combines breathtaking ski sequences of the young Alain Valoir with his rambling personal monologues.
>
> The effect is disconcerting, almost dreamlike. Valoir is so open in his conversation that we believe he is unconscious of the camera's presence, as if the camera were hidden.
>
> Didier, for the most part, is conspicuously absent. While her voice is heard questioning Valoir, she is seen on screen only once. Here, she is nude in bed with Valoir, resting on his chest while he stares into the camera and talks about his bisexuality.
>
> Valoir died last spring in Chamonix while attempting a never-before-tried descent of the famous Auguille de Midi.
>
> As evidenced in the film's title and structure, Didier seems conscious of her participation in the events that led to Valoir's death, yet only obliquely suggests responsibility.

> Late in the film—indeed, the night before Valoir dies—
> Didier asks him, "Don't you know the risks?"
>
> Valoir nods.
>
> "Then why do you go?" she asks.
>
> Valoir drinks some wine, then looks directly into the camera, at Didier, at the audience, and says "I go for you . . ."

An acid taste bubbled up from his stomach as Farrell remembered uttering those same words. The sun beat now on the back of his neck and the year's first insects—tiny black bugs—danced before his eyes.

"She gives us what we want," Farrell said out loud, hearing the threat in the timbre of his voice. His heart raced and he skipped ahead in the fax:

> Members of the climbing community and Valoir's family were outraged at *Elle Le Fera Mourir*. They believed Didier had driven Valoir beyond his capabilities. Even more troubling, they felt the film's title and tone made light of her own role.
>
> "I think she used Valoir for her own ends," said Richard LaFevre, the owner of the climbing store where Valoir worked before becoming associated with Didier. "And she baldly capitalized on the entire mess."
>
> Valoir's sister, Marie, said, "For a long time, I was Inez's biggest defender. I thought she cared for him. But she was cold in that movie. That film was wrought out of my brother's feelings—for the mountains, for skiing, most of all for her. But it was like she didn't feel anything for him."

Farrell read those words a dozen times. For almost two hours he let them collide off everything he knew about Inez. He walked aimlessly back and forth across the butte, examining all the possibilities. By early afternoon he thought he understood her; and with that he came to a terrible conclusion: to stop Inez from assaulting the Grand Teton, to save the others, indeed to save himself, he had to crush her. To crush her, he had to use her techniques.

Chapter 26

F arrell knocked at the door to Inez's room at half past seven that evening. She opened the door wearing tight jeans and a thick purple chamois shirt styled in a drover's yoke. Video monitors glowed behind her.

"Where has you been?" she snapped. "Page and Wave have spend all their own time to put your equipment together for you."

"I just talked to the ranger station at the top of Teton Pass," Farrell said. "The snow pack will deteriorate over the next two days. It won't even get to freezing at night."

Without speaking, she drew back to let him in. She smelled stale after his afternoon among the budding plants. Farrell took a seat on the edge of the credenza.

Inez rolled her head around, cracking her neck. "You give me an ache with all this talk about snow packs," she said. "As Page has said, we do not know until we look."

"You've got Page so messed up he doesn't know which way to turn," Farrell said.

"Really?" Inez said. "My impression, it is the opposite: he knows exactly where he's going."

"Like Henri Rassond and Alain Valoir?" Farrell asked.

The question threw her off guard. She cleared her throat. "Well . . . no," she said. "I consider Page a bit more like yourself."

Farrell felt a draft, as if someone had opened a window in the room. "What's that supposed to mean?"

"Nothing at all," Inez said, getting up. She crossed to a bottle of wine chilling in a plastic bucket and poured herself a glass. "It's just that in Utah you go, so straight ahead. And now, so *reservé*. I think constantly how little I know of you."

"You paid for my athletic ability, not me," Farrell said. He looked around the room at all the electronic equipment. A red light glowed on a camera standing on a tripod in the far corner. Farrell stiffened.

"Yes, that camera is on," Inez said, amused.

Farrell looked away from the lens, then back to Inez. "Maybe it's good that you film this," he said. "The director begins to act."

Inez glanced at the camera, frowning as if she had rethought her decision to film this encounter. She lit a cigarette.

"What do you want to know?" Farrell asked.

"Everything," she said.

"Greed gets people in trouble," Farrell said. "You'll have to share."

"We make the bargain then?" she asked.

"I tell you about me, you tell me about you," Farrell said.

Inez paused, drinking her wine. A door opened outside and music drifted through the air. Inez adjusted the angle of her head to it, as if she were trying to hear the words to the song. She hummed with it, then said, "First you. When you are about to leap off the cliff, what is the first thing of which you think?"

"Easy," Farrell said. "The landing."

"What is the last thing of which you think?"

"That's two questions," Farrell said. He paused to consider his answer. "What it will feel like out there in the air. And that's different every time."

"How?" she asked.

"Sometimes it's direct, like infatuation: your lungs ache, your brain spins, your palms sweat, but you know it's going to be good. Real good."

"Like sex?" She rolled back onto the bed and stared at the ceiling.

Farrell knew what she was up to, but he decided to play along. He said, "No, not like sex . . . like before sex. Like you know you're

going to have your hands all over each other before long and you
want that, but somehow you know the anticipation is better.

"Sometimes the feeling in the air is not like that at all," he continued. "Sometimes it's indirect and that's stronger. Like you visit a
place you haven't been to in a long time, a place you visited last
with an old lover. And there's just the suggestion of a fragrance in
the air, but boom! she's there in the room with you."

"Do you feel that with me now?"

"No," Farrell lied, trying to hurt her. "You were entertainment."

Inez sucked fiercely on the cigarette. She composed herself,
sat up, reached for the wine bottle, and poured herself another
glass.

"My turn," Farrell said. "Why do you like to watch us?"

"I do not know," she said. "It is just so."

"Not good enough, Inez."

She said, "All right, when I see you about to go, it brings something out in me, a feeling, a . . . this I don't understand, that I do not
receive by myself."

"The feeling is good?"

"Good, bad at the same time," she said. "The most close I can
describe it is the state so desperate you fall down into when you
love someone you hate."

She sucked on the cigarette again, then shuffled back on the
bed until she was leaning against the headboard, the wineglass between her folded legs.

"Tell me about your father," Farrell said.

"My choice now," Inez protested.

"You had two questions, I have two questions," Farrell said.

Inez pouted. "My father was brilliant and I know him very little.
Even when he was alive, I see him not much. A photographer. Vietnam."

"The Dividing Line?"

Inez's eyebrows arched in on themselves. "Yes, *The Dividing
Line.* How do you know of this?"

"I used to be interested in photography," Farrell lied again. "It
was in a portfolio of work I saw mentioned in *Life* magazine once. I
put two and two together."

Her jaw moved slightly, then locked left. She sipped from the
wine, stood, and began to talk about her father's theories of pho-

tography. Some of them Farrell had read about in the preface to
the book. Much of what Inez discussed was new: technical argu-
ments, approaches to mood and setting; snippets of her father's
mind that she had gleaned from his letters to her mother and to the
Associated Press photography chief in Paris.

"He thinks you only can capture the real about the person
when they are at their frontiers," Inez said, walking around the bed
toward a cooler. She opened another bottle of wine and filled a
glass for Farrell. He took it, but only sipped at the chilled liquid.

"What do you mean real?" he asked.

"Not the surface," she said. "Their thoughts, their fears, their
hopes."

"Yours or theirs?"

Inez's cheeks hardened. "The camera person and the actor,
they are together, no?"

"If you say so. Your father, did you love him and hate him?"

Inez kneaded the fabric of one of the pillows, but did not look at
Farrell. Softly, she said, "I am a child when he dies. I see other girls
my age with their fathers on the walk to school. I learn to go by
myself."

"When—"

"No, my question now," Inez interrupted. "Your worst memory?"

Farrell answered even though he didn't want to. "The worst?"

"It is required to tell the truth."

Farrell was quiet, conscious of the camera rolling. Finally, he
said, "A boy, eight-years old, gets off the school bus and he's
stricken with diarrhea. He runs to his home, but the door's locked.
He knows his father is inside, but he knows his father is mad. The
father won't let him in. The boy holds it as long as he can, then he
squats and shits all over the back of his legs and closes the garage
door so none of his friends will see. He listens to his father sing to
the radio. He waits for his mother."

"You say it like this happens to another person," Inez said.

"Did I?" Farrell asked, surprised. He thought about it and realized that that was how he always thought of himself—as someone
apart, alone. It saddened him, yet made him more determined than
ever to finish.

"Yes, you did," Inez said. "What does your mother do when she comes to the house?"

"She cleaned me up, so . . ."

"So?"

"So my father wouldn't stop singing," Farrell said.

"Strange, your father . . ."

"I don't want to talk about him," Farrell said. "There are only so many things you can blame on the past. Go on."

"When are you most happy?"

"I don't know," Farrell said. "Probably when I ski."

"Why?"

"Because it happens so fast there are few choices," Farrell said, surprising himself again. "It just happens. There's no anticipation. It's instinct. And when you come out of a bad situation okay, your heart pounds and your breath . . . even the hair on your arms tingles."

Inez smiled, then her expression turned hard. "From where does your money come, Collins?"

The question jolted him out of the lax state into which she had drawn him; he realized that he'd revealed more than she had. "Money?"

"You have money," Inez said. "You do not ask me for any."

"I don't need to," Farrell said, trying to appear at ease. "It's a gauche habit—talking of money. But I'll tell you: I was once very lucky in the markets. I'm frugal now."

Inez gave him a smug expression. "But this is the unusual, is it not—to give up that mode of life, to make much money?"

"Everyone has their fill of such things after a while," Farrell said. "I decided to follow through on the common threat and go to the mountains."

"To find yourself?"

"No," Farrell said honestly. "I wanted to find nothing."

"You do not tell the truth when you say you before you are a tax attorney," Inez said. *"Vraiment* what is it really, the Wall Street, the properties . . . the banks?"

Farrell coughed, feeling color take to his cheeks like a welt. He made a complicated show of standing, walking to the table, and pouring himself another glass of wine.

Inez did not seem surprised. "The banker, then. A strange vocation for someone of your taste for speed."

"One of my problems," Farrell said. "I could never stay interested in handling money just to make money."

"Relationships?" Inez asked. "A wife, a lover? Children."

"My wife left me," Farrell said. "We had a child who died young."

"I feel sorry." Inez frowned. "This was horrible for you and your wife?"

"Things pass and become part of your memory, like the images on film, I'd imagine," Farrell said.

"When it is best, the film is like memory," Inez agreed, "but more like the dream. You are in the dark theater and these situations come on the screen that you are feeling before . . . or you imagine you are feeling before."

Inez stopped and stared into space. Then she said, "It is an accident, the death of your baby?"

Farrell faltered for a second. He saw Jenny's blue hand. But instead of the chill that had always filled him when he thought of her, he felt a steady, warming pressure at the nape of his neck, a pressure which gave him strength.

"No. No accident," he said, in a steady, sure voice. "She died like most people do—for reasons no one quite understood."

Inez seemed disappointed with his response. Before she could speak again, Farrell said: "Tell me about Henri Rassond."

Inez glanced at the wall over his shoulder. "No."

"I thought we were being honest."

"Henry is a specific, like your father. We speak to the general, no?"

"It seemed to me we have become very specific," Farrell said. "No exclusions on details now."

Inez clenched her hands tightly around the glass.

"Now that I know these rules, it goes easier," Inez said cryptically. "Years ago, Henri Rassond is a climber of talent. He allows one event—yes, very terrible, but just one—to shake him. For a time we are good for each other. That is all. You have seen the film, no?"

"I've read about it. They called it art."

Inez waved her hand in the air. "Maybe yes, maybe no. When I meet Henri, he is weak. He needs someone to remind him of his gifts."

"And you were that person?" Farrell asked.

Inez nodded.

"Did you love him?"

Inez laughed, "What is this, love? We join in the night like you and me. But Henri, when we are joined, he takes from me so much. He breaks his eggshell inside me. He takes from me his wings. For a year, maybe more, he is the eagle again."

"People say you used him, broke him, left him," Farrell said.

"C'est merde," Inez said. "He goes to Italy the last time alone. I do not request this."

"So you cared for him after the crash, as any lover would?"

Inez's eyes grew thick and sidelong. "I am there at the hospital. I watch him come to know that he never walks again. I hold his hand all that night while he cries like the baby."

"And then what? Did you cry too?"

"I cry when he cries," Inez said, reaching for the wine. "But these are terrible times. I . . . I do not wish to talk of them."

"Thought you said these are necessary shading devices," Farrell said, and he pointed to the camera.

"I warn you once," Inez replied harshly. "Do not mock me."

They stared at each other in silence. Then Farrell got up and used the bathroom. When he got back, Inez was lying on her back again. She said, "Tell me, Collins, is the concept—right and wrong—*absolu* or *relatif?*" Farrell thought for a moment. "If your talking in a biblical sense, it's absolute. In a legal sense, I suppose it's relative."

"Give me the example," Inez said.

"I don't have one," Farrell said. "You describe the situation, I'll give you an answer."

"How do you say *cambriolage*—when the person enters the house to steal—in English?"

"Burglary."

"That's it. *Absolu* or *relatif?*"

"Absolute, unless the person is starving or naked or thirsty."

"So you make the place for explanations?"

"Survival sometimes demands a bending of the rules."

"Interesting," Inez said. "And the adultery?"

"Unforgivable," Farrell said sincerely. "But something that both sides can learn to live with, I believe."

"In certain cases then," Inez said.

"That's what I said. How about murder?"

"My choice now!"

"No, tell me about Alain Valoir."

"I do not kill him, if that's what you say," Inez hissed. She got to her knees. "I talk of this a hundred times. Alain knew the risks. Constantly we spoke of them."

Inez brushed her hair back from her forehead, a simple act that seemed to compose her. "He fears them, but he said they are beyond his control. He is like you in this respect. What do you say more early, that you feel more alive when you face them?"

Farrell nodded.

"Alain Valoir, he is a genius of the physical, the dancer of ballet on the mountain," Inez said. "On the skis and the climbing rope, much more capable than you or Page. But what he can become is trapped inside. No confidence. He is scarred, we know, by one of his uncles who abuses him as a child."

Farrell flinched.

"So you have not seen that film either?" Inez said. "I treat this situation with the gloves so soft. Alain never tells anyone this, not even me. But I know it is true. I have a sense for this."

She was quiet and played with the stem of her glass. "I teach him to let go his fury, to go where he thinks it is not possible."

"What did you get out of it?"

"Me?" Inez asked. "Nothing. I see him do what he is born for."

"And to die for?"

Inez closed her eyes briefly. "It is unfair for them to turn against me," she said. "I bring him out. I do it not for the fame or the money. This does not interest me. I love what Alain does. I love what Henri does."

Inez drew her feet up and hugged her knees. Farrell watched her closely, sure that she was holding back something.

"But you never told them you loved them, did you?" Farrell asked.

Inez stared at the carpet. "No," she whispered.

"Why not?"

"It does not help," she said. "It is irrelevant."

"Did Rassond ask you to marry him?"

Inez stood up, angry: "How do you know these things?"

Farrell smiled. "Two can play this game, Inez. Did you go to Valoir's funeral? Did you weep by his grave? Afterwards, when you were alone, did you call out his name in the night?"

Inez held her hand to her mouth and hurried across the room where she was out of the camera's range. Farrell followed her, pulling her around by the shoulder so she faced a mirror in the field of the camera lens. Inez shook away from his grasp.

"You don't like the mirror, do you?" Farrell demanded.

"You frighten me," she whispered hoarsely.

Farrell saw her hands, how still they were.

"Me?" Farrell said. "Why?"

She spoke softly, looking in the mirror at his face visible over her shoulder. "When I first hear of you skiing in the woods in Utah, Page and The Wave, they say you are the ice man. Even in the Y Couloir, you look into the darkness and do not blink. Now you blink much, Collins. I think the ice breaks. I think you attack me like this because you have no more defense of isolation. No more singularity. Tell me about it, tell me what happens to you before you come to the mountains in your green truck."

For a split second, Inez almost seduced him. He wanted to tell her everything, to let the past free itself, break away and fly. On the verge of speaking, he glanced down to see the way she ran her bare foot with slow, calculated intent across the carpet. He remembered the dead man and the cripple. He steeled himself and turned away.

Inez followed him across the room, taunting him. "I say once you ski like the cowboy and there it is. I ask myself, why no records about you beyond the papers of birth, of the truck."

"So you tried to research me for your dossier," Farrell said.

"You say it yourself, you are the only mystery I have left," Inez said, smiling.

"I don't like people snooping about me," Farrell said. "I take precautions."

Inez laughed. "But you know, to gather information is a creative process."

Farrell said nothing. He sat down in the chair again.

Inez made a big show of arching her back and stretching her

arms. "Tell me about this estate—no, account! this is the word—bank account in Switzerland."

Blood pounded at Farrell's temples. "You broke into my camper."

Inez nodded. "So interesting what one address reveals."

"I gather you talked to a fat bank manager in Telluride," he said.

"He is fat, the talker?" Inez asked. "No matter. He says he thinks it funny a man who lives in a truck has the Swiss account."

"Pretty good, Inez," Farrell said, but he knew she hadn't gotten far with that line of research. He decided to change tactics, to go on offense. "What is it exactly you want from me?"

"I want to know what you feel," she said.

"What about you?" Farrell asked. "How did it feel to watch your young lover cross that line? I read a little about what you must have seen that day. Valoir's first thirty-five turns down the mountain so perfect. Then he picks his way down another hundred and twenty-five feet. You are above him, safe and warm, letting the camera roll when it comes, an ice boulder, to brush his life aside like a leaf in the wind."

Inez's lips half parted as if she were expelling foul air. Her eyelids drooped. "You do not get to me with this," she said.

"I didn't think I would," Farrell said. "But let me try another story. It's about a little girl who loves her daddy. But Daddy's never around. She sees him every so often when he comes back from whatever assignment he's on, but he's not there to protect and comfort his little daughter the way other daddies do."

"You enter terrain of great danger, my friend," Inez warned.

"And then he dies," Farrell went on, "and he's not there to see her mother take in friends."

He emphasized this last word and Inez jerked backward as if she'd been slapped.

"But maybe they aren't friends. Maybe the little girl's mommy practices a dying art. I read it in Zola once—that novel, *Nana?* She's a courtesan. Only it really is a dead art that doesn't pay well. So Mommy finds out bad things about her friends and uses them. Suddenly there is new furniture and the little girl has nice clothes."

Inez's entire body went rigid. "How do you—"

"Gathering information is a creative act, Inez."

"You have no idea of what cracking ice you walk on," Inez said. The tautness in her face faded as if her skin were made of sand and a sudden gale had blown, erasing all footprints.

"Oh, no," Farrell said, his tone confident. "I think I know exactly where I am. But let's continue with the story, shall we? One day, one of Mommy's friends gets very angry and comes to confront Mommy. Only Mommy isn't home, is she?"

Inez suddenly seemed tiny; she had drawn her legs up tight against herself. She shuddered. "Don't do this . . ."

Farrell continued, ruthless now. "So Mommy's friend hurts the little girl . . . maybe makes her not a little girl anymore."

Inez rushed toward the camera, groping to shut it off. Farrell caught her before she succeeded and threw her back on the bed.

"But our little girl is tough," Farrell said. "She grows up, maybe takes a lover. She's more daring, more talented than him. He is jealous and hurts her. She gets pregnant and leaves him. What happens to the baby we don't know. Does she abort it? Or does she give it away?"

For a split second Inez's shoulders sagged.

"Now we know," Farrell said. "She goes through the agony of childbirth alone. Then she gives her child away.

"She coldly gives it away," Farrell said, enunciating every word, knowing that if he was to break her, it was now. "And after her baby's gone, she stays cold. To the outside world she's forceful, accomplished, even charming when she wants to be.

"But all these things she's hidden inside have dulled her, perhaps rendered her incapable of something basic—the ability to feel, to feel love, to feel fear, to feel pain . . ."

"You do know of nothing!" Inez yelled. *"Je suis compatissante."*

"That's true," Farrell said. "You are compassionate. You *suffer with!"*

"I do!"

"The question is, do you suffer alone?" Farrell asked.

Inez fumbled wildly for the cigarettes on the table, knocking over her wineglass in the process.

"So what does she do?" Farrell asked. He paced the room now, his finger on his lips, looking for the answer. It took Inez three tries to light the cigarette. She smoked it, watching him as if he were a predator and she a cornered animal.

He pointed to the camera. "There it is," he said. "She puts a machine and a lens between herself and reality. And she chooses an unusual subject for her films—the hidden scars of thrill seekers. You ask yourself why? It takes a while, because, as she says, she is compassionate: she cries when others cry; she laughs when others laugh; she aches when others suffer.

"But her tactics have repercussions," Farrell said. "When a good man asks her to marry him, she can't allow herself to taste, to smell, to touch . . . what? Joy? Happiness? Are we getting close, Inez?"

"You are a bastard," Inez said softly. She seemed paralyzed.

"She takes another lover," Farrell said. "A boy really, a boy who's as ripped up inside as she is. But in her need to satisfy herself, she drives him too far and he dies. Did she feel anything for him then, when he crashed down the slope in front of her eyes?"

Farrell pointed at the camera again. "That's what we all want to know, did she care, about the dead boy, the cripple . . . her baby?"

Inez came up again, faster this time. She had her fingernails into his face before he could grab her wrists. They tore into his flesh, but Farrell didn't wince. He held her as she kicked at him and bit and screamed, "I watch their pain!"

Gradually, the fury which gripped her ebbed. And Farrell realized that was the first deep emotion he'd ever seen her express.

"I knew their pain," Inez said as her eyes welled with tears. She pulled away from him, slumping in the chair as if she might be sick. "In ways you never know."

Farrell looked down at her. It was now all clear to him.

"Yeah, you knew their pain," he said, "like an audience knows an actor's, at a distance. You told me you give the audience a peak through the fingers. But I ask you, who is really the audience and what does she feel?"

Inez stared dully at the floor. "She feels much."

"I don't think so," Farrell said. "I think the little girl lost has nothing left inside to give, so she exposes the raw parts of people and takes them for her own. I think she peeks through the hands and feeds on it. I think the little girl is a monster, an emotional vampire!"

Inez stood, her hand over her mouth again, panic in her eyes, and stumbled to the bathroom. Farrell followed right behind her. She leaned over the toilet and vomited.

"Hurts, doesn't it?" Farrell asked as she gasped and vomited again. "Think about that no air feeling the next time you decide to open the doors to someone's closet."

Farrell left her there. He flipped off the camera as he passed it, thinking how water percolates down from the snowfields in spring and with the loss of altitude becomes a rushing torrent. He wanted to lie beside a river in the sunshine. He wanted to die.

"You do not leave!" Inez croaked. She was leaning against the doorway to the bathroom. Her skin was pale and she held a washcloth to her lips. "I have the story to tell!"

"Not interested," Farrell said, without turning. "It's over. No trip up the Grand. Pack your film. Go home."

"This is the fine story," Inez said, and she staggered to the camera and turned it back on. "I say this is the fine story. About the man who travels alone with the nightclothes of a woman. About the man who uses the nightclothes for his pillow."

It was immediate and involuntary: a slight, yet audible catch in Farrell's throat and a waver in his hand over the doorknob. Farrell mumbled to himself, "You've seen her clothes."

"Sit," Inez ordered, wiping the vomit from her chin.

An invisible hand pushed him toward the chair. Inez leaned against the credenza. Beads of sweat rolled off her forehead. "Yes," she said. "The man with Swiss accounts, he sleeps with a negligé. I find it under the bunk and I ask, is it the woman who left him? Is it the Maria he cries for when his penis is in me?"

Farrell fought for air, and as he did, Inez's expression changed: first the corner of her lips rose; then her nostrils flared and her mouth parted as if with pleasure.

"Tell me of the article in the journal in Lake Tahoe," she said.

"What article?"

Even as he'd finished the words, he knew hesitation had betrayed him; people like Inez and Gabriel could read between the lines.

"I think about that night often, you know," Inez said, and the color returned to her cheeks. "You want to touch me again. I can see it. It is there, even though you try to say no. But then you read this article and it is like if you touch me—something with life—it is wrong."

"I said I was tired of the entertainment," Farrell said as spots appeared before his eyes. "You got to be a dull show."

"Bullshit," Inez said. "Remember. I was your audience when you fuck me. I see you go to that other place. Tell me about this article and why you do not touch me again."

He peered at her through the maze of dots and heard himself saying, "I read it because it was unusual. Murder is always unusual. And as for touching you, I just couldn't. You felt clammy."

Inez snorted. "To try to hurt me will get you nowhere. As you say, I lose this ability to feel my pain long ago."

She paused. *"Alors,* you knew him, the dead man. Cordova."

"Never met the man."

"Ah oui," Inez said. "And I think you know why he dies."

"I'm a con man, no killer. That's your field," Farrell said.

"I never say you kill him," Inez said. "But when you read it, I can see: you wish to be there."

"Hardly," Farrell lied.

"Oh, yes. I get nowhere with the accounts. I was at the dead end. But when you read about Cordova, I see that your head goes on the journey. I follow. What do you think I find?"

Farrell did not respond. He seemed to see her down a long tunnel.

"A bank man full of ennui," she said. "A man who before he enters these dull affairs of money, travels to Africa, climbs mountains, skis like a demon. Later, when the world becomes too dull, or too painful, he chases the feeling he loves."

The tips of Farrell's fingers tingled as if someone had pushed a needle into the nerve at his elbow.

"He chases the sensation again and again," Inez continued. "Until after a long time he looks up and sees what his life has become. He is the addict of adrenaline. Nothing else feels so right, so real, as when the liquid stimulant is in his veins."

Farrell stood and took a step closer to her, but stopped, afraid that his knees wouldn't support him. If Inez was aware of his approach, she didn't show it.

"So the man, he sees that he is out of the law, out of the society, out of the limits acceptable," Inez said. Her voice was melodic and pitying; she spoke the language of therapists. "He is trapped there, naked. And he wants so much to go home where there is the security and the warmth."

Inez stroked the side of her cheek. "This is where I lay in my bed and let my imagination play because there are not so many facts that I know of him. But I think he betrays people, powerful, dangerous people. Am I right?"

Farrell searched for a counteropening, but she gave none.

She went on, "For a while, the bank man thinks it all goes his way, that he returns from—how does one put it—the pale? Yes, this is the phrase, he comes back from behind the pale. And he and his wife, so beautiful, will have security once more."

Farrell took another step. Inez reacted this time. She moved behind the camera and swung it toward him.

"Somehow the bad persons, they discover the betrayal," Inez said. "No one is so sure how. Perhaps an informant. And then it is this August day. A Tuesday in August, I believe, and the beautiful woman decides to leave for work before her husband."

Farrell imagined this was what deafness was like: he could see Inez's lips move, but an overpowering wave of silence drowned the nouns and the verbs and the adjectives. The room whirled at a sickening speed. And then a voice, not Inez's, but Lena's echoed. *"No,"* she said, shooing the dogs away with her hands. *"You're not going with me to the hospital, sillies."*

Inez reached for a button on one of the video machines. "It is important to watch close now," she said. "I want the audience to sit forward for your reaction."

Farrell was vaguely aware of the gold bracelet jangling on Inez's wrist as it swung toward the machine. His stomach lurched and his knees buckled as she pressed the play button. The screen flashed white, black, and then the red of fire. Smoke rose in the air. Firemen moved in around a charred car. The camera focused on a white sheet in the grass. And two dead dogs. And beyond, in the garage, a second white sheet.

A police officer put a hand in front of the lens and it cut to a young woman he recognized from a San Diego news station, saying, "Killed in the mysterious bombing were banker Jack Farrell and his nurse wife, Elena.

"Farrell was believed inside the garage when his wife opened the door to their BMW, triggering . . ."

Inez pressed a button again, freezing the reporter's face, distorted now on the screen.

"But you do not die, do you, Jack Farrell?" she asked. The triumph on Inez's face was palpable and depressing.

Farrell sank onto his haunches. He stared at the screen and the black plume of smoke that seemed to rise out of the back of the reporter's head like a question mark. He knew what Inez wanted, a meltdown, a primal outpouring of all that he'd survived. But all he felt was the prick of ice on his skin, as if he'd just leapt into three feet of fresh powder.

"No, Inez, he's quite dead," Farrell said numbly. "It was just as they said, he and his wife died in the explosion."

Inez clapped her hands and crowed, "Such courage, Mr. Farrell. You are everything I hoped you would be. But I'm afraid it is all true. Everything I find points to you."

"Tell them to look again," Farrell said. "Check the coroner's records. The bodies were ripped in half. Neither of them ever knew what hit them."

"No!" Inez insisted, and she stepped out from behind the camera to stand above Farrell. "You are him. But I ask myself, these men, Cordova and Cortez—they kill your wife. You have your chance at revenge and you run. Why?"

Farrell shook his head. Instinctively he reached for the lie. "Your detectives weren't that good. Dig some more in Texas, and you might find I had a different name—a name like Timmons—that appeared in Utah in the late 1970s when Jack Farrell was on the ski patrol. It's the same name that appears on some papers of a shaky real estate deal he was involved in outside of Dallas in the mid-1980s. But me, Jack Farrell? No."

"Fingerprints," Inez said, pointing to the glass.

"Never printed," Farrell said. "Never arrested for anything."

"Photographs," she said, growing anxious.

"Do I look like him?" Farrell asked.

"This is nothing," she said. "The scars: surgery *plastique.* There are records."

"Where?" Farrell asked.

"I prove this!" Inez cried.

"What will you prove?" Farrell asked. "You can point to a person and say you've discovered certain facts. You may try to draw conclusions about them, about their motives, their strengths and weaknesses. But they never add up to any single explanation. You know why? Because in each person there's an ambiguity, an unexplainable sum of the parts, the humanness, the emotions, at work.

"So for the sake of an argument, you might well say I'm Jack Farrell," he went on. "But I know now he's dead, Inez. As dead as you."

"Me? I am as living as I can be," Inez snarled. "Do you know why? Because I am the expert in exploring the little gap where emotions caress cold facts and turn them into something so, so powerful that one cannot capture them with words, only with film. Tomorrow you and I will explore that gap. I climb the mountain with you, Jack, right behind me."

"A participant at last," Farrell said.

"Watch me!" She cried. She tried to slap him. Farrell caught one hand and then the other.

He stood, still gripping them. "I told you I'm not going and neither are the rest."

"Non, non, you climb and you ski tomorrow," Inez said. "Because you are scared now, exposed like that little boy who soils his pants in his garage, afraid of what he has done."

Farrell strengthened his grip.

"I know your gap. You fear now the responsibility, the prison, the dark place with no sunlight," Inez said, squirming with the pain. "The place of boredom where life is the same every day. Every day in the darkness you would think of her and the Latin men. And how someday they find you, how someday they send their guns!"

Farrell wrenched her fingers so violently she squatted and squealed in agony. She panted, *"Mais,* there is an exit! Climb tomorrow and I do not show the police what I find. And when we finish, I let you run."

Farrell wanted to break her with his bare hands. But the thought nauseated him. He wanted it to be January again, he wanted the snow like white ether to drift him away. He relaxed his grip. Inez hung her head and groaned and rubbed her wrists.

Farrell said dully, "What makes you so sure I won't—"

"You say it yourself," Inez said. "You are not the killer."

"Why should you let me run?"

Inez smiled knowingly. "Because I know that on the mountain tomorrow, you will let me be . . . compassionate."

Chapter 27

D efeat had dizzied Farrell. He splashed unaware through the puddles of muddy water in the parking lot and walked in front of a car. The driver blared his horn and yelled at him. He didn't notice. He considered making a run for Canada, but Inez was sure to be watching. There were only a few roads out of Jackson. He'd be caught before Montana. She'd boxed him in perfectly.

In his room, Farrell held the diary for almost an hour, tracing his fingers over the embossed leather until in an act of desperation he opened it to the last entry. He wanted to hear her tell him what she wanted to do after he testified.

August 6

Today is my last day at work. I've told Maddy. She knows it all and this is the hardest part. It will be hard to say good-bye. She's helped in more ways than I probably understand.

I wonder how Jack will take what I have to tell him. Almost three years now. And still I shook with joy and tears when Maddy called last night to tell me the blood test came back. I'm two months pregnant.

So the decision is made for me. I cannot leave a cripple

behind or a baby without its father. Life begins again. I wonder how Jack will take the news?

Farrell slumped to his side, his mind the blank screen he'd so long sought. Only the sensation he'd always anticipated, a chill perfection, the gleaming ice of an ancient glacier, didn't come. Farrell's head burned with a brilliant, searing heat.

A half hour before dawn, a groggy Portsteiner opened the door to his hotel room to find Farrell standing there with Ruby's leash in one hand, two letters, and Lena's diary in the other. Farrell said in a listless monotone, "Going for a climb, Frank. Need you to take care of a couple of things."

"Climb?" Portsteiner responded. He snapped awake. "Jesus Christ, Jack. Have you lost your mind? You said it yourself: Tetons are as unstable now as I've ever seen them."

Farrell shrugged and held out the letters and the diary. "Doesn't matter anymore, Frank. Take care of the dog. Mail these for me. Keep the book safe."

The older man took them. "What are they?"

"The letters are confessions, I guess," Farrell said. "Spent all night writing them. One to my mother. The other to my wife's parents."

"Your wife?" Portsteiner cried.

Farrell nodded sadly. "I couldn't tell you about her because I didn't know how. She's dead, Frank. I had more than something to do with it."

Portsteiner studied him, then spit. "You a killer, Jack?"

"I might as well be," Farrell said. "I finished reading her point of view late last night. Learned things were worse than I thought. Read it if you want. Doesn't matter now."

Portsteiner put the diary and the letters under his arm. He rested his hand on Farrell's shoulder. "Don't go up there with that woman, Jack."

"I'm sorry, old friend," Farrell said. "I got no choice."

Portsteiner said, "Always choice, always hope. The victim of extreme exposure is at risk of shock and coma. But the body can be saved by a gradual warming."

Farrell smiled wanly. "E. R. LaChapelle?"

He shook his head, "Frank Portsteiner."

Ruby whined and tugged at her leash as Farrell trudged away.

"Everyone check their sensors," Page said at the trail head three hours later. They had just signed out at the ranger station.

Farrell reached down to the yellow box the size of a paperback book that hung by thick straps inside his jacket. Each box contained a miniature electronic receiver and transmitter to be used to find each other if they ever became separated. Farrell, The Wave, and Inez carried soft-frame packs to the side of which were strapped skis and poles. Ann, Tony, Page, and the porters were outfitted with heavier, aluminum frame packs laden with food and camera and camping equipment.

"Let's go then," Page said when the check was completed. He led, followed by Inez, Ann, Tony, and the two husky young men in their twenties Inez had hired to carry the extra equipment back to the valley floor; and then The Wave and Farrell. The Wave glanced back at Farrell, who wandered up the trail as if it were all a bad dream.

The Wave slowed and whispered, "She get to you, mon?"

Farrell looked at The Wave as if he should recognize the kid but didn't. "I got to myself," Farrell said. "Story of my life."

"You shouldn't be climbing with that look, mon."

"Why not?" Farrell said. "When you had it, you went farther than you've ever gone before. I guess I'm ready to breach my limits."

He said it with such an air of finality, that The Wave shook his dreadlocks. "Suit yourself, mon. Just be sure you know where them ghosts are before you start down."

"I know exactly where they all are," Farrell said more to himself than to The Wave.

The weather was warm, in the low fifties, the sky was hazy and a moist breeze blew out of the west. They made Garnet Canyon by nine-thirty and continued through it to the Lower Saddle of the Grand Teton. This was the classic approach to skiing the Stettner and Tepee's Glacier that Briggs had pioneered nearly two decades before. In the sunlight, they ran into the gooey snow Farrell had warned about. In the shade, the snow was crusty and the climbers broke through the surface, jerking forward and wincing at the way it cut at their shins. They all stripped to T-shirts, struggling their way upward. Inez had the worst time of it; she was out of shape and wheezed horribly in the thin air. But she never complained even when she slipped around noon and fell, floundering in the wet snow. When Page tried to help her, she pushed him away and struggled to her feet.

They stopped for a break around 1 P.M., a good four hours by Page's estimate from the climbing hut.

"Tougher going than I thought," Page said to Farrell. "Normal day, they say you reach the hut by two."

"It's all your call now," Farrell said. He sat apart from the rest of them and almost cried.

They reached the saddle around five, found the hut in reasonable shape, and stowed their gear. In what light was left, Page, The Wave, and Farrell climbed as far as they could to see whether the snow route east toward the Stettner Couloir was passable. They climbed zigzag up the slope, careful and slow. Twice Page had to call out to Farrell, who veered off course as if he were following the footprints of someone else.

When they returned to the hut, Page said, "I think we've got a go at least as far as the bottom of the Stettner. The climb will be tough, but doable."

Inez smeared Page's cheek with a kiss. "In the morning, all are champions!"

Farrell retired to a corner, arranged his gear for the next morning, and unfolded his sleeping bag. He ate the food offered him, but did not speak. In the darkness he prayed for the first time in years. This, too surprised him, for he had believed himself an agnostic. He found himself carrying on a conversation not with a white-bearded god, but with Lena. And he had the rather comforting thought that perhaps the animists he'd encountered in Africa were correct: We find the two faces of the deity in every object and every animal, in our friends, our lovers, birds, mule deer, elk, the streams, the mountains, and in the air.

The praying made him feel better, as if abandoning himself to a benevolent force beyond his control was his only hope. He sat up in his sleeping bag to look at The Wave, who had ambled over.

"Your quiet scares me, mon," The Wave said.

"Everything's been said. All that's left is to go."

"Then what, another? Ranier?"

"I tend to doubt it," Farrell said.

"Me, too. It's all getting too strange for me."

"I think it's cyclical," Farrell said philosophically. "For brief periods you get used to what has occurred and that's what you call normal. Then it starts over and the sensation of standing outside a fish tank returns."

"Only you're the fish too," The Wave said, scratching at his chin.

"Lake Trout," they both said. They laughed weakly.

"So she . . ." The Wave began.

"Just accelerated the process," Farrell said.

The Wave squinted. "I thought you were stronger, mon."

"Than what?" Farrell asked.

The Wave thought about it for a minute, tugging at his dreadlock. "I guess I don't know."

Farrell patted The Wave on the back and told him he had to take a piss. As Farrell crossed through the room, he ignored Inez. Page offered him a drink of whiskey from a bottle he and Tony and the two porters were sharing.

"No thanks," Farrell said. "I want my head to be clear tomorrow."

"Go with the foggy feeling," Page said.

"Is that how you're taking it?" Farrell asked.

"You'll find it's really not that bad," Page said, but he would not look Farrell in the eyes.

Farrell went outside where the light of the full moon filtered down through the cloud cover. The moonglow was reflected and amplified by the snowpack, so everything—the trees, the rocks, and the mountain itself—appeared soft and inviting. The wet breeze still blew steady out of the south. He dropped into the woods smelling the spices of sap and pollen the balmy weather had goaded from the trees. Farrell pissed, then stood in the clearing for a long time smelling the forest and looking for stars. But the light from the moon had all but obliterated their sparkle. He felt terribly sad for reasons he couldn't explain.

He took a different route back to the hut, stepping quickly through the soft snow. A branch cracked. Farrell stopped and craned his neck, peering through the branches ahead of him. Inez squatted alone. He considered how easy it would be for her to meet with an accident alone in the darkness of the forest. After playing with it a moment, he discarded the thought; he would no longer hurt anyone. He watched Inez until she'd finished, stepping backward when she'd gone to take a roundabout route through the woods to the hut. As he walked, he thought of Maria Robles and Gabriel Cortez and the ways people chose to escape. And then, without understanding why, he said a prayer for all of those who would climb tomorrow, even Inez.

When Farrell entered the hut, Page was sitting at a wooden table against the near wall finishing the rest of the whiskey with The Wave. Inez and the rest of the crew were already in their bags, asleep. Page whispered, "How's the weather holding?"

"Real warm."

"Let's just hope it doesn't rain," The Wave said.

"This country's too high for rain," Page slurred.

"And too late in the season for powder," The Wave said wistfully.

"But wouldn't it be something, though, to wake up to a two-foot dump of superlight?" Page asked.

They all smiled uncertainly. For a moment Farrell believed each of them had the sensation that they were seeing each other from a great distance.

They started out again long before dawn. Page hoped the temperature drop of the early morning hours would crystalize the snow enough to give them support to cross to the entrance to the Stettner without wading. The two porters remained behind to gather the extra equipment for their climb back down to the road. The plan called for them to pick the crew up at the bottom on the far side of the mountain at dusk.

"This shit's like oatmeal," Tony grunted thirty-five minutes into the climb.

"Like wet cement," The Wave grumbled

"The skier of the extreme deals with all conditions," Inez said in a scornful tone.

No one replied. They were working too hard. Soon the sun cast a rosy glow on the narrow traverses they crossed. They moved at different speeds, so that from a distance Farrell imagined they would seem like a caterpillar expanding and contracting as they made their way up the slopes. On one pitch of the climb, they became too bunched together, and Farrell yelled forward to Page, "Don't you think you should have us spread out a bit more?"

Page took his pole and stabbed it into the snow next to him. "Nah, it's solid here. No problem."

At 11 A.M., they reached the bottom of the Stettner Couloir. They all looked up it, humbled and quiet. The right stone wall of the Stettner rose up twenty, thirty feet in places, then flared out toward the center of the shaft so that in some spots it resembled a half dome. Icicles like stalactites hung from the roof. Water dripped off them and splattered on the surface of the snow, all of it echoing, so it sounded like steady rain. Only the water didn't carry the cleansing scent of April; this was the humid, fetid odor of August.

"What a shot this is!" Inez crooned. "Almost like the snow cave!"

"At last," Farrell said sarcastically. "The primal run you've always looked for."

"And you are my caveman," she said, giving him that heavy-lidded expression he'd come to know and fear. "Imagine how the audience in the theater, they take in air fast—whoosh!—as the skier with the criminal past, he weaves down the chute of darkness and light."

The rest of the crew stared at Farrell. The Wave shook his head. "Criminal?"

"Everyone has the secret," Inez gloated. "I have discovered his."

Farrell didn't allow himself to shift his eyes from Inez. They stood that way, stone still, until Tony broke the tension by putting his hand on Farrell's shoulder. "How far do we go until we reach the chockstone you told us about?"

"Ask Page," Farrell mumbled. "He's the guide."

Page pointed up the center of the cavern. "The chute bears to the right at about one hundred yards and then there's another long reach to the stone."

Inez leaned down to her pack and came out with the helmet camera. "You wear it," she said to Farrell. "I want the outlaw's vision."

Farrell grabbed the helmet from Inez and yanked it down over his head. "You're fucking nuts," Farrell said.

"No!" Inez said. "I am the one you look at in the mirror. The fanatic. I want the fanatic's perspective."

"You'll get it, lady!" Farrell said, and without another word, he hoisted his pack, turned, and climbed.

He could not remember the first leg of the pitch; his vision of the world had turned red. But as he rose higher, with Page right behind him, the anger faded into an orange seething. He'd give Inez her desire.

The snow was inconsistent. In places, Farrell and Page floundered in it, gasping for air and grasping for purchase on the walls and on the tiny outcroppings of rock and ice that poked through the surface. In other spots, it was rock-hard, a surface as slick as a hockey rink. At the bend in the couloir the overhang receded, the dripping stopped, and sunshine poured in, refracting through the evaporating water so that violet, blue, and yellow rainbows appeared in the air around them. Farrell led again. Twenty steps up, the firm snow collapsed and his right leg plunged in up to his hip.

"Shit," he groaned. "I yanked my groin again."

Page scrambled up to help him free his leg. Farrell moaned as it it came free.

"You keep going?" Page asked.

"I'll try," Farrell said, massaging the torn muscles.

"You a criminal like she said?"

"Would it matter?"

Page thought about it and shook his head. "At this point, not really. But are you?"

Farrell grimaced and began to climb again. "Yes. I'm a criminal."

"They say starting over begins with admission," Page called after him in a hopeful tone.

"I'd say you suffered a relapse lately," Farrell said, deflecting the attention from himself again.

Page was quiet. He stared after Farrell's retreating pack. "Guess I have."

Because of the injury, Farrell was forced to change tactics: he stopped and took his skis off his pack and held one in each hand. With every step he drove the tails of the metal boards into the hard snow to pull himself upward. The motion was maddeningly slow and painful. But he knew if he stopped now, his muscles would chill and tighten and he might have to be carried off the Grand.

High, high above them, the glacier must have been rotting in the strong sun because now thousands of tiny chunks of granular snow poured forth from the rocks above them and to their left. The crystals cascaded down in twists of turquoise and silver, enveloping the couloir with the sound of grain kernels being poured into a stone mill.

Page and Farrell crouched. The ice chunks pinged off the helmet and then ebbed. When it died completely, Page said, "What's that all about?"

"Dunphy's map showed another couloir above us that dead-ends onto those rocks," Farrell said. He braced himself when another shower of ice spewed down. "The Ford Couloir, I think. Must be nowhere else for the stuff to go but off the cliffs and down into here."

As that shower began to subside, Page leaned his head back to let the tiny ice needles pelt him in the face. "That will sober you," he said. The radio on his hip crackled to life.

"Page? Page, answer me?"

Page grabbed the device and held it to his ear. "Go ahead, Inez."

"Tony is below you, on the right side. He says something about a rain storm of ice."

"Yeah, it breaks off the top every couple minutes."

"I want you both to ski through it."

"Gets pretty heavy," Page said. "We'd be blind coming through it."

"Just do it!" Inez said. "I am at the bottom. Ann is some yards below Tony. Hurry!"

Page fingered the button on the radio. "Whatever you say, Inez."

At noon, they reached the chockstone, a severe pitch of ice and snow and rock that stretched above them for one hundred and fifty feet. Warm wind blew across crevices in the stone, filling the air around them with the rich pitched tones of a flute. Farrell rubbed at his hip and listened to the music. Page mashed down a flat spot at the base of the wall. The action cracked off bits of ice, which bounced down the slope to where they could see Tony strapping himself into an icy cubbyhole on the right side of the couloir, just above the point where the chute became shrouded in darkness. They sat and waited, looking toward the towering dagger of rock called Tepee's Pillar, a thousand feet below and a half mile to the east.

The radio crackled again, but at this height there was interference; Inez's voice was garbled. Finally Tony turned and made a twirling motion with his hands as if he were swinging a lariat.

"That must be our cue," Farrell said, and for the third time that morning snow cascaded into the chute below them.

"Looks like it's going to be like when you were a little kid," Page said, "and you're running through the sprinkler on a hot summer's day. Only this is going to sting."

"You want the helmet?"

"She said it's all yours," Page said. "I'll just duck through quick."

"Page."

"Yeah?"

"I'll see you at the bottom."

Page smiled. "Wouldn't have it any other way."

Page took several long breaths. Farrell could see he was timing his turns, hoping to enter the ice storm in midarc so he wouldn't have to shift his balance blindly. He jumped around on the boards, pointed them into the thick snow, and began a series of whirling turns until he disappeared into the icy spray. Farrell flipped on the helmet camera and followed, trying to weave turns in an opposite composition so he wouldn't get caught in the ruts Page had made and be thrown into the walls.

The stream of rubble spilling from above surged. Farrell skied into it, wrapped now in a silver shroud. The flow of ice chunks, heavier than before, beat about his shoulders and rang off the helmet. He raised his hands to protect himself. The action threw him back on the tails of his skis and he fell through the curtain of snow, wincing at the shrill chatter the helmet made, trying to get his downhill ski to grab at the slope, knowing it wouldn't hold. The jarring motion of the ski vibrated up through his leg to his groin. He cried out.

Farrell slipped by Tony, who tried to reach out to grab him, but missed. He crashed off the near wall and slid again. Now he slipped into the dark part of the chute, his hands splayed out beside him to create friction and slow his rush. Ann was set up close to the upper entrance of the cave and Farrell roared by her, clawing the snow. For an instant, he considered letting go, to become a casualty critics could write of when they reviewed Inez's next film. But then his mind twisted the icy half dome of the cave into the grinning mouth of Jorge Cordova and he knew that more than anything, he wanted to live. Not for himself. For Lena. For revenge.

He arched his back and got himself up on his hip, his hands flat on the slope. Just as Inez came into view—with her camera lights blazing in the darkness—Farrell pushed off the snow with all his might; and he careened toward the mouth of the cave.

He flashed past Inez off-balance, but upright, blinking in the brilliant glare around her. Fifty yards and he was down, propped against a boulder, retching from the bitter apple taste that flooded his mouth, a taste that he realized was once the beloved Northern Spy tartness of adrenaline.

The Wave crouched over Page, who lay pale on the snow. Above Page's right eye was a bruised slash from which blood pulsed in sudden, grotesque bursts. "Bitch," Page groaned. "That bitch of a rock came out of nowhere."

"It must have nailed him when he came through that shower, mon," The Wave said to Farrell.

Farrell knelt next to Page and held snow to the cut until the blood slowed. Page's pupils were round, but fully dilated. A sign of shock. With his knife, Farrell cut an extra T-shirt into strips. He wrapped them around Page's head.

Inez scrambled down from the cave, beaming at them all.

"Incredible!" she cried. "I believe I get the shot of you, Jack, under the icicles just as you come up again. On film, I think it looks like you are behind glass bars! How appropriate!"

She took a step forward as if to hug him. Farrell caught her hands and held them away from him. "Enough," he said firmly. "I've had enough."

"Enough!" Inez laughed. "We just begin! We must hurry now if we want to get the shots on the glacier. The Wave is next. First to snowboard the Grand this early in the year!"

The Wave scowled. "Bag the glacier. We've got to get Page to a doctor."

"Page is fine," Inez said, barely looking at him. "He slides past me and looks right at the camera. I see the blood, but it is not so bad."

"That stone must have hit him like a slingshot," Farrell lashed out. "His right eye's almost closed. He's as good as blind."

"Patch him up!" Inez ordered. "He makes it to the glacier at least."

"I don't think your soul can take another Valoir," Farrell said.

Inez slapped Farrell hard across the face. He took it and the next and the next, just as he had accepted Lena's blows so many months before. When she stopped, blood trickled from his lip.

"Do you get him up or do you want the endless *ennui* of the prison walls?" she snarled.

Farrell looked down at Page. A deep red circle the size of two hen's eggs had formed on the T-shirt. Tony and Ann reached the bottom of the couloir. Ann knelt next to Page and checked his pulse. "He's bad," she said. "Probably a concussion."

"We're going to need a helicopter," Tony said.

"No!" Inez cried. "No one goes anywhere until I say so."

She pointed at Ann and Tony. "Or you don't get your money."

Then she pointed at The Wave. "And you don't find your mother."

And finally at Farrell. "And you rot in jail."

They all froze, staring at her and the jittery way she twirled her finger in the air.

Farrell took a deep breath. "Fuck you, Inez," he said. "I'm calling in the chopper."

He grabbed Page's radio and tried to call, but the only response was dull static. The Wave pointed up at the rocks. "We're blocked off."

Inez smiled in victory. "You see, on the glacier the radio works. We kill two birds with the one rock: help poor Page and get the shots I need."

Page groaned again. "I'm okay to make it there," he said. "But not if we don't move soon."

Farrell grabbed Inez by the collar. He whispered hoarsely, "If he doesn't make it, I'll kill you."

Inez made a kissing noise. "Such emotion, my outlaw. How I wish I had the cameras on."

She struggled free of his grasp. "Who will lead?" she asked.

None of them answered.

"I said, who will lead?"

They just stared at her.

"Fine," Inez said uncertainly. "I will lead."

Inez got her pack on and set off along the ridge. Slowly the others picked up their packs and followed. The Wave, Tony, and Farrell took turns supporting Page. Their route wound across a small ridge behind the jut of a massive outcropping called the Black Dike and out onto a small open snow field. Because of his height and strength, Tony was best able to support Page. So he and Farrell switched packs. The cameraman's load was brutish, and it weighed heavy on Farrell's torn leg muscle. He fell twenty, now thirty, now fifty yards behind the others.

Three-quarters of the way across the snowfield, as the rest of the crew approached a gap between the steeplelike rock of Tepee's Pillar and the great cliff that formed the Grand Teton's east face, the air reverberated around Farrell: *Woomph!*

Snow sagged all around him. His hip seized up and he grimaced, kneeling to relieve the pain. He saw it then: tiny lines running out over the surface of the snow like the support strands on a spider's web. He placed his hands on white crust and froze.

He stayed that way for a full three minutes, sure now that he was in the release zone, sure now that the snow pack would crack and a 100,000-ton load would move off the sleeping bear. But it didn't. By the time he figured it was safe to look up, Inez and the rest of the team were more than a football field away, perched at the crest of the ridge in back of Tepee's Pillar. Farrell struggled to his feet, fixated on the silvery cracks. Gingerly, he took a step and then another and another until he was beyond the farthest gray line.

"Oh, God . . . oh God, thank you," he whispered. He took his time now, stopping every few feet to listen to the snow and his own breath.

"What takes you so long?" Inez demanded when he finally reached them. "The helicopter comes in one hour. We must get to the glacier now."

"We don't go anywhere," Farrell said. "The snow settled back there."

"I feel nothing," Inez scoffed. "You just try to deny me my film."

"It settled, Inez," Farrell insisted. "The whole place is shaky."

"It's two o'clock," Inez said, pointing at the sun, which was approaching the flank of the Tetons. "The shadows, already they are moving on to the glacier. I will lose my beautiful light soon."

"The snow moved, Inez," Farrell said again.

"The snow, she always moves," Inez snapped. "She creeps, she glides, she turns in her sleep. It is normal. Besides, look around you. The helicopter cannot land here."

She was right. It was too narrow and too steep; the only place a helicopter could put down was out there, far down the slope of the glacier where it flattened out.

"All right," Farrell said. "But we wait until the chopper comes and then we move to it."

"No, we film first," Inez said. "We get him down there. We go now."

And before he could say another word, Inez slogged out across the great shoulder of snow that hugged the side of the cliff. Below her spread the Tepees, an eight-lane freeway of white that spilled down the mountain into the forest far, far below. Inez sank in the snow to midshin on every step, so that she moved with the turkey stride of an old man with a cane. Farrell massaged his thigh as the others silently picked up their packs to follow her.

"You coming, mon?" The Wave asked.

"In a minute," Farrell said. "I've got to rest this leg."

"Oh, we can wait no longer, mon," The Wave said. " 'We too take ship oh soul, Joyous we too launch on trackless seas, fearless for unknown shores.' "

"I give," Farrell said.

"Whitman, mon," The Wave grinned, and he set out after Ann and Tony and Page and Inez.

Farrell massaged his muscles for another minute, then looked up. The crew was moving in a tight pack across the snow mound.

He yelled, "You've got them too close together!"

The afternoon wind had picked up, smothering his voice. He got the pack on and lumbered after them as fast as he could go.

Later, Farrell would recall he wasn't sure how he knew. But

within thirty-five yards, he understood he was crossing terrain without foundation; the six of them were perched on a hollow overhang of ice and snow twenty feet high: a rotten cornice, a snow bridge with no support underneath.

"Spread out!" Farrell screamed. "Page! Tony! Ann! Wave! Move back toward me!"

They all heard him this time and turned in their tracks. Tony raised his hand to his brow, trying to block the sun. The dull growl of a waking beast ripped the still air. Farrell saw a swirl in the thick white goo off to his right, an eddy twirling after a retreating wave. The snow around Farrell buckled and ran.

Then the whole thing gave way and him with it. As he went, Farrell instinctively unsnapped the strap that held the pack tight against his chest. There was a split second where he felt the weightlessness of the deep powder turn. He saw The Wave, Ann, then Tony and Page, and finally Inez pitched forward in a violent snap.

An avalanche's force creates so much friction in the first few moments that cold snow can be superheated into blocks, pillars, and spears with the hardness of granite and the keenness of scissors. These violent chunks of snow smashed and cut Farrell's legs out from under him. His left knee tore and he tumbled into a pummeling white. The slide crashed over him. In the darkness there were angry animals with heavy paws, with sharp claws and hungry teeth. The beasts swatted him. They mauled him. All wanted to feed. A powerful force raked him in the stomach and his jaw popped open. He gasped for air. But before he could get any, snow crammed in so far he thought his jaw would split and tear away. He was struck in the lower back. Another blow smashed into the side of the helmet, denting it; and Farrell went limp, sure now that he was finished. He dropped away and in that instant he saw a bright light and Lena stood in it.

Something, a chunk of ice, a bush or a rock, snagged on the shoulder strap of the pack, dislocating his right arm at the shoulder and ripping the pack from him. The action spun him toward the surface where, like a balloon released from deep under water, he burst out on the snowy torrent as it rumbled down the glacier. Farrell whipped and flopped downward. He windmilled twice. Two of his ribs gave way. Then, as suddenly as it had embraced him, the slide flicked him aside like an insignificant bug.

He landed facedown, convulsing on impact. He tried to breath, but his nose and mouth were packed with snow, frozen plugs that wrenched his jaw away from his head like a pig with an apple in its mouth. He tried to scream, but no noise escaped. He managed to roll over, squinting at the sun which shone through the cracked kaleidoscope of his goggles. Farrell had the terrifying thought that he would suffocate in the clean air of a warm spring Wyoming day.

He sat up. His right arm dangled helplessly at his side. He dug frantically at the frozen mass with the fingers of his other hand, but only chips came loose. Next to a rock not far away he could make out a sharp stick. He crab walked to it, ignoring the searing pain. Farrell rammed the stick into his mouth and chiseled at the obstruction until he felt it cut the back of his throat. Still, the air would not come. His head began to swirl.

The rock! Farrell struggled to his knees and cast himself belly down on the sharpest point of the boulder so that it jabbed his diaphragm. The chunk dislodged enough to suck in air. But liquid from the melting plug flooded in, too; and he struggled again at the thought of drowning.

He threw himself on the boulder a second time. The chunk freed. He coughed and spit the awful red tube out, and swooned into blackness.

Farrell had no sense of how long the avalanche had worked his body. Nor could he say how long he lay, passed out, draped over the front of the boulder. But when he opened his eyes, the shadow of the Grand Teton, which had been above him, was now far down the valley.

He rocked to his left and brought his hand to his mouth, cringing at the excruciating sting; his front teeth were shattered. He shivered and knew that unless he moved soon, he'd die of shock. He tried to take off the helmet, but it was badly dented and would not budge. He closed his eyes and with the same stick he'd used to clear his throat, he cleared away the broken glass of his goggles. For fifty yards in every direction, he was surrounded by a jumble of snow blocks and tree stumps and frozen earth. A climax avalanche.

The beast had passed. No movement. No sound. Only the steady gusts of the warm spring breeze.

Farrell wanted to cry, but couldn't. His chest hurt and he reached to feel where the ribs had snapped. His hand closed around the electronic sensor under his shredded coat. He turned it on, the *peep! peep! peep!* noise coming to him like the cries of a newborn bird.

He tried to stand, but a burning pain tore through him and he almost collapsed. Somehow he got himself upright. The swelling had immobilized the knee. He might be able to manage a stiff gait. He took a step, screamed, and stopped, panting. He moved like this through ten yards of the mess, trying to focus on the chirps of the sensor. He noticed that the tone rose when he moved downhill. And after another five minutes, he saw neon green glowing amid the rubble. He hobbled and crawled to The Wave, whose left leg thrust away at an unnatural angle below his hip. The rastaman's face was battered beyond recognition.

Farrell sat down and stroked The Wave's matted dreadlocks. The boy made a choking sound and spit up a wad of bright pink blood. One of his lungs is punctured, Farrell thought. Farrell prayed the kid's spine wasn't broken and slowly lifted him until The Wave lay in his lap. The Wave's eyes opened, his lips moved, and then he shut them again while more blood spilled from his mouth. He gurgled when he breathed. A sucking wound. From his past, Farrell heard priests praying.

At this moment when all seemed lost, over the peeping of the radio transceiver and his mumbled words of prayer, Farrell heard the steady chug of a helicopter. I can save at least one, he thought. He began to sob. He tried to find the chopper in the sky, but couldn't. Farrell got his arms under The Wave and lifted him so the fliers might see the blazing lime of the rastaman's snowsuit. It was a struggle, but Farrell got himself and the kid upright; and he stood there facing down the fall line, feeling the vibration of the great pumping heart which now occupied everything around him.

Epilogue

wenty-six days after Farrell and The Wave were rescued from the glacier, Farrell walked on crutches for the first time. Every ligament in Farrell's knee had been torn or severed. The doctors said it was a miracle he had stood at all, much less hobbled over to save The Wave.

After Farrell had been released from intensive care, Portsteiner went back to Utah. He returned for Farrell's first steps, holding Ruby on a leash. Farrell put the rubber-soled crutches in front of him, grimaced in pain, and stepped forward down the white hall. Nurses stood by with codeine should he need it. As he had every day since Dunphy and the other members of the Jackson search and rescue team had raced from the helicopter to his side, he refused all pain medication.

"Things have been distant for too long," he told Dunphy, who had wanted to inject him with morphine as soon as he had laid him down amid the snow boulders and the uprooted rocks and brush. "I want to feel this for what it is."

When the helicopter touched down at the airport, Portsteiner was waiting. He sat with Farrell on the ambulance ride. Farrell's tongue had swollen to twice its normal size; it took him three times to make Portsteiner understand what he wanted.

"That's a crime, Jack," Portsteiner had said. "I won't do it."

"Fair," Farrell gurgled. "Not fair to them. Wave, Page. Others."

Farrell gripped Portsteiner's hand so violently that the old man finally gave in.

The rescue team found Ann the next morning a quarter mile below the release zone. The coroner said she had died of massive head injuries.

A woman with a probe pole working the very top of the slide path discovered the bodies of Page and Tony the next afternoon, not one hundred feet from where Farrell had last seen them. Dunphy figured they'd been sucked directly down and underneath the snow as if they'd been caught in a undertow at the beach.

"They never knew what hit them," Dunphy said.

They gave up trying to find Inez on the third day, figuring she'd been swept into one of the glacier's deep crevices. A hiker found her pack and smashed camera a week later in a tangle of brush off the slide path. There was a notebook in the pack that contained cryptic entries about the shots in the film, which the local newspaper published under the headline:

Extreme Diary of an Avalanche Victim

A story later that same week detailed the fury of Karl Mann, Inez's German investor, who had arrived in town sure that the publicity of the accident would create a major market for the documentary. None of the film or video Inez was supposed to have shot could be found.

Farrell heard Mann cursing at the nurses in the hallway before he saw him. Mann, an emaciated blond with a scar in the middle of his chin, burst into Farrell's room just as they were changing his bedpan and blanched at the sight of Farrell's toothless smile. Farrell told him some of the truth: that Inez Didier was secretive and didn't tell anyone much about herself or her methods or how she planned to finish the movie.

"I'm as upset about it as you," Farrell said with as much sincerity as he could muster.

Two hospital orderlies had to prevent Mann from trying to see The Wave, who had lain in a coma for four days before awakening, and was still in intensive care. As Farrell had thought, The Wave's left lung was punctured. His femur was broken in two places and he'd suffered a severe concussion, but the speech pathologist predicted he'd regain full control of his language ability.

Indeed, a week after Farrell walked for the first time, the reporters who had unsuccessfully tried to interview Farrell got The Wave to talk. The rastaman held a press conference amid beeping monitors. He was an odd presence on the television screen: the left side of his head had been shaved to let the doctors stitch his lacerations so that he looked like a baseball with part of the cover ripped off—one side smooth and scarred, the other marred by frayed strips of rubber. The Wave told the reporters that during his next scheduled operation the doctors had agreed to set his leg at an angle; so that even if he never walked right again, he'd be able to crouch on his snowboard.

One reporter asked him about the things Inez had written in her notebook and what he thought she was after. The Wave played with a plastic tube that ran into his arm and said, "She was like Rimbaud, mon. 'She saw the sunset, stained with mystic horrors, Illumine the rolling waves with long purple forms, like actors in ancient plays.'"

"You couldn't tone it down even for a minute, could you?" Farrell asked The Wave the next day. He was in The Wave's room to tell him the hospital had decided to release him.

"What and miss my fifteen minutes of Andy Warhol, mon?" said The Wave. "No fucking way."

"You'll be out soon," Farrell said.

"Ten days, mon," The Wave said. "I'll see you."

"I don't think so," Farrell said.

The Wave nodded sadly and shook his hand.

Portsteiner was waiting outside when Farrell was wheeled from the hospital. Ruby barked and wagged her tail. They drove to Dunphy's house on the outskirts of Jackson and had a burning party in an old oil can the guide kept around to get rid of autumn leaves.

"I never stole a thing in my life before," Portsteiner said as the first reels of film and videotape caught fire and belched up a thick black smoke.

"Think of it as returning something that was stolen," Farrell said. "You're Robin Hood."

Portsteiner grunted and threw in another reel. He looked at Farrell, "I went through a lot of it, those files you said she had. Watched a couple of the tapes. Read the diary."

"I figured you would," Farrell said. "You deserved to know."

Portsteiner tugged at his earlobe, as if he knew he should tell Farrell he wasn't responsible for Lena, but couldn't. Finally he asked, "How'd it happen?"

Farrell thought a moment about all the particulars, then said, "I used to think that to ski perfectly, you pulled the boards together and let them fly straight down. Didn't take long before I hit something.

"Now, I wish I skied more like you, shoulders and head in the fall line, but the hips and ankles sensitive, absorbing the terrain."

One by one they fed in the rest of the tapes and the film to the fire. A black smoke belched into the sky, and was taken by a wind that blew off toward the Tetons. Farrell looked through The Wave's file, took a note from it, and committed it to the flames.

In the boxes that Portsteiner had taken from Inez's room and truck, there was also a cardboard portfolio of letters from Henri Rassond, some from as recently as March. Farrell thought about doing the noble thing and not looking; he succumbed and read three. Rassond still loved Inez and wanted her to return to France.

The more recent letters were smudged, stained with drops of water. Farrell didn't burn any of them. The next day he boxed the letters and mailed them to Rassond with no return address included. For some reason he kept the copy of Inez's father's book.

The morning of Portsteiner's flight back to Salt Lake City, Farrell wrote a letter to Page's father to tell him that after everything that had happened, his son still loved him when he died. He knew it was not true, but close. Farrell sent a note to The Wave at the hospital which contained the address of the rehab center his mother was in in Arizona. Next he called the attorney in Switzerland and made arrangements for the rest of his cash to be placed into a trust that would anonymously disburse annual payments to The Wave.

At the airport, Portsteiner made an offer of a desk job back in Utah. There was no enthusiasm in the tender; Farrell knew Portsteiner regarded him with the conflicting respect and unease he would accord any unstable slope. They shook hands awkwardly, then Portsteiner was gone.

Before Farrell drove south out of Jackson, he called Stern in San Diego and told him he was coming in. The agent was furious, wanted to know where he was, to fly there and give him protection. Farrell refused and hung up. He called his mother. She was shocked and then cried when he said Lena was still dead. She told him his father made noises when she showed him his picture, but she'd never known how to explain that his son had died with a wife whom he had never known.

It was eighty degrees, summer weather, and flies buzzed inside the cabin of the truck and Ruby bit at them when they left Jackson. Thirty miles out, he stopped and got out at a rest area above the Snake River, swollen and roaring from the melting snows. He cinched the brace tight around his knee, leaned on the cane, and walked slowly down through the shade of the trees to the edge of the rushing water.

Farrell stared at the swirls of gray and blue, thinking how Gabriel hung off the side of his boat and how Sorolla's paintings showed that life can either be clarified or distorted by brilliant light. He thought that the river was like the dreams he'd had in the hospital after the avalanche. There he'd heard longing voices call to him in the darkness, and he'd turned and called back to them in languages he did not know, but understood. He had stumbled toward the voices, never seeing their bodies. Every time this happened, he woke up sweating and afraid.

A raft appeared on the river, full of tourists shrieking as they entered the rapids. Farrell studied them the way a scientist might observe apes in the wild. He watched one boy who crouched in the front of the bucking raft, his fingers white from the grip he'd taken on the rope, his mouth open to the spray. Farrell understood the boy, but did not smile for him.

He waited until the raft faded from view. He placed Inez's father's book and Lena's diary and her nightgown in the water. He watched them bob for a moment, then climbed back up the hill before the current could suck them away into the chill of the white water.